The Wizard Corps

By
Guy Antibes

STRINGS OF EMPIRE

BOOK ONE

THE CLOISTER WIZARD

By
Guy Antibes

CASIE PRESS
SALT LAKE CITY, UT

The Cloister Wizard

The Cloister Wizard Copyright ©2024 Guy Antibes. All Rights Reserved. No part of this book may be reproduced without the permission of the author.

This is a work of fiction. There are no real locations used in the book; the people, settings, and specific places are a product of the author's imagination. Any resemblances to actual persons, locations, or places are purely coincidental.

Published by CasiePress LLC in Salt Lake City, UT, October 2024
www.casiepress.com

ISBN: 979-8344148557

Cover Design: Kenneth Cassell (modified illustration utilized Adobe Photoshop AI)
Book Design: Kenneth Cassell
Reader: Bev Cassell

Author's Note

In creating a series, one of the things I do is develop an overall story arc. It doesn't mimic exactly the organization that I use in creating a single novel, but there are key events that help define the path the hero will take as he moves through his world. The Cloister Wizard not only is a story about Quint Tirolo in his development as a wizard and a person. I don't have all the steps mapped out before I sit down to write, since Quint's story arc wasn't defined specifically. Just like the predictor strings talked about in this story, everything was murky when I started The Cloister Wizard. While I wrote, a key element of Quint's direction came to me while writing and we will see where clarity that takes us in The Cloister Wizard and in the following books in the series.

— Guy Antibes

The Cloister Wizard

Map of North Fenola

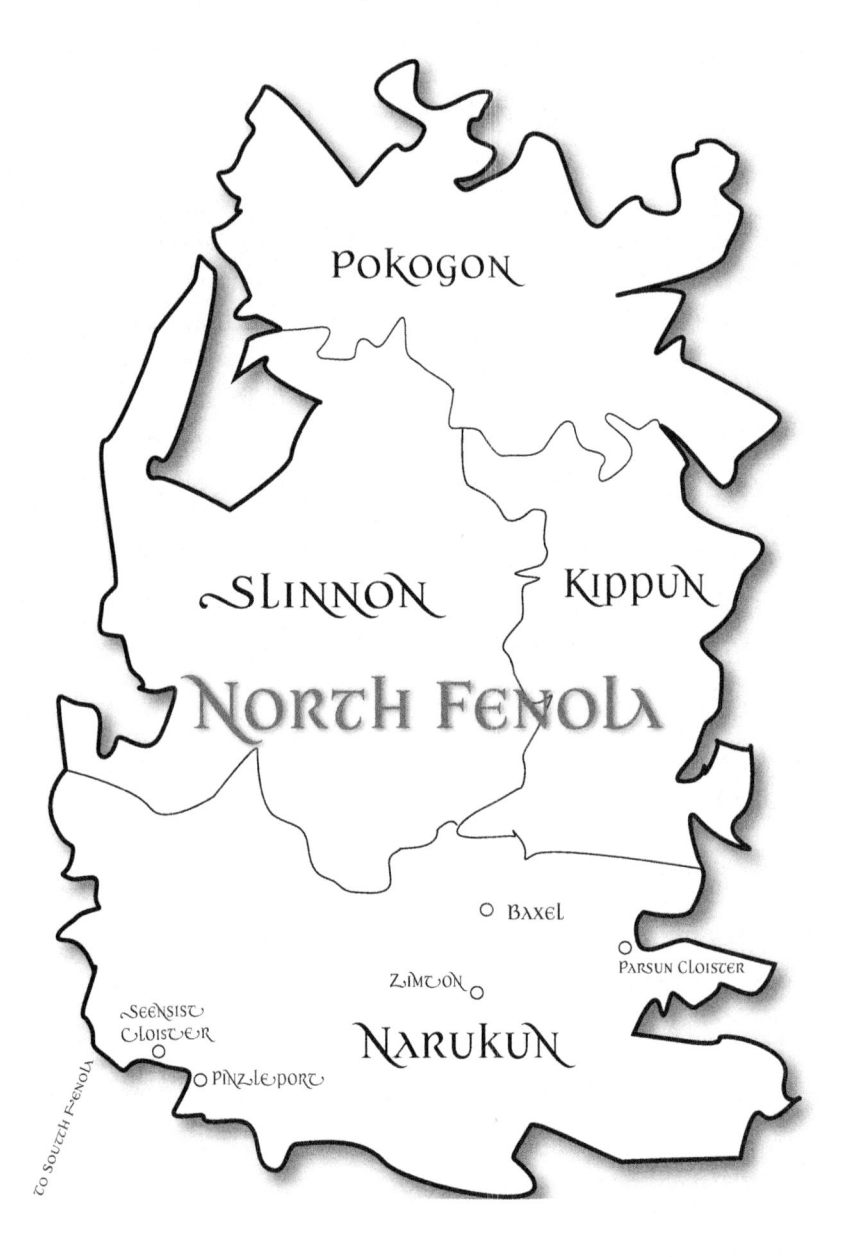

Pokogon

Slinnon   Kippun

North Fenola

○ Baxel

Zimton ○
                                    ○
                        Parsun Cloister
Seensist
Cloister   Narukun
   ○
      ○ Pinzleport

to South Fenola

Strings of Empire
Book One

The Cloister Wizard

Chapter One

Quinto Tirolo followed the soldiers around the walls until he passed a postern door that was beginning to open.

"In here," a robed man said, holding the door open for Quint. He wore a peculiar beard, but his smile seemed genuine.

Quint didn't have an option. Even if there were green-uniformed soldiers inside, he could not fight anyone at this point without exposing his wizardly powers.

After he followed the monk, or whatever he was, inside the door, Quint's escort cast a string against the door. Quint recognized it. "Wood binder," he said.

The monk turned and grinned. "Very good! Follow me. You are expected, young man."

Quint raised his eyebrows. A portent string showed he was coming? There was no doubt the cloister had magic. There were few cloisters in Racellia on the continent of South Fenola from which Quint had just escaped. Quint had never visited one, but the cloister matched Quint's imagination.

The walls were twenty or thirty feet high with crenellations. Various wood and stone buildings were built within the confines of the walls, along with what amounted to a small farm in the center with animals in pens and a large garden lined with fruit trees in front of the arched walkway circling the center courtyard.

The monk led Quint into the most prominent building.

"You will need to talk to the council," the monk said as he nodded to other monks along the way.

Quint was conscious of their eyes following them as they entered the building.

"You can wait inside," the monk said, opening a door to the council room.

The empty room made Quint catch his breath as he realized he had no weapons, no clothes, no sponsors, no friends or allies, and, hopefully, no enemies to contend with. He sat on the first row facing a table with nine chairs elevated on a dais.

The monk's appearance at the door at such a critical moment seemed timed too perfectly for a portent string. The magic of such a string, at least when Quint cast it, didn't present events with that precision. He would have to wait to find out.

In less than half an hour, by Quint's guess, monks began to enter. Some took seats in the audience, and others began to fill the council chairs. There were no friendly smiles or gestures but primarily expressions of curiosity.

The council seat filled as one last monk entered the chamber accompanied by the monk who had escorted him from the exterior door to the room. The monk took the center chair on the dais.

"We are interested in an outlander who decided to seek refuge in Seensist Cloister. What is your name? Our predictor string didn't provide us with one."

"I would rather not give you my name," Quint said. "I have been chased from South Fenola to your cloister and…"

The head monk raised his hand. "We know you escaped from Racellia on a Narukun ship. You were in Racellia's Wizard Corps. It would be easy for us to find out who you are. From what I understand, there can't be that many hubite officers in Racellia."

Quint sighed. The monk was correct. It wouldn't take much effort to find out who he was. A quick trip to Bocarre, Racellia's capital and largest port, and then ask a few questions. If Pacci Colleto's Imperial Gussellian forces had conquered Racellia, it might prompt even more curiosity.

"I am Quinto Tirolo, formerly a captain in the Racellian armed forces. There are few hubites in the wizard corps, and with my escape, there might be none. Racellia was hardly stable when I left. I was being sought by multiple parties and worked my way on a Narukun ship to Pinzleport. The captain said I could seek sanctuary in your cloister," Quint said.

"If you can demonstrate your proficiency as a wizard, we are bound under the cloister rules to accept you."

That was what Quint wanted to hear. "I am a master-level wizard, knowing approximately seventy strings."

Quint heard murmuring among the audience and the council.

"Seventy strings, and you are sixteen, seventeen-years-old?"

"Seventeen," Quint said.

"String proficiency alone doesn't establish your cloister. You must have acquired experience and provide evidence of leadership to achieve the rank of Prior, which is the equivalent of a Racellian master."

"Doesn't a prior run a cloister?" Quint asked. He was almost sure it was the requirement for Racellian cloisters.

"Each cloister has its own rules. For Seensist, you must be at Provost level, fifty strings, to be on the council, and a Prior at seventy-five strings to be the head prior who breaks any ties among the council. However, all decisions require at least a majority of the council members. My duties mostly revolve around being a referee."

That seemed fair to Quint. "What rank am I now?"

"Probably a deacon. Additional strings can push a monk to a higher level, and if you truly know seventy strings, then your entry rank would be a deacon. However, in our cloister, your duties will start at novice. We can talk about all that later. My question is, what are your intentions now that you have landed in Narukun?"

"I want to survive. I have been attacked numerous times since my magic manifested itself, and the latest attack was while I sailed to Narukun."

That brought some gasps and more murmuring behind Quint.

"Then Oscar, the monk who let you in, will lead you to a cell."

Quint's eyes grew wide.

"Not a jail cell, a monk's cell," the Prior said. "You will be issued robes, tested, and then we will determine how you can best contribute to the community."

"I appreciate the opportunity to join your order," Quint said.

"Be careful what you wish for," the head prior said. "You won't be eligible to join the order at this time. Once you are tested, I will meet with you to discuss what the predictor strings said."

§

Quint spent a sleepless night in his cell. It wasn't large, but he'd been relegated to smaller rooms in the wizard corps. He had no possessions, so there wasn't anything to crowd the space. The large, empty bookcase was encouraging. He didn't know what he'd have to do to fill it.

Oscar tapped on the door less than half an hour after dawn, just as a bell began to ring. Quint was already awake. He put on the same clothes he wore on the ship.

"Breakfast before you meet alone with the head prior. I'll give you an orientation after we eat and get you some proper Cloister clothes."

Quint handled breakfast without complaining. The food was plain and under-seasoned, but he saw other monks shaking something on their food in the refectory. Oscar wasn't one of them. Quint's escort ate with the ghost of a smile. There was little talk in the refectory.

"Is there a restriction on talking while eating?" Quint asked as they left the refectory.

Oscar nodded. "Any sound is discouraged at breakfast. Early mornings are a time for personal reflection."

Quint noticed some of that, but plenty of quiet communication was going on.

"Time for clothes." Oscar led the way to a building called 'The Monk's Warehouse.' "Anything you can talk the issuing monks out of is fair game."

They stepped inside to a long counter. Four issuing monks stood waiting for customers. Oscar grinned and went to a monk, who gave him a nod and a grin.

"You are the new outsider? I couldn't go to your welcome," the monk said.

Quint would hardly term the grilling he went through as a welcome, but he was here to get his clothes, and he needed a monk friendly with the issuers. "I am. Quint Tirolo."

"Tirolo. That's a South Fenolan name?"

Quint shrugged. "I suppose so."

"He'll need four sets of robes, socks, and boots to match. A set of underwear and a lantern for his cell." Oscar turned to Quint. "He might need a shaving kit. Make that two. One always needs a spare."

"Coming right up," the issuing monk said, winking at Oscar. He leaned over to get a better look at Quint and nodded before he disappeared in the back.

They waited for a while before the monk returned with two sacks. One was smaller than the other. "Here we go. I put a set of robes, boots, and the shaving kit in this one."

Oscar pushed the larger sack toward Quint and took possession of the smaller. "Can you find your way to your cell? Change into cloister clothing, and I'll return to your cell to give you some additional orientation."

Quint left the warehouse while Oscar remained with the small sack. Oscar was benefitting from taking Quint to get his clothes. He didn't like the petty dishonesty, but Quint didn't know the cloister's rules.

The clothes were made better than Quint expected. He envisioned rough stitching, rough cloth, and rough sizing, but everything fit well enough, and the fabric was as soft as anything the wizard corps issued. The monk also slipped in a couple of soft trousers to wear underneath the robes. Quint was more comfortable with that.

After quickly finding places for his clothes and going to the lavatory to test out the shaving kit, he returned to find Oscar napping on his cot.

"That's a good one," Oscar said, patting the thin mattress as he rose, yawning.

Quint wouldn't characterize his bed quite that way. "We are going to discuss the cloister rules?"

Oscar nodded. "There are five bells: morning, midday, dinner, evening, and vespers."

"And what is vespers?"

"For those inclined, there is a quiet service in the refectory. Perhaps a tenth of the cloister will rise for vespers. It isn't a religionist service but on the qualities that make a respectable monk. Refreshments are served and are seasonal in nature. In the winter, a hot drink and a biscuit or cake. That's when I go," Oscar said. "We get up at the morning bell and go to bed at the bedtime bell. Lights out at evening bells."

"And lights on at the morning bell?"

Oscar grinned. "You are catching on. You are to faithfully carry out the duties assigned to you by the cloister council."

"There are penalties for not adhering to the rules?"

"Yes! Various penalties for various infractions. A common punishment is you might miss meals or copy books in the library. Monks are expelled for serious infractions, and most of those occur when we are permitted to visit Pinzleport once a month."

"What about the Green guards?" Quint asked. "Aren't they a problem?"

"When outsiders are expected to enter the cloister."

Quint frowned. "Am I in danger of being captured if I leave the security of the cloister?"

"You are currently. I'm sure the Prior will restrict your outside activities for some time. I don't have any idea how long."

Someone opened Quint's door. "I'm here to take you to the Prior."

"I can do that!" Oscar said excitedly.

"I'm sure you can, Viznik, but it's my assignment this time."

Oscar rose and gave them each a bow before leaving the new monk with Quint.

"How did you and Oscar get along?"

"For a morning, well enough," Quint said. "Am I going to be under his wing?"

The monk gave Quint a knowing smile. "It's up to the Prior, but probably not."

Quint had the impression there was more to the answer, leaving it up to the prior to tell him.

"Let's go," the monk said.

They crossed the courtyard to the council building. Monks worked the growing part of the farm, and others tended the animals.

"Second floor," the monk said as they entered the building's foyer.

Quint followed him up stone steps and stopped. The monk tapped a code on a door, and the Prior gave permission to enter his office.

"You may leave us, Brother Kentor," the Prior said. He turned his gaze to Quint. "And you may sit." The prior pointed to a chair.

"You had a good night?"

Quint pursed his lips. "It's a new place. I guess I'm not used to everything."

"To be expected on your first night. What did Viznik tell you?"

The prior learned about Quint's morning.

"You may find that your mattress has been changed out," the Prior said. "Your clothes won't be stolen for a few more days."

Quint frowned. "And Oscar's small bag?"

"His payment for showing you around. That isn't an official cloister exchange, as I'm expecting you to know."

"It didn't seem like it was. I can use magic to lock my cell?"

The prior nodded. "It's expected." He waved his hand to signal a change in subject. "What didn't you tell the council yesterday?"

"I didn't want to bore everyone," Quint said. "I'd do better if you ask me questions so I can give you more precise answers."

"How were you treated as a hubite in a willot country? I know you aren't treated equally."

Quint nodded. "I was beaten, attacked, and given the worst kind of assignments until I was able to show my abilities to a few officers who recognized that my abilities outshone my background. I was first put into the Wizard Corps, sweeping floors and emptying trash and worked my way up from there. I've been in situations where my wizardry only gained me so much."

"And your rank?"

"I ended up as a captain, but I was assigned to a unit outside the wizard corps that plucked intelligence from periodicals."

The prior nodded. "You were a spy?"

"I probably supported spies. I went on a single assignment to Gussellia, joining a negotiating team. The emperor of Gussellia took a liking to me, but I think I showed up on a subordinate's portent string and was asked to join him."

"Turn traitor?"

Quint shrugged. "Sort of. I left him after we toured the hubite area. Racellia is unstable, and a general decided to eliminate all the hubites." Quint's eyes watered at the memory. "My family was murdered. I left the Gussellian emperor and returned to Bocarre until the Gussellians were about to invade. The capital was in turmoil, and I decided it was time to leave."

"You joined Captain Olinko's ship?"

Quint raised his eyebrows. "You know the captain?"

The prior nodded. "He is known in Pinzleport. His was the only ship from South Fenola to arrive at Pinzleport the last few days. You had to have been on his ship."

"I was," Quint said. "Feodor Danko and his daughter tried to kill me, but they failed."

"Lucky you, for now. I doubt if Danko will forget you. He is high up in the Green organization. You are presumed dead?"

"I was," Quint said.

"I know enough for now. It's time for testing," the prior said, rising from his chair. "Come with me."

§§§

CHAPTER TWO

QUINT SIGHED AS HE FACED THREE MONKS seated at a table. The head prior left as soon as he gave introductions. Demonstrating all his strings was a tedious exercise, but Quint was sure it wouldn't be the last test.

He went through the strings. Two of the monks documented the strings and Quint's results.

"I'm sure I know a few more, but without my string book..." Quint shrugged.

"Seventy-eight, by my count," one of the monks said. "I documented what you did and wrote in the name we use in Narukun for some of the strings we describe differently than you do in Racellia. We can give you a copy."

"I seriously doubted you had mastered that many," the monk in the middle said. "I'm sure we can recommend deacon status for you. However, just as you were told before, your cloister duties will start at novice, but you should move up quickly."

"Does the cloister have the ability to teach me more strings?" Quint asked.

"We have more than three hundred documented. I doubt you can learn them all. We all have our limitations."

Quint nodded. "I know that," he said non-defensively. "But I can learn more?"

"It's up to you. The cloister has three prior-level monks and a retired Abbot who once knew over one hundred strings. I am a council member, but I am provost-level. Perhaps one of them can help you. It is up to you to ask. They may turn you down, but there is always the library. With a deacon status, you have access."

Quint managed a smile. "What do I do now? Do I get a different cell?"

The middle monk shook his head with a smile. "Our cells are no better than yours, I'm sure."

"Will Oscar be my guide?" Quint asked.

"No." The reply was emphatic. "Oscar has other duties he is suited for and his allegiance is in question. We will assign a younger monk to guide you through your assimilation."

Quint would not miss Oscar. As excited as the man was to usher him into the cloister, Oscar didn't elicit trust. It looked like that behavior wasn't missed by the senior monks.

"We have one more thing to discuss," the provost said, "the predictor strings, what you call portent strings."

Quint nodded. "I was wondering about that," Quint said.

"You have an exceedingly bright future. Some people can change the world. You could be one of them."

"If I survive," Quint said. "I've heard that before, but my future hasn't kept my present out of trouble."

"And it likely won't. If you could keep your potential a secret, you'd have a better chance, but wizards with the ability to cast predictor strings aren't uncommon," the provost said. "You may not be with us for long."

"You've seen that?"

The provost smiled. "I have. You experienced our proximity to peril when you arrived yesterday. We are almost under siege by the Greens, and that will last until the royal authorities ever re-occupy Pinzleport."

"You've seen that happening?"

The provost laughed. "It happens every few decades. Your actions, on the other hand, are murky. I could see some actions, and then the spell would blur. Other than arriving at Seensist's back door, your time spent with us is a little vague. If you are familiar with predictor strings, they aren't always correct."

Quint nodded. "I am restricted to the cloister until then?"

"Voluntarily, we hope," one of the other monks said. "Greens still stick their noses where they don't belong throughout the year. No one is forced out of the cloister to visit Pinzleport; however, there are advantages to a trip to the market or to some of Pinzleport's better restaurants."

"I have more than enough to learn in the short term," Quint said, meaning what he said.

"Good. Return to your room, and your assigned companion will show up."

Quint found his way to the room and removed the wood-binding string. When he opened the door, Quint didn't see anything amiss. He sighed as he sat in the single chair, looked out the second-floor window at the grounds below, and then snorted. Maybe they didn't trust him with a window that looked outside the cloister. Quint didn't mind. If he remembered correctly, the outside windows were tiny compared to this one.

He stood when he heard the knock. He opened the door and looked down into the face of a young woman. Quint groaned.

"You are displeased I am a female?" the girl said.

Quint smiled. "Kind of. In Racellia, two of those most active against me were young women," Quint said. "I hope it won't be three."

She giggled. "I'll do my best to stop that from happening. May I come in?"

Quint turned the chair and offered her a seat while he sat on the bed. "I'm Quinto Tirolo, but I go by Quint."

The young woman smiled. "You can call me Sandy. My formal name is Sandiza Bartok."

"Even Sandiza is nice," Quint said. "What is your level?"

"I'm a deacon with thirty-one strings. I was accepted into Seensist Cloister when I was thirteen. That was eight years ago."

"That makes you twenty-one. I'm seventeen. One of my villains was sixteen, and the other was about two years older than me."

"So, it's not an older woman thing?" Sandy asked with a smile.

"Not at all. Calee tried to kill me twice. I ended up saving Amaria a few times despite her foul deeds. What are we to talk about?"

"I talked to Oscar while you were interviewed," Sandy said. "Oscar is acolyte-level." She cleared her throat. "I'm amazed you claim to know over seventy strings."

"I tested at seventy-eight, but I know more. Strings come easy to me."

Sandy shook her head in amazement. "And I thought I was a prodigy."

"You still are," Quint said. "I'm a prodigy, too."

"A prodigy two levels higher, but I think they chose me because we are both younger and more accomplished than most of the young monks in the cloister," Sandy said.

"What will I do? I was told I'd be doing novice things."

"Do you like gardens or stables?" Sandy asked.

It didn't take much for Quint to figure out where this was headed. "Gardens. My father lived in a forest and made wagon wheels."

"You took care of horses?" Sandy smiled and nodded her head.

"One. I did all kinds of chores. Probably similar to what novices get to do," Quint said.

"Then let's get you a plot to take care of," Sandy said.

They walked across the large courtyard and stopped in front of a plot of dirt. Not a thing grew but weeds.

"This has been harvested. It is all yours."

"What do I plant?" Quint asked.

"The master gardener will talk to you about it. The council found that the yield is better if a monk is responsible for their plot rather than splitting up the work any other way. Let's find him."

Quint followed Sandy to a split door opening onto the courtyard.

"Eben!" Sandy yelled after opening half the door.

An old monk sauntered to the door. He looked Quint up and down. "My new novice?"

"Quinto Tirolo," Sandy said. "He's a deacon since he knows many strings, but he's young, new, and yours for the open plot."

"You know anything about gardening?" Eben, the garden master, asked.

"I grew vegetables back home, but I think you grow different kinds here."

"Where was home?" Eben asked.

"Southeastern Racellia," Quint said.

"Come back tomorrow after breakfast, and I'll have your personal piece of paradise designed for you." The monk wrote Quint's name with the notation: New Plot.

"How many hours do I spend with the plot?" Quint asked Sandy as she led him back across the courtyard.

"It varies, but a few hours a day once the plants start to grow. I managed a plot one season." She smiled. "I thought it was fun. The library is next. The librarian is an ex-professor at Pinzleport University. He decided that being a monk was less political than working in Pinzleport and became a monk a decade ago. He doesn't teach classes, but he teaches younger monks. If you are honest with him, you'll get the best results."

"Honest?" Quint asked.

"You'll see."

§

Hintz Dakuz was a short, grizzled monk. Partially bald, the man seemed to have a perpetual frown stamped on his face and an angry mood to match it. Quint guessed he was about fifty years old.

"This is the new deacon?" Dakuz snapped. It sounded like Quint was an unwanted burden that was about to be placed on the librarian's shoulders.

"Quint Tirolo from South Fenola."

"I know who you are. I was sitting in the back of the council chamber when you were interrogated," Dakuz grumbled. "You'll be wanting a study plan?"

"Yes," Quint said, taking his cue from Sandy, to be honest. He was very tempted to dissemble to keep the man's lousy humor from boiling over, but perhaps honesty meant forthrightness.

"What do you know?"

"Not much that applies to North Fenola. I was an analyst for the military, perusing journals and looking for trends in how people thought."

"A desk-bound spy?"

"Some could call it that."

"I do," Dakuz said, lifting his chin and then rubbing his whiskers. How much Narallian do you know?"

"I don't know what Narallian is."

"The language we use in the cloister and the language of those who rule others in Narukun. You'll have to learn that since most of our best books are written in Narallian, not the common tongue."

"The willots in South Fenola have their own language, too. Is Narallian a spoken language?" Quint asked.

Dakuz's eyebrows shot up. "Now, that is an excellent question from an outsider. The answer is conditionally yes. Legal documents of any import are written in Narallian, but most people speak in common. If you flitter around the villages surrounding Seensist Cloister, you'll find they generally speak common, and if they are lucky enough to have learned how to write, they write common, too."

"How do I learn Narallian?"

"That's why you and I are talking. If you already knew it, I'd give you a reading list, and that would be that. Sandiza can be your study partner. I don't have the time to waste on drills, but speaking, you've got to do it to learn the language."

They continued to talk about what Quint did in the Wizard Corps, his abilities to learn strings, and how to make them.

"Tomorrow after your gardening experience," Dakuz said. "We might discuss your impression of Feodor Danko and his daughter Calee."

"You know them?"

Dakuz nodded. "He is the worst of the worst. I hate the man, and his daughter isn't far behind in sharing Danko's place of dishonor. If anything, she is less innocent than her father."

"I have my own stories," Quint said.

Dakuz's face softened for a moment and then hardened again. "Then we can share. Be off! I have things to do."

The conversation occurred at the door to the older monk's office, and Dakuz shut it without another word.

"Do you come with me to learn Narallian?" Quint asked.

Sandy made a disagreeable face. "No! I can only take tiny exposures of Hintz Dakuz." A bell sounded. "Time for our midday meal. I will treat you today."

"Treat? Aren't the meals free?"

Sandy shook her head. "Not at all. You must earn everything you consume. Since you are new, the cloister gives you two weeks to learn how to earn," she said with a smile.

Lunch was an experience that Quint decided he'd have to get used to. The basic cuisine wasn't appealing. When lunch was served, everything was boiled, and the few bites he tried were woefully under seasoned. He would have to find someone to get him one of the spice packets he saw monks use on their food.

Sandy followed his gaze and pulled out a spice packet from her robe.

"Are you looking for something like this? Take this. It's yours."

"To make the food edible?" Quint asked. "Yes!"

She tossed it to him. "Try out the spices and let me know which ones you want. When you've been here for a while, you can go out to a village or Pinzleport market and buy your own."

"I get money?"

"You have to work for it," Sandy said. She produced her own packet and liberally sprinkled pinches of various things on her lunch. After taking a bite, she closed her eyes and smiled. "Think of meals as blank canvasses and the packets as paints you use to create masterpieces."

Quint didn't think he'd be that kind of a connoisseur. Now he understood why the Dankos preferred Slinnon cuisine to what was cooked in Narukun.

Sandy held out her hand for Quint's packet and sprinkled something like what she used on Quint's food. "Try that."

Quint tentatively tried the food and felt an explosion of flavor in his mouth. The bland food seemed to expand in his mouth as he ate. "This is much better!"

Sandy nodded indulgently. "Some people never get the knack of how to season, and then there are the poor souls who don't use packets."

Quint didn't want to be a poor soul. "You'll have to teach me what you just used."

"I can do that. Maybe you can dedicate a small corner of your plot to growing herbs and some spices. You can't grow everything in the courtyard, but enough to save you money."

"Who owns what I produce in the plot?"

"The monastery, but you get a percentage of what you grow for your use, to eat, or to sell," Sandy said. "You'll figure it out."

§

After a tour of the monastery, Sandy left Quint to his own devices. He wandered to the library and was relieved Dakuz wouldn't return until the next day. A younger monk sat at the desk.

"Can you take me around and tell me the rules? I am to meet with Hintz Dakuz tomorrow morning after my gardening experience," Quint said.

The librarian chuckled. "Gardening experience. It sounds like managing your plot is a novelty. If it starts that way, it won't end up as one. All of us have managed plots or worked with the animals when we were novices."

They were the only monks in the library, so Quint got a thorough tour. Unlike the libraries in Bocarre, Narallian books were mixed in with those written in the common tongue. Quint's eyebrows shot up when he realized that Narallian was like willotan, the original language of the willots.

The librarian helped Quint select a dictionary, a pronunciation guide, and a few history books. Quint had something to fill the rest of his afternoon as he returned to his cell and began to study.

The alphabet was almost the same, with two new consonants and a new vowel to learn. As he took a history book and plowed through the first few pages, Quint found the conversion wouldn't be as smooth as he thought. Most of the words had usage differences.

He surmised that Feodor Danko and perhaps Calee would have learned the differences so they could play dumb if his hosts spoke willotan. Danko was the kind of person who would take advantage. But then, Quint realized he had done the same thing when Pacci Colleto interviewed him in Gussellia. Perhaps Quint would have to accept the fact that he was more of a spy than he thought.

Quint spent the rest of the afternoon making notes of the changes and couldn't get through the history books. His pronunciation would have to be honed by sessions with Sandy.

His studies were interrupted by a knock on the door. Sandy poked her head into the room and spotted the books. "You've been productive?"

Quint nodded. "Willotan, the language the willots take to be their own, is similar to Narallian. I should be able to pick the reading part on my own, but the speaking part is another story." The bell sounded.

"A story we can tell each other in practice sessions," Sandy said breezily. "It's time for dinner. I'm to deliver you to the head prior's table. You will find it's a chance for other councilors to interrogate you."

They walked over to the refectory, joined by the other monks.

"Unlike breakfast and lunch, we eat together for dinner," Sandy said. "I will leave you at the table and sit elsewhere."

Quint was left standing in front of a round table elevated above the others in the refectory. The head prior sat in the back.

"Tirolo, please sit there," the prior said pointing to the chair with its back to the room. "This is the council table, and we will let you ask questions this time."

That seemed fair to Quint. He sat, and within a few moments, the refectory buzzed with conversations. The quiet rules for breakfast and lunch didn't seem to apply to the evening meal.

The last councilor sat down, and the head prior stood and clapped his hands three times and uttered a religious prayer, speaking in a language Quint thought familiar and assumed it was Narallian. The pronunciation was very different.

"We have one item to present to you this evening. We have a new novice, Quinto Tirolo, from Racellia on South Fenola. He is a refugee with talents that Seensist Cloister can use in the future." The prior nodded to Quint and signaled him to rise.

Quint turned to the monks. There were two hundred and sixty monks, according to Sandy.

"Say something, Tirolo," the prior said quietly.

"I'm Quinto Tirolo, but I generally answer to Quint. I was in the Racellian Wizard Corps until my home country burst into a civil war. Most hubites in Racellia were murdered, so I took refuge on a Narukun ship heading for home. I am good with strings, so that I will be a deacon, but like the rest of you, I assume I get to perform novice duties. I've already got my garden plot," Quint said with a smile. His comment was met with laughter. He hoped that was a good sign. "Please help me be successful among you."

The prior clapped, followed by the rest of the refectory, and Quint sat down. The sounds of many conversations began to fill the room again. One of the councilors held his hands out and wove a string. The sound from the rest of the room subsided into faint background noise.

"Does the spell go both ways?" Quint asked.

The councilor pursed his lips. Quint didn't mean to offend the councilor, but the monk's face didn't appear congenial. "It does."

"Quint," the prior raised his eyebrows at Quint. "I can call you that?"

"All of you can," Quint said, "but I'll answer to Quinto and Tirolo, too." He smiled and a few councilors didn't seem amused.

Becoming a novice didn't make Quint a member of the Seensist community, it seemed.

"It's time for you to ask us questions," the prior said.

"Do I know strings that aren't used on North Fenola?"

"There were some," one of the councilors who tested him said. "We would like you to help us understand them. We share our strings with you, and you are expected to do the same."

"I'd be happy to do that. I had to leave my spellbook behind," Quint said. "It documents all the strings I know with thread diagrams and the weaving process I use to make the string."

"Can you duplicate it?" the same monk asked.

"I intend to, anyway. I'll make a copy for the cloister. I'm not sure if anyone can duplicate all my strings," Quint said.

"I understood that when we tested you."

"Can I ask another question?" Quint asked.

A young man served dinner to the table, and they stopped to eat in silence. Quint turned to look at the rest of the refectory and saw that the prohibition on talking still operated while everyone ate.

When most of the meal was eaten, the prior nodded to Quint. "You may proceed."

"Where did the Narallian language come from?"

A monk who appeared to be a supporter or at least someone who tolerated Quint raised a finger. "It is an archaic language. I grew up thinking it was the precursor language of Narukun, but it has existed for millennia. Narukun is not regarded as a secret language, but that doesn't apply to all hubite countries. Take Racellia. You never learned it."

"I withdrew a few Narallian books this afternoon. The willots of South Fenola call it their ancient language, Willotan. The alphabet is three characters smaller than Narallian, and from what I can tell, the pronunciation varies quite a bit."

"After an afternoon looking at our unique language, do you consider yourself proficient in Narallian?" the offended monk asked sarcastically.

"Not at all. The languages have diverted from their original source. I will still have to learn words, how to use the new characters, and figure out how to speak Narallian. It may be easier for me since I have a frame of reference."

"Are other South Fenolan hubites as accomplished as you?"

Quint frowned and blinked away watering eyes. "I doubt there are any hubite wizards on South Fenola at this point."

"I forgot about the genocide in Racellia," another councilor said.

"One more question," Quint said. "Is there a turnover of monks in the cloister, moving to other cloisters or leaving wizardly orders altogether?"

"The answer to that is yes," the head prior said. "We don't consider ourselves a fighting order, but all the cloisters will defend their monks should they be captured by factions in Pinzleport or move between cloisters. The factions tend to collect wizardly monks; sometimes, we must take matters into our own hands to free them."

Quint wanted to ask more about that, but he decided it would be something he could talk to other monks about in a different setting.

§§§

Chapter Three

"I CAN TAKE YOU TO A LOCAL VILLAGE to get seedlings. Growing from seeds will take weeks longer," Eben, the master gardener, said. "I thought you might like to grow string beans. They are simple to grow if your growing frames are sturdy. I have plans for easy ones."

"What about growing herbs?"

The gardener grinned. "I always have good starts. Do you know what to grow?"

"I'll get the list from Sandiza Bartok. Some of what I want are spices and don't they come from trees?" Quint asked.

"Most, but we can work on it. String beans aren't currently being grown and they will bring you a good price. We'll go out in a few days."

Quint didn't have a choice but to trust the gardener. He thought he wouldn't be able to leave the cloister, but perhaps Sandy meant leaving by himself.

"For the rest of the morning, turn the soil. I suggest a shovel, a rake, stakes, and twine to make straight rows."

Quint went to work. It had been a few years since he worked on his mother's vegetable garden, but hers was about the same size as his plot. The dirt wasn't hard. It hadn't been worked on since harvesting, but Quint was done with half of it by the time he had to leave to eat lunch and wash up . It was time to meet Hintz Dakuz at the library.

§

The irascible Dakuz expressed his dissatisfaction with a monk as Quint walked in. The monk was red in the face and looked embarrassed, even more so when Quint showed up. He quickly beat a retreat when Dakuz dismissed him.

"You haven't decided to escape yet, eh?" Dakuz said when Quint approached.

"No sir," Quint said.

"I'm not a 'sir,' young man," Dakuz said.

"My military training. What would be an appropriate honorific?" Quint asked.

"Dakuz will serve," the librarian said. "I understand you stole books from the library yesterday."

"I signed a receipt, Dakuz," Quint said.

"How do you think I knew?" Dakuz said sarcastically. "What did the books tell you?"

"That Willotan, the formal willot language, is similar to Narallian. I suspect that a long, long time ago, the tongue was the same, and then it diverged. The two languages are not identical."

"And you can read Narallian already?"

"I can puzzle my way through it slowly if I have a dictionary I can refer to often," Quint said.

Dakuz picked a book out of a stack on his desk. Quint could see it was in Narallian. "Show me."

Quint picked out a page and could translate less than a quarter of the words. "I have a way to go," he said.

The librarian pursed his lips. "Not bad. You aren't playing games with me, are you?"

"I'm not," Quint said. "Why would I waste time studying a language I already knew?"

"You are still willing to waste time, as you phrased it?"

Quint nodded. "I am."

"Then continue with what you are doing. The books are out on loan for two weeks, no more. I don't have a solution, but you'll have to wait two weeks after you bring them back before you can get them on loan if no one else has checked them out," Dakuz said. "Those are library rules. You'll have to work through them."

"I'm happy to do so," Quint said to Dakuz's grumbling. "What about magic instruction?"

"You know seventy-something strings! You should be teaching me!"

Quint frowned and was rewarded with Dakuz narrowing his eyes. "I was told last night that the cloister has a list of three hundred strings."

"And you think you'll be able to do them all? Magic doesn't work that way, boy."

Quint was getting irritated, but he took a deep breath and plunged on. "I can do more than most people, and I won't know what I can or can't do until I try."

Dakuz stared at Quint through his still-narrowed eyes. "I'll show you the spell books. They are secured."

"I promised to document the spells that the cloister doesn't have that I demonstrated."

"And how will you document them?" Dakuz said, softening his anger.

"I'll show you now, or I can bring a spell sheet to our next meeting."

Dakuz pursed his lips. "Tomorrow will do. What else do you think you need to know?"

"Narukun history and the current political situation," Quint said.

"Is that something a monk should know?" Dakuz asked.

"It is for me. I'm not going to say I'm more than a monk, but—"

"You are going to tell me you are more than a monk. I've heard about the predictor strings," Dakuz said.

"That wasn't what I was going to say, Dakuz. It's apparent that the political factions affect the workings of the Seensist cloister and likely all of Narukun's cloisters. I'm new to your country and need to know where I should next place my foot on this new path of my life."

Dakuz laughed. "You have a well-oiled tongue, that's for sure. You need to learn Narallian better to read political tracts and newsheet articles like you did in Racellia. Your best friend Feodor Danko writes such things."

"I've read his book on empires," Quint said.

"And what did you think?"

"It opened my eyes."

Dakuz frowned. "It is a pile of manure; that's what it is. He and his cursed daughter left out half the stories. "

"That affects his main idea?"

"What is his main idea?"

"That empires can't last long and inevitably crumble," Quint said.

"Do you know that two-thirds of the Baxel continent is an empire that has been intact for almost three thousand years?" Dakuz asked.

"I've never heard of it," Quint said.

"You wouldn't, not being from South or North Fenola. I've got a few books written in the country of Honnen on the continent of Amea and smuggled into the cloister a few hundred years ago. I've had word since that the empire is still going strong."

"What kind of empire does that?" Quint asked.

"Here is where I agree with Feodor: the emperor is not related to the previous one by law. A large part of longevity is choosing competent leaders. I don't know much more about it since it is mostly closed to the outside."

"So, Feodor Danko should have spent more time investigating the Baxel-based empire?" Quint asked.

"Absolutely. It is apparent, isn't it?" Dakuz said. "Whatever they have or whatever they do could be duplicated."

"But what if the Baxel empire has objectionable practices that no one in North or South Fenola would ever agree to? You can't duplicate success unless the circumstances are amenable to local change," Quint said.

Dakuz stared at Quint again. "Who taught you how to think that way?"

Quint shrugged. "In the past two years, I've done a lot of research. I had to do a good job, or I'd be fired, which was almost the same as a death sentence," he said. "I paid attention to the advice my bosses gave me."

"Continue to do that," Dakuz said. "Spend time with Sandiza Bartok and become more proficient at Narallian. Your learning about all things Narukun will only be realized when you do. I'll give you a few periodicals to puzzle over. Remember, not all monks come to Seensist knowing Narallian. We will talk more tomorrow, and bring one of your spell sheets on one of your more challenging strings." Dakuz rose. "Let's get you something current to read."

Quint left his first session with Dakuz with a newsheet, a Red-oriented political tract, and a Green-influenced pamphlet on agricultural policy. Both were published in Pinzleport. Quint was glad the session was over. Dakuz grumbled and grimaced the entire time, but he wasn't as bad as Quint expected.

§

Quint arrived a few minutes early for dinner. He didn't have anyone with him. The councilors' table was full with another person in the seat he had occupied the previous night.

"Looking for a place to sit?" Sandy said, nudging him from behind.

"Actually…" Quint said.

"Follow me." The young woman led Quint to a table in the back and sat next to him. "If you are late, you get to serve the next evening."

"Have you been late?"

Sandy sighed. "It's inevitable, but serving isn't so bad."

"Tables aren't assigned?"

She shook her head. "No, but peers generally end up sitting beside each other."

"Are we peers?"

Sandy gave him a quick smile. "We are both deacons. Everyone at this table will likely be a deacon. I can introduce you. Youngish deacons are generally rising in the cloister hierarchy. Older deacons have peaked, but most have responsible positions or duties."

"Oscar Viznik?" Quint asked.

A dark cloud metaphorically appeared over Sandy's head. "He is an acolyte without a responsible position, and that's because he isn't perceived to be responsible. I won't talk about him if you don't mind. He hasn't contacted you, has he?"

Quint shook his head. "I shouldn't seek him out?"

"I wouldn't, and that's all I'll say."

Two young men sat at the table, and the Oscar conversation ended. Sandy looked relieved to have the subject changed. She introduced Quint to her fellow deacons, and soon the table was full. Quint answered a few questions, but the group began discussing the cloister. Quint was happy to sit back and listen to the gossip and discussions on the factions.

As he listened and watched, Quint could get an idea about who went with what faction. None of them seemed like fanatics, and none of them appeared to be strident Reds or Greens.

"Were you escaping from Greens when you came here?" one of the monks asked.

Quint was surprised he was asked a question after being ignored for a few moments.

"I was. I had a run-in with Feodor Danko in Bocarre, if any of you have heard of him. He told my ship's captain that Green guards would be waiting for me at the dock where the ship put in. The captain had me rowed ashore to the beach below the cloister and said I'd do better coming here."

The monk snorted. "You have that right! Stepping into the cloister is not something a Green guard would do alone."

"There aren't any Greens in Seensist?"

"Plenty," Sandy said, "but there are Reds as well as other factions that wouldn't put up with a single Green imposing their will. Monks want peace and quiet so they can pursue their studies and their projects. Incorporating factional nonsense in the cloister only leads to ruin and unrest. We do what we can to avoid it."

All but one of the monks seemed to agree. Quint had put the dissenter down in his mind as a Green but didn't know why. The room went quiet as the head prior stood and said a different prayer, but still in Narallian, over the food. After a brief buzz, the food was served, and the refectory settled down to the business of eating.

Conversations began to increase as diners finished their meals. "Thank you for putting up with me," Quint said as he stood and noticed others in the room leaving. As he reached one of the doors, Sandy caught up to him.

"What do you think of my group?"

"The factional nonsense was toned down," Quint said. "I noticed one of the group is a dedicated Green."

"Zopik?" Sandy asked. "He is. Did you classify everyone else?"

"No one is as rabid a partisan as he," Quint said. "I'm not sure they are Reds, either."

Sandy sighed. "We will have to have a conversation on cloister factionalism. You can be forewarned about what topics to avoid, but it seems you have no problem identifying alliances."

Quint laughed. "It was what I did for two years: identify trends and opinions. The knowledge didn't help me when Bocarre started to crumble into a civil war."

"I'll bet it did."

Quint sighed. "I suppose I made fewer mistakes. The ones that fooled me were the Dankos, but then they were in Bocarre on their own mission, and it didn't include me."

"They were the ones who put the Green guards on the docks?"

Quint nodded. "I don't have any political opinions and would like to understand Narukun's environment better. I don't like authoritarians," Quint said.

"You aren't a Green, then."

"Most likely not, but then I don't know what they truly believe. I'll have a better chance after I do some reading. Hintz Dakuz is having me translate periodicals and papers."

"From Narallian? I thought you didn't know the language."

Quint told Sandy about his discovery comparing Narallian and Willotan. "I'll be relying on you to teach me the pronunciation. It is very different. I could only pick up several words when the head prior prayed at dinner."

"I know your schedule, but you don't know mine. Can we talk at lunch tomorrow?"

"Is that permissible?"

"It is easier to take your meal out of the refectory and eat outside."

§§§

CHAPTER FOUR

Q UINT SAT IN THE REFECTORY AT LUNCH. The previous day, his work on the garden was ruined by rain that started close to midnight, and he was still working on flooding out the cloister. Dakuz was pleased with Quint's format for his string book pages. "Pleased" was a relative description, thought Quint, after enduring criticisms of just about everything from Quint's choice of paper to his penmanship. Quint's style of writing was different than what was taught in Narukun.

His translation was acceptable but not even good at this point, but Dakuz said it was a start. Quint took that as a compliment.

Sandy walked in soaking, grabbed a tray of food, and sat down. She smiled. "You could have cast a predictor string to see if it was going to rain," she said good-naturedly.

"I try not to cast those," Quint said. "I'm afraid of what I might see."

"Really?"

Quint nodded. "Really. Everyone says I will do great things, but I don't want to be influenced by what might be in my decision-making."

"You think ahead!" She said it too loudly and clapped her hand over her mouth.

"I restrict that, too," Quint said. "My garden is a sodden mess, but I think I made a few inroads with Hintz."

"You are calling him that, now?" Sandy asked.

"No," Quint said with a smile. "He said my assignments were a start. He said he would have rejected what I did last night."

"I know a quiet place we can talk, if you can eat fast."

Quint had the ability, and now the motivation, to do that. Sandy led Quint outside. They stood underneath the porch of the front of the refectory.

Sandy sighed. "It's not going to let up, is it?"

Quint shook his head.

"We are going to the council building," Sandy said before sloshing through the puddles as she crossed the courtyard. Quint passed by his plot. He hadn't thought it would have turned into a lake. Perhaps he could grow fish, he ruefully thought.

Inside the council building, Sandy led him into the basement and opened the door to a bare, stone room and cast a light.

"Dakuz would have eventually told you about this. It is for string experimentation. Monks have died in the room," Sandy said.

"I'm sure the cloister is old enough to have had monks die just about everywhere."

She brightened. "Good observation, but I don't think it makes me feel any better."

"It does me," Quint says. "Perspective has a way of doing that."

"Maybe for you…"

She walked to a square table surrounded by four chairs. "We can talk here until someone decides to practice strings."

"I can show you some of my advanced ones if they need proof that we are working in wizardry," Quint said. He created a string and brought up a set of lights that went from one end of the room to the other.

"I've never seen that before," she said.

"It was a string a Gussellian wizard had in his spellbook. You duplicate threads to get multiple lights," Quint said, taking a seat. "Is it too bright?"

"No! No, no, no," Sandy said. "I still don't think of you as a powerful prior-level wizard."

"I can go through fifteen or twenty strings if you want to see more."

Sandy laughed. "No need. We are here to expand your horizons, not mine. You wish to know about the factions."

"We are," Quint said.

"Let's start with the Greens. They have a large following, but most of them don't know that much about Green policy. Greens believe that a council is the best form of government, and that council comes from the elite, who are generally well-educated. Citizens are in place to serve the elite families, who run the government."

"The elite families rule in perpetuity?" Quint asked.

"That is the idea."

Quint frowned. "It isn't any different from a hereditary ruler except it's a group that rules and group dynamics being what they are, someone will run the group, and they could become the emperor or head councilor or whatever. Who creates the rules?"

"The council," Sandy said. "The Green monks insist Seensist Cloister is ruled the same way."

"Except one's family and friends aren't on the Seensist council, so an exception is that hereditary elites don't rule the cloister, just elites," Quint said. "What about personal property?"

"The state owns everything. The council establishes pay scales, where people are housed, and who permits whom to move around Narukun."

Quint frowned. "None of which Seensist cloister chooses to emulate."

"Not yet. My imagination can take me from there. It makes for an orderly society, and those who make decisions are rewarded handsomely and live exceedingly well."

"What about the Reds?"

As Sandy described their principles, it struck Quint that the Red faction was basically set up to promote nobles rather than the elite and their social goals gave 'lip service,' as Sandy said it, the people. They supported a monarchical government with property rights, speech rights, and the ability to create a business and keep the profits. The monarch had the right to modify the rights as necessary.

"What about taxes?" Quint asked.

"For the Reds? The king decides."

"And if the king decides to raise taxes that put people out of business or evicted out of their homes for non-payment of unfair rates?" Quint asked.

"The Reds aren't perfect either," Sandy said. "For many, it's a matter of who you trust more."

Quint was just about over his head with evaluating the two factions. "I doubt it," Quint said. "I'm not a university professor, so I don't know much about alternatives, but I support a freer environment, and so does the cloister. They give us a plot to work and allow us a bit of freedom to sell our excess. I suppose similar incentives exist for those who do the other crafts."

"More or less," Sandy said.

"What other factions are there?"

Sandy settled in her chair. "Some are single-purpose factions, like only addressing the needs for farmers or teachers or things like that."

"May I ask you what your faction is? Don't answer if it's too personal."

"I lean slightly toward the Greens. My family never liked the kings in Baxel, and some of that rubbed off on me, but I'm no fanatic."

"What kind of government does Narukun have?"

"A monarchy. It is a mostly Red country at the top."

"Almost?"

Sandy nodded. "People don't like our society being closed at the top."

"The king of Narukun supports the Reds?"

"For all intents and purposes," Sandy said.

"Self-defense," Quint said. "He is doing the rational thing. If Feodor Danko is anything, he is a fanatic Green. If I were the king of Narukun, I'd probably match the Greens move for move."

"Probably," Sandy said. "You figured this out just now?"

Quint shrugged. "It's a logical extension. I thought of the Reds as reactionary to the Greens, but it's all a matter of where the leaders come from and then who gives the most freedoms to the common people. I could be wrong."

"But you are right in the general sense. I'm impressed that you picked it up so easily. I've had fights with family and friends, and no one seized the bigger picture like you did," Sandy said.

"I've had some experience that you haven't had. I'm sure you can do many things that I can't, like speak Narallian."

"There is that," Sandy said.

Someone knocked on the door. "Are you about done?" The monk looked at the line of lights. "Was that from one string?" he asked.

"It was," Quint said.

"Impressive. You are the monk from South Fenola."

"I am," Quint said.

The monk grinned. "Perhaps you can show me how to do that."

"Another time," Quint said, getting to his feet.

"I had to leave, anyway," Sandy said. Once in the hall, she told Quint they could get together for another session in two days.

That was convenient since the master gardener had told him that rain or shine, tomorrow they would be heading for New Baziltof, a good-sized village in the opposite direction of Pinzleport.

§

Eben didn't know where the old Baziltof was. The "tof" meant community in Narallian, so the gardener said. Quint would have to look it up.

The village was good-sized. There were three parallel streets in the central part of the village. They were bisected with a large green used for markets two days of every week. Market stalls filled the green.

"We can look for herbs and spices?" Quint asked the gardener.

"This market has a better selection than the market in Pinzleport; although there are specialty shops at the port, none have the volume that Baziltof has."

Quint took out the list that Sandy had given him. "These are the ones I want the most of," he said.

The gardener took Quint to the farmers' section of the market first. Quint bought his beans. There were three varieties that the gardener recommended. Then they collected extra starts for plants that the gardener said would sell well in the cloister, other than the string beans. The gardener then filled up the wagon with produce and replacements for plants that had been washed away by the previous day's storm.

"Now, the herbs," the gardener said.

They both bought an ample supply. "What you don't use fresh, you can dry. All the monks know how to do it."

Quint also bought a selection of herb starts he'd try to grow.

"Spices that aren't grown around here are in another section of the market."

Quint collected more spices than on Sandy's list. Some were familiar, grown in South Fenola, and others he wanted to try.

"What else do we need to purchase?" Quint said.

"You don't have any money, but I can lend you some of mine. Is there anything else you'd like to buy?"

"I'd like my own copies of Narallian texts. A dictionary and a pronunciation guide if one is available."

Eben drove the cart out of the market and down one of the main streets, stopping at a bookstore. Quint noticed shops had Narallian script instead of the common tongue painted on their signs and windows.

Quint walked in. "I'd like to buy some books on Narallian," he said.

He walked out, spending all the money the gardener had lent him. He now had two dictionaries and a pronunciation guide that looked of dubious worth to Quint. The history books were old, used, and probably more accurate than anything newer. They covered the wagon with light canvas and headed back to the Cloister.

As they rode into a patch of woods, Quint pursed his lips.

"Have you ever been attacked on the way back to the Cloister?"

"Not going to or returning from Baziltof," the gardener said.

"Today is not your lucky day," Quint said.

He looked back and saw two horsemen enter the road at the start of the wood. Four more entered the road ahead of them.

"You do know we are about to be ambushed," Quint said.

Eben looked ahead and then behind. "They aren't after me!" he said as he jumped off the wagon and ran into the woods.

Quint grabbed the reins and urged the two horses forward. He put the reins in his teeth and began creating a string on the bouncing carriage. As they approached the four horsemen, with the rear pair still far behind, Quint stood and cast a fan of flame into the riders. As the men and horses began to stop, Quint grabbed the reins from his teeth and urged the horses through the burning attackers.

None of the ambushers attempted to attack Quint, more intent on quenching the flames. The two riders in the rear stopped to assist their cohorts in crime, and Quint continued toward Seensist Cloister.

"Where is Eben?" the monk who opened the gate asked.

"He ran into the woods, and when he didn't show up, I decided he could walk back," Quint said as he snapped the reins and proceeded to the garden building.

When he had unloaded the wagon and put the horses and wagon away, he began to plant the beans in his plot. The master gardener showed up when Quint was through with the string beans and planting his herbs.

"You didn't come back for me!" The gardener said, huffing, puffing, and red in the face from his long walk and anger.

"I wasn't going to stick around when there were two highwaymen still able to attack me," Quint said. "As you said, they weren't after you. How did you know that?"

Eben hemmed and hawed. "Why would they want me? No one wants starts; they want produce. The only valuable commodity on the wagon was you."

"And you deserted me," Quint said. "With my deserting you, I'd say we were even, don't you?"

"You won't get away with this!" the gardener said.

"Shall I let you get away with setting me up?" Quint put his hands on his hips and stared at the gardener, who couldn't withstand Quint's gaze.

"We are even. Perhaps I exercised bad judgment," the man said, admitting he had told someone that Quint would be traveling to Baziltof.

"Perhaps you did," Quint said. "I'll forgive you if you forgive me," Quint said. "You saw what I did to the ambushers. I didn't fight the two men behind us. No need since they stopped to help their friends." Quint extended his hand.

Eben stared at it for a moment and then shook Quint's hand. "Let me see your work," the gardener said.

Quint thanked the gardener for his reluctant compliments on Quint's orderly rows and accepted Quint's work. After finishing with the herbs, Quint watered his plot and took his new books to his cell to peruse for the rest of the afternoon.

The dinner bell would strike in an hour, but Quint had enough time to compare his new dictionary with the library book and deemed it a worthy replacement, although he had no way to evaluate the pronunciation of texts. Perhaps Sandy could do that.

§§§

CHAPTER FIVE
~

DINNER WAS UNEVENTFUL. Sandy was missing from the table, and the others said it wasn't unusual for any of them to be gone. One monk thought Sandy had gone into Pinzleport with another monk for dinner. The monk raised his eyebrows when he said it. The others laughed. It was clear they thought Sandy had a paramour among the younger monks.

Quint could not help feeling his face heat up. It wasn't that he had consciously had feelings for Sandy, but the thought of her with another monk shocked Quint. He recovered. Quint reminded himself that everyone had a life before he arrived and would continue to live their lives after he left. Quint didn't feel the sense of betrayal that he had felt with Calee Danko. This was a simpler reaction, and Quint had to recognize it as a touch of naivete he faced as a seventeen-year-old.

He walked out into the evening after dinner and sat on a bench within a flower garden on the other side of the courtyard's animal pens and garden plots. The faint whiff of manure assaulted his nose as he took in the moon rising. Quint reviewed his day. It would have been a resounding success if the assassins hadn't shown up. Quint dismissed his disappointment with Sandy, but although he said he had forgiven the gardener, the forgiveness didn't account for the lingering distrust.

He spent the rest of the night translating and finishing the Green agricultural policy tract. It was clear the Greens wanted to rule Narukun with an iron fist. Everyone should bow to the Green council, and they would get their just reward for doing so. The reward was being a serf. Quint could envision an entire country becoming like southeastern Racellia. Life would be worse; Quint was sure of that.

The next day, Quint made sure his starts were taking to their new environment and his herbs were doing the same. He arrived a bit early for his session with Dakuz.

"Here is my translation of the Green policy tract. I bought some history books at Baziltof yesterday when I went with the master gardener for plants and supplies. I also bought a dictionary, so I don't have to get one on loan every two weeks."

"You aren't supposed to leave the cloister," Dakuz said.

"I thought it would be permitted if I had an escort."

"Eben is a Green. If I were you, I'd avoid Greens where possible. They are not on your side."

"Am I to engage every monk with a philosophical discussion to determine which faction they favor?" Quint asked.

Dakuz stared at Quint as if he were an idiot. "As much as you can. I would vet anyone who offers to escort you outside. Consider the head prior's instruction for you to stay within the cloister for the next six months. Things must cool off regarding you, and yesterday's attack proved you are still in danger."

"How did you know about the attack?"

"Eben told the guards that you deserted him a mile from the Cloister. Assume everyone will know of your fight," Dakuz said. "He should have kept his mouth shut about the attack. How did you fend them off?"

Quint described the encounter.

Dakuz went silent for a moment. "Keep as much to yourself as possible, you fool! Not only were you outside without the head prior's permission, but you used magic to injure or kill. You could be removed from the cloister for that. Luckily, the version I heard didn't mention magic. The fact that some sympathetic Green monk didn't march into the prior's office and blurt out the magical details of the attack proves the cloister's complicity. The less said, the better. Do you understand?"

"And if someone asks me?"

"Give them no details. Say the gardener ran, and you rode through them." Dakuz grumbled to himself. "Let's go over your feeble attempt at translation, and then let me examine your history books to see if they are better than useless, which I suspect they aren't.

§

Quint smiled as he ate lunch in silence. He sat at the table with Sandy's friends. They welcomed him and asked about his trouble on the road from Baziltof. Quint gave them the story that Dakuz suggested, which seemed to satisfy them.

Sandy showed up late and asked Quint for some time after the midday meal to discuss his progress. They stepped into the manicured garden area and found an empty bench.

"I made a mistake," Sandy said. "I should have stopped you from going out of the cloister. It was my fault for not realizing the head prior had restricted your movements. I'm glad you survived the attack."

"I think it was an assassination attempt," Quint said. He was tempted to tell her he fended the bandits off with his magic, but Dakuz's warning stopped him. "The master gardener might have told someone I was out and about. He jumped off the wagon when the attackers began to close. I grabbed the reins and ran them down."

"You were lucky. They could have jumped on the wagon," Sandy said.

"Luck was certainly at play," Quint said, "but it should have never happened."

"I stopped by your garden plot. I was impressed by your work. Your mother taught you well."

Quint smiled. "Indeed, she did. My father also emphasized following her instructions. I have been good at doing that in my life, maybe too good. What's next in my orientation?"

Sandy shrugged. "Continue to do what you are doing, but no outside experiences for six months or until the head prior says you can leave the cloister. I don't think you'll be attacked inside these walls."

Quint looked around the large courtyard and at the buildings that surrounded them. "I hope you are right, but I'll be prepared. I bought a dictionary and a pronunciation guide. I'd appreciate your comparing the guide to the one from the library. The dictionary seems to compare with the one I borrowed."

"I can do that right now if you have the time."

Quint thought for a moment. "I can make time. It shouldn't take long, and I'd like to get started on pronunciation lessons. Dakuz said you'd be the best person for that."

"He did?" Sandy said, sounding like she was impressed.

"I assume your diction is good?"

"It is," she said, standing up. "I'll meet you at your cell in half an hour."

True to her word, Sandiza brought a bag filled with thin books.

"I bought these in Pinzleport yesterday." She pulled them out. "They are Narallian primers for new learners."

Quint looked at the covers. "These are for children."

"New learners," Sandy said with a grin. "Not only do they have spelling, but they also have pronunciation for the words in each chapter."

"You don't want to work with me?" Quint asked, a little confused.

"That isn't it. You can work on these at your own pace and on your own time. I think you'll move faster to fluency since you have a head start knowing the language of South Fenola."

"Willotan," Quint said.

"Right, willotan. Let's review a chapter, and then you can show me your translations. I'm not taking the place of Hintz Dakuz, but helping you speak Narallian sooner. You have other things to learn from him."

"I do," Quint said.

Quint's diction was awful as he tried to read the first few paragraphs of the first primer. Sandy couldn't understand most of what he said.

"Now, follow along with me," she said.

They continued to go through the first chapter, and then Sandy reviewed the pronunciation marks at the end. Quint showed Sandy his pronunciation guide, and Sandy showed him that the guide's marks assumed a general knowledge of Narallian pronunciation.

"You would have spent years trying to get the diction right," Sandy said. "Let's look at your translation."

Sandy caught about the same things that Dakuz did. "You are better with written Narallian, but I expected that once you said there was a similarity between what you read in Bocarre and what we speak here. With new learners, it is generally the opposite," Sandy said. "I'll leave you to your work. We can talk in two days. Get as much work done as possible, but speed won't help you. Focus will."

Quint spent the rest of the afternoon reviewing everything he had done with Sandy and Dakuz. What he thought would be easy because of knowing willotan wasn't going to be the case.

§

"I am concerned about your well-being," the head prior said in a private meeting with Quint just before the midday meal three days after the assassination attempt.

Quint gave the head prior a small bow. "I am fine. I wasn't injured."

"It isn't an injury I'm concerned about. I suspect you used magic to separate yourself from the assassins?"

Quint took a breath before objecting, but the prior raised his hand.

"You won't be punished for doing so. Your life was at risk, and our cloister isn't a suicide cult. I'm much more concerned about Eben's action than yours."

"I talked with him the day of the attack and this morning while I worked. We have everything worked out, and since you know what he did, his influence can be diminished," Quint said.

"Within the cloister?"

Quint nodded. "I now distrust what he says, and since you know he betrayed me to the Greens, he can be watched and punished if needed. I wouldn't punish for this." Quint was interested to know if the Greens would do some punishing of the master gardener on their own. "I didn't know I couldn't leave the cloister under any circumstances."

"A misunderstanding. I'm just glad your ignorance didn't cost you your life," the prior said. "I have a punishment for the misunderstanding, not the magic usage. Your head will be shaved."

"Shaved?" Quint asked. He had seen other bald monks around the cloister. "Are all those with no hair being punished?"

The prior laughed. "No, not at all. For many, it is a symbol of their dedication to the order. You won't be out of place if you remain inside the cloister. In six months, when your hair is grown out, you may tell Sandiza Bartok and Hintz Dakuz of your punishment, but for all others, it will be a sign of dedication to your improvement. Am I understood?"

"You are, Head Prior. I won't let you down."

The prior pursed his lips. "Perhaps that will come in the future."

"My predictor strings?"

"People like you are too big to stay here for long."

"People like me?"

"Achievers," the head prior said. "At some point, there will be a compelling reason for you to leave, and you will. Your destiny does not lie in taking my place at some point."

"I never contemplated…"

The prior stopped his comment with his raised hand again. "There is plenty of time for circumstances to become clearer in the future." The prior looked at the old wooden clock on his wall and nodded. "We have spoken more than needful. Sandiza will show you where to shave your head. Do it after lunch. There isn't any kind of a ceremony attached."

Quint found an empty table and ate alone for lunch. On the way back to his cell, Sandy walked up behind him.

"You are headed in the wrong direction. The cloister barber is back that way." She pointed behind her with her thumb. "I've been asked to accompany you."

"You are getting your head shaved, too?" Quint asked with a hint of a smile.

"No! Of course not. I'm your guide. I suggest the story should be you are doing it as a symbol of dedication to your studies."

"Does Dakuz know the story?"

Sandy grimaced. "Actually, he suggested it. If we both support that, there should be no controversy."

Quint sighed. "I was wondering why there wasn't a mirror in my cell."

"Only because he took it with him when the previous monk left the cloister. You buy your own."

"Something to look forward to, I imagine," Quint said.

When they stepped into the barbershop on the second floor of the building next to the refectory, the barber-monk was snoring in one of the two barber chairs.

"Awake!" Sandy said. "I have brought another victim."

The monk blinked his eyes and sat up before yawning. "Not you, Sandiza?"

"Not today," she said. "This is the new monk. After a week to think about it, he has decided to dedicate the next six months to learning, contemplation and honest work."

"Tolo or something?" the monk asked.

"Quint Tirolo," Quint said.

"Sit here," the monk stepped away from his napping couch.

"Shaved heads are the easiest to start but a pain to maintain. You should learn to shave your head." He looked closely at Quint. "You need to learn how to shave your face at the same time," the barber said, chuckling. He whipped out an apron and tied it around Quint's neck. "Close your eyes and go to sleep. It won't take long."

Quint closed his eyes, and a moment later, he felt a spell make him relax, and then he fell asleep. When he woke, he felt his head. His hair was gone, and his face was shaved, too.

Sandy handed a few coins to the barber and handed Quint a mirror.

"I'm not the same person I was when I walked in," Quint said, already rubbing his head and missing his longish hair.

The barber walked in from behind a curtain in the back of the shop. "Here is a straw hat. You don't want to stay in the sun too long on your first day. Gradually let the sun tan your cranium."

Quint thanked the barber, although he didn't feel very appreciative. Once they entered the sunlight, Quint put the straw hat on.

"At least it fits," he said.

"I bought you a little present at the cloister infirmary." She gave him a small white bottle with a cork stopper. "Put a thin coat of the salve on your head before you go out. It will give you some protection, but it will also help with the tanning."

"I don't know what to say, and it isn't thanks," Quint said. He managed a smile so his poor joke wouldn't be misinterpreted. "Luckily, hair grows back. Won't it?"

It was Sandy's turn to smile. "It will. You pay the barber the next time, whenever that will be."

"Will he spell me to sleep every time, even after it's grown out?"

Sandy giggled. "That is up to you. Are you in the mood to go through your schoolwork?"

"Maybe not today," Quint said. "I think I want to think about everything, and I can do that working in the garden plots. If I finish quickly, I can always pull other monks' weeds."

"Ask first. Some monks also use that time to cultivate their spiritual selves."

Quint nodded.

§

Sandy went elsewhere while Quint watered his starts and examined all his plants. He found a monk toiling in a much more mature plot.

"Mind if I give you some help?" Quint asked.

The monk looked suspiciously at Quint. "Do you expect to be paid?"

Quint shook his head as he took the straw hat off. "I have to get mentally used to this." He pointed to his bald head.

The monk chuckled. "I did that once when I was younger. I'd be happy for the help."

As they worked, the monk asked Quint about South Fenola. "Who do they worship?" the monk finally asked.

"No one. Most of South Fenola is secular. No religion is practiced. Are you a religionist?" Quint asked.

"I wouldn't use that term, but I suppose I am. My sect believes in divine interventions. Most sects recognize Tizurek as God and Tova as Goddess. Past that, there are lots of variations. My sect believes that Tizurek is the supreme god and Tova is his handmaiden."

"They aren't married?"

"We don't believe they are. Other sects worship Tova with different roles and Tizurek in different manifestations as well."

"Just like factions?"

The monk nodded. "You can say that and won't be too far off the mark. As I said, we believe that Tizurek speaks to humans. Most of it is by impressions. If you want, you can attend our meetings on Felsday."

"You don't meet at Vespers?"

"Not here," the monk said. "Vespers is a secular service at Seensist. It is more a social gathering than a spiritual communion."

"We would call Felsday Second Day in Racellia. Tizuday is First Day named after Tizurek. I understand it was originally the holy day of the week. Pulday is Third Day, Yaxday is Fourth Day, Lictday is Fifth Day, Wozeday is Sixth Day, and Homeday is Seventh Day. Today is Yaxday," Quint said.

"You did well," the monk said. "I am Pol Grizak."

"Quint Tirolo," Quint said.

Pol grinned. "I know who you are. I'm from the eastern shores of Narukun, close to the border with Kippun. Kippun is populated with hubites, too, but centuries ago, they assimilated into the Pogokon culture. I think they have become more polennese than the polens who inhabit Slinnon and Pogokon. We can talk again. Let's finish weeding because I have a magic class to attend."

Quint could feel the warmth on his head and put his hat on for the last row of weeding. He said farewell to his new friend; at least Pol seemed like a friend, although he was probably thirty.

When he reached his cell, Quint washed his head and put another thin coating of the salve before continuing to translate his publications.

§§§

CHAPTER SIX
~

DAKUZ FROWNED. "What irritating sounds you are making," the older monk said. "People won't talk to you, even if they do understand the squawking."

"Sandy said my pronunciation is getting better."

"It is improving, but I wouldn't call it better yet," Dakuz said. "Ask the Head Prior to sit in on council meetings. They often will talk in Narallian unless there are non-speakers present."

"Are there other meetings or groups that do the same?" Quint asked. "Pol Grizak has invited me to a religious group meeting on Felsday. Would they speak Narallian?"

Dakuz gave Quint a dirty look. "Why don't you ask him, someone who knows, rather than me, someone who doesn't."

Quint took that for a "yes." He wanted to talk about religion, but Dakuz forced the conversation around the current events in Narukun. Living amid factionalism differed from learning about what was happening in northeast Narukun, where the capital was. If he hadn't lived in Bocarre, the events he read about daily working for the late Colonel Julia Gerocie wouldn't mean as much to him when he put his reports together.

Quint sighed as the image of Colonel Gerocie's body came to mind. She didn't deserve to die. Feodor Danko was on the side that murdered her. Perhaps Master Pozella encountered the same fate. Another sigh accompanied the thought that Quint may never know.

"Now for some magic."

"A question, first. I know you don't like the Dankos. I wondered how Calee could be able to kill me at sixteen."

Dakuz lifted the corner of his mouth in a wry smile. "Who said she was sixteen?"

"Her father did. Is she a year or two older?"

"Try twelve or thirteen years older," Dakuz said. "Your list of strings doesn't include any cosmetic spells. Did you know that category of strings even exists?"

"She is almost thirty?" Quint said, utterly astonished.

"Cosmetic strings aren't particularly good for one's health," Dakuz said. "It eventually ruins the recipient's skin. Let's talk about them for our magic segment."

For Calee to appear sixteen, Dakuz guessed she had to use three or four strings to make her young age convincing and minimize the damage. Two would be illusion spells, but the skin strings used on her face were advanced strings that stretched and held the skin tighter. To be convincing under close observation, illusions would be judiciously utilized depending on Calee's true appearance.

"Can I darken my hair and skin?" Quint asked. "I used peat stain once in Bocarre, and it didn't last long."

"I'm sure there is something. Vain wizards would certainly have developed a string to darken their gray hair." Dakuz stroked his wispy graying beard. "Not something I would use myself. Do you want to try a few?"

"I'd start with dark hair, but…" Quint rubbed his bald head. "That will have to wait."

"Camouflage?" Dakuz said. "We might be able to do better than that. If you are strolling in a market, an illusion string would be easier, and you wouldn't worry about your skin."

"At my age? I think my skin can take some abuse for a while," Quint said.

Dakuz grunted. "Everyone is different. You could cast a youth string, and when you reverted, your skin might have suffered terrible damage."

"How long does a string last?"

"Illusions, no more than a day. The transformation strings may last a few days before they must be recast. Shall we spend a week on those?"

"I'm interested and can see how I could use them to avoid being attacked."

"Or assassinated," Dakuz said.

"Same thing." Quint pulled out his notebook and wrote "Cosmetic strings" on the next blank page.

§

"I've heard of cosmetic strings," Sandy said when they met two days later at Quint's garden plot after lunch. "They take a high-level wizard to cast. You, for example."

"Is there are way to find out who has the best magic between Feodor Danko and his daughter?"

Sandy nodded. "I'm sure they would be tested. Everyone tested in Narukun, including you, is now registered in Baxel." She shrugged her shoulders. "I can write to the registrar. Testings aren't secrets if you pay a search fee like everyone else."

"I don't have much money," Quint said.

"Don't worry. I get an allowance for you. I'll send it out on the post. It will start its way to Baxel tonight."

Quint smiled haplessly. "I don't know why I'm interested, but I am. Calee tried to kill me twice, that I know of. I suppose father and daughter could be counted as my enemies. I need to be less forgiving."

Sandy looked across the plots at the master gardener talking to a couple of monks. "Look at them. If they were my enemies who tried to kill me, I wouldn't stand for it."

"You'd kill them?"

"I'd do more than forgive them, Quint. You should have found a way to punish Danko. If he gets in your way again, you should. Sending messages through actions is an old Narukun tradition."

"I've barely been here!" Quint said. "I thought I'd be expelled if I did something like that."

Sandy sighed. "You are probably right. The old traditions can get you into a lot of trouble." She smiled. "Something for you to think about when you meditate."

"I will," Quint said. "Shall we go over some Narallian words? I brought a sheet full of them. I can meditate after I've figured out how to pronounce all these."

They spent almost an hour with Quint making notations in common script pronunciation next to the words.

"Not bad. I detect some progress being made. Keep at it," Sandy said.

"Let's try for a compliment from Dakuz by the end of next week."

Quint laughed. "That has little chance of happening in the next year."

Sandy left Quint to play around with his garden plot, but that didn't take long and wouldn't for another few weeks. He retreated to his cell and repeated each word that he practiced at the garden plot five times before he turned to the assignments that Dakuz had given him.

Only a few of Sandy's friends showed up for dinner. Pol Grizak tapped Quint on the shoulder.

"Want to join my group? I can introduce you to some people you will meet again on Felsday."

"I could do that. Why are so many monks missing?"

Grizak laughed. "The menu. We are having a Kippun-style dinner tonight. It can be an acquired taste. Are you up for it?"

Quint shrugged. "I suppose so. I haven't prepared an alternative."

"You will once you've been here for a month or so."

Grizak led him to a table with an assortment of monks and introduced Quint to each one. It appeared that they all knew who Quint was. He made sure he remembered all their names when they were served. The table paused, and one of the older monks spoke a prayer in Narallian. Quint understood some of it, but before he started his language studies, he wouldn't have recognized it as close to the willotan tongue.

"We will speak Narallian at the service," Pol said.

"I'm trying to learn, but it isn't coming fast."

The monks laughed. "Give yourself a year or two to learn," one of them said.

Quint looked down at his dinner. He could see a resemblance to Slinnon cooking, but it looked like everything sat in a pool of grease.

"Is there a way to eat this and not consume all the oily stuff?" Quint said.

"I slice my bread, scoop the top on it, and eat it that way. You want to eat quickly before the fat begins to solidify."

A few others laughed and nodded. The rest of the monks dug into the pile of meat chunks and vegetables smothered in a greasy sauce on top of a mountain of rice. The taste wasn't so bad, but the presentation was awful.

"It is served in the traditional Kippunese way," Grizak said, dolloping the meat and vegetable on a slice of bread. "The other way to eat it is to skim the top and eat half the rice. That's what most of us do."

That was what the other monks had done. Quint tried both ways and liked the rice method better than the bread.

"You did well, boy," one of the monks said when they were finished.

"I've had Slinnon food before in Racellia. It wasn't genuine Slinnon-style, but close enough. It is better than this."

"Our hubite brothers in Kippun adopted Polennese ways and added their own twist to the cuisine. It went in the wrong direction. At least it's filling," one of the monks said.

Quint returned to his cell to resume his studies, but he sat on his bed, looking out the little window and thinking that Grizak's friends seemed nice enough, but then the master gardener initially did, too.

§

Felsday finally came. An hour after dinner, Quint showed up at the entrance to the building where Grizak's religious meeting was to be held. He nodded to a few of the monks who Quint had met at the dinner table until Grizak finally showed up and led Quint to their third-floor meeting room.

Thirty chairs have been set up in rows, pointing to a podium standing at the front. Quint counted twelve empty chairs and took one of them. Grizak sat next to him.

"Our leader is a council member," Grizak said quietly. "He runs the meetings, but our religious leader is a senior monk. He rarely eats in the refectory, preferring to buy and cook his own food."

"Where does he do that?"

"The kitchen staff let him. He pays for the privilege."

The council member entered the room and sat on one of two chairs behind the podium, followed quickly by a monk Quint had never seen before. The man had white hair but looked between fifty and sixty years of age, still older than Dakuz.

A few stragglers arrived before the council member rose and stood behind the lectern.

"Welcome to our service," the council member said in common. "We have a visitor in our midst. Because of him, today's service will be spoken in the common tongue. Pol, could you introduce Tirolo?"

Grizak gave a quick introduction. It was what Quint had shared with Grizak. There was a smattering of applause, and an embarrassed Quint sat down.

"We have no announcements, so I give the rest of the time to Brother Shinzle Bokwiz."

Bokwiz, the religious leader, stood and smiled at the tiny congregation. He called on a monk to begin the meeting with a prayer. Quint noticed that most of the prayer was formulaic with the end praying for recent events. The end invoked the condescension of Tizurek.

Quint looked around. Everyone but him bowed their heads, closed their eyes, and folded their hands on their laps. At the end, they placed both hands over their hearts in a salute to their god.

"Thank you, brother," Bokwiz said. "Since we have a visitor, I will depart from what I prepared to say and provide a quick history of our religion before I return to my message. Is that acceptable, brother monks?"

Mumbles of consent rose from the congregation.

Bokwiz nodded. "At one time, there were a myriad of religions in our world. People worshipped gods of all kinds in many ways. There was a great darkness that filled the land. Some legends speak of a ball of fire that struck the world. A god was exercising vengeance on those committing evil. Many people died from the fire and the extended darkness. When the darkness was about to lift, a voice boomed from the heavens. Those who survived weren't merely the righteous but the unrighteous as well. Everyone had a chance to return to the bosom of the god who called himself Tizurek.

"From that point onward, all the religions in the world worshipped Tizurek as their god. Over time, the name of Tizurek changed from culture to culture, each adding their flavor to what they perceived Tizurek to be, even changing his name. Men and a few women have taken up a standard and have claimed to be representatives of Tizurek. String magic was developed, and some pretenders were powerful wizards who were soon exposed as charlatans. People lost confidence in Tizurek, and cultures of the world began to forget Tizurek until now.

"There is always the hope of a true standard bearer rising among the people of the world, but alas." Bokwiz sighed. "We all stand waiting to hear the words of Tizurek booming from the heavens once more."

Bokwiz looked at Quint from the lectern. "You are welcome to attend our congregation to see if our way of worshipping Tizurek seems right to you. We adhere to common sense principles of looking out for each other, minimizing our infidelities to the truth, and living chaste lives. Pol is knowledgeable in our teaching, and he can answer your questions. Our meetings are a time to gather and listen to a thought or two on what we feel Tizurek wants of us, and for the rest of the week, we contemplate how the teachings can improve our lives. So, it has been said."

"So, it has been said," the congregation said in unison, placing both hands over their hearts.

Bokwiz drank water from a goblet behind the podium and continued presenting a sermon on loyalty to men and Tizurek. He gave examples of disloyalty and ended the meeting with a prayer in Narallian. The meeting lasted less than an hour.

The congregants rose and talked about the sermon. Pol let Quint sit for a few minutes as he greeted his friends. They all spoke Narallian and Quint was just as glad they let him alone because he could only understand bits and pieces of what they said.

Shinzle Bokwiz finally made his way to Quint.

"Are you overwhelmed, Brother Quinto?"

"Quint. Call me Quint. I wouldn't say I'm overwhelmed, although it is new information. I know little about gods and goddesses and have never heard of the fire and darkness. Is it a legend or recorded history?"

"Probably a little bit of both. The announcement by Tizurek to all the world is in all the accounts. For many, it is the hardest to swallow, but his proclamation is the most consistent part of all the accounts."

"Was common spoken then?" Quint asked.

Bokwiz chuckled. "Absolutely not. He spoke directly into everyone's minds and hearts. It is the source of our hands over heart sign."

"Pol said Tizurek still speaks to men?"

"To few," Bokwiz said, a touch of disappointment in his voice. "He has not spoken to me, although I have felt confirmation of his existence. Most of our congregation has, too, in varying degrees. I have felt feelings that were not my own on a few occasions. It is no delusion, although others scoff when I speak of it. Other sects claim it is Tova that touches our hearts." Bokwiz shrugged. "It may be true, too. I have no idea."

"Do you have a holy book? I've read of such things in novels."

"We have writings and transcriptions of sermons that have been assembled. Pol can supply you with those consistent with our vision of Tizurek."

"Other sects get the same feelings?" Quint asked.

Bokwiz frowned. "Alas, that is so. We cannot claim exclusivity, but what is ours is what we call the Code of Tizurek. It is an explanation of behaviors that we ascribe to. We all fall at times, but we pick ourselves up and improve our lives to tap into the promise of living with Tizurek after we die."

"And no one has ever been back from the dead?" Quint asked.

Bokwiz smiled slyly and shook his finger at Quint. "That is where faith comes in. We must exercise faith in Tizurek to activate the possibility of our elevation."

There was too much being said and unsaid for Quint.

"Thanks for inviting me. I'll certainly seek Pol with more questions."

"Please do," Bokwiz said.

Grizak was talking to other monks in Narallian. Quint made eye contact, nodded, and left the meeting. He had already learned bits and pieces from Dakuz but hadn't had an overall summary of religion in his world.

Quint didn't know what he believed and what he didn't. The monks in the meeting seemed sincere, but there were nearly three hundred monks in Seensist Cloister and maybe ten percent were believers. He talked to Dakuz about the religious aspect but didn't expect Dakuz to be religious. So far, the monk seemed to be honest with him.

Quint's cell seemed a refuge as he felt overwhelmed by his cloister experience. He was doing well until the religion discussion and the monks speaking Narallian. For the moment, the cloister didn't feel like the sanctuary he expected. Quint felt he needed to talk to someone, but it was late, and he had no idea how to contact Sandy other than at the refectory.

A knock interrupted Quint's confusion. When he opened the door, Grizak stood grinning with a bottle and two ceramic goblets.

"I thought you might want to talk about your experience tonight. You looked somewhat bewildered when you left the meeting." Grizak raised the bottle. "I brought something along to soothe your nerves."

Quint let the monk in and offered him the only chair in the cell. Grizak poured and handed Quint a goblet.

"Drink, even if you don't usually imbibe," Grizak said. "Perhaps it was rude for us to launch into our after-sermon discussions in Narallian, but I got the sense that wasn't what put that look on your face."

Quint took a sip of wine. It wasn't too strong. He thought about his response. "It was a new experience for me. I'm not a gregarious person, and the only person I knew was you and a few acquaintances from sharing the dinner table in the refectory so that you can put some of my awkwardness to shyness. The concept of religion is foreign to me. I admit a certain intimidation when Shinzle Bokwiz talked, and everyone put their hands over their hearts. I've never felt that way before. I've been intimidated plenty of times in military meetings, but then I was a target. Here I was a bystander, which made it different, I guess."

"I can see that. You are a youngster compared to the rest of us. Did you feel an affinity to what Brother Bokwiz said?"

Quint sighed. "No. I felt awkward and ignorant. I can't judge something as far-reaching as some kind of miracle that happened thousands of years ago. I can understand the darkness as some kind of physical disaster, like a volcano erupting and covering the world with clouds or something worse. The voice?" Quint shook his head. "The rest of it seemed like it made sense. I'll have to do some research on my own. That is something that I've learned to do along with critical thinking."

"You can't explain everything objectively about religion, Quint."

Quint nodded. "The belief part. Wanting to put your hands over your heart kinds of stuff, I understand. The messages from Tizurek can be intuition. I do believe in intuition, but more from the magic side, like uncast predictor strings."

Grizak laughed. "You are what we call a rationalist. Where we have our faith, you have your rational, objective, secular view of life. That kind of thinking can only get you so far if you seek spiritual guidance."

"If I want to seek spiritual guidance. I will do more research but with an open mind. How is that? I won't return to one of your meetings until I can speak Narallian better."

"Fair enough. We are still friends. You will still join us for dinner?"

Quint laughed, relieved by Grizak's response to Quint's soft, he hoped, rejection.

"Of course. We generally speak common, anyway." Grizak filled his goblet again. "If there are any other things about the cloister that you want to know, you can talk to me. Sandiza doesn't have to be your only contact, although she is more pleasant to look at than I."

"Too old for me!" Quint said.

"Really? How old do you think she is?"

"She said she was over twenty. I'm still seventeen."

Grizak laughed. "Sandiza has been in the cloister since she was young, entering as a prodigy with early magic. I don't think she is too old. You are much more experienced."

"How many strings does she know?" Quint asked.

"She is a deacon. That means thirty strings. But as you know, strings aren't the only qualifier for levels in the cloister."

"But she is far from being a novice?"

Grizak nodded. "If she is your cloister guide, I'd guess she is. I try not to keep track of such things. Do you think she minimizes her strings?"

Quint thought. "We haven't had many conversations on strings since I know so many, but she definitely said she was years older than me."

"I don't mean to be personal, but are you attracted to her?" Grizak.

"You are being personal, but I will answer your question. I'm going to have to restrain myself and not let her know what you told me," Quint said. "I am drawn to her as a friend, and I don't think her misstating her age is a reason to stop letting her help me around the cloister. A romantic relationship might get in the way of that."

Grizak took a few sips from his goblet. "I think that is wise. Give it until your hair grows back again."

Quint finished off his wine and set his goblet next to Grizak's. "Thanks for coming over. Our Sandy discussion helped put the meeting into some kind of perspective."

Grizak took his goblets and his bottle and stood. "I won't take up more of your time. We can talk again."

"I'd like that," Quint said, realizing he meant it.

§§§

Chapter Seven

The following afternoon, when Sandy arrived to help Quint with diction, he looked at her face more closely. He wasn't a great judge of ages, but her face seemed a little smoother than before. He laughed to himself. Quint had thought Calee looked sixteen, and he hadn't really noticed. Sandy's age made no difference if Quint didn't look at her as a potential girlfriend.

His diction was getting better, but he admitted the trouble he had when attending Bokwiz's sermon.

"That is great!" Sandy said. "The more you integrate within the Cloister, the better for everyone.

"They spoke more common because I was there, but when the sermon ended, they reverted to Narallian, and it was disheartening that I couldn't understand much of what they said," Quint said.

"It's common. When one learns Narallian, the instructor and the student talk much slower with a smaller vocabulary. It is a natural thing to do. The monks spoke Narallian at a conversational speed which is higher than speeches and announcements. I'm sure they lost you quickly if you tried to listen."

"Which I was."

"The only solution is more drill and put yourself in places where they speak Narallian," Sandy said.

"And where are those places?" Quint asked.

"You found Bokwiz's sermon. There are other gatherings around the cloister. I'll make a list of groups who are likely to speak Narallian. Dakuz can provide more, but he will probably advise studying more."

"I need more study," Quint said. "Have you ever thought about religion?"

Sandy frowned. "That is a little too personal. I said I consider myself to be on the secular side, but there is a small part of me who respects Tizurek and Tova. We won't discuss it right now."

"I'm sorry I brought it up."

Sandy waved a hand. "Don't feel sorry. We can talk about it another time and place."

That was more than he got out of Dakuz earlier in the day. Dakuz claimed to be a confirmed secularist, but he thought keeping his friendship with Grizak was an excellent idea. According to Quint's teacher, exposure to religion was better done when one was young so it could be discarded sooner. Immersing oneself in Narallian was also an excellent idea, but as expected, Dakuz wanted Quint to learn more basic Narallian before he did too much immersion. Going to Bokwiz's sermons was a harmless way to prove Dakuz's point.

Sandy showed up early. Quint asked, "Do you want to learn some strings?"

"You want to teach me?"

"The only thing I have over you is the number of strings I know," Quint said. "Now that I'm more settled in the cloister, it's time to reproduce my string book. I'll start with that, and you can see if there are any strings you'd like to learn. I know I'd like to learn some cosmetic strings. I'm assuming you know a few."

"Just a few," Sandy said. "Do you have enough paper and ink for your book?"

"Enough for a start."

"Let's go over to the cloister store and get you enough to do the job. It will be my treat. As you said, we are done for today."

Quint thought Sandy was irritated by his offer, but she seemed over it by the time they stepped inside the store. Quint had only been inside the store once, and he still had no coinage to buy much of anything.

"Who owns the store, the cloister or an enterprising monk?" Quint said as they looked at various bundles of paper.

"An enterprising monk," Sandy said. "Everyone does what they can to earn extra money."

"All I know are my strings," Quint said. "I could provide analysis, but I don't think there is a market for social research inside the cloister."

"Strings? Like teaching me strings?" Sandy said. "Wizard-wise, you are at the level of a Prior. Why not? I suggest you talk to Dakuz about that. You'd be competing with him."

"He teaches for money?"

She nodded. "I'm getting paid to escort you while you are integrating into the cloister, after all," Sandy said.

The admission startled Quint. "Is everyone getting paid for something? Is Grizak being paid to recruit me?"

Sandy shrugged. "His spiritual leader, Shinzle Bokwiz, is, I'm sure, and the council member that sponsors the flock is."

"I'm being paid for gardening my plot for the cloister, and I can get paid if I sell my private produce?"

"And you can make money teaching spells. You'd make more teaching than selling your string book. Anywhere you can turn your actions into a service is something you can charge more for."

They bought paper and writing materials and headed back to Quint's cell.

"Can anything be bought and sold in the cloister?"

"No, of course not, but before the services selling began, the cloister struggled to keep all the monks fed. That was a few centuries ago. It started letting the cloister sell produce in local village markets, not Pinzleport, and no one has gone hungry since."

"What is the purpose of the cloister, then? Does it exist to make money, or does it promote wizardry?" Quint said as they walked up the stairs to Quint's cell.

"It promotes wizardry, but there is less of that than there used to be," Sandy said. "Call it a more 'balanced' environment."

"I'll bet," Quint said. "What is the cloister's plan for me?"

"Watch. You have a future that might or might not come true. They want to see how circumstances bend. Will they move in your favor or against you?"

Quint unlocked the door to his cell and let Sandy in. She sat in the chair, arranging the purchases on Quint's table.

"There are those who think I will fail?" Quint asked.

"Some do. Most of us, including myself, are interested in how you develop. You learn at a rapid rate. Some never thought you'd make any kind of progress in speaking Narallian."

"I haven't."

Sandy chuckled. "Don't sell yourself short. Your translations get better every time you try. Many of the rest of us grew up hearing Narallian spoken. Give yourself six months to progress, and then let's see how well you do." She rubbed her head and laughed. "You have a natural clock on your scalp. It's time for me to leave. Talk to Dakuz about it. He might give you a different perspective. Whatever he tells you, there will at least be a kernel of truth hidden beneath all the bluster."

She put her hand on Quint's shoulder. "There are those who believe in you." She patted his shoulder and left the room without another word.

Quint touched his shoulder. She had never touched him before or said twice in the same conversation that she hoped he would succeed. At least, that was how Quint took it. He shook his head and chided himself for reading too much into her words and actions. He sat in his chair and began to duplicate his string book.

§

"Interesting," Dakuz said when Quint showed him the first five pages of his string book. "How did you come up with this format?"

"I came into possession of a master's string book. It was a smaller format, but it had everything but the diagrams. I learned how to diagram a string from a magic teacher in the wizard corps."

"I'm impressed. A competent wizard could use this to see if they could make the spell work."

Quint nodded. "That is the purpose. These five vary in difficulty. I was wondering if you know someone with the ability to understand these."

"You are sure they work?"

"I tested them when I finished the paper. They work."

Dakuz took a sheet and examined it. "Let's see."

Quint guessed that Dakuz could successfully create that string. He watched as the wizard duplicated the instructions. Quint let him fail.

"It doesn't work," Dakuz said.

"It doesn't work because you made three mistakes. Your worst one was how you manipulated the threads." Quint pointed them out on the document.

"Oh, I did, didn't I?" Dakuz tried six more times, getting coached by Quint for each attempt before he created a pink magic light that floated in the air. "I don't like the pink, but I like the concept." He moved the light with his finger. "How long does this last?" As he finished the question, the light blinked out.

"A few moments," Quint said. "You'll need to exercise more power to make it last longer."

Dakuz looked at the sheet. "You need to make a few comments like that on these sheets."

"But that's true of all strings," Quint said.

"A reminder, then, about a wizard's strength. Some won't have the power to do more than get a flash of light."

"And that's a differentiator between a powerful wizard and a weak wizard," Quint said.

Dakuz shook his head ruefully. "You are right about that. What are the limits of your powers?"

"There are strings I can't do. A few were listed at the back of my old string book. My magic teacher could do them easily. I'm sure that's the case with most wizards."

"Who are of a certain level," Dakuz said. "You want to teach all your strings?"

"Why not? I helped you learn a new string."

"And I would have given it up as a failed string without you."

"What would that be worth?" Quint asked.

"Twenty rubles?" Dakuz asked.

"What is the most you would pay for the pink light spell?"

Dakuz rubbed his head. "Fifteen, but that's because I don't know how long I'll be able to spell the light."

"In advance?" Quint asked.

Dakuz smiled. "You sly puppy. Have them pay in advance, and you can charge the twenty rubles or," the man shrugged, "twenty-five."

"Will I put you out of business?" Quint asked.

"I'm not the only one who teaches magic or teaches strings. Your worth is that you know strings that others don't. Your diagrams are unique in the cloister. You won't find out how popular you are until you try. Teach specific strings and not magic principles, and you won't be stepping on any toes."

"How do I get people to know what I'm doing?"

"You need permission first. I'd start with the head prior. The cloister is going to want their fee."

"Fee?" Quint asked.

Dakuz laughed. "You are naive, Quint. They promote the exchange of services because they get a little tax on each transaction. How do you think they make their money."

"On the plots of land."

Dakuz nodded. "You work for little, and the cloister makes big profits."

"What do they charge you for teaching me?"

"I charge them, and then they deduct ten percent. People who buy and sell commodities they purchase outside the cloister don't make a lot of money. Your service and my teaching, on the other hand, make us enough money to pocket more of what we charge, but our ability to earn is still limited."

"Then that's my next step. I need to make more copies of my string book."

"Complete your string book first, and we can go over what strings would be good sellers," Dakuz said.

"That service is for teaching you the pink light," Quint said.

"One more. Teach me one more, and it's a deal."

Quint laughed. "It is a deal."

"Now, it's my turn to make money. Show me your latest translation."

§

Quint entered the council room. The last time he was here was the day after he had gone to shore from Captain Olinko's ship. Four councilmen were present, including the head prior and the council member who helped with Grizak's religion meetings.

"You have a proposal for us?" the head prior said. "We can negotiate for the council. You do know our arrangement with monks providing services for pay?"

"I do," Quint said. He explained his idea for teaching strings and handed a copy of a common spell formatted like his spell book to the head prior. "This is what I will use as my learning resource."

"This is an interesting format. Your students would get one of these?"

Quint nodded. "I know the handout will cut into my market because the spell document explains how the spell works, but wizards make lots of mistakes when they create strings, and I can see those mistakes and work to correct them. If you want to know how well I do, you can talk to Hintz Dakuz. He was my trial student."

"And what happened during the trial?" one of the council members asked.

"It took him seven tries. If he was working alone, he might have given up and concluded he couldn't manage the string," Quint said.

"He would confirm this?" another monk asked.

Quint nodded.

The religionist monk looked at the sheet when it came to him and tried out the spell. "Amazing! I've cast this string many times, but not like this. I might want you to help me with some spells I struggle with."

"I'll help where I can," Quint said.

The monk said to the other, "He can add some fresh insight to string casting at Seensist."

The other monks nodded when the head prior looked at them.

"Our fee would be fifteen percent," the head prior said.

"I was told the standard is ten percent," Quint said.

The head prior blushed. "Well, let's start out with ten percent and see how well you do. We can't have our monks making too much money."

"Do you ever lower the cloister fee?" Quint asked.

"Ah, that is a private matter," one of the other monks said.

Quint knew he was treading on soft ground and bowed. "I will keep a log of my appointments. Where can I advertise my services?"

"In the cloister it is by word of mouth. I suggest you make more friends who can spread the news of your new venture."

"Do I get something in writing?" Quint asked.

"There are five of us who witnessed our agreement. That is sufficient in the cloister."

Quint bowed to them. "How often do I pay you?"

"At least every six months unless you make more than five hundred rubles. If you do, we will ask for ten percent of the previous month's profit to be paid by the middle of the month. See the person at the foyer desk for details," the head prior said. He stood. "I guess that's it. I wish you well with your new enterprise. This doesn't take the place of your gardening duties."

"I assumed it didn't," Quint said.

§§§

CHAPTER EIGHT

~

By the time Quint's hair had grown half an inch, and he no longer considered himself bald, his string business kept him busy. He decided to set up a few fixed times to work with monks. Eben, the master gardener, had begun to reassert himself and demanded more time for Quint to work on his plot since his plants were getting closer to harvest. He was already selling his herbs to the cloister store. He didn't make much on the transactions, but it wasn't subject to cloister fees, and the transaction was simple.

He had learned something else. One way to avoid cloister fees was to trade his service for another. Dakuz had traded learning a string for spreading the news of his service, and that was the beginning of learning about the barter system within the cloister.

Quint quickly learned to talk to his clients - he couldn't think of them as students - to see if there was a barter opportunity. Dakuz told Quint not to be assertive. There were informal rules about bartering, and not being overt was one of them.

His next client knocked on the door. He let Eben in.

"You want to learn a new string?" Quint asked. The hardest part of his new enterprise was determining a challenging string that the client could learn.

"I want to give you a warning," the master gardener said. "You are to stop teaching heretical strings."

Quint looked at the gardener, trying to keep his temper in check. "Which of my strings are heretical?"

"All of the strings from South Fenola that aren't practiced in North Fenola."

"And how am I supposed to know what is or isn't used in the rest of the North Fenola countries?" Quint asked.

"Then you are to shut down your business, or else."

"Or else what?" Quint said, taking a step toward the master gardener.

"You will be killed," the master gardener said.

"And who ordered my assassination?" Quint asked.

"I'm not going to tell you that."

Quint grabbed the gardener's robe and lifted the smaller man on his tiptoes. "If anyone tries to hurt me, you will be the first I'll be looking for. I gave you a chance the last time, but there won't be another pass. Tell your people that I will not keep this threat secret. Come with me."

Quint almost dragged the master gardener down the stairs into the vast courtyard and across to the council building, picking up a crowd following them.

When he dragged the master gardener up the steps, he turned and told the crowd what happened in his cell. Two of Quint's clients stepped up and took the master gardener on each side. Quint quickly cast a shield string, something he should have done before he stepped outside his dormitory. He walked into the administration building and approached the female monk behind the counter.

"The master gardener threatened me with death. I demand he be arrested and interrogated to see who ordered him to do so," Quint said.

The foyer was filling up with monks.

"And what am I to do? Arrest him?"

"What is that you normally do?"

"Nothing like this has ever happened before," she said.

"Then I suggest you find a council member," Quint said.

The woman's eyes went to the top of the stairs to the next floor.

The person at the top cleared their throat. "I suppose I qualify," the head prior said. Two other council members stood behind him. "What happened, Brother Tirolo?"

Quint told him.

"He lies!" Eben said. "He can't prove anything."

"Is that right?"

Quint sighed. "We were alone."

"I will keep your encounter with the master gardener in mind. You have finished your plot and now have another source of rubles, so your cloister position will change. Harvest what you can in the next few days and wait for another assignment," the head prior said.

"As for you, it would appear this is your second betrayal of the cloister if Brother Tirolo speaks the truth. If there is any other trouble Brother Tirolo reports, you will be expelled from Seensist."

The master gardener gnashed his teeth and glared at Quint. "You won't last the day," the gardener said.

"Expel him now!" the head prior said. "Why did you threaten Quint after I had warned you?"

"He is a danger to the cloister!" Eben said.

"A danger to the Greens?" Quint asked.

The gardener pressed his lips together as he was led out of the foyer.

"Upstairs," the head prior told Quint.

As Quint followed the head prior, a spear of fire splashed against Quint. He turned to see a monk he didn't know struggling with other monks. Grizak put his hand on the attacker's neck, and the assassin crumpled into the arms of Quint's defenders.

Quint turned and walked back down. "Does anyone know him?"

Grizak worked a string and cast it at the unconscious monk. His face changed.

"Baldur Wetzel," a monk in the crowd said. "He's a Green. I know that much."

The head prior looked down at the monk. "Brother Wetzel has also been warned about his behavior within the cloister." He looked at Quint. "You aren't the only one the Greens like to intimidate."

Quint didn't think the head prior would classify an assassination attempt as a little more severe than intimidation.

The head prior looked disgusted. "Put him in jail and find some monks who will guard him. Throw Eben in with him."

"How do you incarcerate a wizard who can cast fire?" Quint asked.

"In a metal box. You'll see. Come with me."

Quint followed the head prior to a small brick structure behind the council building. Monks dragged Wetzel's limp body into the building and into a room lined with thick metal. The door was solid except for two boxes.

"The large box is for transferring meals and removing waste. The smaller one is for communication. There is no line of sight for the guards," one of the monks said.

"Toss in another mattress," the head prior said.

Once Wetzel was dropped on one of the mattresses, the master gardener entered, struggling with his guards.

"Inside," the head prior said.

"No! He will kill me!" the master gardener said.

"That is a problem you will have to solve." The head prior took a deep breath when the door shut as Eben began to curse the cloister, the head prior and continued to warn anyone who heard him that Quint was a danger.

Most of the council members had shown up. Quint was asked about his encounter with the master gardener in his cell. Quint was afraid he would be blamed for something but was finally released to return to his dormitory cell.

Grizak joined Quint on the way back. "What will you charge me for that shield string? We don't have a protective string that powerful. I want to be first in line."

"I forgot to cast that when I left my cell with Eben, but I had a moment to execute the string when I paused on the steps of the administration building."

"That was masterful," Grizak said.

Quint was about to say he was a master, but that was much too boastful, even thinking about it.

"I'm lucky Baldur Wetzel didn't attack me until moments later."

"I saw."

Quint pursed his lips. "Do you know the spell that Wetzel used to change his appearance?"

"I know of it," Grizak said. "Do you want to trade strings? I can show you how I can cancel the spell."

"Sandiza Bartok was going to find the string, but sure. We can trade. Let's start with yours."

Quint showed him the format of his spellbook pages as he documented Grizak's string. "Let me try it."

Quint created the string and cast it against the wall. It felt effective.

"That felt right. I'll have to bring the monk who knows the string so you can practice on him to make sure."

"Let's do that," Quint said. "Now it's your turn."

§

"That was a bold act," Dakuz said when Quint visited his teacher after starting to harvest his plot.

"I'm sorry I lost my temper, but I wasn't about to let a coward tell me what to do. The shield was something I should have done earlier, but it served its purpose."

"You eliminated two of your enemies," Dakuz said, "but you revealed that you possess a powerful protective spell." Dakuz rubbed his hands. "Something we can trade, right?"

Quint smiled when he realized Dakuz wasn't going to castigate him for an irresponsible act.

"Do you know the spell that Baldur Wetzel used? You intimated that you didn't know any cosmetic spells."

Dakuz looked out the library window. "It is a secret that I do, but it is a worthy trade. It is better than casting a collection of cosmetic strings. However, a mask string only lasts for a few hours."

Quint quickly taught Dakuz the shield spell. "The shield is stronger…"

"The more power you put in it," Dakuz said. "I know, we've been through that before. How do I test it?"

"You find a shield of some kind. A metal shield will work, but I suppose you could use any sheet of metal. You have to hold it close, and I'll cast a fire spell, a weak one. If the shield works, the fire will act differently."

The exchange was made. Quint needed another page of instructions on how to visualize the mask. It was an illusion but an exceptional one.

They turned to Narallian practice. In the few months that had transpired since Quint's meeting with Grizak's group, Dakuz said Quint had made strides. Quint was now translating publications almost as well as he did for Colonel Gerocie in Bocarre. His speaking improved, but Sandy still tried to hold back smiles as he read. At least he was speaking well enough to have an accent.

Just before dinner, Grizak showed up with a familiar monk that Quint remembered from the religious service. "Time to see if my string works," Grizak said.

The monk turned his face into Grizak's. Quint paid close attention to see if the string was like Dakuz's spell, and it was identical. Without any discussion,

Quint cast the spell Grizak gave him, and the two Grizaks returned to one.

"You pick strings up better than anyone I know. If you are doing many trades, your string count must be soaring," Grizak said.

"There aren't as many trades as you may think, but my spellbook is growing."

"Spellbook?" Grizak's friend said.

Quint showed him the page he sketched for the illusion-canceling string.

"You even document the threads," the friend said. "I am impressed. How many strings do you really know?"

Quint looked at Grizak and grimaced. "Over ninety, now," Quint said. "There are more, but I'm not very proficient with those. There are currently eighty-four in my spellbook. The head prior gets a copy."

"You should be running Seensist," Grizak said.

"I've learned there is more to administering a cloister than the number of strings you know. I'm too young to do much of anything."

"But you are learning more all the time," Grizak said.

"I must, to survive. I have done enough trying to be defensive all the time. I realized that I couldn't let the master gardener get away with threatening me. Perhaps that was a turning point."

"Your Narallian? Is it better?" Grizak asked.

"Better, but not good," Quint said in Narallian.

Grizak laughed. "Not good, but I can understand it," Grizak returned in Narallian.

They both laughed.

Grizak and his friend left Quint to get ready for dinner.

Quint arrived at the refectory. Grizak's table was already full. A monk that Quint knew from the garden plots waved Quint over. Quint didn't know him very well, and he wasn't particularly friendly. Quint looked for Sandy, but she hadn't arrived. Quint wasn't comfortable sitting with strangers so soon after he had been attacked, so he turned around and quickly cast a shield string.

He glanced at Grizak's table, and his friend had raised his eyebrows. Grizak had noticed. He was introduced to the other monks. It was clear to him he wasn't among friends. The head prior walked in to make his comments.

"I'm sad to announce the death of Baldur Wetzel," the head prior said. "It appears that our former master gardener kept Brother Wetzel asleep until early this morning when Brother Wetzel was killed in their cell. The surviving brother was immediately taken to Pinzleport and turned over to the city authorities." He uttered a prayer over the food and the servers began to bring the food out.

"Proud of yourself, aren't you?" one of the monks at the table said. "Two good men are as good as dead."

"Because I refused to die?" Quint said. "Is there no justification for self-defense in your eyes?"

"Not when it involves my friends," the monk that Quint knew said.

Quint pushed back his chair and stood. "I'll find a more hospitable table," he said.

Two monks rose with him, taking larger, sharper knives out of their robes. They lunged, but Quint was expecting an attack. He would have gladly put them to sleep but couldn't have a quarter of the refectory going under.

"I'm sorry, head prior," Quint said as he flamed one of the monks with a needle-shaped spear of flame and then the other.

The other three monks climbed over chairs and the table and grabbed Quint's wrists before he could cast another string.

The action brought back the feeling of hopelessness he had before when fellow Wizard Corps members attacked him. Rather than curling into a ball, his basic defense when Quint was younger, he kicked his assailants. His larger size made an assault on his attackers more effective. He was soon to be eighteen, after all. Quint twisted and freed up one hand, which he balled into a fist and punched one of the monks in the nose.

At that point, other monks joined Quint as few monks in the room sided with the Greens, as Quint now thought of them. The fighting continued for a few minutes before Hintz Dakuz cast a string that sent a shock of pain through Quint. The effect didn't last long, but the spirit of the fight was broken as monks tried to shake off the effects of the spell.

Quint backed up and began to push his allies back. Others in Quint's group did the same. The Greens stood where they were, but their bodies relaxed, and the fight ended. The Greens took the two monks Quint had injured away to the cloister infirmary.

"Sit, all of you," the head prior said. He nodded at Dakuz. "Thank you, Brother Dakuz, for your quick action."

Quint would have to learn that spell, but he didn't know what Dakuz's price would be.

"Another attack on Brother Tirolo," the head prior said. "I had my eyes on that table since I knew a few monks allied with Eben. We will continue with dinner. If your food is knocked to the floor, you will leave the refectory and find sustenance elsewhere. I will let this episode pass. The attackers received suitable punishment from Brother Tirolo."

Quint saw his plate broken on the floor. He had some bread, cheese, and a bottle of wine in his cell. That would tide him over until breakfast.

A monk ran into the room and whispered something in the head prior's ear.

"It appears that the murdered monk was Eben. Baldur Wetzel killed his jail mate and assumed the master gardener's robes. He was assisted in escape and is now at large in Pinzleport."

The monk who invited Quint to his table sneered at Quint and grinned at his one remaining friend. Quint sighed. Another enemy at large. Quint was sure to have others.

"Brother Tirolo, we have an open seat on the dais. We can get your side of the story if you join us." The head prior looked over the refectory. Those without food can leave now. The rest of you can finish your dinners."

Quint found Sandy's eyes in the back of the room. She smiled and waved before sitting down. He didn't know if he cared if she saw his plight or not. There were two empty spots at the council table.

"Next to me," the religionist council member said.

A server brought a new plate of food, and the council began to eat. After a few moments, one of the council members asked Quint for his story.

Quint's account didn't take very long.

"It appears that you present a problem for the Greens," one of the council members said. "What do you intend to do about it?"

"I can't just say 'I intend to survive,' can I?"

Another councilor shook his head. "No, you cannot. We are lucky all you've caused are a few burns and bruises for the bystanders. You are not allowed to kill everyone who insults you."

"I didn't kill them, even though they would have considered it a triumph to kill me," Quint said. He looked at his food. Quint hadn't lost his appetite but couldn't eat while under this interrogation.

The refectory was quiet. A few people continued with their dinner, but most of the monks kept silent, trying to hear what was said on the dais. Quint looked down at the rest of the monks.

"Perhaps we can meet elsewhere and discuss my strategy. It wouldn't do to announce it to those," he nodded to the room, "who might be Green sympathizers."

The head prior raised his eyebrows. "I hadn't even thought."

Quint felt the prior should have, but the situation was probably unique.

"After dinner, we will reconvene in the council chamber for a closed session." The head prior emphasized the "closed" so that the rest of the monks heard it.

"After dinner?" Quint asked.

"Yes, my boy," the religionist said, putting a forkful of food into his mouth.

§§§

CHAPTER NINE

"THE INJURED MONKS WILL SURVIVE, but some will take ugly scars to their graves," a healer monk said to the seated council.

Quint sat off to the side and didn't know if he was relieved or not.

"You've had a few moments to think about your next course of action," the head prior said after the healer had left the chamber.

"Do I sit or stand?" Quint asked.

"Whatever you please. This isn't an official hearing," the head prior said.

"I have no place to go," Quint said, feeling defensive.

"We haven't decided to expel you, Brother Tirolo," the religionist council member said.

But they could at any moment, Quint thought.

Quint did have an idea. It was more of an offer to help the cloister and Quint's situation. "I have a proposal to make," Quint said. "Give me the assignment to determine the loyalties or affinities to different groups within Seensist. I have experience putting information together from different sources. That will allow you to know who a Green is, who is a Red, and what other kinds of allegiance there are in the cloister."

"An invasion of privacy? I'm sure the monks wouldn't stand for it."

"Are you willing to lose your power? The Greens had the audacity to try to kill me in the foyer of the administration building and again in the refectory. Aren't you embarrassed about that? If you know where everyone stands, you will automatically have more power in Seensist."

"Won't that give you power?" one of the councilors asked.

"It won't if I share everything with you, and I promise to do so. Sister Sandiza can look over my shoulder while I work. Hintz Dakuz can, as well if you wish."

"Not Hintz Dakuz," another councilor said.

"Whatever you decide. The only thing I ask is that you permit me to defend myself and the discretion to use killing power if the situation warrants."

"You want to become an assassin?" the head prior asked.

"No! If I have the power to choose how to defend myself, I can discourage those who want to be my enemies. As for me, I want to be left alone to study."

"And sell spells?" the religionist councilor asked.

Quint shrugged. "I haven't seen the harm in it. Of the spells I've sold, my clients can manage less than fifty percent of the strings I've sold."

"Much less," the head prior said. "And I think that's a good thing. I don't have any objections if the rest of the council and those here agree. We will review the agreement when you have been here six months."

"Two months to go?" Quint asked.

The head prior smiled and lifted his chin. "Your hair should look very presentable, then."

Quint rubbed his short hair and returned the prior's smile. "I suppose that will give me a goal to finish my analysis. Two months, and we reassess."

The councilors agreed, save the one who asked about Quint's power.

"I'd like the permission in writing, and have it posted where everyone can see. The more who know, the more hesitant attackers will be," Quint said.

"I'm unsure about that, but I will approve the posting. Write out what permission you want. We will send you our version." The head prior yawned. "I am ready to retire."

A few smiles came to some of the councilors' lips, and Quint was dismissed.

He returned to his cell and wrote out the permissions he wanted, making them as simple as he could. Quint also wrote out an agreement, again, simple, that gave him two months to assemble an allegiance evaluation on the cloister. He did make sure it was plain that his report would be a best-efforts analysis.

Quint didn't sleep well. He wondered if the council would have someone cast another predictor string. It didn't matter to him unless they expelled him on the spot.

After breakfast, he delivered his two documents to the head prior, who accepted them graciously and gave Quint the impression that the cloister would consider it a serious matter.

Sandy caught him as he left the building. "What happened last night?"

Quint told her.

"They allowed you to do that?"

"I can either lock myself up in my tiny room, or I can publicize myself as a threat to life and limb and live an open life. It's only for two months, anyway. You will be assigned to oversee my work."

"Not oversee," Sandy said. "I'm an observer. The head prior made that clear to me before you showed up. They cast another predictor string and didn't find anything detrimental to the cloister between now and then."

"What about after?" Quint asked.

She shrugged. "I wasn't told, if they even looked. When do you start?"

"I already have," Quint said. "I've been sizing up monks when I meet them. I have to do a more thorough job."

"But you haven't written anything down."

Quint shook his head. "It's time to do that. It's time to see Dakuz. Want to come?"

Sandy smiled. "No, I have a winemaking class to attend."

"You want to become a vintner?"

"A more knowledgeable wine drinker." She waved as she walked off.

§

Dakuz frowned. "You are sticking your neck out, and there are those ready to chop your head off."

"I couldn't think of an alternative in the time they gave me. I needed something that could give me some leverage in the cloister. I don't want to be scolded every time I'm attacked. If I did nothing, the attacks would become a regular thing, and I don't think they will stop until they are successful."

"You are right about that! You could have just left. You've got a little money to get you wherever you want to go," Dakuz said.

"Not yet. Maybe in two months, but I doubt it. My Narallian isn't where it should be," Quint said. "I don't feel ready to leave."

"Nor do I," Dakuz said. "I think you need more followers."

"More followers? Who do I have right now?"

"Grizak and a few of his friends and Sandy," Dakuz said.

'They would follow me?" Quint asked.

"I believe if you left and said you'd let them come with you, they would come. Maybe not now, but in a few months. You'll be eighteen by then. That's an adult in Narukun."

"I'm eighteen today," Quint said. "It's my birthday, and I'm in no mood to celebrate."

Dakuz grumbled. "You'll have enough celebrations in the future. Enough to make up for it. You can ask me now."

"Ask you what?"

"Who is aligned with what faction," Dakuz said.

"You've already done that? Does the council know?"

Dakuz frowned. "Why should they? That gang wouldn't know what to do with that kind of information, but you would."

"Maybe," Quint said. "I might find some more candidates for followers." A smile blossomed on his face. "You'd really give that to me?"

"I would. Consider it a birthday present, but you should verify my observations," Dakuz said. "Enough about that. I'll deliver my notes to you this afternoon." The older monk rubbed his hands. "Now, let's talk about how mechanical things work. You've been gawking at clocks all your life. Do you know how they work?"

Quint was surprised by the subject. "It's not something I've thought a lot about. They have wheels that turn. They are connected, so minutes and hours are synchronous. I took a broken one apart when I was twelve. I never could get it back to work."

"Some clocks are sun-powered, some are water-powered, but the best ones are spring-powered." Dakuz plopped a book in Narallian on the desk. I want you to read this and interpret it. We can discuss what words you can't find, and there will be plenty of technical ones that won't be in your dictionary."

"Killing two birds with one stone?" Quint asked.

"The more birds, the better," Dakuz said grumpily. "Take three days. I need some time off from you, and then we can enlighten each other with what we've discovered. Go now. Shoo."

Quint returned to his cell. He had the rest of the morning to himself and began writing a list of monks and his first impressions of their allegiances while still thinking of that assignment. The book on clocks had lots of illustrations of the different designs of clocks. He could tell it wasn't a particularly scholarly work, but the diagrams had labels indicating he had many Narallian terms to learn.

A few minutes before lunch, Sandy arrived with a portfolio containing the new agreements. The council had modified each of the documents, but not enough to concern Quint. They also inserted a roster of the monks. It was printed, which surprised Quint. The council had used the list enough to require many copies, and it was current enough to have his name listed.

"This looks like I didn't scare off the council with my demands," Quint said.

"I never saw your originals, but your actions tell me the agreement is acceptable?"

"It is," Quint said. "I'd rather have the posted announcement express the menace of my wizardry a little more strongly, but it will serve."

"More of a warning?" Sandy shivered. "I think the point is plain enough," she said. "When will you get started?"

"This afternoon. Dakuz is bringing over his observations about the monks. That will save me some time, but I won't take what he gives me without verifying where I can. I will cite him as a source, although I know one councilor who doesn't like my teacher."

"You'll ask Dakuz about documenting him as a reference before you use his information, won't you?"

Quint smiled. "I'd be risking my life if I didn't."

The lunch bell rang, and the two of them walked across the cloister. Shinzle Bokwiz stood at the entrance to the refectory.

"Will you allow me to eat lunch with you, Brother Tirolo?"

"You can call me Quint."

Bokwiz smiled. "And you can call me Brother Bokwiz," the religionist said and then laughed. "Shinzle is my name. I was just teasing."

"In that case, you can join us," Quint said.

They walked in and found a small table for four. As they sat, Pol Grizak asked if he could join them.

"Am I liable to receive a sermon for lunch?" Quint asked.

"No, no, no," Bokwiz said. "I heard you were classifying monks according to their allegiance, and I thought I'd catch you before you got too far into your project."

"You succeeded there," Sandy said.

"Good!" Bokwiz said. He winked at Sandy. "I'd appreciate your adding a little wrinkle to your list."

"You want me to hand out invitations to your sermons?" Quint said.

Bokwiz frowned. "Too obvious, don't you think, Grizak?"

Pol nodded.

"I'd like you to note if someone is a religionist or not," Bokwiz said.

"How will I find that out unless I become even more obvious? Handing out invitations would be easier, not that I intend on asking anyone about their affiliations. I am planning on using an indirect method," Quint said.

"But you will be talking to monks?" Bokwiz asked.

Quint nodded.

"Then do your best. That's all I can ask. You don't expect to have a perfect list?"

Quint shook his head this time. "I don't want to offend monks, and I don't intend on engaging with everyone."

"I misunderstood," Bokwiz said.

Quint didn't believe that the religionist had been confused.

"Why don't you come to my next sermon and see who shows up? You can record their presence," Bokwiz said.

"I'll help you identify them," Grizak said with a grin.

"I can certainly accept your offer."

"Bring Sister Bartok with you," Bokwiz said. The cleric looked at Sandy. "You will come, won't you?"

Sandy looked trapped. "Of course. Anything to help with Quint's project." She smiled weakly.

"Then I'll be getting on my way."

"We haven't gotten our lunches yet," Sandy said.

"I generally fix my own. See you next Felsday," Bokwiz said as he headed toward the door.

Quint sighed. "At least I got a personal invitation," he said.

"You did. He's quite a monk, isn't he?" Grizak said, watching Bokwiz stop a monk outside for a chat.

Quint followed his gaze. "He's right. I'll need you to identify your congregants. I forgot everyone's name amidst all the Narallian talk. This time, I won't be so lost."

§

Dakuz showed up shortly after Quint arrived back from lunch. He carried a disheveled portfolio of papers shoved in one way or another.

"You might have to do some organizing," Dakuz said without embarrassment.

"I have to look at them all, anyway," Quint said.

Dakuz growled. "Quite so. How is it going with the clock text?"

"I started," Quint said. "I'm glad there are lots of pictures. They will help me figure out the terms."

"Don't get your hopes up," Dakuz said, "but give it a try first. What did Bokwiz want with you?"

"You saw us at lunch?"

Dakuz grunted a yes.

"He invited Sandy and me to his next Felsday service. I think I'm finally ready to face all the Narallian that will be spoken."

"Good! Did he ask you for anything else?"

"He wanted me to ask everyone if they are a religionist."

Dakuz pursed his lips. "There are more sects than his at Seensist. You know that, don't you?"

"Pol Grizak told me. It would be an interesting point to add, but I'm not sure I can get honest answers from everyone," Quint said. "Some will say yes to appear pious, and others will say no to hide their beliefs."

"And that will be the case with the factions, too."

Quint patted the portfolio. "But I have a head start."

"You might have to be more creative. What will you do when your two-month probation ends?" Dakuz asked.

"I suppose I won't know until the time comes. They might let me stay if I don't have to fend off assassins. If not, perhaps it will be time to move on."

Dakuz worked his lips. "I'd hate to see that," he said.

"That's a compliment coming from you. I'm glad you feel that way," Quint said. "I'd rather stay if that helps."

"I don't know if it will," Dakuz said. "Read a little from the Narallian clock text. I want to see how you do with a technical book."

Quint read a few pages slowly. Dakuz provided technical words and their pronunciations and definitions.

"Not bad, but not good. It is all practice now, anyway. Lots and lots of practice." Dakuz rose from the single chair in Quint's room. "Happy birthday, Quint."

And that was the extent of Quint's eighteenth birthday and the only recognition of his moving from a youth to an adult that he received. A bolt of sadness hit him, wishing he could have celebrated in Racellia with his parents and siblings, but that wish would never come true.

§§§

CHAPTER TEN

Sandy disappointed Quint by declining to attend Bokwiz's service. He could understand why she backed out, but she understood Narallian much better and could back up his lack of mastery. Grizak was too much a congregant to give him a frank opinion of whatever was said.

Grizak waited at the door for him and frowned. "No Sandiza Bartok?"

Quint shook his head. "She was otherwise engaged."

"I would have been pleasantly surprised if she came." Grizak sighed but brightened. "But you are here. Come in. The entire service will be in Narallian, this time. Are you ready?"

Quint grimaced. "No, but I'm not sure I'll ever be truly ready."

They walked in, took seats, and waited for the councilor and Shinzle Bokwiz to arrive.

"They are always late?" Quint asked.

Grizak gave Quint an amused smile. "I think they believe it adds to the mystery of the service. I'm okay with that. It makes the start of the service more formal."

They didn't wait long. Both arrived together. Quint struggled to understand the sermon, but with some help from Grizak, he was able to get something out of it. If anyone expected some kind of spiritual conversion of Quint, it wouldn't happen until Quint made some significant strides in the language.

The conversation after wasn't as bad. Some of the congregants spoke in common so Quint could join in on the discussion. He asked questions about the sermon and about what else they did to observe the tenets of their religion. Quint struggled to take it all in since all the monks were excited after Bokwiz's sermon.

Quint stayed until the other monks began to leave. It was time for bed, but Bokwiz stopped him.

"Can we talk?"

Quint shrugged. "I tried to keep up with your sermon, but I could not get all that you said."

"I don't mean to test your Narallian. I wanted to talk to you about the cloister and what you intend to accomplish while you are here."

Quint didn't know why Bokwiz would want to know what Quint wanted to accomplish other than have the choice to leave or stay in two months.

"Go on," Quint said.

"Let us sit," Bokwiz said. "My bones aren't as young as yours."

"I'll agree with that," Quint said with a smile.

"What is your goal until the head prior asks you to stay or leave?"

Quint frowned. "I didn't know it was up to the head prior. I thought I had some say in what I would do."

Bokwiz stroked his white beard. "It might have been at one time, but that changed after the refectory attack. I suppose someone neglected to tell you."

"Do you know what will affect the decision?" Quint asked.

"I think the goals are a little flexible, but the possible outcomes have hardened up. Complete the assignment the head prior has given you. You have started on the classification of monks in the cloister?"

Quint snorted. "I have begun my research. I'm doubtful that all the monks will tell me the truth. I've decided to include religion in the mix like you suggested, but is that separate from the political factions?" Quint sighed. Bokwiz should be smart enough to know that Quint was getting frustrated.

"Internal politics and external politics," Bokwiz said. "That makes three classifications, and I think those make sense. You will see some alignment between the three, but the mix won't be consistent."

Quint closed his eyes at the increasing complexity of a project that he only had eight or nine weeks to complete. "I don't know how I can do all that on my own. Is it acceptable to do my best?"

"I'm not sure," Bokwiz said. "It's up to the head prior."

"What is his classification?" Quint asked.

Bokwiz nodded. "That I do know. Will you accept my help? I may involve others in collecting what you need."

Quint had Dakuz's analysis. "I have some information from another party, so I suppose I will accept help from whoever is willing to work with me. Is there a cost to your help?" Quint thought he knew the answer.

Bokwiz chuckled. "I'm not going to make you go to my services," Bokwiz said, "but I will insist that we have discussions."

"So, you can convince me to join your flock?"

The religionist shrugged. "Not necessarily. You might end up converting me to something else."

"A different way to worship Tizurek and Tova?" Quint asked.

"I'm open to that. My sermons don't require an intolerant view of hubite deity." Bokwiz narrowed his eyes and looked intently at Quint. "Some predictor strings show you have something to contribute to the spiritual world, but everything is too hazy to know what."

Quint felt like he had been exposed, yet he had never contemplated such a thing. He had purposely tried to avoid asking about his future. "I'm going to be a religionist leader?"

"Perhaps not a leader, but let's call it the possibility of a spiritual facilitator," Bokwiz said.

"A sponsor?" Quint said, trying to find a semantic way out.

"That's a possibility. As I said, the future isn't clear where you are concerned."

Quint looked away from Bokwiz. "The murkiness of my destiny is what is keeping me from being expelled as we speak?"

Bokwiz nodded. "I think that might be partially true. I have looked into your future and see positive things where you are concerned. Positive from my point of view."

"But not others?"

"The Greens don't like what they see. Why do you think they so urgently desire you dead?"

"Because they have looked, as well, and found that I am firm in the belief that authoritarian approaches are not good for any society."

"And you had a commoner upbringing."

"Less than common for a hubite in Racellia," Quint said. "I'm uncomfortable with the attention. I'm far from being capable of leading anyone. I just turned eighteen."

"It's true," Bokwiz smiled. It almost looked like a grimace. "You need a lot of seasoning, but you also have a knack for surviving."

"I can't survive the way I did in Racellia. In my own way, I could hide. But that worked there, but it won't work in the cloister. Am I destined to lead the cloister?"

Bokwiz shook his head. "I'd be disappointed if you did. Your future is more expansive."

Quint made to object, but Bokwiz raised his hand. "That's all I'll say. You told the council that the Gussellian emperor had a similar viewing so I'm not revealing something you don't already know. I heard your story."

Quint took a deep breath. "I can't worry about that now," he said. "I will focus on making money with my spell exchange and getting the cloister monks classified. How can you help me with the classification?"

"Leave that to me. I will take on the religion classification. How about that? I already have a good idea of where most of our brothers and sisters stand. I just need to document it."

"Dakuz gave me a head start on many of the monks' political views, but I'm going to have to broaden that to include cloister status. Does every monk have a strong opinion about the outside?"

Bokwiz smiled. "No. Some care nothing for either. We have to document them, too."

"It's a deal. Does this conversation count as one of our discussions?"

"It does. I'm convinced I didn't make a mistake in talking tonight. That was what I wanted to find out. We can talk about deeper subjects another time."

Quint frowned. "There isn't much time. Can I tell Dakuz and Sandiz Bartok?"

"And Grizak. My people will know because I will use them to find out about people they know."

"I'm glad I don't have many secrets," Quint said.

"For now," Bokwiz said. He smiled and rose, giving Quint a deep bow. "I hope I can prove worthy of your friendship, Brother Tirolo."

Quint felt a shiver go up his spine. He returned Bokwiz's bow. "Call me Quint, or I'll never be comfortable around you."

"Thank you, Quint. I like being called Bokwiz better than Shinzle, by the way. I always have."

Quint watched Bokwiz walk away before he returned to his cell. The discussion was less comfortable than if the religionist urged him to join his congregation, but the offer seemed genuine. He would have to do some interviews with people he didn't know to verify Bokwiz's list and Dakuz's, too.

Sandiza might help him do that. He didn't fully trust her since she was a paid helper, but that would come. Quint smiled as he walked up the stairs to his cell. He had the impression he was picking up a set of followers. Grizak, Sandy, Dakuz, and Bokwiz. Quint guessed they were doing it because of the predictor strings' result and not because of being around him. He lay in bed and put his arm behind his head. As Bokwiz said, it didn't matter who helped him if it was help. Verifying their contributions would prove his helpers' fidelity.

§

Quint reviewed some of Dakuz's reports, and they held no real surprises for the monks Quint knew. That was a good thing in his mind, but Dakuz had mixed up external and internal politics with his evaluations. Quint's tutor also didn't address a third of the cloister's monks. That left one hundred or so judgments that Quint would have to make.

After working on translating another journal, this one on brickmaking, Quint brought his latest work to Dakuz along with a good sampling of Dakuz's evaluations.

"Now what?" Dakuz said as Quint walked in.

"My translation," Quint said. "I learned a lot of new words."

"And your visit to the religious service?"

"Illuminating in a few ways."

Dakuz furrowed his brow. "You aren't going to join them, are you?"

Quint laughed. "Not yet. I talked one of them into joining me."

"Pol Grizak?"

"Shinzle Bokwiz. He's going to help me categorize the religions practiced or not practiced in the cloister. We decided that we needed three points of information to make the assignment useful for the head prior."

"We?"

"As I said, he offered to help."

Dakuz sighed. "He cast a predictor string?"

"He did, or someone he knows did. Bokwiz thinks I'm going to have some kind of influence over religionists. It must be something far into the future," Quint said, "because I'm not really interested in Tizurek or Tova. There was no religion in Racellia."

"You mentioned that before." Dakuz stared at Quint for a moment. "You are young enough that every thought you have now could change in the future."

"Don't you have the same opinions now that you had when you were my age?" Quint asked.

Dakuz pursed his lips, hiding half a smile." Sometimes, I feel like the same me, but my perspective on things is quite different. Some core principles of my youth have persisted, but when I was your age, the world I perceived is not the one I perceive today."

Quint had to think for a few moments before he understood Dakuz's comment, although he couldn't see that he would think drastically differently. Good was still good and rare. Evil was evil. The Dankos were evil. Most people were a combination.

"Bring me what I gave you, and I will adjust. The internal politics is independent of external attitudes."

"I don't know how different they will be, but the analysis should help the head prior know what is going on within these walls," Quint said.

"Rate yourself," Dakuz said with a frown before folding his arms, showing some defiance. What Dakuz was defiant about, Quint didn't know.

"Internal politics - unaffiliated, but I support the head prior. External politics - unaffiliated, but I don't support the Greens and I'm not sure about the Reds. Religion - unaffiliated."

"And you are a male and rated a deacon."

"Yes. I forgot about that. This wouldn't make much sense if the results were anonymous, would they?'

Dakuz shook his head. "The survey would be a curiosity but of limited value. What am I?"

Quint raised his eyebrows. "Internally - unaffiliated as far as I know, but I can't tell."

The answer brought a smile to Dakuz's lips. "That means I am succeeding, at least with you. I generally support the head prior, but there are other council members who I don't. I can't say I would trust any of them with something important."

"What about Bokwiz?" Quint asked.

"He's not a council member, but Bokwiz seems unaffiliated, but I don't think that's a correct reading. To me, he is a cipher like me. He doesn't want to show his affiliation, or it might affect the size of his congregation, but I'd say he is at least pink, if not fully Red, in his external politics."

"You aren't a religionist? I have no idea."

That brought a smile to the older man's face. "I believe and practice my own religion. Surprised, aren't you?"

"I am," Quint said.

"I was brought up a reformed believer. We believed in the equal standing of Tizurek and Tova. I have never seen evidence of a need to change that. There is the conservative faction of which Bokwiz is a proponent. Reformed people think the two gods are married and jointly rule the heavens and the earth, and the Enlightened faction, their name, not mine, believes that Tizurek serves Tova," Dakuz said.

"But what about someone who believes in a greater power that created everything that isn't Tizurek or Tova? Or someone who thinks that god is a collective of all things that live in the world?"

"Go crazy with that, Quint. I call them universal believers. I think Bokwiz does, too. Factions of universalists ebb and flow throughout history. Most of what they think is based on fads at the time. Tizurek and Tova have persisted for as long as humans have existed," Dakuz said.

"Let's go with five classifications, the fifth being the unbelievers," Quint said. "I'll tell Bokwiz the next time I see him. He wants to meet with me outside the services. You don't have any objections?"

Dakuz chuckled. "Why would I object to a man I almost trust? Remember, I don't trust anyone. Go ahead and talk to him. Are we finished with the spiritual talk?" he said. "Let's get down to lessons. If you truly may be here for two months and must leave, we will change our lessons so there are three subjects: Narallian, Geography, and Politics."

"So I can survive on the outside?"

The older man nodded. "Exactly. We can start by going over your translation."

§§§

CHAPTER ELEVEN

NOTES WERE STUFFED UNDER QUINT'S DOOR when he returned from lunch. He had gone directly from the library to the refectory. Quint had borrowed books from Dakuz and had lugged six of them to lunch and then up the stairs to his cell.

His spell exchange business hadn't dropped off. There were exchange proposals, a few of which looked interesting and straightforward spells that only required training. Quint drew a signup chart with times he would be in his cell and pinned that to his door. The notes would require personal visits, and Quint would take advantage of those to get more data for his classification efforts.

A knock came on his door as he was about to open a Narukun geography book.

"Bokwiz," Quint said, surprised the religionist would come to his cell.

"We have a few things to talk about," Bokwiz said. "May I sit? Old bones, remember?"

Quint quickly straightened his desk and turned the chair around to face the bed. He pointed to the chair. "Please sit."

Bokwiz smiled. "Gladly. I thought we should get some of the religion definitions clear."

"Dakuz and I talked about that this morning. I thought we would classify religion one of five ways." He told Bokwiz of his classification.

"I might term things differently, but I think that will work for the head prior's purposes. What else are you collecting?"

"Name, level, internal affiliations, external affiliations, religious affiliations. I think that is more than enough."

"He will change things around to suit his perceptions, anyway," Bokwiz said.

"Are you here for anything else? Is there something that demands my immediate attention?" Quint asked.

"Ah, you caught me. Something I heard might happen, and you should be aware of it. One of my flock overheard talk of another attack by the Greens. This is a more ambitious attack, and you remain their target."

"Shouldn't you go to the council with the information?" Quint asked.

"I'm not sure the council can be trusted to protect you," Bokwiz said.

"I've been shielded outside my cell."

Bokwiz nodded. "Sometimes, shields are not enough. Wizards often lose their protection when the enemy crowds them. Strings can't be cast and," Bokwiz shrugged, "bad things can happen when you lose control of the situation."

"I know that happens. I've been surprised enough," Quint said. "I'm not invulnerable."

"I can ask a few of my people to accompany you."

"Bodyguards? I need bodyguards?"

Bokwiz nodded. "You do. Some of my people reside in this building. Meet with the head prior and see if he will move them close to your cell."

"It's bad enough that I'll need a defended space?"

Bokwiz looked around. "This isn't very defensible, is it?"

Quint shook his head.

"Then ask for one. There are groups of empty cells elsewhere in the cloister. You will need six, at the least. All the cells are about the same size, anyway," Bokwiz said. "I'd see the head prior now to get it arranged. There isn't much time to lose."

"It won't happen today?"

"Or this week, but any time after that."

Quint sighed. "I'm going to be kicked out for sure."

"We will see. It might be easier to identify some of the factions if there is an incursion," Bokwiz said. The religionist stood. "I have to leave. Walk with me downstairs, and then we can go our separate ways."

On the way downstairs, Bokwiz looked up and down the corridor on

Quint's floor and nodded. "The other place I thought of is more defendable than this."

When they walked outside, Bokwiz wished Quint good luck with the head prior and walked away. If Bokwiz was trying to lure Quint outside, he succeeded. Quint cast a shield thread and walked over to the council building.

"Are you done so soon?" the head prior asked as Quint walked inside the prior's office.

"Barely started, but I do have a start," Quint said. "I will categorize three things: the religion, the external affiliations, and the internal affiliations."

"Why bother with religions?" the head prior said.

"So I can see if there is a connection between how a person believes and how a person regards their political alignment. I don't expect a one-for-one relationship, but I do think there might be some indicators, and this will likely be the only time anyone will bother to gather that information."

"That sounds good to me. Do you need any resources?"

Quint shook his head. "Not yet. I don't have much time, but I have more helpers than I thought I'd have. Even so, there will still be monks refusing to give me any information."

"Do you need council orders to back you up?"

Quint hadn't even thought of asking for authority. "I would accept them. I have one other request that is related but is a bit more personal. I'd like to move to a more defensible place in the Cloister. Something made from stone, preferably with six cells or more. A few monks have offered to act as bodyguards, and they should be near."

"You think someone will attack you in your cell?"

"I've been attacked outside the cloister and inside the cloister multiple times. Nothing has been done to discourage them."

"I'd say your attackers were dealt with."

"But the strength of their hatred overcomes what we've done so far."

"I can think of a few such places. You'd have to clean them. They haven't been occupied for some time. There is a reason they are vacant, and being very cold in the winter is one of them. "

"I'm only looking short term. Maybe two months." Quint looked directly at the head prior.

"Oh. I see what you mean. The deadline." The prior cleared his throat and brushed off a few invisible particles from his robe. "You will have at least two to choose from. See me tomorrow after breakfast, and I'll have someone show you what is available."

"That will be great. I'll put together a sample of what I'll be putting together and see if the format will be acceptable."

The prior chuckled. "I keep forgetting you used to provide written reports in the Racellian Wizard Corps."

"And to the Racellian Foreign Minister and his staff," Quint said.

§

"You aren't waiting to get started, are you?" Sandy said as she arrived at Quint's cell a few minutes after Quint returned from the council building.

"I feel a sense of urgency," Quint said. "Two months may seem like a long time, but it's not."

"Are you going to have time for your studies?" Sandy asked.

Quint nodded. "It's a high priority. If I must leave the cloister, I want to survive on the outside. Dakuz has modified my courses. If I stay, my education won't be wasted."

"What can I do?" Sandy asked.

Quint discussed his problems gathering information for the head prior's report. She offered to use her connections, as limited as they were, to gather information, and her circle would be different than Dakuz's and Bokwiz and his congregation's.

A knock on the door interrupted them.

Quint let a monk in and introduced him to Sandy, his cloister escort. The monk wanted to buy a spell.

"Level?" Quint asked.

"I'm an acolyte. I know twenty-one strings."

"I'm not sure you will be able to cast the hot air string you want," Quint said. "If you buy the string, you get a paper with everything written, but no refunds."

The monk nodded and nervously looked at Sandy.

Quint wrote out the spell using the same format he had learned in Racellia but changed a few terms to match how magic was taught in the cloister. He rolled up the spell and tied it with a string, conscious of the connection, a string around a string, and gave the monk a price.

"That's fair if it works."

"You get a try in my presence for your fee," Quint said. "Here is a demonstration."

The string would create a bubble of hot air that would heat a room. He turned to Sandy. "Would you open the window? It will get warm in here."

Quint made sure his shield was still intact before he invoked the string. Instantly, a distinct pop filled the room, and Quint felt the warm air dissipate. He smiled. A cold cell could be heated with magic no matter where he ended up in the cloister.

"That works!"

"Of course it does," Sandy said, fanning the warm air out of the room.

"Your turn. Do you remember what I did? You can refer to your sheet after you pay the price."

"Can't I find the same spell in the library?" the monk said.

"You can, but this one is better," Quint said.

"How is it better?"

"I've tweaked the string, so it is easier to reproduce. You won't get that in the library."

"What if I sell this to someone else?" the monk said.

"I don't think you want to know what I can do."

The monk looked nervous. "I know what you can do."

"Are you going to pay me and try the spell, or are you going to leave us?" Quint said. "Make up your mind." Quint held the rolled-up document and tapped his palm.

"Here," the monk said.

Quint observed the monk look at the instructions and tried to duplicate the string and failed.

"You didn't faithfully replicate the threads in the order I specified."

"Threads have an order?"

Even Sandy rolled her eyes.

"They do indeed. Have you really mastered twenty strings?"

"I might have been exaggerating."

"And you are a novice rather than an acolyte?"

The monk frowned. "I said I was exaggerating."

Quint showed the novice how to manage the threads and made sure the young man could do that step. "That wasn't so bad, was it?"

The monk was sweating. "No." He managed a smile. "I think I can work the strings." The monk cast a string this time and the pop wasn't as pronounced as when Quint performed the string, but the cell undeniably warmed up, just not to the extent of Quint's string.

"The difference is in the strength of magic. Put more magic in, and the volume and heat will increase."

The money was exchanged, and the novice rushed out of the room with his treasure. It wouldn't be worth very much now, but it would be in four more months when the weather changed.

Sandy clapped. "Impressive. What else can you do with that string?"

Quint laughed. "I've created a very close version that mimics the smell of flatulence when used. He may make a mistake and create quite a stink in his cell."

"Naughty boy," Sandy said. "I didn't have you down as a joker."

"I'm still a teenager," Quint said. "In Racellia, hubites couldn't joke around. The wrong prank could mean one's life. I gave him the means to avoid embarrassment. We made a fair deal."

"More than fair with you making sure he could perform the string."

"I've had plenty of sales where the monk couldn't perform the string in front of me, and quite frankly, the monk was incapable of weaving the threads that an advanced string needed," Quint said.

Another knock on the door, and an older monk walked in without Quint's permission.

"I haven't seen you before," Quint said.

"Oh. I've been around, youngster."

"How can I help you?"

"Die!" The monk quickly threw a fire spear at Quint. The fire split into two that followed the contours of the shield Quint wore.

Before the monk could react, Quint put him to sleep. He turned around and extinguished two blazes with a water string. Sandy had shriveled into a corner away from Quint and couldn't escape. She looked down at the sleeping monk.

"He is a Green," Sandy said. "And he is a follower of Tova. He hangs around with Brother Bazika."

Quint grimaced and stepped over the monk to help Sandy out of the corner. "Do you want to repeat that?" He jotted down the information. "Shall we dump him out the front door," he said, "or out the window?"

After the documentation was done, Sandy followed Quint down the stairs, holding onto the monk's feet.

"You were so exposed!"

"I have a better shield than anyone in the Cloister, and I'd never sell that string," Quint said, "so I wasn't as exposed as you think. I can also cast spells more quickly than anyone."

"You've made a believer out of me. Are you going to continue selling strings?"

Quint pursed his lips. "I'm not sure. I'm not going to have any possessions left if I get more fire-happy monks, and I'm more motivated to identify all the Greens in the cloister. Staying away from them is better than fighting them. If two or three were jammed into my cell, I might not have escaped unscathed."

"You knew exactly what to do. I am more than impressed."

"I've had more practice than I've wanted since I've been here," Quint said. "Let's go over my Narallian pronunciation. I still have some periodicals that I haven't translated yet. We can read along together."

Sandy pursed her lips. "Just this time. I think it's time to be transferred to another job."

"Is it something I've said?" Quint asked. "Am I too high a risk for you?"

She nodded. "I didn't appreciate the risk until today. No, I promised if there were certain things that happened between us, that I would withdraw. Escorting you has been very lucrative."

"Certain things?" Quint sighed. "Boy-girl things?"

"You feel the same way? My attitude changed when I saw you handle the novice."

Quint gave Sandy half a smile. "I don't feel the same way today, but I know my feelings could change. You've been nicer to me than anyone in the cloister, but part of that is your job, so I've restrained developing anything other than a neutral relationship. I do count you as a close friend, though."

Sandy looked relieved. "I was warned, strongly warned," she said. "Let's go over your diction, and then I'll leave. Don't worry about your project. I will continue to work on that."

They both struggled to go over Quint's pronunciations. Sandy kept smiling and being more solicitous than ever before. Quint got distracted and began to do worse.

"I think I better leave. As far as I'm concerned, we are still friends after this awful session?" Sandy asked.

"Sure," Quint said with a smile.

She left him, and Quint was bewildered by how quickly everything happened. When she said she had feelings for him, Quint's own feelings responded, but he was careful not to tell her. If she was warned, Quint was sure Sandy would receive a punishment of some kind for getting too close to the outsider.

He was sorely disappointed when he realized he had to hurry to create a form to manage the information about the monks. Quint stared at the notes he made about his attacker. He thought of Sandy cowering in the corner and sighed. Things had changed between them with her confession and there wasn't a thing Quint could do about it.

§§§

CHAPTER TWELVE
~

AT DINNER, QUINT WALKED UP TO THE COUNCIL DAIS and gave his form to the high prior.

"I understand you left a sleeping monk on the ground outside your dormitory," the religionist council member said with a smile.

"He became unruly, and I had to fight or put him to sleep. I couldn't exactly work in my room with a belligerent monk asleep."

A few of the council members chuckled at Quint's remark.

The high prior pursed his lips and gave Quint a mildly disapproving look. "I'm disappointed with you." Quint couldn't understand the comment. "Here is a map of the cloister that we discussed earlier," the prior said. "The person I asked to accompany you declined to help." The prior shrugged his shoulders. "It happens."

Quint took the document and left, finding a seat at Hintz Dakuz's table.

"What was all that entertainment about?" Dakuz said drily, nodding toward the council members.

"I had a client that wanted to learn how to heat his cell followed by another client who wanted to heat me. I had my shield spell working and put him to sleep before he could try twice. Sandy and I dragged him outside the dormitory building so I could continue my Narallian diction lessons."

"A reasonable move," Dakuz said. "What did our beloved head prior give you?"

Quint raised his eyebrows. "Do I get a 'please show me?'"

"Please show me," Dakuz said in a way that mocked Quint.

"I'm thinking about changing cells along with some monks volunteering as bodyguards. I could have used some help this afternoon."

Quint unfolded the document as Dakuz pushed into Quint's shoulder to get a better look at the map.

"The areas outlined in blue?" Dakuz asked.

"There are three sections of the cloister that I can use. Can you look over these with me? I'm not experienced at finding things wrong with cells."

Dakuz grunted. "I'm probably not much better than you at deciding, but I've more experience living in cells of all kinds, and as it happens, I have nothing pressing after dinner."

Dakuz knew the cloister better than Quint and led him to a set of rooms above the refectory kitchen. The smell of cooking permeated the rooms, and most of them were currently used as storage by the kitchen staff.

"I don't think you'd be interested in smelling good cooking and bad at all times of the day," Dakuz said. "It looks like a good place to pilfer, however," he said as he opened a few boxes and baskets to see inside.

"We can take this off our list," Quint said.

"For now," Dakuz said. "You haven't seen the other two possibilities. All of them must have problems to be unused."

The second set of rooms was adjacent to the stables. They were smelly as well.

"The cells are larger and face away from the stables if you don't mind living close to the livestock," Dakuz said.

"I grew up caring for animals," Quint said. "The smell is the same as the courtyard where the livestock is kept." He looked at the cells that shared back walls with the stables and found voids in the mortar. "We can minimize the smell by plugging up the mortar that has fallen out."

"That is too big of a job," Dakuz said.

"No, it isn't. We can plaster the walls connected to the stables, if we wish," Quint said. "The walls are solid. I am guessing every place we look at will have to be cleaned, anyway."

"This is better than the kitchen cells?"

Quint grimaced and nodded. "On to the final candidate."

The last set of rooms was up four flights of stairs, and the cells on one side of the space faced the ocean with many-paned windows framing the view. Not all the panes had glass, letting a cool wind blow into the cell.

"Drafty and cold," Dakuz said. "The ocean is pretty, but I'm sure the cold and the damp from the seaside exposure drove the previous monks out when the cloister expanded, and there were better places to live."

"The climb up the stairs is daunting," Quint said, "although it will give us exercise."

"Don't include me in 'us,'" Dakuz said. "I won't be joining you, however, the monks can use magic to heat the rooms since none have fireplaces and the windows can be resealed."

Quint looked at the thick windowsill. "Or install another window on the inside," Quint said. "It is the most defensible. Traps could be installed on the stairwell, and if worse came to worse, we could let down ropes and escape the cloister."

"This is the best for defense but the worst for livability," Dakuz said. "Are you sure you want to move? Your spell exchange business will suffer."

"I've thought about that, and there are blank spaces around the courtyard where I can meet monks," Quint said. "I'm exposed, inviting them to my room."

"You are exposed wherever you are."

Quint stepped into a cell and looked around. "We only need to seal up the windows to make these work. The kitchen won't be happy to have its storage rooms displaced, and I'm not sure the stable smells aren't permanently embedded in the stable cells. My purpose for moving is defense, and this is the best. The remoteness of the cells only makes them more secure."

"You'll have to convince your candidates for bodyguard to put up with the inconvenience."

Quint tapped on the window, and the pane fell out toward him. He caught it and laid it on the deep sill. "This is the one."

§

The following morning, Quint had to wait an hour before the head prior could meet.

"I'd like to take over the cells at the top of the sea wall," Quint said. "They need some cleaning, but we can do that. Are there any glaziers among the monks? The windows need attention."

"Replacing the broken windows along that wall has been on the list of many head priors," the monk said. "You can provide the labor?"

"I hope so. The cleaning, for sure. Those cells are the most defensible in the cloister."

The head prior nodded. "You are sure? I'll give you and your monks a six-month trial. After that, we will re-evaluate. That doesn't affect your decision in eight weeks," the prior said, "but if you leave, the remaining monks should benefit from their labors."

"Understood," Quint said.

"Dakuz knows who the glazier is. He may request helpers."

"I'll make sure he gets them," Quint said. "Is it acceptable to board the windows while the windows are being repaired? That way, we can move in a few days."

"It is acceptable. I have another appointment, so if you will excuse me," the head prior stood, forcing Quint to rise and leave. A young monk sat on a bench facing the door to the head prior's office. The prior called him in after Quint had left.

Quint found Grizak in the library and organized an impromptu meeting with Grizak and Dakuz.

"I'll show Grizak the new cells," Quint said.

Dakuz snorted. "They are hardly new," he said.

"I know where they are. Shall we go up and look?"

"Count me out, but I'll stroll over to Kozak, the cloister carpenter, and have a chat," Dakuz said.

After a night to think about it, the cells looked even more defensible. The cell walls needed washing, and floors were uneven and cold, something Quint hadn't considered.

"We can bring the straw mats from our current cells, which will help warm up the floors. You will have to teach everyone the hot air spell," Grizak said. "Let's check the windows."

The ocean windows needed some work to open and close, but Quint could use his binding string to straighten the window frames enough to work. All the windows in the line of cells facing the courtyard were stuck in place, but Quint used the same technique and achieved the same successful result.

They heard someone coming up the stairs and Dakuz had brought a friend.

"Brother Kozak wanted to see what he was facing. Since I knew you were still here, I dragged him up to find out how much work he needed to do," Dakuz said.

Kozak stepped into the first cell and looked out at the ocean. "Pretty until it is stormy or foggy," the carpenter said. He opened the window and looked at the frame. "This has already been worked on."

"I straightened the frames so the windows would open and close," Quint said.

"You saved me more than a week's worth. How did you do it?"

Quint told him about using the locking and unlocking string for wooden doors as a method to crudely true the window frames.

"And I don't have to remove the windows to do the work. Clever. I know the string, but I didn't think to use it like you did. Who taught you?"

Quint shrugged. "I thought of that on my own."

Kozak nodded and grinned. "You are showing me why you are so special. Good work! I use magic in my work, but now I have something new to learn."

"Would it be beneficial to install another window inside the first? Would that make the cells more comfortable?" Grizak said. "It's another one of Quint's ideas."

"You certainly have a deep enough sill. I could do it quickly if I didn't have to match the pane design," Kozak said.

"Then do it. Something else that might work," Quint said.

"How many are moving up here?"

"A minimum of six," Quint said.

"There are ten cells. I've always wanted to try out a winch system. I've had a winch sitting in my shop as long as I've been here. We can make one of the cells a winch room. That could hold storage for the ones up here," Kozak said.

"How long will it take?"

"A day a window and two or three days for the winch. We might have to remove some stones. I've got boards to cover the windows in the meantime. The monks will have to use candles or magic lights during the day, but they do that at night anyway."

"How many helpers do you need?" Grizak asked.

"Three. Any more, and they will be getting in the way. It would be better if they've had some building experience, but…" Kozak shrugged.

"Grizak can take care of that. I'll walk down with Brother Kozak, and you two should find your bodyguards. I'll excuse Quint from class today." Dakuz said, letting Kozak roughly measure the ocean windows and the courtyard side windows.

Quint left them to it while Grizak and he sought out the volunteers.

§

They ended up with six volunteers. Two had helped build family projects, and a third had spent a few years learning to be a stonemason as a hobby. Quint thought that was a perfect match. Grizak said Tizurek was looking over them, but Quint had his doubts.

The three helpers were sent to Kozak's workshop.

The other three bodyguards, plus Grizak and Quint, lugged buckets filled with water, brooms, mops, and rags and began cleaning the cells. With all five, each cell took an hour, and in two days, all the cells were as clean as they were going to get. If they stayed longer, the plastered walls would get another coat, but they had done all the cleaning they could to the bare stone walls for now.

The straw mats currently in the monks' cells were dragged up the stairs and laid out. They were happy to realize the new cells were longer on all sides than their old ones. The next day, they were stopped from carrying their furniture up four flights of stairs by Kozak and his helpers.

"It's time to see your lift," the carpenter said. Kozak led them to the first cell on the courtyard side of the corridor and opened the door. The room that Kozak had forbidden them to enter revealed a large opening rather than a window. A contraption was bolted to the floor and the walls. "This is a winch," the carpenter said, pointing to a cylinder with rope coiled around it. The lift, this platform, is lowered to the ground and then one or two of you work the winch and bring whatever on the platform up four stories. Then you bring it in, sliding the platform along this track. You can remove things the same way."

"Like a drawbridge," Quint said, seeing the lift for the first time along with the other three cleaners. He clapped his hands. "Let's get to work."

Bringing up everyone's goods was still work, but everything went much faster. By the time the dinner was close, the cells were furnished.

"The window work can begin now," Kozak said.

The dinner bell rang, and everyone went down the stairs. Quint looked up at the lift secured on the fourth floor with shutters covering the opening. The cell wouldn't be warm, but it would be dry, and they had an easier way of lugging up anything into their secured living quarters.

Quint had taken the last cell on the ocean side. His window only had one pane missing, so he had pasted a small cardboard pane over the hole. The cell was just enough larger than the others so that he could have two chairs in his room. Tonight would be the first night sleeping in their tiny compound.

His mind was on the winch, and he was glad that the attitude of his floormates was positive. Their living in an isolated section of the cloister required exercising camaraderie, plus they were guarding against attack on Quint.

After dinner, they took chairs into the corridor for a group meeting. Quint asked Grizak to do most of the talking about securing their floor. Once the ideas started to flow, Quint had to appreciate the benefit of a group working through ideas. It reminded him of the meetings in the Wizard Corps in the strategic operations group once he was promoted to lieutenant.

Quint took notes, and he reviewed the group's output when the ideas began to fade. Some ideas were considered too expensive, time-consuming, or unworkable. Still, when they finished, they had identified low-cost traps for the stairwell and a set of procedures for securing the floor including the lift. Everyone recognized it could be a weak point if the lift were on the ground at the time they were attacked.

Everyone retired for the night, and the group's general attitude was still very positive in the morning. With his personal security improved, Quint needed to address the project for the head prior. He had lost five days, he estimated, and now it was time to start assembling the information that he had.

§§§

CHAPTER THIRTEEN

After a morning of recording data on his chart, he checked in with Dakuz.

"Did you sleep well?" Dakuz asked.

"Surprisingly well. Except for the window work, everyone is moved and happy to have a little more room. The lift was a great idea."

Dakuz grunted. "Kozak demonstrated for me before he showed you and your group. I thought it turned out nicely."

Quint related the excitement of the bodyguards and the results of their security meeting, showing Dakuz his notes.

"I'm not going to interfere, but you can take a couple of other measures. You should have a duty board that shows which two monks are supposed to be with you. Having a secure place to sleep doesn't protect you walking around the courtyard," Dakuz said.

"A duty board. I like that. Then, my monks can trade places when they need to. I like it," Quint said.

"Complete your list, and then take Bokwiz and me on a tour."

"Why Shinzle Bokwiz?" Quint asked.

"Bokwiz has a history and is more experienced in defensive measures than I am. He might have some more ideas, but after you are ready to do extra things. If everything is a work-in-progress, you won't complete anything until after your probationary period," Dakuz said.

Quint nodded. "Another good idea. Now, I have something else to show you." He unfurled his chart and showed Dakuz how he intended to present his research into monk affiliations.

"That is good enough for the head prior," Dakuz said. "He doesn't have any idea of what he wants, but that should work. It allows you to show blank spaces for those you didn't get all the information, and the councilors can work on that if they are interested."

Quint frowned. "Is this a make-work project? I never thought of it that way."

"That's because the stakes are so high for you. That's exactly what it is, but you have to do your best, or you won't be able to make a choice."

"A choice is valuable," Quint said.

"Especially for you. Every choice you make might affect the future."

"That again."

Dakuz nodded. "Yes, that again, and get used to it. Your life will affect many other lives, which is your lot."

"As revealed by portent strings."

"Exactly. So, you know the future can shift, meaning your choices can be meaningful."

"I'm going to concentrate on my survival and getting this chart finished, then."

"And make sure you also give your bodyguards a chance to survive. Now, schoolwork. Have you had a chance to do translations?"

Quint hadn't and was loathe to admit it, but he had a reply. "I've been speaking to my bodyguards in Narallian. They aren't reluctant to correct me and suggest new words."

Dakuz furrowed his brows. "Not what I assigned, but in this case, I'll make an exception. Here," he handed Quint two more publications. "Get these translated, and let's have our next library session in two days. Tomorrow, I want a tour of your new cells. Perhaps we should test the lift to see if it can lift an old man up four floors."

"A test!" Quint said. "We can make that happen as long as there are enough monks available to pull you up."

Quint helped Dakuz off the lift the following day and into the storage room. Grizak had helped Quint haul Dakuz up the side.

"Nice. We might see more of these in the cloister," Dakuz said.

"This wall has the worst stairway," Quint said, "but look at the cells."

Dakuz poked his head in a few of the cells. "These are bigger than they looked. I can feel the extra chill, though."

"Windows will be coming in every day this week," Quint said. "It will be better, but a little magic can heat the cells while they are occupied."

"What is the hook for?" Dakuz asked, looking at a hook embedded in the stone under a window looking at the ocean.

"Escape on the sea side," Quint said. "It doesn't make sense to do that on the courtyard side since if we are attacked, the attackers will be waiting in the courtyard."

"Then put hooks on the inside cells, too, so if someone attacked from the sea, you could make a quick exit down a rope," Dakuz said.

Grizak nodded. "We can do that."

"Dakuz has some other ideas," Quint said.

"I think this will be a popular place for monks when there become vacancies," Dakuz said. "I've seen enough. I'd rather take the stairs down. An old man is still heavy enough to make the lift perilous."

Quint showed where the traps would be as they descended the stairs. Dakuz looked impressed, but that might have been for the benefit of Grizak. Dakuz never held back where Quint was concerned.

"Go back and get those documents translated," Dakuz said. "I think if you are smart about moving around the cloister, you are secure enough to last more than a few months.

§

Bokwiz showed up at lunch. Dakuz had to return to the library after his tour.

"I brought all I could gather while you and our friends worked on your new cells. I'm sure it is more than what you expected. My congregants aren't of one mind politically within and without the cloister, so their friends expanded my contribution. I have fifty monks in that portfolio. Most of the boxes are filled in, but there are gaps."

Quint was anxious to see the papers, but Bokwiz put his hand on Quint's wrist. "Not here. I did find something else that my findings don't show. Everywhere, the allegiances are shifting. Everyone who helped me warned me that the cloister was in a transition period. Nobody knew why except it might have something to do with the fights in the council building and the refectory. Some people were attracted to the action, and others were repelled."

"Affiliations shift, even in Racellia," Quint said. "I will submit the information given. Why don't you join us for lunch?"

Bokwiz smiled. "I have more to do, but I wanted you to get started now that you have a secure place to work. I may pop by tomorrow evening after the services."

Quint looked in the portfolio, tempted, but he resisted pulling the paperwork out.

"Show us what you have tonight," Grizak said. "We will do our part with the research, but I'd rather not bother those our fellow worshippers might have already contacted."

"Good idea," Quint said.

After lunch, when Sandy joined him, Quint was returning to the seawall cells. "I haven't seen you since you've turned into a carpenter."

"A cleaning person more than a carpenter," Quint said. "Do you want to see my new cell?"

"These are your bodyguards?" Sandy asked.

Quint introduced two of the monks living on his floor to her.

They walked up the stairs. Quint could see the start of some modifications. He didn't know what they were but hoped Kozak was having fun with all the work Quint loaded on him.

"I've been on this floor once on a dare from another sister," Sandy said. "It was scary and cold, but you've made this into something that has some appeal, not that I'd want to live all the way up here."

"Good. A woman would distract the monks."

Quint showed her his cell, and one of the monks asked Quint to follow him. The monk opened the door to one of the unused courtyard-side cells. Inside was a table surrounded by eight chairs. It was a tight fit, but the inhabitants now had a meeting room. Quint decided to keep the work in progress from the project in the flat file that was squeezed into a corner.

"We thought this would be drier than an ocean-facing cell."

"And the window is intact," Quint said. He looked at Sandy. "I can show you what I've done. Have a seat while I get more papers from my cell."

Grizak stood at one corner, looking at the papers spread out on the table. "We should count how many monks we've already interviewed."

Sandy joined in, and there were two hundred-seven monks listed. Danko's contribution had the most blanks, but now Quint had evidence that he might be able to submit the project on time and with an analysis, which wasn't demanded by the head prior.

"Now, what can I do?" Sandy said.

"Compare these names to the master list that the head prior gave me. There could be duplicates, too," Grizak said.

Quint stayed in the project room after he showed Sandy the master list, looking over Bokwiz's contribution as he tried to determine how he could see any shifts in affiliation. He failed after a quarter-hour. He would need all the bodyguards to look at the names they knew and see if they had any sense of what Bokwiz said to watch for.

Sandy stayed almost three hours before she finished.

"Two sisters out of twenty-eight. I'll have to get to work on those," she said.

"If you can, see if you notice any shifts in the last few months. Bokwiz said that some seemed to soften their affiliations one way or another after the Greens attacked me. That isn't evidence, but the more consistent stories we have, the better report I can make to the head prior."

"I'll do it but give me until the rest of the week. I will return in two days. Has Dakuz given you more assignments?" she asked.

"He has," Quint said. "I'm trying to fit them in. I haven't stopped reading and speaking Narallian during the construction."

"You are doing a great job, Quint. I'm sure you are learning some leadership principles."

Quint laughed. "If I am, it's unintentional, but thanks. Everyone had done a great job pitching in, but all the monks are volunteers."

He walked her down the stairs and watched her scurry to another assignment. As he returned to the cells, he noticed a smile on his face. He wiped it off with his hand, but it returned.

After dinner, with all the monks speaking Narallian, Quint spoke to them in the meeting room, showing them the project and discussing what they were looking for. The monks caught the vision of listing, and they spent the rest of the evening comparing the boxes with their impressions of all the monks that they knew. They found an additional twenty-three monks that weren't entered. With Sandy's twenty-eight, the master list was almost complete, but with more empty boxes than Quint thought might be acceptable to the head prior.

A storm blew in after midnight. The windows leaked, but they were prepared and kept the dampness to a minimum. Quint slept fitfully as lightning lit up the room and thunder rattled the windows. He'd be more comfortable when Kozak was finished.

§

After the storm, the meeting room was tight and dry. That put Quint in a good mood as he ate lunch and headed to the library and another one of his sessions with Dakuz. His two bodyguards brought their own study materials and found out-of-sight tables in the library.

"Were you flooded out?" Dakuz said as Quint walked into his office.

"No standing water and all the ceilings were dry," Quint said. He reported on a productive afternoon with Sandy's help. "She promised to get information on the cloister sisters."

Dakuz sat back in his chair, steepling his fingers. "It's been a week since you met with the head prior. Remember what you told me he said?"

"No attacks for a week," Quint said. "We always have two monks with me and two monks in our cells. I've taught them all how to cast shield strings, which all can do."

"Have you taught Sandy?"

"No," Quint said.

"Then do," Dakuz said. "There is general uneasiness throughout the cloister. I think the Greens are doing some aggressive recruiting."

Unfortunately, that might have matched with Bokwiz's warning. "She will be by tomorrow."

Dakuz nodded. "It may be time to start your own faction. You can look at your list to find possible candidates. I'd stay away from both Reds and Greens. They are too set in their ways."

Quint didn't like what he was hearing. "Is there anything I can do to reduce the tension?"

"Bokwiz came by last night with a monk who can cast predictor strings. The spell confirmed the tension and the possibility of a larger fight, but your presence blurred his vision. He couldn't see what the outcome was. Anything could happen. He didn't know if you'd stay in the cloister or be expelled."

"I can't imagine a predictor string being so vague with a short-term viewing?"

Dakuz frowned. "Neither could the string-caster. What outcome do you desire?"

"I'd like to stay for at least a year, but I think it won't be any longer than that because I doubt the Greens in Pinzleport will stop."

"I agree. I'd be prepared to leave at any time."

"Even after all we've done to make the ocean cells livable?"

Dakuz waved Quint's comment away. "That is your contribution to the cloister for putting you up for these past months. Now, let's do some geography. Where are the closest cloisters?"

§

Grizak, Quint, and the bodyguards sat together at lunch. A server came with their orders and slipped a note next to Quint's plate. Quint looked up at her, but she quickly scuttled away. He watched her disappear through the kitchen doors.

"What is that?" Grizak asked.

Quint opened the note. His heart began to race as he read the message in Narallian. "Sandy has been kidnapped, so says the note."

"And?"

"I'm to go to the cells behind the stable in two hours, where I'll get more information," Quint said.

"Greens!" one of the bodyguards said. "We don't have time to check the place out."

"I'm to go alone," Quint said, "and not notify the council." He tried to tamp down his alarm, but he couldn't stop breathing heavier.

"Cowards," Grizak said. "We won't desert you."

Quint frantically thought about what to do. "Who would have some armor on short notice?" Quint asked.

"Kozak," the stonemason bodyguard said. "He even has weapons. Does it say come unarmed?"

"For a wizard? That would involve the removal of the wizard's hands," Grizak said sarcastically.

"We need defenders at our cells," Quint said. "They won't be able to break into our meeting room unless they burn our rooms down."

"We can go," one of the monks pointed at one of the others, who nodded. "As soon as we finish lunch."

"The rest be in proximity. We don't want any deaths or even serious injuries if we can help it." Quint looked at the stonemason. "You and I will stop at Kozak's shop before I fetch Sandy."

"What if she isn't there?" Grizak said.

"There will still be a fight. The head prior expected something a week after the last attack. I think he thought they would be licking their wounds until now," Quint said.

"He was right," another monk said.

§§§

CHAPTER FOURTEEN

Quint made sure those with him had paper and pencils to document who came out of the stable area, if for no other reason than to identify the kidnappers. They weren't to chase unless Sandy was brought out when they tried to escape.

They found Kozak working on a wagon wheel.

"Sandiza Bartok has been kidnapped to draw me into a trap. I wondered if you had armor or mundane weapons I could borrow."

Kozak stared at the stonemason. "You have a big mouth."

"It may help save two lives," the stonemason said.

Kozak sighed and looked at his work. "I have to finish this by dinnertime, so I can't go looking right now."

Quint smiled. "My father was a wheelwright, and I was his apprentice," he said. "I'll finish this if you can find me at least a breastplate. They won't make the mistake of sending only one wizard to kill me."

"I can't turn that offer down." Kozak took his work apron off and tossed it to Quint. "You better be right about knowing wheels."

The stonemason followed Kozak back into the carpenter's shop while Quint examined the wheel. It had been years since he worked on a wheel, but this was a simple wagon wheel with two cracked spokes. Kozak had already broken down the wheel. The iron ring that held the wheel together was intact, and everything else looked good except for the hub. Kozak had missed seeing a crack.

Quint rummaged around a bin full of wheel bits and found a match that only needed greasing. He began to dry fit the spokes, and after shaving a bit off the new spokes, the newly reset spokes stuck out of the hub. Quint worked on the rim, and then he put the iron band on the fire Kozak had built. As Quint worked, his thoughts began to simmer down, and he regained control over his emotions.

The last step was one that Quint could never do himself since he was much smaller when he worked for his father. He put on thick leather gloves and was able to slip the band over an edge, then he quickly used a mallet to pound the band around the rim and finally seating it to the rim before hammering an edge around the side enough to keep it from slipping.

The band was on, and Quint poured water around the rim to cool it, and as it cooled, it tightened the wheel. When he was done, he stepped back to wipe his brow with Kozak's apron. He heard clapping behind him.

"We decided to observe your work," Kozak said. "Very good." He tapped the wheel with the mallet. "It will tighten some more. Take your armor and return it when you are done."

The stonemason urged Quint to splash some water on his face and hands to look more presentable to his enemies.

The armor consisted of a leather breastplate, a little too large but wearable. Leather gauntlets covering thin metal plates.

"He had a nice helmet, but it would have made you look too obvious."

Quint nodded as he let Kozak help him with the breastplate, which he covered with his robe.

"I don't have a sword, but I do have this," Kozak said, giving Quint a long knife. "I think your magic is better than a knife, but you might find it a cold comfort to have some sharpened steel on you."

"I will," Quint said. "I hope I can get this back to you before dinner."

"Good luck, Brother Tirolo," Kozak said, putting a hand over his heart. "May Tizurek fight on your side."

The invocation made understanding why Kozak was willing to help them easier. "I thank you," Quint said, "for the armor and the sentiment." He couldn't bring himself to call it a prayer.

They walked quickly toward the stable. Before they were in sight, Quint instructed the stonemason to stay behind and not to enter the cells' courtyard until Quint called.

"Be careful you aren't caught off-guard by another unit of Greens."

"We won't," the stonemason said.

§

Quint looked at the roofs and didn't see any monks hiding on the roofs of the cells or the building on the other side. It didn't mean no one was there, just that Quint couldn't see them. He cast his best shield string, took a deep breath, and walked in.

"Sandiza?" Quint called.

A monk stepped out from a cell at the far end of the stable row. Quint could smell horse manure and looked toward the wall where his cells were, the fourth-floor windows peeking over the roof. He was ready with a string pulsating in his right hand.

Quint opened the first door to an empty cell. He did the same with the second. When he turned from the man standing with his arms folded at the end of the stable, his adversary went into a crouch and cast a fire spear. Quint let it splash futilely against his shield.

"Third door," Quint said as he opened it. Two monks cast tongues of flame. Quint attacked them both with spears of flame, piercing both of their shields and washing against their legs. It was up to them to smother the flames while they were rolled on the floor, and Quint had to put his attention elsewhere.

He armed himself with a wind string, and when the monk shot a new flame at him, Quint's wind spell forced the fire back onto the caster, and the monk's robe erupted in flames. Another four monks emerged from the other side of the courtyard.

"Where is Sandiza Bartok?" Quint called.

"At the end," a smiling monk pointed to the cell where the first opponent emerged.

Quint cast another fire spear. This time, it splashed against the newly appeared monk's shield. He quickly cast a sheet of flame at the other monk, who promptly hid behind the monk with the shield, but the monk behind him erupted in flames.

"I'll give myself up if you show Sandy," Quint said.

The shielded monk laughed. "That won't work with us because your sister-friend isn't here. We want you dead, so you won't destroy our cause." The monk quickly looked at his three remaining companions. "Rush him!"

Quint backed up, but three more monks had jumped into the courtyard from the first cell. It was seven to one and Quint wouldn't be able to survive this without help. He ran to the new monks, hoping he'd be able to get past them, but two were shielded after a quick attempt. Then Quint set fire to the gate. Hopefully, the smoke would bring his bodyguards.

He spun, casting a last spear of fire before the Green monks reached him. Two more were down, but that left five to deal with. It was still too many. He needed to stall for time, but they grabbed his robe and began to kick him. One tried to flame Quint, but Quint's shield turned back the flame and burned the caster. He was down to four.

Quint struggled as the monks began to beat him. His hand was taken and stomped on while he struggled. His hand turned numb. Quint wished he knew how to cast a one-handed string like his Wizard Corps instructor Geno Pozella claimed to do, but he did have the knife, Kozak's cold comfort, in his belt, but he felt he would not make it through the fight. There were still too many.

His hand was getting some feeling back, but Quint wasn't ready for wizardry yet. An opening gave Quint the chance to scuttle away. He pulled out the knife and kept the remaining monks away. Another spear of fire bathed his shield, which was getting weaker.

He waved the knife back and forth and backed up against a cell door. He knew he would be cornered, but the pillar of smoke from the burning gate had to be plainly in sight of someone.

He opened the latch and almost fell into the dark confines of a windowless cell. Quint secured the latch but didn't know if the metal and old wood would hold against the monks and their magic. He shook feeling into his hand and joined the wooden door to the frame and the latch to its plate on the frame.

Quint sheathed his knife and tore off his robe. Kozak's breastplate was scratched, and his wrist guards were seriously scuffed. Someone had tried to use a knife on him, and amid the fighting, he hadn't even noticed. Quint frantically looked at his surroundings. The roof was tile, with small holes, but nothing big enough to blast through. He thought about a sleep spell, but he had to have a line of sight to his assailants, and that wasn't going to happen.

The door began to shake from whatever the monks tried to tear it down. Quint leaned against a wall to regain his breath and work his injured hand. He still had magic left, but he didn't have any confidence in his weakening shield until he cast a new one.

The sounds of pounding stopped, replaced by yelling. Quint tried to unlock the door, but something was holding it in place. He needed to join the fight, but the exit was sealed until he remembered he had a string for decomposing stone. Quint had never used it for practical reasons, but now he had one. He focused his magic on the wall by the door and cast the string. He stopped and pushed. An area of the wall wasn't as stable. Quint cast another string, and the mortar had lost its sticking power.

Quint donned his robe and put the hood over his brushy head before running into the wall and shouldering through into the cell courtyard. The fighting stopped for a second while Quint's dramatic appearance diverted everyone's attention.

Three Green monks immediately attacked Quint, but the refreshed shield held, and Quint's bodyguards fell on the men from the back. The second shielded monk shrugged a bodyguard off and pulled out a knife the size of Quint's.

"I'll make sure you die if it's my dying breath," the monk said as he lunged toward Quint.

Quint had thought of a possible solution while in the cell. He pointed to the ground and cast an earthquake string. Quint focused it as much as possible, and the ground shook underneath the monk's feet.

The assailant's eyes grew as he lost his balance and fell to the ground. Quint quickly touched the man's wrist, putting him to sleep. The fighting stopped as monks flooded the courtyard led by Sandy and the head prior.

"Someone put out the gate fire," the head prior said.

An older monk used a water spell and soon the pillar of smoke became a thin thread that rose above the rooftops until it hit the wind and dissipated.

"What happened?" the prior asked Quint, still nursing his injured hand.

Quint described the fight as best he could. Once he was in the cell, Grizak took up the story until Quint broke through the wall, distracting friend and enemy both.

"This is the leader," Quint said.

The head prior leaned down and cast a string. The monk's face changed into that of Baldur Wetzel. "He sneaked into the cloister and set his trap," the head prior said. "He has already been judged and sentenced to death for the murder of Eben."

Quint stared at the man's face. It was too familiar to him. "My bodyguards might have recognized the face he stole. I suggest you find him to see if he is all right. The master gardener wasn't allowed to live."

Sandy was standing to the side. "You are all right?"

"Bruises," Quint said. He felt a sting on his cheek and rubbed it. "A few cuts as well. They damaged my hand, but I could revive it enough to cast strings."

And a mighty string that was," the stonemason said, examining the hole in the cell wall.

Quint turned to look at the door. The face of it was scorched and shredded, but the wood was thick enough to delay the monks and when Quint tested it, one of the monks had joined the wood on the exterior side. They had wanted Quint safe for them to kill after they had taken care of Quint's bodyguards.

"You saw the smoke?" Quint said to Grizak.

Grizak nodded. "We did. That's when we attacked."

"What about the cells?" Quint asked. "It looks like you all were here."

"Dakuz and Bokwiz volunteered to guard our quarters and told us to join the fight," one of the bodyguards said. "I'm glad we didn't take this section." His head turned around to look at the damage. "You've done enough damage, Quint."

"Our companions?" Quint asked Grizak.

"Two need assistance to the infirmary, and the rest of us need a day of rest."

"I'll take care of the Green brothers. It was plainly a conspiracy to murder you," the head prior said.

Quint nodded. "Did you spot the fire, too?"

"No, Sandy went to your floor, and Dakuz informed her that she was abducted by the Greens and likely needed help. She ran to the council building, and we are here to make sure the fighting stopped," the head prior said.

Quint turned to Sandy. "Thank you. I'm glad you are uninjured. Once they told me you weren't with them, the fighting turned ugly."

"And what saved you?" the head prior asked.

"A superior shield, Kozak's armor and knife, and an unlocked door," Quint said.

By the time Quint had examined the other attackers, Baldur Wetzel had died. The head prior seemed unfazed by the death, and Quint thought the prior was expertly covering his relief that an escaped murderous monk had breathed his last.

"Any surprises?" Quint asked the head prior. "These had to be Greens."

"None at all, although I am surprised, they were willing to risk all. You have become a formidable foe to the Green organization," the prior said.

"With a lot of help," Quint said. "I had a hard time reviewing strings to use. The stress of being attacked from all sides shrunk my memory. Fire strings were what came to mind, but some of them had shields, and I thought it was the end."

"I'm glad it wasn't the end," Sandy said, shivering.

Quint had the urge to put his arm around Sandy as if he were protecting her, but he successfully restrained himself. "That goes for both of us," he managed to say.

§§§

Chapter Fifteen

Almost two months later, the Greens hadn't launched another attack. Quint resumed his string exchange business, and his hair had grown out. Their floor spoke Narallian all the time, and Quint felt he had made a lot of progress. He was ready for his interview with the head prior after lunch, so Quint arranged to meet Bokwiz and Dakuz in the library to go over his final version of the report.

"You have an entry for every monk in Seensist Cloister?" Bokwiz asked.

"Even the two young novices who entered in the past month. Sandy is their escort and gave me estimates."

Dakuz clucked his tongue in mock sympathy. "Do you miss her following you around like a puppy dog?"

"A bit," Quint said. "But I'm learning to get over it. This is our final review. You've both read through my paper that goes with the chart?"

"In Narallian. That was rather bold of you."

"Grizak edited my work. He said the paper is mostly coherent," Quint said.

"I thought it was insightful," Dakuz pronounced with an unexpected compliment.

"The head prior is one who can appreciate the thoughts you made. I doubt if any of the rest of us could do a proper analysis like that. I can do the thinking, but not organize my thoughts as well. My report would be significantly less coherent than yours," Bokwiz said.

"Then it's time."

Dakuz nodded. "Have you made up your mind about what you will do if the head prior accepts you or rejects you?"

"I have Parsun cloister in mind," Quint said. "I'm not confident enough to find my place in Narukun, but I'll concentrate on that for the next six months regardless of the prior's decision."

"Are you going alone?" Bokwiz asked.

Quint shook his head. "My bodyguards have unanimously decided that they will go wherever I do. I can always use a few more followers. I know it's presumptuous to ask, but that includes you two."

Bokwiz laughed. "I told you weeks ago that I was willing, and I still feel that way."

Dakuz shook his head. "You are too much trouble," the librarian said. "How can I leave all my books?"

"The cloister's books," Bokwiz said.

"You both know what I mean. Count me out."

"It's an open invitation," Quint said. "It could be today or six months from today, but it will happen."

The lunch bell rang out, and the two bodyguards who escorted Quint to the library showed up to escort him to the refectory.

They joined Grizak and the others at their usual table. Quint ate sparingly, nervous about his appointment. He still hadn't assembled the words he would say if the head prior gave him options.

In half an hour, Grizak sat on one side of Quint and the stonemason on the other on the bench in front of the head prior's office.

"I'm ready for you," the head prior said, sticking his head out of the door.

Quint stood and straightened up his robe, helped by his two companions.

"I'm with you whatever happens," the stonemason said.

"So are we all," Grizak said.

Quint nodded and sat in front of the head prior's desk.

"You have completed your project?"

"I have, but I'm sure you already know that."

The prior nodded. "I do. I've heard about your work. Some speak favorably, and others think you have stolen their most private information."

"It might be for some," Quint said, "especially the religious question, but I thought it would be a useful data point, and I hope my analysis proves my point." Quint stood and gave the thick portfolio to the head prior.

"I hadn't expected something so thorough," the prior said.

Quint sat back down and nodded. "Since I have experience doing similar analyses, I thought it was necessary to do a good job. I'm sure you realize that allegiances shift over time, affecting the details, although the larger perspective won't have changed since I've been working on this."

The prior shuffled through a few pages. "It looks complete enough to me."

"Like a news sheet, the facts can change, and I might not have been told the truth."

"So I should toss this?" the head prior asked.

"No, don't do that. It is still an analysis that can lead to some conclusions or at least perspectives on the cloister population."

"Then I will regard it as a study of estimates."

Quint nodded. "That is what I would do. I would like to acknowledge helpers who assisted in collecting information. My bodyguards helped a great deal. Hintz Dakuz, my instructor, gave me a list of people he knew, and I confirmed most of what he gave me. Sandiza Bartok collected information on the sisters, and Shinzle Bokwiz gave me information on many of the older monks in the cloister."

"And I contributed my estimation of how my council colleagues think."

"You are included in the acknowledgments at the end of the analysis," Quint said. "I had originally thought it to be easy, but it took all the time you gave me."

"We should be thankful the Greens were chastened enough not to try anything since the stable attack."

"My bodyguards and our remote living location contributed to the difficulty in attacking me."

The head prior nodded. He thumbed through the analysis. "I can't give you my answer on your future with Seensist until the council has had a chance to review this. Return in a week at this time and I'll have some feedback on this and our decision. You have proven yourself resourceful and resilient in overcoming a difficult situation. I noted that your paper is written in Narallian. I assume you did most of the work yourself?"

"I had one of my bodyguards read through my paper and offered grammatical corrections. I took most of them," Quint said.

"Your knowledge of Narallian is a matter of concern for some council members. You may go. We will meet in the small council chamber in a week."

Quint bowed to the head prior and left the office, deflated that he'd have to wait another week before learning his fate.

"Well?" Grizak asked.

"No decision will be handed out today," Quint said. "We have to wait another week, and it will be a council decision."

"No!" the stonemason said. "You don't have the unanimous support of the council."

"How much do I need?" Quint said. "There are two Greens on the council and a Red. The rest have different political affiliations on the outside."

"So we can't tell?"

Quint shook his head. "I'm in the same position as after lunch. We are going to have to exercise some patience."

He tried to be optimistic about the situation, but in actual fact, the delay made Quint think more strongly about leaving when the decision was communicated to him. He wondered if the high prior was involved in some game with Quint being the sole playing piece, but Quint had no idea how to play or what the stakes were. At this point, it seemed he had one move to make. Stay on the board or get off. Getting off had appeal, but his gut told him he was missing something he needed before leaving Seensist Cloister.

§

"A week will go by quickly," Sandy said to Quint as she sat behind him in the alcove where he exchanged strings. "Was the head prior impressed by your work?"

Quint shrugged. "I don't know. He just looked at the pages but didn't read any. I thought the head prior was supportive. However, I'm not so sure at this point."

"You intend to leave immediately after you find out?"

"Probably. None of us have much to take with us. Grizak suggested we pool our money and buy a wagon to carry our possessions. I'll ask for a week to leave, I suppose."

Sandy played with a strand of her hair. "You haven't asked me to go with you."

"Not directly," Quint said. "Do you want to give up Seensist?"

"Maybe," she said. "I'd need a direct invitation."

"Then come with us. We will be heading to Parsun Cloister."

"And hope they will let you in?"

Quint didn't know what to think about Sandy's request for an invitation. He was uncertain if his bodyguards would accept a woman, but she wasn't following them. Everybody was following him.

"I identified it as the best-suited cloister for me and had Dakuz check. He knows some of the monks. They have empty dormitories and haven't admitted a novice in three years."

"It's dying?"

Quint nodded. "And we can help revive it. Bokwiz is going."

'And Hintz Dakuz?"

"No, unfortunately," Quint said, sighing. "Would you consider coming?"

Sandy smiled. "I'm not sure, but since I have an invitation, It would only be proper to give you a reply."

"You should," Quint said. "When I leave, and I'm not sure when that will be."

"So, you said."

"So, I said," Quint replied. "Shall we do some diction while we wait for a client?"

"I'm ready if you are."

Quint read from a periodical on current trends in pottery design. The subject of design was something Quint had never thought of before. Like a lot of the papers and articles that Dakuz gave Quint, it gave him exposure to a facet of Narukun life that he hadn't considered. He probably wouldn't have been exposed to the subject if he were reading general textbooks. For the first time, he realized that Dakuz's documents provided Quint with a very rounded education that could help him outside the cloister.

"Do you have a favorite design?" Quint asked Sandy in Narallian.

Since they had just finished an article on the subject, Quint and Sandy were able to converse on the subject. Quint found that Sandy did have a pottery preference. She didn't like partially glazed pottery.

When Quint admitted he didn't have a preference, Sandy chided him. "You need to spend more time acquiring likes and dislikes."

"There is food that I like better than others," Quint said. "Doesn't that count?"

"It counts, but I'm talking about appreciating the design of things, or sounds, or even appreciating the weather," she said.

"I've never had time for that kind of thing," Quint said.

"You haven't had time for a lot of things," Sandy said. "You should spend a few minutes with Brother Kozak. He has a sense for design and can show you what he's made purely to see if he can make pleasing shapes."

"Aesthetics!" Quint said in Narallian. "I don't have a feel for it, do I?"

"Not yet, but people can develop one if they put their mind to it."

A very young monk walked up to the table. "I'm here for Sister Sandiza."

"One of your charges?" Quint asked.

Sandy gave the boy a grin. "He is, and I have to get back to work."

"Aren't you still being paid for helping me with my Narallian?"

She smiled and patted Quint on the head. "You, brother, are a labor of love."

Quint watched her take the young monk in hand and walk away. The two bodyguards broke into laughter.

"You aren't supposed to listen in," Quint said.

One of the guards still had a smile on his face. "And miss Sandy throwing so many signals at you? For being as smart as you are, you miss them all."

"I got the one about the invitation," Quint said.

"Ah! Improvement. Improvement is good, but that isn't enough," the bodyguard said. "Remember, we can hear everything you can." The guards chuckled again. "I like the pottery with the glaze drizzled down the sides and the jugs with wide bottoms."

"There isn't enough business this afternoon to stay," Quint said, getting up abruptly. "Let's pack up and go." He hoped his face wasn't too red with embarrassment.

§

The bodyguard contingent followed Quint into the council room. The audience seats were half full. Sandy, Bokwiz, and Dakuz sat together in the back. Quint even spotted Kozak chatting with another monk. Quint took his seat on the otherwise empty first row.

The council members came in as a group. Quint guessed they made their decision just before the meeting started.

The head prior called the meeting to order and began the proceedings.

"We are here to rule on Brother Quinto Tirolo's project." The prior looked over the audience. "I didn't expect there would be this much interest in a young monk."

The comment brought a little laughter in the room.

"The project, first. Brother Tirolo conducted a survey, with the help of other monks, on attitudes within the Seensist Cloister. The subject was mine to give. The survey was remarkably thorough, and the presentation of the findings exceeded my expectations. Brother Tirolo wrote an assessment and analysis of his survey. The results weren't particularly surprising, but the way the information was summarized was unique in our experience and gave us a lot of things to think about."

The religionist council member rose at the head prior's urging. "I found more religious monks among us than I thought. There are enough to renovate the chapel that we haven't used since before I arrived."

Another council member stood and reported on how diverse political thought was in the cloister and proclaimed that wizardry brought everyone together.

"You get the idea," the head prior said. "We've always known there are undercurrents within the cloister, and now we can better observe them. As a result of our examination of Brother Tirolo's work, we have decided to accept him within our community with full rights and privileges."

Quint waited to hear a condition, and then it came.

"There was a concern brought up by some council members about Brother Tirolo's ability to attract trouble. They agreed to release the probationary status with one exception. If there is another attack within the cloister, we are afraid Brother Tirolo will be expelled."

That was more like Quint expected and he was prepared to accept that. He didn't like putting people at risk any more than the council did. It also meant he was determined to be ready to leave the cloister at any time. In his mind, the council's decision put a target on Quint's back. He hoped he could last the next six months so he would feel more prepared.

Quint walked up to the council members after the head prior dismissed the meeting.

"I appreciate the vote of confidence," Quint said.

"You accept the terms?" one of the council members said. A Green, as Quint remembered.

"I do. I will have to stay in my quarters more than usual, but I like being here," Quint said.

"I'm glad you will," another council member said. "I haven't been to your string exchange. I have a few you might be interested in, and I'd like to learn some of yours."

"My hours are sporadic, but if you chance by, stop, and we can do business," Quint said.

The head prior took Quint aside. "It was the best I could do and get you passed. I hope you understand."

Quint understood how weak the head prior was, but he kept that to himself. "We both know it's only a matter of time before the Greens attack again. They will do so just to get me expelled, if nothing else."

"Well, you have more time to prepare. Without the project, you will have more time to prepare. Your Narallian in the analysis was very impressive."

"I had a good teacher and a good helper," Quint said.

A council member dragged the prior away for consultation on another matter, giving Quint an excuse to learn his friends' reactions.

"I don't think you could have expected more," Bokwiz said. "I'll be arranging my affairs starting tomorrow. I suggest you do the same."

"I have already made the decision to do the same. I don't know if the Greens will make a big statement or a small one," Quint said.

"A big one and that includes another attempt on your life. Your bodyguards will have to be on high alert all the time."

Kozak came up to Quint. "If you need any more projects, I can let you do any wheelwork that comes into my shop," Kozak said. "Sister Sandiza mentioned that you might be interested in looking at my woodworking pieces."

Quint restrained, shaking his head at Sandy's audacity. "Of course. She said I need to develop a better sense for aesthetics."

"Only if you want. You have other talents, my boy," Kozak said.

Dakuz had already left the room, and Sandy had attracted both her charges, so she was sitting describing the council process to them. Quint waved to her before leaving the room with his bodyguards and returning to their floor.

Quint's floormates assembled in the cell they used for the classification project.

"Why don't we leave now?" one of the bodyguards said in Narallian.

"I'm not ready," Quint said. "It's not that I owe the cloister anything, but I don't feel ready. We all have to practice the defensive and offensive strings now that we have the time."

"You are going to hold sessions?" the stonemason asked.

"Why don't we do that?" Quint said. "Let's get a list together of what we should know. Shields is at the top. Many of you know one or two. You need to practice fire strings and then anything else we can manage. I used the earthquake string to stall my attacker, for example. Not all of you can create all the strings. But let's find out what each of us can learn."

"What about weapons?" Grizak said.

"I'm not sure that an intensive training program would be appreciated by the head prior, but we should do just enough training to stall any assailants," Quint said.

"I know enough to do that," one of the monks said.

"Then you can be the trainer. My skills aren't great, but I know how to wave a knife." Quint turned to the new trainer. "Work with Kozak to make staffs and procure knives. He might have more ideas."

§§§

Chapter Sixteen
~

The training sessions began in the stable cell courtyard where Quint fought. The trainer knew more about weapons than he let on, and the monks responded.

In the evenings, Quint worked on teaching strings and, more importantly, when to use them in a fight. After the first week, he also worked with the monks in the stable courtyard. Everyone had two or three defensive strings to use. Quint made sure they could put an enemy to sleep, and all but one monk could master that string.

Kozak arrived with staffs, a few swords, and knives for everyone. The trainer picked up a sword and said, "I never thought I'd pick one of these up again. Fate has its way, just about every time."

"You mean Tizurek," Grizak said.

"Fate, Tizurek. Does it matter?"

"It does to me, but go on," Grizak said. "I think I'll need to learn to swing a long blade."

The other monks laughed at Grizak's description of the sword.

"I read a novel that kept calling swords long blades," Grizak said. "I wanted to hear how it sounded."

"Are you intending to leave us and take up pirating?" Quint asked.

"No!" Grizak said. He put the sword down but, in a moment, picked it back up. "I'll be a hero!"

§

Grizak woke Quint in the middle of the night. "A couple of squads of

Green guards were let into the cloister by your old friend Oscar Viznik."

"My savior?" Quint said, sitting up. "Where are they?"

"On their way here. There are too many to be stopped by our traps once they find out where you live. They are looking for you."

"Then I'll have to leave by myself," Quint said. "The group needs more training time before we leave. Tell Dakuz, Bokwiz, and Sandy that I will return."

"Good luck," Grizak said, tossing the escape rope out the window. "Now. Here is a purse of money and our beloved stonemason gave me this to give you if there was an emergency."

Quint opened the note and read. "I've got a place to stay in Pinzleport. Perhaps I'll stay there a few days," he said. "Pull up the rope after I leave and tell them you don't know where I went."

"I didn't read the address. I can do that without lying or even if the Greens cast a lying string."

"If they don't ask in the right way, I'll have some time to look around the port and return."

"Do you think you should be going out alone? I can go with you."

Quint paused for a moment. "No. I need you here to calm the boys down. This is not the time to practice fighting. Stay calm."

"May Tizurek be with you," Grizak said.

Quint had thrown his clothes on. He grabbed his robe but didn't intend to wear it outside the cloister. Quint opened the window wider and let himself down, having to jump the last six feet. He wasn't far from where he climbed up from the beach, but he didn't want to use that route. He headed north along the cloister wall, crouched down, and ran into the woods beyond.

Pinzleport was southeast, but Quint guessed the guards would watch the road from the cloister to the port. He found a path that led east and followed for an hour until it intersected another that went south. He stumbled along, almost falling asleep as he walked.

In a few minutes, he walked into the outskirts of a village. Quint ditched his robe and kept to the outskirts, finding a stable with a clean stall filled with fresh hay. He found his bedchamber until dawn.

"Hey, you! Wake up," a farmer said in Narallian, holding a pitchfork with sharpened tines. "What are you doing in my stable?"

"I was traveling to Pinzleport, but I misjudged the distances and ended up here rather than there," Quint said. "Can I pay you for half a night's sleep? I wasn't sleeping more than three hours."

"A ruble or two will work or an hour's labor."

Quint grinned. "I'm an able body," he said.

The farmer's suspicions vanished as he planted the handle end of the pitchfork into the dirt of the barn. "Good. Clean out the stables, and we will be even. You've already tested out my hay."

"Indeed, I have," Quint said.

"You have experience?"

"We didn't have four horses, but I guess if you've cleaned one out many times, that's enough to know how to do it."

"Then I'll leave you to it. I'll have my wife make a meal, and you can eat it on your way to Pinzleport. It's about three hours walking south of here."

Quint waited for the farmer to leave the stable and used strings to separate manure from hay. He used the pitchfork for the rest of the job. It was an experiment, and Quint was happy that it worked. He could teach the application of the string to the monks of the cloister. Perhaps it would be a going away present when he left.

"All done?" the farmer said as he answered the kitchen door with a napkin tucked underneath his chin.

"You can inspect it."

The napkin was torn from his neck, and Quint followed him into the stable.

"I put the manure on the pile."

The farmer laughed. "I can see that, and you freshened up the stalls. That's good enough for today. Let's get you your edible wage, and you can be on your way."

"Thank you," Quint said to the farmer's wife, a tall, thin woman with an unexpected giggle. "I thank you both for the opportunity to work for my breakfast. I'll be on my way and wish you a nice day."

The wife gave Quint a skin of watered wine and a bag of food. "You have an interesting accent. Where are you from?" she asked.

"I grew up close to Pashun Cloister to the northeast. My father was a wheelwright. We lived in the forest since he cut his own lumber. He was from South Fenola."

"Not many hubites there."

"That's why he ran away and came to Narukun. I guess I picked up the way he talked."

The farmer clapped Quint on the back. "Have a good hike into the port."

"I will. I'm going to see one of Dad's friends."

"A job awaits?"

Quint shrugged. "Maybe I'll go to sea."

The farmer's wife shivered. "I hate the water. Good luck to you, lad."

Quint left them on the stoop of the kitchen door and gave them a wave while he turned toward the main road through the village.

A tear rolled down Quint's cheek. Although the couple didn't look like his mother and father, they acted with the same kind of generosity his parents would have. He wished his parents would have run away from Racellia and headed north. His life would have been simpler, and he wouldn't have to feel such a hole in his heart when he thought of them.

As much as he would have liked to clean up, Quint couldn't fully trust that the farmer wouldn't tell anyone about his nighttime visitor. Quint walked through another village.

He found a road taking him east of Pinzleport. He saw a squad of riders coming from the south through a copse of trees. Quint didn't want to be caught on the road and ran for cover.

The riders galloped by with their green tabards flapping in the wind. Could they be looking for him? That was the last thing Quint wanted to know as he scrambled back up the road and began jogging toward the port. A wagon struggled to make it on the road. Quint slowed down before he approached the wagon.

"Can I help?" Quint asked.

The farmer grunted. "You could help if you had four feet and hooves."

"Maybe two feet and a young back," Quint said.

"I'll grant you permission to try," the farmer said.

"Good." Quint began to unload the wagon, and the farmer caught on to what Quint was doing and helped.

"I didn't think of that," the farmer said.

"Maybe it's the young mind looking out for the young back," Quint said with a smile.

With the wagon unloaded, the horse dragged the wagon on the road. Quint helped the farmer put his produce back in the wagon.

"Are you headed to Pinzleport?" Quint asked.

"I am. Are you in need of a ride?"

"I am," Quint said. "I'm interviewing for a post at sea."

"You should be a farmer. Honest work, and you get to eat all you want."

"In a good year," Quint said.

"Are you a farmer as well as a young smart aleck?"

"I've worked the soil enough for my tender years. I'm tired of dirt underneath my feet and fancy to feel the roll of the waves."

"So you can feed the fishes with your latest meal?" the farmer said with a grin. "Get on. We can discuss the philosophy of life on our way to the port."

No one challenged them when they rode through the Pinzleport east gate, and the riders never returned along the road. Quint helped the farmer arrange his goods in the market stall.

"It's time I left you," Quint said.

"It was a pleasure solving the world's problems. I wish you well," the farmer said.

For all his talk about philosophy, the farmer mostly complained about his wife and the drudgery of farming, but he did like market days so he could get away from it all and chat up all the friendly customers. The farmer proclaimed that he included Quint in the "nice customer" category.

Quint walked through the streets until he found the address he wanted. The house was very close to being a mansion, but no one was home. With time on his hands, Quint walked back to the market and found the dry goods section. As he strolled along, he knew his clothes didn't match the port as well as it matched the village where he bought his present suit of clothes. He purchased two changes in the Pinzleport style from a used clothing stall and a bag to hold his old ones. Quint finished his purchases by buying some personal items and a hat he'd seen many young men wearing.

It was time to return to the house. Quint returned to the house and rapped his knuckles on the door after casting a shield string. A woman about his mother's age answered.

"I don't want to buy what you are selling," she said, staring at Quint's bag.

He doffed his hat. "I'm from the cloister," Quint said.

"Oh, that makes it a different story. Come in. Come in," the woman said, opening the door wider.

Quint stepped in and looked around the foyer. It wasn't decorated in a grand style, but Quint could feel the quality. He wondered if he might have some sense of aesthetics after all. She took him to a sitting room about as big as his cell in the cloister. It was an intimate affair, but the chairs were not like the cloister's at all. He sank into soft velvet cushions.

"I'm sorry my house isn't as severe as Seensist. I have been there before. My late husband was a donor."

"I am sorry for your loss," Quint said.

"No worry. My husband left this world eight years ago. I have come to terms with his death." She sighed. "Now, what about you? If you are who I think you are, you have been stirring up a hornet's nest in the cloister and in Pinzleport."

"I am Quinto Tirolo."

"Brother Tirolo." She gave Quint a curt nod. "I am kept apprised of what goes on there, but not from that snake of a head prior," she said.

"He has treated me fairly enough," Quint said.

She snorted. "Only because he has no idea what to do with you."

"The head prior has a shaky hold on his position. The Greens want him at their beck and call, but even with the head prior's vote, they are outmanned on the council."

"He isn't a Green?" Quint had the head prior down as a Green. At least he was a Green sympathizer, no matter how much he had tried to hide it.

"The second he declared his allegiance, he'd be bounced out of the cloister," the woman said.

"Isn't there anyone to replace him?" Quint asked.

"No. There are a few candidates, but no. One of them is a member of your little group."

"Grizak?"

The woman pursed her lips and made a face. "Too pious. Now, who gave you this note?"

"A monk who fancies himself a stonemason. He is younger than Grizak and is part of my group of followers in Seensist Cloister."

"He is the son of a prominent builder in Pinzleport. The boy left his father's business behind when he found he had magic, and that day, he walked down the road to Seensist. He isn't a Green or a Red, and I've kept track of him while he has been in the cloister."

Quint was hopeful he could talk to the woman more before he had to leave. She might not be objective, but she seemed to be a reasonable observer of people. He asked her for her name.

"Wanisa Hannoko. Hannoko was my husband's name. He came from Kippun as a teenager disenchanted with the faux-polennese attitudes of the citizens. You may proceed."

"I will, Lady Wanisa."

The woman laughed. "Call me Wannie. You are called Quint, right?"

"I am." Quint gave her a rundown of his time in Narukun.

"No one told me you could do so many strings. I knew you were a master-level wizard, but you could take the head prior's position if you wanted."

Quint laughed. "How could I do that?"

"I know a way," she said with a sly smile.

"I'm not interested. I'm too much of a target. That is why I want to leave this area."

Wannie pursed her lips. "You'll always be fighting against the Greens while you are in Narukun."

"Will I have to fight a war with them?"

She laughed. "You tell me! You are the master. I'm sure you know a predictor string or two."

"There is more than one?" Quint said the fib to see what the woman would say.

Wannie looked satisfied with herself. "I know something a master doesn't? Yes, there are six that I know of, but they are all specialized, and all suffer from the same unpredictability. I'm sure you know about that."

"I do," Quint said.

"How did you get to Narukun from South Fenola?"

"On a ship captained by Goresk Olinko. He was waiting for Feodor Danko in Bocarre, the Racellian capital, and I was able to come aboard as an assistant purser."

"You worked for Horenz Pizent?"

"You know him?"

"I do, and Olinko is in port for a few weeks, waiting for cargo that has been delayed. Do you want to escape aboard his boat?" Wannie asked.

"It is called a ship," Quint said. "It got corrected all the time I was aboard."

Wannie giggled. "You passed my basic nautical test. Do you want to see your captain? I can invite him for dinner. Pizent, I'm not so sure he'll come. He is a closet Green."

"And you are a Red?" Quint asked.

"I'm not sure what I am. The Reds are becoming more like Greens while they share power in Pinzleport. What are you?"

"Something else. I don't like people in power intimidating the populace."

Wannie snorted. "What have the Greens or the Reds done for the man on the street?"

"I don't know," Quint said.

"Taxes, fees, and unfair laws! So, they can enrich themselves," Wannie said.

"We might be closer to the same faction," Quint said.

"Is that your goal?"

Quint thought for a moment. "It might be. I don't know what the future has in store for me. I could be stabbed on the street tomorrow, so even my future could be very short."

"Think more positively." Wannie rose from her chair. "I'll show you the library. My husband accumulated an impressive wizardry section. I had to fight Seensist to keep them here after he died."

Quint was taken to a study. It was two floors high and lined with books. The second floor had a ledge with a railing that allowed one to find books unreachable from the main floor.

"The magic section is over there, behind the desk," Wannie said. "I'll have the cook bring in a snack while my maid freshens up a room for you. I have a dinner party to arrange."

The magic library was a mix of old books and portfolios and new books and thin folders with shorter treatises. Quint was interested in the old portfolios.

He brought an armful of the portfolios to the desk in the room and began to go through them. The treatises were ancient, with some of the crumbling parchment pages glued to stiffer, newer backing. Most were in Narallian, but a different version than Quint had learned. It took him longer to figure out what they were about. He saw familiar strings discussed as new discoveries.

He opened another portfolio and raised his eyebrows. The pages were covered with a familiar script, willot. The pages were all ancient, but to Quint's surprise, the language had changed much less than Narallian. The strings were notated much differently, but Quint could pick out the documentation.

"Did you find something interesting?" Wannie said, carrying a bottle of wine while a maid brought a food tray. "This might be a little rich compared to cloister cuisine, but I'm sure you will like it." She leaned over to look at the portfolio. "You can read that? My husband bought it because it was so old. He couldn't find anyone to translate it. That's all I can tell you."

"I learned how in the Wizard Corps. The willots of South Fenola claim this is their native tongue, but I learned that it was probably the original language of the hubites."

"And Narallian? That is supposed to be our mother tongue."

"It's a mystery, isn't it?" Quint said. "I don't know what's true. There were some events in ancient times that confused everything. It doesn't matter to me other than what is inside this."

"Try to solve it by the time Captain Olinko arrives. It will be an old reunion."

"Not that old," Quint said, "but I'm happy to see them again."

"I'll leave you to your discovery," Wannie said.

Quint looked at the food and decided it couldn't wait to be eaten and the portfolio didn't care, so he ate enough of it to satisfy his hunger. The cuisine seemed to be a mixture of Slinnon and Narukun. The best of both, he thought as he finished the plate and sipped wine. He needed to concentrate on what he read, so he kept it at a sip.

The portfolio had various documents, all in willot. One set of documents had some strings, but it also had something else: a description of one-handed spells. Was this what enabled Pozella to cast strings even though he couldn't manage the use of both hands? Quint read the ancient script multiple times, found paper and pencil in the drawer, and copied the one-handed description. It was four pages long, and some terms had lost their meanings over the centuries or millennia, or however old the document was.

Quint slipped the transcription into his coat pocket and continued to read. There was a description of the fall of South Fenola to a willot uprising and the hubite migration to Baxel. It spoke of other hubites joining with a group of grans headed to North Fenola to settle in uninhabited polennese lands on the southeast part of North Fenola.

The document was centuries old, maybe millennia old, and Quint wondered if Narallian was willotan with polennese influences. That might make sense, but Quint would need to learn polennese to know. Willotan would have taken a long time to change into Narallian, but the portfolio was ancient enough for that to have happened.

Another document described a sea voyage, but before the end and before Quint could find out where the travelers came from and landed, the writing was illegible, and the page had crumbled.

Wannie walked in. "Making yourself at home? Did you find anything interesting?"

"This is so ancient," Quint said. "It talks about the migration of grans and hubites. I think this was written in South Fenola and taken to Frosso."

"Frosso? How did my husband get it?"

"If he deemed this valuable, he could have had someone retrieve it for him," Quint said.

"He was proud how old it had to be," Wannie said, "but he didn't dare look through it, fearing to tear the pages."

"You should have someone transcribe it. Someone you trust to do the job," Quint said.

"And you can read it."

Quint nodded. "Any educated willot in South Fenola can."

"Oh! We can't have that!" Wannie said. "The Reds and the Greens would destroy this if it went against their version of history."

"Some people would," Quint said. "Most people that I know would. That's why you need to keep it close to you and make a copy. Some of the pages are already fading into nothingness."

"I'll put it somewhere safer," Wannie said.

Quint gathered the pages, carefully slid them into the portfolio, and handed them to his hostess. She left for a few moments and returned.

"Our guests will arrive in two hours. Why don't I take you to a room that you can use while you are in Pinzleport?"

"Happily," Quint said. "It has been a long day."

"I'll wake you in time for dinner," she said.

A maid stood at the door. She was probably there the entire time Quint spoke to Wannie, and he hoped she was trustworthy. The maid would have heard why the portfolio was significant.

He followed the maid to a large room on the third floor of the house.

"My mother likes to have fun," the maid said, letting him into the room. "So do I."

The room smelled of cleaning soap and polish. "You are smart enough to know I heard more than I should have. Don't worry. My father's portfolio will be safe, and I will likely be the one to do the transcribing. Mother wouldn't trust herself not to make a mistake. There are better clothes laid out on the bed. Mother likes people to dress for dinner."

Quint laughed. "We didn't do anything like that in the cloister; before, I always wore work clothing."

"An interesting euphemism for the wizard corps, Captain Tirolo," the maid said. "I will leave you to rest up for a while."

Quint stared at the door Wannie's daughter used to leave. Was Wannie the cook, he wondered? Maybe not. It didn't matter to him. The daughter's casually slipped-in mention of his former life surprised him, but Captain Olinko knew his past and perhaps had trusted Wanisa Hannoko enough to tell her.

§§§

CHAPTER SEVENTEEN

DINNER WAS A SURPRISE. Captain Olinko brought Horenz Pizent with him. While they sat in the sitting room, another pair showed up. Quint was astonished to see Grizak as the stonemason walked through the door. Wannie's daughter showed up wearing a dress and looked much more like a lady than she did as a maid. She walked over to Grizak and greeted him like an old beau. She also seemed to know the stonemason since they didn't introduce one to the other.

"You are the only one who has not eaten at my table, Wannie said to Quint, "although you know everyone here, Brother Tirolo."

"I haven't been properly introduced to your daughter," Quint said.

"Her full name is Andreiza Ylizabeta Pormodor Hannoko. You may call her Andy," Wannie said. "Brother Grizak and she are old friends. There was something there once, but Pol wanted to live the monastic life. I think Andy has never given up on him."

"He doesn't look like he's given up on her," Quint said, looking at them smiling and joking with one another. "Does she know the other monk?"

"She should. Dontiz is her younger brother."

"And your son?" Quint asked, amazed that the hands-on monk grew up in such a fancy house.

"Grizak convinced him that his magic needed polish, and he could get it at the cloister."

"But he's a stonemason."

"My husband built houses and buildings as a hobby and taught his son everything he knew. Donnie liked working with stone the best. They haven't been here for a few months. Did you have anything to do with that?"

"Maybe. Ask them. I got to know them well during that time."

"And they you," Wannie said. "We haven't stopped writing. Between Donnie and Goresk Olinko, I know as much about you as anyone."

"You flatter me," Quint said.

"It isn't without self-interest, but we can talk about that at dinner," she said as a different maid showed up and proclaimed that dinner was ready.

The dining room was large, and the party sat at one end of the table with Wannie at the head. Grizak and Andy sat beside each other with Donnie farthest away from Wannie. Quint sat next to Wannie with Olinko on the other side and Horenz, Olinko's purser, on the end facing Donnie, the stonemason.

"We know each other. Children, I took the initiative and let Quint know your names and relationship with me. I hope you don't mind."

Both shook their heads. "So," Wannie rubbed her hands. "I'm sure Quint is anxious to know what happened in the Cloister after escaping."

"Escaped was the right term," Donnie said. "They finally made it through the traps to our floor and pushed us around a little. When they turned the place over, and you weren't there, they asked about the ropes at the windows. We said it was in case of a fire on the stairways."

"At least one of them was smart enough to figure out that you left Seensist," Grizak said. "They pushed us around a little more and broke a few chairs in the meeting room before they left. No injuries other than a few bruises. We didn't think it was worth a fight."

"It wasn't," Quint said. "Is everything back to normal?"

Donnie shook his head. "We are back to having guards march around the walls day and night, and the main gate has guards examining every person and everything that comes into the cloister. They even nailed the door you originally used to enter the cloister shut. Oscar Viznik came out as a Green after all."

Quint had to laugh. "A bit of self-discovery, I imagine. So, I'm stuck here for a while?"

"As long as you need to," Wannie said, patting Quint's hand.

"They don't know where you are," Grizak said. "I wouldn't parade around Pinzleport and Donnie, and I won't tell the head prior or anyone else where you are."

"Have I been expelled now that I'm gone from the Cloister?"

Donnie shook his head. "Not that I know of. Everyone knows you ran to escape a horrific beating or death. There are enough smart people on the council to know that you won't return if Greens are prowling around outside."

"How did they get into the cloister?" Captain Olinko asked. "They've never invaded before."

"Quint draws Greens to him like flies to carrion," Grizak said.

"Not at dinner, please," Andy said.

Grizak shrugged and nodded.

"I still have an opening for a ship's wizard," Olinko said.

"I'll give you up for that," Horenz said.

Quint smiled. "I appreciate the offer, but I have other things to do." He looked at Grizak, who nodded. "We, my bodyguards, and I, were going to leave Seensist before the end of the year, anyway. We thought we'd make our way to Parsun Cloister."

"Do you think the Greens will leave you alone if you take up residence on the other side of Narukun?" Wannie asked.

"No," Quint said. "But it will take them some time to find us. Are there Greens in Kippun or Slinnon?" He knew the answer, but he wanted to ask.

"They aren't as strong. Greens and Reds are the scourges of Narukun. Their reach extends over the seas, but Pinzleport is where the greatest concentration of either faction is," Olinko said.

"More Reds in the capital," Wannie said. "The king is rumored to be a Red, Quint."

Quint knew that, too, but he nodded as if it were new information.

"If we are to hold to the monastic life, Parsun is the only place for us. Seensist has shown it is a weak refuge, and Parsun needs younger blood."

Andy raised her hand. "I'll be a Sister."

"That would be lovely if you had a thimbleful of magic," Grizak said.

"Then I'll follow you into Kippun. I have Kippunese blood."

"Hubites are hubites no matter what they think," Grizak said.

Andy frowned and sat back, looking defeated.

Dinner was served.

"I have followers," Quint said, opening the conversation while everyone began to eat.

"Even some older monks," Donnie said.

"Why are they following you? That developed fast," Olinko said.

Quint told his story. He didn't know how much Wannie and Andy knew, but he gave his ex-shipmates a different perspective than he did Wannie.

"This Sandy is your girlfriend?" Horenz asked with a sly smile. "Is that forbidden in the cloister?"

"Discouraged but not forbidden," Donnie said.

Grizak frowned as Andy squeezed his arm. "There is hope for me yet!" she said.

When Quint reached the point of knocking on the Hannoko door, he ended his story.

"I can't imagine a wizard selling spells," Olinko said. "I've never seen it in Pinzleport."

"Narukun wizards are jealous of what they know," Grizak said. "Quint conducted an exchange as well. How many new spells did you get?"

"A few. More than I thought," Quint said, "but I haven't had time to verify them all."

Olinko clucked his tongue. "Modesty, modesty."

"But his modesty always comes with results," Grizak said.

"Not always," Quint said. "I'm learning, but I can only hope to survive the education."

That brought laughter to the dinner table. Olinko stood up with Horenz. "I'm afraid Horenz and I must leave. Ship sails at midnight, and there are a few details we must attend to on shore."

Olinko shook Quint's hand. "You have until midnight to decide if you want to return to the sea."

"I don't want you to be disappointed, but no. I hope the offer will be open."

Horenz grinned. "It will be until we find another wizard."

"One thing I did learn," Quint said. "Calee Danko is thirty years old. She uses a masking string."

Olinko nodded. "I found that out when I reached port after dropping you off at the cloister. The Danko's are an evil lot. Stay away from them," Olinko said.

"I will as long as they stay away from me," Quint said.

Everyone wished the two seamen calm seas, and they left. Donnie, Grizak, Andy, and Quint ended up in the sitting room. Wannie was seeing to clearing the dinner and had other things to do.

"She doesn't want to be around when I'm pursuing Pol," Andy said.

"I don't know why you are still interested in me," Grizak said. "I have settled on my vocation."

"Not when you've decided to follow Quint wherever he wants to go. That means you are still flexible," Andy said.

Donnie laughed. "She'll never give up. Andy can't touch you as long as you stay in the cloister."

"But I can touch you now," Andy said.

"Only my arm," Grizak said.

"I've always known that your order doesn't demand a commitment to celibacy," Andy said.

Grizak clamped his lips shut, looking harassed.

Donnie kept smiling. "Did you look through Dad's book collection?"

"He can read that old portfolio that Father couldn't translate," Andy said. "Except it appears that a large percentage of the population of South Fenola can read it."

"Is that true?" Donnie asked Quint.

"It is. There are a lot of arcane words, but I figured most out. There are a few strings mentioned, but they are variations of common ones the three of us know. The most interesting piece was a section on making strings with one hand. It's almost a different kind of magic, but I can't vouch for the topic or the accuracy. It might be a hoax, or I'm missing a key part of the string creation."

"That gives you something exciting to do while you're stuck in this pile of bricks," Donnie said.

"It does. I had a teacher in Bocarre who didn't have the use of an arm. Perhaps he knew the secret."

"Then find out. I can't think of a better wizard to discover ancient knowledge," Grizak said.

§

Quint woke up the following morning with a hollow feeling. He had missed some genuine friends while in exile from the cloister. Olinko was as he expected, but Grizak and Donnie were tied to Wanisa Hannoko, which was why the address had been forced on him.

He dressed in the clothes he bought at the market and returned downstairs.

Andy wasn't in a maid uniform, but she was fixing her own breakfast in the kitchen.

"Is your mother out?"

Andy nodded. "She always goes out in the morning with the cook. She expects you to start on your one-handed spell work. Mother thinks you would honor Father if you could make it work."

"I suppose that can help pay for my stay," Quint said.

"You don't owe us anything. I'm just happy to have seen Pol again."

Quint frowned. "He is committed to monastic life," he said, "and he is a religionist."

"We all are in this house, and I know Donnie goes to the Tizurek services. He's not as committed to Seensist as Pol, but they have always been close friends."

"I didn't know that. I didn't take them for pals or anything, but they were in the same group who became my followers," Quint said.

"I'm surprised you could peel them away from Shinzle Bokwiz," Andy said.

"Bokwiz is a follower, too," Quint said. "It has to do with predictor strings and me."

Andy stood. "Mother believes that you are something special. She has talked to a few members of the council. She told me that the Greens see you as a threat, or you would be welcomed with open arms rather than held at arms' length."

"That sums it up nicely and the reason I must leave Seensist. I'm not actively gathering followers. Grizak and your brother and their friends attached themselves to me, especially after I needed some helpers."

"And they helped you fight and helped you escape."

"Exactly," Quint said. "I still can't convince myself I'm worthy to have people look to me to lead, but…" Quint shrugged.

"I have a job to go to."

"What do you do?"

Andy raised her eyebrows as if she was surprised Quint would ask. "I help in a printer's shop. I don't do any printing, but they like a pretty face at the front counter, and Mother doesn't discourage me from paying a little bit of my way around here." She left Quint by himself.

The maid from last night came in and filled a bucket with water from the pump at the sink and gave Quint a nervous smile before darting out of the kitchen. That meant Quint could eat whatever he found. He wasn't a glutton, but he did locate leftovers that worked for breakfast and took his meal upstairs to his room to see if he could unlock the mystery of one-handed wizardry.

The maid peeked into his room and was going to withdraw immediately, but Quint stopped her.

"Is there anything to drink on this floor?" Quint asked. "I'd rather not go up and down the stairs for something to sip on while I work."

She smiled at him and scrunched up. "As long as you don't tell anyone, Master Hannoko kept a modest wine cabinet on this floor. You are in his private bedroom and study." She walked past him to the closet and twisted something on the closet wall. A panel slid open, revealing wine racks. Quint guessed there were fifteen bottles. He felt a breeze of cool air from the secret chamber.

"There is magic involved, but cooler basement air is moved through a pipe into the cabinet and back down to the basement. The cabinet is always cooler and sometimes cold. Feel free to use the wine. Put empty bottles in the cabinet, and I will discreetly replace them from the wine cellar."

Quint couldn't imagine what string would do that unattended, but he could feel the flow. He asked the maid for a suggestion for a light wine to sip. She pointed one out.

"The goblets are washed every week or two," she said. "Just put the used ones in the cabinet, and I will take care of them."

"Did you do the same for your master?"

"I did. If you are wondering, Lady Wanisa said it was all right if I shared this with you." Her smile was more relaxed, and she didn't scurry when she walked out of the bedroom.

Quint smiled as he poured a goblet of wine and sipped. It was excellent, according to Quint's limited palette. He couldn't drink too much of the wine, or he wouldn't be able to concentrate, just like he wanted to avoid drinking in the library downstairs the previous day.

The four pages that he had copied needed closer examination. The process of creating a one-handed string stretched Quint's understanding of the concept of magic. Pozella had always said there was more to strings than following a set of rules, which might have meant more mental force. Quint often changed the intensity of his strings, but with the one-handed method, although still requiring threads woven into strings, it was will that did the final shaping of the string, and it was will that cast it.

He read through the entire transcription three times and felt he understood most of it, filling most of the words he didn't know with words he did by analyzing the context. It was a skill he developed in Bocarre working for Colonel Julia Gerocie doing much the same thing as he wrote reports on trends in willotan, where he didn't know all the words.

Once he learned how to do one-handed spells, if he succeeded, the trick was to develop the skill to shape the string. He didn't know how he was going to do that. The document wasn't a set of instructions but an outline of how the process worked. He decided to start with a simple fire string.

Quint looked out the window at the back garden of the house and spotted a bench beneath a tree. He didn't want to bring down the house if his magic went astray, so he tucked the transcripts in his pocket and exited the house, sitting on the bench. The weather was pleasant. He looked around and found the spot secluded enough from the other nice dwellings on either side and in the back.

After rereading the transcripts, he looked at his hands and decided to learn with his left hand. That would give him the ability to cast strings with one hand while holding a weapon in the other.

His first exercise was to create a ball of threads in his left hand. Quint had learned to do that with Pozella and then he combined with threads on his right hand, but he had to combine them to create strings. He quickly learned the trick to one-handed magic was holding the increased number of threads with one hand. Quint had to reduce the number of threads he created with his magic and had barely begun to try when Lady Wanisa summoned him for lunch.

"Did you find my back garden pleasant?" Wannie asked as she showed Quint to sit at the kitchen table with Wannie, the cook, and the maid.

"I did. I'm practicing magic. It's been a while since I had the opportunity," Quint said.

"Did you find something interesting to try out in my husband's library?"

"I did," Quint said. "I copied the pages, so I'm not using the fragile paper, and it may take me some time to get the process right. Magic has changed a little, and I might learn something interesting if I can get the technique right."

"The technique is?" Wannie asked.

"Single-handed strings."

Wannie raised her eyebrows. "That would be a change."

"So far, I haven't gotten past the first step," Quint said. "It's better than sitting around."

"You can read more of my husband's library."

Quint smiled. "I'd rather do something. I'll feel like I'm cooped up if I'm reading the whole time."

"I see your point," Wannie said. "Eat up. Make sure you have plenty of strength."

"I'll follow your advice," Quint said with a grin.

§§§

CHAPTER EIGHTEEN
∽

THE AFTERNOON SESSION WAS MORE PROMISING. Quint had to develop a different mindset to make smaller threads, and after a few hours of practice, he had a palmful of twisting tiny threads. Now, he had to organize them. The rest was more straightforward since weaving threads into strings was the same technique. With fewer threads, the resulting string was smaller. Quint cast the string on the stone-paved walkway, and the strings flashed, and a column of fire six feet in height burned for a moment.

When Quint was ready to run for a bucket of water, it died down and extinguished itself like a similar two-handed string would. He hadn't put much power into that string, but the technique amplified its effect.

He stared at the blackened spot on the pavement and tried to absorb what he had learned. Smaller wasn't necessarily weaker. He couldn't experiment with fire in the back garden again. It was too dangerous. For his next string, he would cast water. The air was humid enough to be a source of moisture, with Pinzleport next to the ocean.

The process was the same, but Quint could feel resistance with the threads. The key to control of the spell might be how the threads were produced rather than how the strings were woven. He stared at the threads in his hand. These would produce water from the air. It was a more complex string, and the threads that his magic produced looked like his two-handed version. Weaving the string was more challenging, and he had to start over a few times, but the effect was like the fire. A deluge created puddles in the back garden.

Quint felt the back of his hands and could feel dry skin and he could sense the dry air from the string, pulling moisture from the air. The humidity didn't take long to return, but the one-handed approach was more powerful but much more complex to control. He looked around and found that he had worked through the afternoon, and the sun was setting. He rose from the bench to see Andy leaning against the doorframe of the kitchen door, looking at him.

"You solved something," she said, "although I don't know what you were solving."

"One-handed strings. They are much different from two-handed strings and much harder to create."

"Is that why our garden is soaking wet on a sunny afternoon?"

Quint smiled. "It is. I did a simple fire string and blackened some paving stones. I had to use something to clean the soot off."

"I can see from here that you have a bit more to go," Andy said. "How much harder is it?"

"I'm not sure. I have to run through more strings. No one lower than a deacon can probably handle the water string and not much less than that for the simple fire string that you can usually use to light a candle. My string could start a house fire," Quint said. He yawned. "The spells draw more energy."

"Just because they are one-handed?"

"I don't know. I practiced for hours, making a handful of threads. It's harder to make a small amount than a normal amount."

"Maybe they are more concentrated," Andy said.

Quint shrugged. "That might be. Something's different. I'd like to find out, but I don't want to experiment in your back garden with more powerful strings if I can't control them."

"Do you fancy a picnic on a secluded beach tomorrow?" Andy asked.

"Wouldn't Grizak be jealous?"

It was Andy's turn to shrug. "Would that be a bad thing? We can take a large lunch if you need more food to power your spells. I'll have Mother and the cook put together a basket. We will need to do something about you."

Quint smiled. "Don't worry about me. I can put on a mask."

Andy clapped her hands. "You know cosmetic strings?"

"I do," Quint said.

§

Quint created a mask resembling one of the lieutenants he shared a flat with in Bocarre. Andy couldn't recognize him, even after staring for a whole minute. Quint took the basket and followed Andy to a secluded beach halfway between the Cloister and the outskirts of Pinzleport. They had to climb down a cliff using a secret path, so Andy said, to arrive at the beach.

"Have you been here often?" Quint asked, taking off his shirt to get some sun.

"Before Grizak found his 'calling,' Donnie and Grizak would bring me here to wade in the water. The rocks and the shape of the sand bottom create tides too treacherous to swim. But it is a serene place with little vegetation. I thought it a perfect place to watch a true master at work."

Quint laughed. "I'm hardly a true master. I'm a novice when it comes to one-handed magic."

"Novices can't read an ancient document and interpret a different kind of magic, can they?"

"Probably not," Quint said. "It takes an understanding of the theory of two-handed magic and a high degree of competence to control threads and strings."

"Which you have."

Quint nodded. "I was blessed with innate competence, and I had a great theoretical teacher. He always taught me the reason why we do something as well as how to do it. You'd be surprised how that isn't part of magic instruction, even in the cloister."

"So, our ancestors were more powerful than we are today?"

Quint shook his head. "No way to find out, and theoretically, I have little understanding of why the two one-handed spells are more powerful."

Andy peered at Quint.

"Your staring is uncomfortable."

"I'm trying to figure out why you can't walk back to Seensist with the face you are currently wearing. Who is going to recognize you?"

Quint grunted. "The spell to eliminate the mask is simple, easily learned. An observant person would see it as a mask. Look at the hairline and the neckline."

"Oh. If I knew that, I could tell without magic."

"The effect is smoother than a real mask, but it can be detected. One of the Green assassins had a mask on. When he died, the mask disappeared. I didn't have the time to look closely," Quint said. "I wouldn't want to risk getting caught. But walking with a young woman down a beach is something no one would question. Am I right?"

"Close enough, Master Quint," Andy said. "I'll get the picnic set up under the shade of that cliff and you do your thing. I brought a book, should I get bored."

Quint started with the fire string. This time he put more power into the thread and made sure the strings were perfect when he cast it into the surf. A pillar of fire almost as high as the cliffs appeared on the water, but the pillar began to turn to steam at the bottom, and the fire shrunk into a misty cloud.

He did the same thing with the water, and when he cast the string, it sunk into the water, and then a hump appeared on the surface of the water and exploded with the sound of a crashing wave and splashed water almost to where Andy was watching. Quint was soaked.

To make sure his regular strings were unaffected, he duplicated water and fire, and Quint couldn't see anything abnormal. Andy clapped from her spot.

"You should charge admission. It is an impressive show."

"I've got some more to try," Quint said.

Lightning was next, and as before, the one-handed lightning string shot out more than one hundred feet over the water. Quint cast a conventional lightning string, and the bolt shot out fifteen feet before it fizzled.

Quint was concerned that the one-handed technique was too powerful to use, so he spent the rest of the morning making progressively smaller amounts of threads until the threads were encased in a small grape-sized ball of blue light that he could weave into a small string. He tried fire, water, and lightning again, and they looked like two-handed strings.

"That's enough for today," Quint said, dropping onto the thin blanket that covered the sand.

"I began to read an hour and a half ago," Andy said from beneath a broad-brimmed hat she had brought. "Somehow, I'm comforted you learned to control those strings."

Quint smiled. "Let's see if I can get a lightning bolt to go from here to the water's edge."

He created a ball of threads the size of an apple, like he usually would, and wove the string and cast it towards the open sea. In Quint's mind, the bolt went past the edge but not too far past before it dissipated in a cloud of sparkles.

Andy clapped. "I think I like that the best of what you've done today. That mound of water was too strange."

"But that's what a water string does. It takes water from around it to create a flood of water. I can control it to fill a water bottle, but that isn't as interesting. When I cast it into the ocean, it absorbed the water around it and created the mound."

"It's still creepy," Andy said. "Have a lot to eat. Your body probably needs it and then have a nap."

Quint didn't realize how hungry he was until he began to eat. He drank too much wine since Quint neglected to bring any fresh water or a container to hold it, and he fell asleep on the blanket.

§

"Time to wake up," Andy said in the common tongue.

There was something strange about her voice, Quint thought. He opened his eyes and saw men standing around him. Two of them wore the green tabard of a Green guard.

"We've been caught?" Quint said to Andy.

"That is what I think," she said. "I fell asleep next to you, and they woke me up and told me to do the same to you."

"What are you two doing here?" one of the guards said in Narallian.

Quint just looked at Andy with his eyebrows raised.

Andy sighed. "It's a secluded beach. He's a man, and I'm a woman. What do you think?"

"You, I know," one of the men said, this time in common. "I've never seen this one before."

"I arrived a week ago," Quint said. "South Fenola."

"He looks a bit like a willot, doesn't he," one of the men said.

"Who did the magic?" a guard asked.

"I did. I only know a few strings, but I know them really, really well. I wanted to show Andy what I could do."

"With magic," Andy said, looking at Quint.

Quint nodded. "With magic."

A couple of the men chuckled.

"Get off the beach," a guard said. "Consider beaches a restricted area for the present. There is a dangerous monk on the loose." The man looked at Andy. "You know him, don't you?"

"Brother Tirol-something?" Andy said. "I've never met him, but my brother who lives in Seensist has."

The guard grunted. "Get on your way. Now."

Quint put his shirt back on while Andy quickly put everything into the basket, and they had to hurry up the cliff with all the guards at their backs.

"Time to meet my Mother," Andy said, grabbing Quint's hand and walking briskly toward the port.

Quint looked back. The guards had already begun to walk toward the cloister and disappeared over the edge again to another beach.

"That was too close," Andy said as they continued to hurry back to the Hannoko house. "Your mask worked this time."

Quint snorted. "And I was going to remove it when I got to the beach."

"Why didn't you?"

"Premonition, I guess," Quint said. "I learned enough today, anyway. I have a lot more experimentation, but I've got to practice making small amounts of threads. There has got to be something else that I'm doing to draw so much power into my strings, but I don't know what it is. The four pages that I read don't mention it."

"Did you finish reading the portfolio?"

"Enough of it to know that it doesn't talk about the effects of the strings," Quint said.

They went into the house and were confronted by a frantic Wannie.

"What's wrong?" Andy asked.

"Who is that man with you?" Wannie said, with fear in her voice.

Quint cast the string to remove the mask. "It's me."

"We were violated. Just after lunch, a squad of Green and Red guards appeared on the doorstep looking for Quint. I let them in and prayed to Tizurek that you wouldn't return while they were here."

"Looking for me?" Quint asked.

Wannie nodded. "They roughed up our beloved servants but left me alone. I was scared to death. Your father would have fought them, Andreiza," Wannie said.

"Are they all right?" Quint asked.

"They are, but they are in as much shock as I am. We've put everything right. You'll have to wear that mask inside and outside," Wannie said.

"I can do that, but I won't stay to put you at risk," Quint said. "I'll have to figure out a way to get back inside the cloister and appear as an itinerant monk or something."

"But you can't afford to be detected," Andy said.

"I can't put you and your staff in danger. I didn't think they would be searching houses," Quint said. "Perhaps I'll leave tonight."

"But won't that be dangerous?"

"At this point, anything I do is dangerous. I've been through this before in Racellia," Quint said.

He went upstairs while dinner was being prepared and gathered his meager possessions. He didn't have a robe, which was an advantage in this situation. Dinner was a somber affair.

"Fix some food that can be bundled up so it looks like I've been traveling," Quint said. "I'll be the same person I was on the beach."

When it was dark, Quint set off for the cloister. When he was close, someone walked up silently and yanked on his collar. A magic light appeared.

"I thought you were the fugitive," the guard said.

"No, I'm the person with bad timing. I'm an itinerant monk and have been traveling for some time. I've already been accosted on a beach with a girl I met in the port. Her parents didn't want me in Pinzleport, so I decided to see if the cloister would put me up for the night."

"You'll have to speak to the chief. He's by the gate."

Quint didn't want to leave a sleeping guard on the cloister road and let him lead on. He hoped that being this close to Seensist, he might be able to talk his way inside. They didn't have far to walk and soon they were in front of a table set up in front of a tent erected at the side of the cloister gate.

"I found him walking to the cloister," the guard said.

Quint gave the same story he had used before.

"What level are you?"

"A permanent acolyte, I'm afraid. I don't have much aptitude, but being a wizard gives me an advantage with some of the ladies," Quint said. "I don't carry a robe for that very reason."

The chief laughed. "I wouldn't either. Go on in. What's your name?"

"Denzil Adzirak."

The chief wrote the name down and let Quint go in. He walked directly to the seaward wall where their floor was and walked up the stairs. It had been repaired. He peeked into the meeting room and there were only four chairs around the table. His room was straightened up, but the rope by the window was gone, and there was a different study table in the room.

The bed was made better than Quint usually did, so he laid down and fell asleep.

"You!" Grizak said, using his foot to wake Quint up. The moon hadn't moved much, so he had just fallen asleep.

"Just get back from Bokwiz's service?" Quint asked.

"You are Quint! How did you get in?"

"Do I look like Quint?" Quint asked.

Grizak shook his head. "You don't, but you sound like him."

"I'm an itinerant monk," Quint said. "I don't know how long I can wear this mask before some Green monk magically removes it with a string."

"Well, we can deal with that in the morning. Everyone else has gone to bed. I was checking out the floor like usual and found you snoring away. Sleep tight," Grizak said, closing the door behind him.

§§§

CHAPTER NINETEEN
~

QUINT HAD TO REMOVE HIS MASK and use the string to get it back on. Donnie and Grizak could tell it was a mask, but the others couldn't.

"We will be moving up our departure from Seensist," Quint said. "The Reds and the Greens have joined to patrol Pinzleport together. I'm afraid Seensist will be taken over sooner than later."

"I'll talk to Bokwiz's sponsor on the council," Grizak said.

"And I'll give Dakuz a visit," Quint said, wearing one of his other robes.

He saw his bodyguards off. Quint didn't want to risk exposure during a meal, and left for the library as soon as he thought breakfast would be over. He found Dakuz munching on a hunk of bread.

"I was wondering if we could have a word?" Quint said, trying to disguise his voice.

"Well, I was wondering when you'd return from wherever you went after escaping," Dakuz said. He looked up and smiled at Quint. "Wearing a disguise, I see. That will fool the guards but not many on the council."

"That's why I didn't go to breakfast."

"Want some of this?" Dakuz held out his half-eaten loaf.

"No thanks. My guards are bringing me something. We are leaving as soon as we can get everyone ready. Tomorrow or the next night," Quint said.

"Still thinking Parsun Cloister is the place to go?"

"Better than Seensist. The port is infested with Greens and now Reds. They were jointly going through the houses in Pinzleport."

"That isn't a good development."

Quint nodded. "From what I've read, the area around Parsun is safer for us. I was ready before I had to escape."

"How was your escape? Grizak hinted that you found a secure spot in Pinzleport."

"I did," Quint said. "While there, I was able to read an ancient portfolio. I learned this…" Quint built a weak water string with one hand.

Dakuz looked stunned. He was unable to come up with a suitably sarcastic remark. "You learned that on your own?"

Quint nodded. "The instructions were in an ancient hubite language that I happen to know. Willotan, of all things. I'm far from being proficient. If you use your normal magical strength, the strings are too potent. I'll learn to control it before I'm comfortable teaching the technique to someone else."

"What brought you back? I thought you'd wait a little longer before you returned. The Greens and Reds have set up a perimeter around the cloister. How will you get out?"

"That's the main reason I'm here. I'll need a diversion. Do you have any ideas?"

"Like me creating it?" Dakuz asked. "I could start a fire or something."

"The fire thing is too dangerous. I don't have any animosity toward the cloister," Quint said. "We can't escape out of the windows. There is a squad stationed below them."

"What about the postern gate that you came through? Everyone knows the story about how Oscar Viznik let you in. The door has been secured from the inside. Take the security off, then leave in the middle of the night."

"That is a good idea. I'm going there next."

Quint left Dakuz and took a roundabout route to the door in question, and made sure no one was around. The door was magically sealed with metal bars sunk into the door frame that kept the door from opening. Quint quickly checked the frame and found it wasn't bound to the stone.

He used his woodcutting spell, which wasn't powerful enough to separate the wood from the stone, but Quint remembered another bartered string for cutting quarry stone. He created the stonecutting string with his customary power and concentrated on creating a cutting beam as thin as a needle. The string cut through stone as if it were butter.

Quint guided the beam along the door frame and stopped at the corner. He cast another string and ran the beam along the top and then another that cut the other side. Quint shook the frame, and it gave enough, telling him it could be pushed out when he cut the corners. It didn't matter how much metal banding bound the door.

Now that he had confidence that he had an egress point, he returned to his room and waited for his team to return.

§

"It's going to be dangerous," one of the bodyguards said. "We should leave tonight."

"What about Sandiza and Brother Bokwiz?" Donnie asked.

"We leave them a message," Quint said. "I'll take them to Brother Dakuz."

"No need to expose you any more than you are," Grizak said, "mask or not."

Quint had to agree. "Then tonight it is, just us."

The bodyguards switched tidying up their affairs as best they could in shifts. Dakuz had the messages with an urgent request not to hand them out until lunchtime the next day.

Quint was waiting for dinner when there were shouts in the cloister. He stepped into the lift and looked out to see something he never had expected to see. Across the courtyard, Red and Green guards were fighting monks. Monks were fighting monks. This wasn't an invasion to find Quint, but a war.

The fighting was still in the courtyard, some distance from their wall. Quint couldn't stand watching. He grabbed the armor still under his bed and ran down the stairs. Any of the uniformed guards were fair game. The monks were problematic. He didn't find much resistance until he stepped into the courtyard. The fighting was concentrated at the refectory, and few were looking his way.

A skirmish in front of the stable cells was getting started. Quint ran to help three monks surrounded by five guards, four green and one red. They were casting flames, but none of the monks could project much power, and the fire splashed against the guards' armor. Quint didn't understand why they didn't aim for the guards' faces as the monks were driven back and would soon have a wall at their backs.

Suddenly, from behind the monks, Oscar Viznik, Quint's savior at the postern door, sent a fire spear into the back of one of the monks, who dropped to the ground. Savior or not, Quint jumped into the fight. His fire spear missed, but Oscar ran away from someone with more power than he had.

The guards looked at Quint as he cast a spear, splashing at the feet of the guards. They didn't want to fight someone who would fight back and retreated toward the refectory.

"Go to your cells and lock the door any way you can. If you can't lock them, shove your beds against the door. You shouldn't be fighting."

"We were on our way to the refectory," one monk said. Quint had exchanged strings with him and sighed. There was no way the monk could handle the string Quint had given him if the fire string was any indication. "If you look out your window, see if you can tell who is on what side."

The monks fled and entered a dormitory building Quint had never entered. He turned toward the refectory. He picked up a sword dropped by one of the fleeing guards and used the weapon to slash at the odd guard. His magic shield had protected him from the monks fighting on the side of the Greens, but the shield would not protect him from the sharp edge of a sword.

The fight spilled out even more when Quint crossed the courtyard. It couldn't have started long before he looked from the lift.

Quint began throwing fire spears at the guards. Few had shields and they were dropping to the ground. Quint didn't bother with the nicety of wounding them. Not when the bodies of monks were beginning to litter the grounds.

He watched the head prior kill one of Bokwiz's congregation.

"You are on the side of evil?" Quint said, confronting Seensist's leader.

"What is evil?" the head prior said. "It is the opposite of whoever is in power."

The prior cast a lightning string at Quint, whose shield barely stopped the attack. Another one or two of those would kill him.

The head prior grinned. "You are ready to die? I'll be a hero!"

Quint raised his free hand and beat the prior to the next string. He guessed the head prior's shield wouldn't withstand a fire spear cast with a single hand. Quint had no compunction killing the prior. The prior fell back, his clothes smoking. He didn't know if the prior was dead or not. The battle raged on.

The unaffiliated monks began to make headway against the guards when Quint spotted his bodyguards escorting Sandy and Bokwiz in a tight-knit group heading his way.

"Time to leave," Grizak said.

Quint nodded. "A quick trip to the cells, and then we leave."

They approached the wall that held their cells to see a couple of Green and Red squads milling at the entrance.

Quint sighed. "We leave with what we have." He led them to the postern door when he heard steps.

"No, you won't," Oscar Viznik said with four monks behind him.

"Shields!" Quint said.

As he said it, the enemy bathed them with flames. Quint was glad his friends had anticipated the need for protection, and they attacked the monks. Sandy cowered behind the bodyguards, but Bokwiz was up to the fight. The monks were too close to cast strings, and the battle was close quarters. Monks with fists, Quint thought.

When the conflict became physical, Quint's people overcame their attackers.

"Stand guard while I get the door clear," Quint said.

He turned to the postern door and used his cutting string to separate the rest of the doorframe from the stone. With no one alive aware of their location, two of the bigger bodyguards physically forced the frame through the stone wall.

Grizak and another monk dragged the attacker's bodies away from the door while everyone else left the cloister and took up defensive positions. Two monks, including Quint placed the door back into place once Grizak returned. Quint sealed the door to the stone with magic, and they headed along the cliff's edge to the fishing beach below and into the woods.

They found a trail to take them north and trotted away from the cloister in the twilight.

"Stop right there," a voice called from within the woods.

Bokwiz stopped and put a protective arm around Sandy. The other monks were ready to fight.

"Show yourself, knave!" Quint said, smiling.

Dakuz walked out of the woods overloaded with bags.

"Is that our stuff?" Donnie asked.

"What I could carry of it. I didn't have much time to sort out money from the other possessions, but this is what you get," the librarian said. "I somehow knew you'd all escape, except I'm surprised Sandiza Bartok and Shinzle Bokwiz tagged along."

"The attack was at dinner," Grizak said. "I made sure they were protected as we tried to fight our way to our cells."

"I saw uniforms pass my library window and expected you'd take advantage of that diversion. I almost didn't make it out of your building before a few squads showed up, but I still have a few tricks," Dakuz said. "What's next?"

"I think I killed the head prior," Quint said. "He had me complete the affiliation study so he could separate his people from the unaffiliated. I saw him attack one of Bokwiz's people, and that was my last fight before I went looking for my bodyguards."

Dakuz grumbled. "Let's stop talking. I can't go very fast lugging all this stuff."

§

With the bags distributed, they set off north. Quint intended to head north of the village he had visited with Eben before heading east. Their priority was to get as far away from Seensist as possible, but the attack on the cloister came as dinner was starting. Everyone was hungry except Dakuz, who had brought enough for himself but not enough to share other than give everyone a small piece of bread.

After a very uncomfortable night on a bed of leaves in the middle of the woods, they were back on the trail at dawn. They came close to a small village.

"I'll pick up supplies," Bokwiz said. "I always wear normal clothes under my robe," he said, pulling off his robe. "I have enough money to get something for us to eat."

"I'll go with you," Sandiza said. "I'll be your daughter." She took her robe off, wearing a feminine version of a vest, shirt, and trousers.

The rest of them found a comfortable clearing to wait. Bokwiz and Sandy returned with an unexpected companion. All three carried food but no supplies.

"Who is he?" Grizak asked.

"I am Helmut Turicek, the headman of the village your friends just visited. I have a letter for Brother Quinto Tirolo. Brother Bokwiz says Tirolo is among you," Turicek said. "I was awakened in the middle of the night and asked to watch out for Brother Tirolo."

"That's me," Quint said, stepping forward.

The headman's eyebrows rose. "You are the youngest here, except for perhaps the sister."

"He's the right person," Dakuz said in a grumble. "Give him the letter."

Quint looked around. "The rest of you can eat while I read."

There were two letters in the envelope. The first was from Bokwiz's council member friend, and surprisingly, Wanisa Hannoko wrote the second. Quint read Wanisa's first.

> I hope Donnie is safe and sound, in your custody. Cooler heads prevailed in Pinzleport, and the battle at the cloister finally ended when the port police joined the monks. I wouldn't call Pinzleport safe, but the cloister is. Give Donnie my best, and I recommend following Brother Croczi's advice.

"Donnie, is this your mother's handwriting?" Quint asked.

"Is this true?" the stonemason monk asked.

Quint nodded. "I will read Brother Croczi's letter next, but I'll read this one aloud."

> I've sent this letter and the one from Lady Wanisa to all the villages close to Seensist. Whatever path you've followed isn't as fast as a horse and rider on a mission. A miracle occurred. Pinzleport's police, which hadn't distinguished itself from letting the Red and Green guards do whatever they wanted, finally developed some courage and joined us in putting down the attack on our cloister.
>
> Unfortunately, many of our brothers and sisters perished before the assistance arrived. I am confident that you and your small group survived your escape. I am asking you to return to us. We need you and members of your group to help us restructure our cloister. I was asked to offer Dakuz and you memberships on the council as enticements.
>
> Our head prior did not survive the battle, and I am now acting head prior. I asked Lady Wanisa to write a note to verify I wrote this note.

"What do you think?" Quint asked the group.

"If it weren't for my mother's letter, I wouldn't believe what Croczi wrote.

He could have been forced, but I believe my mother. I'd say let's go back. If we don't like how things work out, we can leave under less hasty circumstances."

"I don't disagree with that," Dakuz said. "Only Croczi would invite me to be a council member."

Bokwiz asked for the acting head prior's letter and pointed to a small mark after a paragraph.

"That is Croczi's mark. He wouldn't have made that if he was writing under duress. I agree with Council Member Dakuz," Bokwiz said with a sly smile.

Dakuz grumbled something Quint couldn't quite understand.

"The rest of you?"

Everyone agreed to go back. Quint felt some relief. He had left too much behind, including the confidence that he could lead any group of people through a wilderness all the way to Parsun Cloister.

Quint shook the headman's hand. "Thank you for looking out for us and for the food."

"I paid for that food!" Sandy said.

"Then thanks for selling it to us," Quint said.

§§§

CHAPTER TWENTY

~

QUINT WAS SURPRISED BY TWO MORE MONKS volunteering that the new head prior was a Red. Neither of them said anything about Bokwiz or Sandy or anyone else.

"I'm not the best interrogator," Quint said.

"Give yourself some time to practice," Donnie said. "It's time to have a chat with Grizak."

They found Grizak talking to Kozak, the carpenter. "Ah, what timing," Grizak said. "I thought we might see if our friend here could make some wagons."

"Where would we get horses?" Donnie asked.

"Buy them from the cloister," Kozak said. "You could leave some money behind if you couldn't get the new head prior to sell them to you."

"Or we could have someone go into Pinzleport and buy our own to keep in the stable," Quint said. "I'm more comfortable doing that, and I think we could get better animals."

"That works, too," Kozak said. "We were discussing how big the wagons needed to be. One normal-sized wagon would be a tight squeeze."

"Then two. They need to be sturdy enough for rough roads," Quint said, "and the sides high enough for protection from projectiles."

"Goes without saying, knowing that you'll likely be attacked along the way to wherever you are going."

"Parsun Cloister," Quint said. "Want to come along?"

"Me?" Kozak said. "That would be unfair to Seensist."

"And why is that?" Donnie asked.

"I'm the best carpenter in the place," Kozak said with pride.

"And where were you when the fighting began?" Quint asked.

"Me?" Kozak turned red. "I'm a builder, not a fighter."

Quint looked at the affiliation list. No one could ever figure out who Kozak sided with.

"The invitation is open," Quint said. "Do you need help with wheels?"

"I always need help with wheels."

Quint laughed. "Then I'll do the wheels if you give me a drawing or something. Is there a standard size in Narukun like in Racellia?"

"There is, and that is what you need to build. Then, if something goes wrong, we can replace it," Kozak said.

"We?" Donnie asked.

Kozak grumbled to himself. "I did say that, didn't I? I'm doing some thinking while we are standing here."

"And what does your brain say?"

Kozak shook his head. "Not my brain, my heart. When you escaped, Brother Tirolo, I was excited for you. An adventure. Something different from overbearing guards invading our cloister from time to time. Not that I'm affected, but…"

"So, you'll come with us?" Grizak asked.

"I'll think about it," the carpenter said. "These old bones aren't too old for one last adventure."

"Good!" Quint said. "I'll get started tomorrow. Donnie and I have to get the monks on my list interviewed."

"Interviewed? For what?" Kozak asked.

"We want to make sure all the monks aren't getting depressed about the battle. Croczi is having the councilors talk to everyone."

"Talk to everyone who is scared out of their wits and can't get un-scared?" Kozak said.

"That's it."

The carpenter nodded. "I know those who hid with me are fine. We had a good time in our hiding place. It helps to have it stocked with some bottles of wine."

"Any on this list?" Donnie asked.

Kozak examined the list at arm's length before he put spectacles over his nose. "Four and two sisters." He looked for his fellow hiders. None were on his list.

"Was Brother Croczi hiding?" Quint asked.

Kozak frowned. "I didn't see him fighting, either. I suspect he was holed up like me."

"You weren't underground?" Grizak asked.

"No. There are a few empty cells overlooking the courtyard that I know. We picked the largest and watched the battle. It became a little gruesome for the ladies," Kozak said. "Croczi wouldn't expose himself to danger. He prefers to work from the shadows."

"What do you mean?" Quint asked.

Kozak looked around his shop to see if anyone was in earshot. "You do know he is a Red. For most of the time, Reds and Greens don't mix. He and the old head prior were enemies until recently."

"How do you know that?" Donnie asked.

"I have my ways," Kozak said. He grinned at Quint. "I never had a chance to do a string exchange while you were in business. I'm sure I have a few strings to trade."

Quint smiled back but could talk about strings later. "You are sure he is a Red?"

Kozak nodded. "Positive. I wouldn't be surprised if all the surviving councilors are Red sympathizers."

"Then why did two of them leave the council?" Quint asked.

"Who left? Kozak asked.

Quint read their names from the affiliation list, and the carpenter's face darkened.

"I saw both of those monks killed in the courtyard. Red guards handled those swords."

"They were shielded?" Quint asked.

Kozak closed his eyes. "Yes. The monks fought back, but…" he shook his head.

"Did you see Brother Dugo fighting?" Donnie asked. "He said that Bokwiz is a Red."

"Dugo?" Kozak pursed his lips. "Dugo emerged from his hiding place toward the end and joined the police in putting down the guards. He was injured in the fight."

"He was on the police side?"

"Oh, yes. He saved a few police lives and paid a price for it."

Quint looked at Donnie, shocked by the revelation. He didn't want to hear the answer, but he had to ask the question. "We were told that Shinzle Bokwiz is a Red. Is that true?"

Kozak shrugged. "He's a monk I rarely talk to," the carpenter said. "However, if he is a crony of Croczi's, I'd be careful." Kozak's eyebrows rose.

"Bokwiz was one of our group!" Donnie said.

Quint nodded. "I'll make sure about him, then." Quint's stomach turned. Dugo's accusation now had an independent confirmation. There was more to check on, but he clearly couldn't believe anything Croczi told him.

Grizak accompanied Donnie and Quint back onto the courtyard, where Donnie explained what they had heard from Dugo.

"I've worked with Brother Dugo on a few projects, and we attended a few classes together. I wouldn't expect him to tell lies," Grizak said. "Dugo's fighting was verified?"

"Yes, it was," Quint said. "Now, we need to talk with Sandy. I'm not sure Bokwiz or Croczi will own up to their involvement if they truly are Red spies."

§

They found Sandy talking to her two youthful monks. Neither of them looked as if they had been in a battle recently, and the discussion seemed to be low-key.

"We need to talk to Sandy," Quint said to the boys. "Can you excuse us?"

"Sure!" one of them said. "We are impressed you came back and happy you brought Sister Sandiza with you."

The two left, for where Quint didn't know, and Sandy didn't tell them.

"This is important?" Sandy asked, looking at the three monks.

"Very," Grizak said.

"I'd like you to tell us exactly what happened when Bokwiz and you went into the village for supplies.

"Exactly?"

Quint nodded. "It's important."

She giggled nervously. "You've put me on the spot."

"Just tell us what you saw," Quint said.

"We walked into the village. I thought we'd head for the nearest store, but

Brother Bokwiz said we should get information from the village headman. I asked him what kind of information, and he wanted to know if any soldiers had been in the village."

"He didn't go directly to a store?"

Sandy shook her head. "The village wasn't that big, so finding the headman's house was easy. He was eating breakfast."

"What happened next?" Quint asked. His stomach was flip-flopping. What she told him next was very important.

"He had me stand outside to make sure there weren't any soldiers. I was to run into the house if I spotted anything. Brother Bokwiz went inside. I had to wait a while until they came out."

"You didn't see the headman give Bokwiz the letter?"

Sandy shook her head. "Is that important?"

"You didn't hear what they said?"

"Not until they both came out. We went to the store after that, and I led them back to the clearing. By the way, Bokwiz made me pay for the food."

"You didn't see any soldiers or guards?" Donnie asked.

"No, but there were curious people walking past the headman's house."

"Of course. A pretty girl was standing in front," Quint said with a smile.

Sandy blushed. "What is this all about?"

"Someone Donnie and I interviewed said Bokwiz was a Red sympathizer," Quint said.

"You mean he's a spy?"

"That is what I'd like to find out. What you just told me hasn't cleared Bokwiz. In fact, what kind of person would leave you alone in front of a house when the opposition could ride by at any time?" Quint asked.

"I admit I wasn't comfortable standing around for that long," Sandy said, "but Bokwiz is a religionist leader!"

"Sometimes your political views outweigh the religious," Donnie said.

"I can't speak to that," Quint said, "but that might be the case here. We know that Croczi is on the Red side. That has been confirmed, and Bokwiz and Croczi are close friends. I would have thought Bokwiz would be a better council candidate than Dakuz, but Bokwiz remains in the shadows."

"I wondered about that, too, since the acting head and Bokwiz are so close," Sandy said. "Could it be true?"

"We were concerned you were a Red, too," Donnie said.

Quint wanted to hit Donnie. It wasn't the time to ask that question, but the damage had been done.

"I've never concerned myself with the two major factions," Sandy said. "I'm not interested in who can be more dominant. Neither of them are for the people, just the power. I'm surprised they cooperated to take over the cloister."

"And they never did find me," Quint said.

"The fools," Grizak said.

"If Bokwiz is a spy, they were able to lure us back," Sandy said. "Who are the fools?"

Quint lost his breath. Bokwiz had made a fool out of him, and he and Dakuz were the prime victims.

"Now it's time to talk to Dakuz and see what he says."

"Could he be in league with Bokwiz?" Grizak asked.

"Now's the time to find out," Quint said.

They found Dakuz in the library with his assistant, looking over a disheveled pile of books.

"Someone shirked their duty while I was gone," Dakuz said through his teeth. He glared at his assistant and then gave Quint a weak smile. "Can't you see I'm busy? Come back later."

"It won't wait," Quint said.

Dakuz gave the assistant a stream of curses combined with instructions to put the books back onto their proper shelves and took Quint and the others into his office.

"How can I be a council member and have that person be in charge of the library," Dakuz said.

"Leave Seensist," Quint said.

"Has something happened?" Dakuz said. "Is it about Bokwiz?"

"What about Bokwiz?" Quint asked.

"I've been doing some thinking. I never went to Bokwiz's services, but I knew that Croczi and he were close. I expected Bokwiz would be a councilor, but surprisingly, I was selected. I'm no councilor," Dakuz said. "I'm a surly, cantankerous wizard. I do my best in that role. Something was fishy, but I thought I could get a nicer cell. It turns out the old head prior was punishing himself. His cell wasn't any better than mine."

Sandy repeated her story about the village headman.

"That does it, doesn't it? Bokwiz asked to be a follower, right?"

Quint nodded his head.

"How out of character is that, regardless of your future?"

"I thought it was touching," Sandy said.

Grizak grunted. "Or devious."

"I vote devious," Donnie said.

"What are you going to do about it?" Dakuz said. "Don't look at me? My instinct is to run."

"Wagons," Quint said. "We leave as soon as the wagons are finished. I have some ideas, which I will keep to myself. I've almost gotten my contact-the-monk project done, so I'll have the time."

"Oh, that," Dakuz said. "I suppose I'll distribute the recruitment ideas and call it a visit."

"At this point, I don't care," Quint said.

"As if it matters," Dakuz muttered.

§§§

CHAPTER TWENTY-ONE
~

KOZAK WAS HARD AT WORK.
"Can we buy wagons?" Quint asked. "We might want to use them sooner."

Kozak shrugged. "There are plenty to purchase in Pinzleport. You can get your supplies there, too."

"I'm going to have to leave the cloister," Quint said.

"Is that smart?"

Quint shook his head. "Not smart at all, but tell me what I should look for."

"I'll go with you," Kozak said. "If I'm going to repair them, I want to choose."

"Is that smart?" Quint said with half a smile.

"Not smart at all, on the one hand, and very smart on the other."

Quint enlisted Donnie to accompany them, ostensibly to visit Lady Wanisa. Quint told Croczi that he had met Lady Wanisa while he was gone from the Cloister the first time and Donnie invited him to return. Kozak would join them en route. Quint paid one of Sandy's monks to deliver a message to Wanisa Hannoko.

"You are sure about this?" Croczi asked on the morning of the following day. "You are at risk in Pinzleport."

"I am. I'll be wearing a mask," Quint said. He had a hard time even looking at Croczi and had not seen Bokwiz except for dinnertime the few days he had returned from the battle, and then the religionist didn't even talk to him. Something was wrong.

Quint accepted a short sword from Kozak that would fit underneath his new oversized robe, hiding his armor. Donnie wore two robes. He had everything he wanted at his home and would return to the cloister with weapons and armor.

Donnie and Quint walked out of the cloister on the very familiar road leading to Pinzleport. They were halfway there when ten Red guards stopped them on the part of the road through heavy woods.

"Where do you think you're going?" the officer leading the squad said.

"To visit my mother, Lady Wanisa Hannoko," Donnie said.

"I'm afraid I can't let you proceed," the officer said.

"Why not?" Donnie asked.

The officer nodded at Quint. "He isn't allowed in Pinzleport. Mask or no mask."

"Why not?" Quint asked.

"It isn't for you to question."

"Why not?" Kozak said, emerging from the woods alongside less than a dozen Pinzleport policemen and twenty or more sailors led by Captain Olinko's first officer.

The Red guards looked nervously at their officer.

"Why not?" the leader of the police said.

The Red officer pursed his lips and motioned for his people to retreat.

"We will escort you to Lady Wanisa's house and then your sailor friends have our permission to take you wherever else you need to go this morning," the police leader said.

The contingent went a little faster, arriving at the Hannoko residence, followed by the squad of Reds in the distance.

"Donnie," Wannie said as she rushed out of the house. "I hear you will be leaving us."

"Who?"

Wannie looked at Quint. "He sent a note asking for a police escort and saying you were about to leave Seensist for good this time."

"I am, but I'm not going into exile, Mother. I'll be in a different place, a bit farther away."

Quint walked up with Kozak. "We will leave Brother Hannoko with you while getting supplies in Pinzleport," Quint said. "Thank you for alerting Captain Olinko. His assistance was needed."

"It was my pleasure," Goresk Olinko said as he stepped to the front door, holding a steaming mug in his hand. I'll supervise Dontiz while you are gone."

From Goresk's glance at Wanisa, Quint realized that perhaps Dontiz should be the supervisor.

"We don't have much time," Quint said.

Kozak and Quint walked down the street guarded by friendly sailors. Kozak knew Pinzleport better than Quint and had mentally sketched out a route to follow. They went to a stable and bought four horses and then rode those, still followed by sailors on foot, to a wagon maker and bought two new wagons with the sides high enough to suit Kozak with frames for canvas covers.

Quint eyed a squad of Green guards milling about a hundred paces away.

The market was next where the carpenter bought new and used tools to take on their journey. The carpenter didn't feel right about removing his favorites at the cloister. Before purchasing food and food preparation supplies, the pair stopped at two weapon suppliers where Quint and Kozak selected edged and non-edged weapons for the trip including bows and arrows.

Just before noon, the wagons rolled in front of the Hannoko's house. Their Green shadow remained half a block down the street.

"Come in for lunch. I've prepared lunch for your bodyguards," Wannie said, ushering Quint and Kozak into the house.

"I'll eat with my crew," Olinko said, passing them at the front door, carrying a large tray covered with a cloth.

"I have what I need in two bags," Donnie said, meeting them in the dining room. "I would have only needed one, but Mother decided to help." He gave Wannie a pained smile. "By the way, Croczi forged the note from Mother. I don't know who did the writing, but they are a master forger."

"Why am I not surprised?" Dakuz said.

Lunch was a quick affair. Wannie asked about what they were taking and didn't inquire about their plans.

"I have a much closer relationship with the police after the recent unpleasantness. Our city fathers have changed places, so the Pinzleport police are back to being a neutral power in the port enforcing the law," Wannie said.

Quint, Kozak, and Donnie walked out of the house. Wannie gave Donnie and Quint hugs, and Olinko quickly stepped in line to receive one for himself.

"Some of my men need to get back to the ship. We had a brief discussion with your Green followers, and it became a bit more active than you would have preferred, but…" Olinko didn't finish his sentence.

The sailors were a few men shorter, but they accompanied the wagons to Seensist. At the gate, Quint saw the rest of the bodyguards, Dakuz and Sandy, along with her two charges, standing amidst a pile of bags.

"Croczi didn't waste any time shedding his friendly skin and kicked us out of the cloister. We bundled up your things and are ready to go," Grizak said.

We picked up a couple of extra monks?"

"Their choice," Sandy said. "They didn't want to have anything to do with Seensist."

As they loaded one wagon, the folded canvas cover began to move. Andreiza Hannoko emerged, brushing dust off her clothes.

What are you doing here?" Grizak asked. "You need to return to Pinzleport."

Andy shook her head. "Not going to happen, Grizak. I'm going where you are going."

Grizak covered most of his face with a hand in exasperation.

"She's not exiled," Quint said, recalling what Donnie had said to his mother. "We can always send her back if she doesn't behave. Besides, I'm sure Sandy wouldn't mind a female companion."

"If they can get along," Donnie muttered.

They were about to leave when Dugo, the monk who had enlightened Quint about Croczi and Bokwiz, showed up with a few bags.

"I'd like to go if you'll have me," Dugo said.

"Welcome aboard," Grizak said.

"And Bokwiz?" Quint asked Grizak.

"Our spiritual leader decided he would be needed ministering at Seensist," Grizak said. "He extended his apologies. No one will leave the cloister to wish us well."

"That confirms his true role amongst us," Quint said.

"It does, unfortunately. Your bodyguard contingent has unanimously decided to follow you rather than him. Is that all right?"

Quint nodded. "We are ready to go?" Quint asked the group.

Everyone nodded, and once the wagons were loaded, they left Seensist.

Quint doubted if he'd ever return to the cloister, although Pinzleport might see him again.

§

The wagons ambled on until dark. They continued until they came to a stretch of woods and found a clearing that had been used as a campsite before.

The bodyguards went to work raising the framework and stretching the canvas tops over both wagons. As Quint helped, he realized that he had been too busy to think of Sandy now that Andy had joined them. He smiled. Sandy and Andy. They would have to buy a tent for the women.

Quint elected to sleep outside as did the bodyguards. The two young monks were assigned to sleep with Dakuz and Kozak in one wagon, with the two women using the other covered conveyance.

Neither Sandy nor Andy volunteered to make a meal out of the supplies. There were a few other monks who could cast water strings, so Quint didn't have much to do. He decided to explore the woods to make sure their campground was safe from large animals. Just before he entered the undergrowth, Sandy joined him.

"We haven't had a chance to talk in private," she said. "I thought this would be a good opportunity, away from the cloister and from the bodyguards."

"Is there anything specific?" Quint asked.

"I have a confession," Sandy said. "Brother Bokwiz convinced me to help him spy on you before we left Seensist during the battle. I had no intention to do so until we reached that village."

Quint pursed his lips but didn't say anything. She had to have more to say.

"I agreed, but he promised nothing would happen to you if we returned to Seensist." She frowned, and her eyes misted. "I thought he would continue to be a friend, and I was going to tell you of his duplicity, but," she turned to look away, wiping a tear, "I never imagined he would go against his word. When I heard you were attacked going to Seensist, I gathered my things. I was going to leave the cloister if you returned or not." She fell to her knees. "Please forgive me. Bokwiz has a certain power over individuals."

"You felt it?" Quint asked.

Sandy nodded, but then her eyebrows rose. "Could it have been a string?"

Quint nodded. "If it was the slightest bit unnatural, I'm sure it was. It was how he kept his congregation together. I wouldn't be surprised if some of his congregation were feeding him information on a regular basis."

"What about the bodyguards?"

"Not them," Quint said, "or I would have noticed by now. We haven't been together since our escape, or I would have noticed it in you. Since he isn't here to reinforce his string, I imagine his spell has faded."

"Dugo was unaffected?" Sandy asked.

"I think Dugo is unaffected by many strings," Quint said, helping Sandy up. "He is a unique person who has been slighted in his life. Our journey will allow me to talk to him, but we need to talk about us."

"Us?" Sandy asked. "You still consider me to be a friend?"

Quint smiled. "Do I look angry? I suspected you, of course, but I'm relieved that you were likely coerced to cooperate with Bokwiz. He ignored you once we returned?"

Sandy nodded. "At first, I was hurt, but then I avoided him. Guilt, I suppose."

"I doubt if Bokwiz can feel guilt. I'm not sure if he is a true religionist," Quint said. "I'd like you to stay with us. I think we are amenable to each other, and I'd like you to continue to Parsun if you are willing."

"I am," Sandy said. "I am 'amenable,' as you say." She gave him a smile that was more like the Sandy he knew.

"I have three responsibilities for you. Keep care of Andreiza Hannoko and those two monks of yours. Haven't they got parents?"

"Orphans," Sandy said. "They aren't fully into their magic yet. One of the monk's parents died in a boating accident. They were both from Seensist. The other is off the street and showed some magic at his age. He is only twelve. No one knew what to do with either of them, so since they had magic or were likely for it to develop, they were placed in Seensist. Better that than the streets of Pinzleport."

"Then they are your charges. Keep the boys out of trouble and keep Andy out of a different kind of trouble. I don't want Grizak to be too confused. She is after him, and he wants to resist her."

"That won't last long," Sandy said. "Andy is relentless."

"I suspect it won't, but let's help the situation go more slowly than Andy wants."

Sandy frowned, but beneath that was a smile. "I'll do what I can. Am I going slowly enough?"

"What?" Quint said. He felt his face warm. "Regarding us?"

She nodded; the frown had disappeared. "I know you feel something."

"But I have to lead the group," Quint said.

"You have lots of people with experience to help. Lots of monks have girlfriends."

Quint felt a tinge of desperation. "Slow is a good thing," he said.

§

The sleeping arrangements worked out, but the tent for the women would be much better. Quint, Grizak, and Kozak spent the night under the wagons. Breakfast was a quick reheating of the meal the night before, and not long after dawn, they were on their way east again.

Quint had an opportunity to walk with Dugo, a fair distance from the wagons due to the dust.

"You have a resistance to strings?" Quint asked.

Dugo nodded. "Psychic strings, mostly," Dugo said. "I can't cast them, and they don't like me. That was the reason I left Bokwiz's services. I'm a religionist at heart, but even though I didn't think him sincere, I liked the early version of Tizurek that he preached. I have felt guilty about my lapsed faith and hope to correct that at Parsun. I can't stand two-faced leaders."

"You didn't like the previous head prior?"

Dugo loudly grunted. "He was the worst! I saw him talking to Greens enough, and since I knew what to look for, I caught him passing messages that made it to fellow Green monks. I was hating my time in the cloister. I thought you were like him, but I learned otherwise."

"From whom?"

"From my observations. Not as much from you as from your followers. You weren't using magic to bind them to you, and they look up to you more than they ever did Bokwiz."

Quint nodded. "I think you're right."

"I know I am," Dugo said. "What can I do on this journey?"

"Keep me humble," Quint said. "I don't think I've succumbed to the adoration yet. Let me know if I change."

"And Sandiza? She is a very pretty face, not that Miss Hannoko isn't as well. Do you want to discourage her?"

Quint laughed. "I think she's the one with the string," Quint said. "No, I'd like that to develop at the current pace, slow."

"What else?"

"Are you handy at anything other than resisting psychic strings?"

"I know how to cook. I worked in a Slinnon restaurant before I joined the cloister."

"Then help Kozak if your injury permits. His cooking is serviceable," Quint said. "Neither of the girls has expressed an interest. If your cooking passes everyone's opinion, then you can take over. Kozak's talents are going to be tested elsewhere on our journey."

"That is a reasonable approach. Where did you learn to be a leader?" Dugo asked.

Quint laughed. "I'm just halfway to my nineteenth birthday," he said. "I'm doing my best."

"You haven't been perfect. You were an idiot to return from your first escape, but I think you are doing well enough. You have my vote to continue."

Quint smiled. "I appreciate that," he said, clapping Dugo on the shoulder.

§§§

CHAPTER TWENTY-TWO

Halfway or more to Parsun, they stopped for the night close to a large estate. During breakfast, a well-dressed man with three guards rode into their camp.

"Who is the leader?" the man said.

"I suppose that is me," Quint said.

The man looked around the camp. "Other than the two boys, you appear to be the youngest male here."

"He is our leader," Dakuz said. "Ask anyone else."

"And you are?"

"Hintz Dakuz. This is Quinto Tirolo," Dakuz nodded to Quint. "And you are?"

The man took a breath and drew himself an inch taller. "Zim Pilka. I'm the lord of the surrounding area. What are you doing in my domain?"

"Passing through," Quint said. "We are headed to the northeast coast."

"To the cloister there?"

"Yes," Dakuz said. "We are monks seeking to align with another cloister."

Pilka stroked his chin beard. "Parsun is the only one directly east of here. It has recently been shut down. You will be disappointed when you arrive."

"What happened?" Grizak said, walking up to the impromptu meeting with Donnie.

Pilka sighed. "I have relatives close to Parsun and have previously visited the cloister. The place was run by old monks called the 'Elders,' and the rules became less flexible, driving out the younger monks. That reduced the number of monks, and the elders didn't bother to repair the cloister. A storm blew off the ocean this summer, and the walls facing the sea collapsed. I don't know the details, but that was the last blow, ha, ha, and the elders proclaimed the cloister defunct."

"What happened to the monks?" Dakuz asked.

Shaking his head, Pilka sighed again. A man full of sighs, Quint thought. "Twelve monks showed up on my doorstep looking for a place to live and build a new cloister that treated the miracle of magic as a thing to study with rules more suited to study than severity. I put them up in one of my villages. I've let them make what they can of a lumber mill and furniture factory I had closed."

"I have a master carpenter in my group," Quint said. "Perhaps we can visit them on our journey east and help them get set up." Quint wanted more information about Parsun. He would have liked to trust Pilka but found it hard to believe a cloister died, as Pilka claimed.

"Then spend a few weeks in my domain. Parsun won't dissolve in that time. I'd like to hear your story."

"We have not left without making a few enemies," Quint said. "I'd rather continue to move on."

"A few days, then. You are close to the one town under my watchful eye. I will protect you and pay for your lodging and food for a few days. How can you refuse?"

Traveling for the week wasn't that rewarding, Quint thought. He had hoped the journey would bind everyone together, but that didn't seem to be the case.

"I won't. A few days and then we are off to Parsun. If it is as you describe, then we may return and join the monks that we meet if they seem amenable to adding us to their group," Quint said.

"Whatever happens, happens," Pilka said. "I wouldn't mind another's perception of the monks, anyway."

"You want us to be your spies?" Quint asked.

"Not spies. Just your unbiased opinions."

"We can do that," Dakuz said. "I, for one, would like to taste some different cooking for a few days. I think the rest of us would, too."

"And a bed," Grizak said, "would be nice for a change."

"I'll leave one of my men to guide you to the town's inn," Pilka said.

"The monk's village is an hour away from the town. My man will guide you there once you've been settled. I will treat you all to dinner in the town's best restaurant."

"We can't say no to that," Donnie said.

Grizak nodded enthusiastically.

"Then we will finish breakfast and take you up on your gracious offer," Quint said.

Pilka nodded goodbye, conferred with his guards, and left one behind as he took a trail into the woods.

The guard accepted a plate of remnants from breakfast as everyone else prepared to leave. Quint stayed with him.

"How did Zim Pilka, Lord Pilka, I suppose, know we were in the forest?" Quint asked.

The guard was gobbling down the food. "Lord Zim likes fresh game for lunch and dinner, so we send a few hunters out, some of us guards, into the woods before dawn. This morning, the hunter came upon your group. Lord Zim thought you were more monks from Parsun and came to investigate."

"So, Parsun is really falling apart?"

The guard shrugged. "I can't say that's the case, for sure. The monks brought the news, but Lord Zim may still send someone to investigate. I think he is as unsure about their story as you are."

"Oh?" Quint said. "He didn't give me that impression."

The guard smiled. "Lord Zim's mind spins and whirls. He may tell you one thing and do another."

"He is untrustworthy?" Quint said, knowing he was overstepping.

The guard waved his hand in front of him. "Not at all if he trusts you, but he has peculiar methods of divining the truth. Be honest with him, and he ultimately will be honest with you."

"Ultimately?"

The guard nodded. "Most of us have been tested from this direction and that. Those that fail are quickly dismissed."

"I hope he doesn't dismiss us," Quint said. "I haven't been as forthright as I might be, but I have told him no falsehoods."

"Then you don't have anything to worry about."

They left the clearing and, in less than an hour entered the town, Zimton, almost as big as Pinzleport. It was bordered on one side by a lake that fed into a river that ended up in the eastern sea. The inn was better than any Quint had seen in Racellia, being six stories high with a lift that carried people to the top three floors. Kozak was very impressed.

Quint, Grizak, Kozak, Dugo, and Dakuz were escorted to rooms on the top floor. Quint and his friends looked out at the lake above the rooftops of the buildings below from his room.

"Lord Pilka knows how to impress simple wanderers," Dugo said.

Quint had a different opinion. "Lord Pilka knows how to impress wizards who can cast predictor strings," he said to his friends. "If Lord Pilka didn't want to impress, he would have given us directions to the village holding the monks."

"You distrust him?" Dakuz asked.

"No. Not at this point," Quint said. "He has his own way of evaluating that which happens around him. He may use magic, or he may use his wits. I think he uses both."

"Should we be worried?" Grizak asked.

"Not about someone who has ordered the making of that lift," Kozak said.

Dugo grunted. "How do you know Pilka ordered its manufacture?"

"I asked," Kozak said.

Dugo grunted again. "Show me how it works."

"I will, with pleasure," Kozak said.

Dakuz stood at the window as Grizak went with Kozak and Dugo to more closely examine the lift.

"What do you intend on asking Pilka at dinner?" Dakuz asked Quint. "He will be expecting questions."

Quint raised his eyebrows. "I suppose he will. I've been thinking of the advantages of settling here over the Parsun cloister. I've been thinking of the disadvantages. The major one is our proximity to Baxel, the capital and center of the Reds. We are a little over three days away. Where would we go if lords in Baxel decided to exterminate us? One of Parsun's attractions is that it is a neutral cloister and more remote than most others."

"If it still is a cloister," Dakuz said. "Why don't we send some boys east to find out? They could be there and back if we rent them horses. Donnie could go."

"Why don't you take care of it," Quint said. "I think Donnie would appreciate some time away from his sister, don't you think?"

Dakuz chuckled. "I think it is an exceptional motivating factor."

"Then we can offer it to him before dinner. I'll tell Lord Pilka that is our plan. He might even send a guard to go along with them."

"To test out what our guide told you?"

"And give Lord Pilka some confidence in whatever they discover to the east," Quint said.

"Aren't you picking up deviousness a little too quickly?"

Quint smiled. "I think it is a mental defense. My mind has taken a beating while I've been in Narukun."

§

Pilka had arranged a private room at the inn. Quint's group had arrived, and they were waiting for the lord of the domain to arrive. There were four empty chairs at the long table. Finally, the door opened, and a young man and a beautiful young woman, no older than Sandy, entered, followed by a matronly woman and Pilka.

He had brought his family. Quint was impressed. Pilka was craftier than Quint thought, or he was comfortable with a group of travelers he had met earlier in the day, or perhaps Pilka was both.

"I sent my oldest son along with your men to Parsun," Pilka said before introducing his family.

"That's what I understand," Quint said. "Let's make introductions."

"Good idea," Pilka said, seating his wife before he took a chair close to Quint.

Introductions were made. His wife was named Silla. Gallia, the daughter and Pilka's youngest son, Criz, was perhaps a year older than the oldest of Sandy's two monks. Pilka's oldest son was Donnie's age and was currently riding east to Parsun.

"Would you like me to accompany you to the monks in Tova's Falls, the village where the wood mill is?"

"Maybe one or two of your people," Quint said. "I'd like the monks to know we've talked to you, but I'd rather make up my own mind. If you are there, they might not be as forthright."

"I agree with Quint," Dakuz said. "You understand?"

Pilka smiled. "I do, indeed. I took the privilege to order. Our food should arrive soon. While we wait, why don't you give me your version of what happened in Seensist? I received some information from Pinzleport this afternoon."

"May I?" Dugo asked. "I'm more of an independent observer than anyone other than our two young monks."

Quint nodded. "Go ahead. There will be some things left unsaid that I can fill in later."

Although incomplete, Dugo's account was as accurate as Quint's.

"I had escaped from a Red-Green takeover of the cloister when they came through the cloister to capture me. I spent a brief time in Pinzleport at the home of the parent of one of my bodyguards and returned to Seensist," Quint said. "I don't know why the head prior let me go when I escaped the first time, and nothing happened, but when I returned, they returned with the intent of culling non-aligned monks out of the cloister."

"I was one of the non-aligned," Dugo said, lifting his healing arm.

"We decided to leave a few days later when we found out the new head prior was secretly a Red. The old head prior was secretly a Green. One of my original group, a religionist leader, turned out to be a Red spy in my group. He wasn't invited to join us."

"And you think to run away from the factions?" Pilka asked.

"We intend to find a place we can make defensible against attack, but I have no illusions that I can destroy either the Reds or the Greens. We may consider joining your monks if we can be secure," Quint said. "The Reds control the capital and the crown, but the Greens are centered in Pinzleport and are more aggressive."

Pilka nodded. "You would term me non-aligned, but I am careful not to offend the Red faction, or I might find my domain ripped from me. You, Brother Tirolo, represent an unknown factor. People don't like the unknown. You showed up on one of my wizards' predictor strings as an extraordinary figure, but amazingly, your future is a cloud of impressions without details.

"You retain master wizards?" Dugo asked.

"A wizard doesn't have to be a master to cast predictor strings, but it does take a powerful one. Not all wizards are suited to the monastic life in a cloister," Pilka said. "You should know that."

"I do," Dugo said, "but master-level wizards are powerful. I thought…"

"You thought correctly. Both wizards I retain are masters and supervise a small force of fighting wizards, but you are more familiar with those, aren't you, Brother Tirolo."

Quint nodded. "I am. Is that why you aren't concerned about the monks setting up a residence in the furniture mill?"

Pilka shook a finger at Quint. "You are correct. I can set up a meeting with my masters once you return from Tova's Falls." Pilka cleared his throat. "Now, if you please, would you enlighten us all about life in Racellia and South Fenola?"

Over dinner, Quint explained what the life of a hubite was like in Racellia. Unfortunately, it was all in the past tense. Pilka's daughter asked most of the questions, including living in Bocarre's international quarter.

Quint couldn't help but be taken by the girl's intelligence, demeanor, and looks. He glanced at Sandy from time to time and didn't see a particularly happy face. He thought living close to Pilka might not be a good idea for personal reasons.

"We will leave tomorrow after breakfast," Quint said. Could your people be ready by then?"

"Of course," Gallia said. "I'll take you there."

"Good," Quint said. "I won't take all my people with me. They might want to spend some time in a town. Is it safe here?"

Pilka nodded. "Much safer than Seensist or Pinzleport."

§

Sandy sat next to Quint at breakfast. "I want to go to Tova's Falls," she said.

"Don't you want to look around at what middle Narukun offers?"

"I'll do that when we come back," Sandy said. "Who else is going?"

"Kozak and Dakuz," Quint said. "The boys can accompany the bodyguards. Would you like Andy to join us?"

Sandy pursed her lips. "Not this time," she said. "She's well-liked by the bodyguards. What about Dugo?"

"I'd rather have him here to walk around and listen."

"I understand," she said.

Pilka walked in with Gallia, his daughter, and another man.

"This is Olinz, one of my stewards. He carries a note of introduction if it is needed."

"That will ensure we won't get lost," Quint said with a smile. "How far away is Tova's Falls?"

"An hour and a half. One could ride there and back in a morning or an afternoon," Olinz said.

Quint nodded and introduced Kozak, Dakuz, and Sandy to Olinz. Pilka and his entourage sat in the lobby until Quint's group finished breakfast, and they were soon heading northeast, away from Zimton. Sandy insisted on riding at Quint's side, and Gallia was happy to ride with Dakuz, who seemed softened while he talked to the young woman. Olinz and Kozak talked about the mill and Parsun Cloister's collapsed wall.

The road led them up past a plain filled with villages and farmland into foothills and to the southern edge of a spine of mountains that ran northward two-thirds of the length of North Fenola.

After at least an hour and a half, they emerged from a thick forest and looked up at a cliff from the mountains ahead of them. A veil of falls fell from a lake above the cliff, falling hundreds of feet to another lake below.

The large village surrounded the river exit from the lower lake. A large stone building with a non-operating water wheel sat on the other side of the river accessible via a wide stone bridge. There were a few workers on the bridge in the cool mountain air.

Kozak stopped and everyone let him look at the mill for a bit while he stroked his chin beard. "We can move on," he said.

The village was sleepy before noon, but there were three wide roads leading to the town and another out of sight behind the mill.

"Where does that road lead?" Quint asked, pointing at the mill.

"Ultimately, Baxel, our capital. On market days there is lots of traffic since Tova's Falls is the market village in this area. There is also a lumber auction on the other side of town," Olinz said.

"Then what happened to the mill?"

"It is haunted," Gallia said, stopping and turning back on her horse. "The spirit in the mill said it was on holy ground, and that was that. Father is considering building another mill a few miles south of the village."

"Haunted," Dugo said with a snort.

"I wouldn't be so smug, my friend," Olinz said. "The spirit has been seen recently by more than one person."

"Were they the new monks?" Dakuz asked.

"Most of the recent sightings," Olinz said, "but there were experiences with the spirit in the last twenty years, even before the mill was built and before the monks moved in. We used to have pilgrims bother the mill when the spirit sightings first started, but when the mill shut down, the sightings stopped, and the pilgrims dropped to a trickle and then stopped altogether. The monks have agreed to keep their sightings secret."

"Who owns the mill?" Dakuz asked.

"Lord Pilka. He didn't want to tear it down, so he wondered if it was turned into a cloister…"

"The spirit would be satisfied and leave?" Quint said.

Olinz nodded. "Exactly. At least if it was satisfied by having monks rather than workers."

Quint thought a bit. "More monks, more holiness?"

"That's what father thinks," Gallia said.

Quint wasn't much for spiritual manifestations, but his own experience with predictor spells had confused him, as well as his talk with Bokwiz. Still, he didn't know if Bokwiz was a total charlatan or if he genuinely was a religionist.

"We've come this far," Quint said. "We might as well size up the tenants… the non-spiritual ones." Quint was glad none of the religionist bodyguards had accompanied them.

Olinz and Dakuz laughed, the girls smiled, and Kozak shuddered.

The bridge looked to be in decent shape. A workman was replacing broken cobbles.

When they crossed to the other side, a horn blew from a top window.

"The spirit?" Dakuz asked.

"Monks alerting the others that there are visitors. They probably recognize Gallia and me," Olinz said.

A gate opened, and three monks gawked as they rode into the courtyard.

"The saw machinery is still here," Kozak said with interest.

"Lord Pilka will remove it when he builds the new mill," Olinz said.

The oldest-looking monk raised his hands. "Welcome to our monastery."

"Not a cloister?" Quint leaned over, whispering to Olinz.

Pilka's man shrugged. "Last time I was here, they called it a cloister." Olinz straightened up. "I bring visitors to Lord Pilka's domain. This is Brother Quinto Tirolo, formerly of Seensist Cloister. He has brought about ten monks seeking a new place to study and practice wizardry."

"You are young for a leader," the man said.

"I'm a master of ninety strings," Quint said.

The monk raised his eyebrows and asked Kozak and Dakuz if Quint's claim was valid.

"I tested him myself," Dakuz said, "although I can't claim near so many."

"Come in and take a tour. We have our, uh, difficulties in this place."

Olinz held a hand up. "In case you're wondering, I've already told them about the spirit."

The monk sighed with relief. "Better you than us. We had a visitor last night, in fact."

"Do the visitors ever appear during the day?"

"Oh, yes," one of the other monks said. "If you are lucky, you might see one. We can arrange a tour before lunch. We will feed you, so at least there is one thing good out of your journey. You came from Zimton?"

"We did," Olinz said. "Lord Pilka had other matters."

The monk bowed. "Of course."

§§§

CHAPTER TWENTY-THREE

THE TOUR TOOK MINUTES, NOT HOURS. Kozak would have liked to have examined the tools and machinery, but the only place they lingered was the machinery running the waterwheel. The monks turned the wheel on for them for a few minutes.

"Everything works," a monk said.

Quint didn't see anything untoward about the monks. They seemed barely organized and wondered how they would exist if Lord Pilka weren't supporting them. They grew nothing or made nothing for sale. If it were his cloister, he'd be making wood products for sale to the market.

They walked into a large hall. The place looked older than the rest of the mill.

"This is the existing building," Olinz said. He smiled and looked at their host. "Sorry to take over."

"You know more about it than we do," the head monk said. "Go ahead and tell them the rest."

"This hall was standing before Tova's Falls was a village. It is centuries old. Some said it was a church dedicated to Tova, hence the name of the falls," Olinz said. "Lord Pilka couldn't tear it down, although it was used as a furniture workshop before the brothers moved in. They converted it into their refectory."

"Only a corner. As you can see, we take up a small piece. We hope to fill this hall."

"And how will you do that?" Dakuz asked in his usual surly tone.

"By spreading the legend of the spirit of Tova."

Olinz coughed. "The spirit is Tova?"

The lead monk shrugged. "It can be. The spirit doesn't talk, it just appears. Often in different aspects."

"Won't the spirit be displeased?" Quint asked.

Gallia took a step closer. "It has never uttered a word, only feelings. Feelings can't hurt anyone."

"But one can hurt another's feelings," Sandy said. Her first utterance on the tour.

Quint smiled, which seemed to irritate Gallia. Her appeal was sinking quickly during the exchange.

"We can have an early lunch," the lead monk said.

Lunch was simple. A meat stew, bread, butter, and a weak wine. Quint thought it to be quite forgettable and worse than most of their meals on the road. After the tour, the monks claimed they had no issue with his group joining theirs. The monks even admitted they could step aside if they had a say in creating new cloister rules. Quint rose when finished and walked along the walls, looking at the textures of the ancient stones.

§

Quint felt a shiver and seemed to be drawn into the wall. He looked back to see all movement had frozen in the hall. He was almost pushed by a force and stumbled into a lived-in room. It was warmer, with carpets covering the floors and overstuffed chairs.

"Sit," A tall, severe woman ordered. She was almost beautiful except for her angular features.

Quint had the urge to sit in one of the chairs.

"That's better," the woman said. She was ageless with white hair set off by bronze skin. Her clear blue eyes were more hubite than Quint imagined his own to be.

"Where am I?"

The woman laughed. It was almost a giggle. "You are no longer in the world," the woman said.

"Tova?"

She lifted her chin. "Some have called me that."

"You are the spirit of the mill?" Quint asked.

"You are supposed to be quaking, bowing down, and asking forgiveness to be such a mean and lowly thing."

"Why?" Quint asked.

"I don't really know," Tova said. "I've heard others tell their congregants those are my rules. I don't have any rules like that."

"You appear to them?" Quint asked. He thought he should be frightened, but this woman didn't make him afraid.

"I don't appear, but I sent spirits to stir them up. The spirits are my own creatures and only live for a few moments past their purpose."

"Which is?"

"To communicate with humans. Tizurek was so much better at that than me," she said. "We don't have much power these days."

"Your days are gone in the world. Few believe," Quint said.

"You believe. Don't tell me you don't."

Quint took a deep breath. "I believe that you, whoever you really are, stand before me. You have vastly more power than I do," Quint said, "despite your claiming to have lost it. Do you always change the truth to suit your situation?"

Tova sighed. "I am sorry you feel that way, but I had a hand in your creation, and in my own way, I led you here."

"What if I didn't go to Narukun?"

"You would have died, and I would have had to raise another. You see, I have a problem. The god you call Tizurek is lost, and I have raised you up to find him."

Quint blinked in disbelief. "How can I find a god, or whatever you are?"

"Denying my existence, still? A skeptic to the end?"

"I hope this isn't my end," Quint said. "I'll accept that you are an incredibly powerful entity that calls herself Tova, for now."

She shrugged. "That is good enough for me. I'd like you to find an entity that calls himself Tizurek. Your reward will be great power."

"I don't want power," Quint said.

"You are going to get it one way or another. I rather like the fact you don't seek it. I will give you a few clues that I have been able to glean. My visibility into your world is murky as yours would be into mine," Tova said. "Tizurek has sought refuge from his arch-enemy by becoming a resident in your time and place. He has vague memories of life here, but" she sighed, "you will find him and lead him here. The wall in my old house in your world is thin. When you leave, you will know the string to pass from one world to another. You do not have to restore his memories, although that will not restore his power. That can only be done here."

"What of the mill?" Quint asked.

"Oh, that. I'd like you to take up residence there for a time. Create a more stable cloister. It doesn't have to be a place of worship. I won't bother the inhabitants very much. My creatures will accept your presence. The monks will feel that."

"You said I'd have a few clues?"

Tova nodded. "I know he is on the continent of Votann and likely masquerading as a gran. He has white hair like me and gray eyes. Although we are both much older, Tizurek will appear like a man in his late forties." She favored Quint with a sly smile. "Will you do it?"

"His name?" Quint asked.

"He used the name Simo Tapmann, but he goes through names and identities since he still knows he is immortal and your kind are like a match, bursting into flame and dying a short time later. You don't have to rush to Votann any time soon."

Quint was wondering at this point what he had eaten to produce this dream. "How much time do I have to find him?"

"A lifetime. I can give you no more, but I feel you will take far less."

"I hope so. I have a life to live."

"You will," Tova said. "Along the way, you may achieve great things. Don't rush. You aren't ready yet, anyway."

"May? Everyone thinks I will."

"They have a different concept of 'great' than I do. I have told you enough. I would consider it a favor given, if you rededicate this church to Tova worship."

"What about Tizurek or Simo Tapmann? Can he be worshipped too?"

"In Tova's Falls, it is permissible to worship both of us. Rise so you won't fall."

Quint stood up, and the next moment he felt like he was pushed back and had to take a step to maintain his balance. He was facing the same wall as before his vision. He took his pocketknife and scratched a line in the rock he had been led to before turning to the rest of the group, still frozen.

Quint shivered. Was his vision more than a dream? He took a steadying breath before time had caught up to his mind.

"What do you think, Quint?" Dakuz said. "Shall we give this place a try?"

Quint fought with himself. Was the vision real? Did one of the spirits who inhabited the mill plant a dream in his mind? He thought of the string that would return him to Tova's presence. The string burst into this head. The threads and the weave of the string were nothing like any he had seen before.

"A moment, please," Quint said.

He turned back to the stone with the scratch and cast the string. The pushing feeling returned, and he was back in Tova's presence.

"You didn't believe me?" she asked.

Quint smiled. "I needed to make sure I had control over this dream. Even a little." He suddenly knew a different string filled with potential that wasn't of his world and found himself back in the hall.

He turned around. "Let's draw up an agreement. I'm sure Tova would be pleased." Quint smiled on the outside and was ice cold with fear on the inside. He instantly fought against being a religionist, but how could he deny Tova and Tizurek now?

§

The second tour of the mill was twice as long. Kozak split off from the rest to get a deeper look at the mill machinery. Having a working mill made sense when one was in the middle of a forest. Quint wondered what Pilka would want in return for operating the mill. Olinz seemed to think the market was large enough for two mills, but Kozak wasn't so sure when he returned. A specialty mill might be more appropriate for a cloister. He thought a return to furniture making might make sense, having the mill process unique wood species.

Quint wasn't a businessman, but he did have a feel for the trade, having spent his early youth as his wheelwright father's apprentice. He wondered what the current inhabitants of the mill had to say about reviving the operations.

Olinz, Gallia, and Quint's people sat down with the three senior monks in the ancient hall.

"We don't want to be overcome by you and your group," one of the monks said.

"My group is the same size as yours," Quint said. "There is currently room for all, but we will need to build more dormitories. Shall we have a council government?"

"We had an Elder running Parsun. It worked until he became senile. I don't know if they are even a cloister at this point," the monk who seemed to be the leader said. The man looked at Quint. "I'm afraid we can't accept you as our leader. Your youth and inexperience are disqualification enough."

"Then a council. I would like to sit on it since I am probably the most powerful wizard, but I don't feel the need to lead," Quint said. "Perhaps a council of five? Two from your group and two from mine who vote on a leader and a replacement. I will disqualify myself as the lead monk."

The three monks looked at each other and nodded. "We will agree to that. Perhaps you aren't so inexperienced after all."

"As long as I can practice my magic. I'm not a religionist like others in my group, but we would like a religionist faction within the cloister," Quint said.

The negotiating went on into the late afternoon, and it was time to return to Zimton. They were putting their notes together when an apparition emerged from a wall.

It was the form of a woman cloaked in golden mist. She took a few steps and stood looking at them. It wasn't Tova's face, Quint knew. He could feel a sense of well-being emanating from Tova's creature. The spirit dissipated in a cloud of sparkles.

Olinz bowed his head, as did a few of the monks. Gallia jumped to her feet. Sandy grabbed Quint's hand, but Kozak was the first to say something.

"Did you all experience the warmth that I did? That was no evil ghost," Kozak said.

"Peace and goodwill," Olinz said with a note of reverence. "Was that Tova?"

"Tova has a short life if that's the case," Quint said. He realized he shouldn't have spoken.

Gallia grunted. "I had the feeling we should convert this back into a church," she said. "I'll talk father into making it a condition of living here."

"I agree," the lead monk said. The other two nodded. "We've never felt such a strong feeling before. I'm sure it was acceptance of our joining to create a new cloister."

"We can discuss it further tomorrow. I think we have most of what we need," Quint said.

"I agree," Olinz said after a deep breath. "I think we have gotten Tova's message."

Kozak gave Quint a questioning look, but Quint had no answer he was willing to give in everyone's hearing, and he didn't want to talk about the experience on the ride back. Gallia was another matter. She wouldn't stop talking about the apparition and recounted the experience at least five times before they left Tova's Falls on the down-sloped path to Zimton.

The experience only confirmed Quint's meeting with Tova. He could never put it down to a momentary delusion.

"What else will we need to negotiate?" Sandy asked Quint as they rode together in the twilight.

"There are three parties to the agreement," Quint said. "We need to show our notes to Lord Pilka and incorporate his demands into the agreement. That takes precedence."

"I'm glad you came up with that on your own," Olinz said. "I think the old monk underestimates you, Brother Tirolo."

"Quint. You can call me Quint."

Olinz nodded. "You don't have the kind of airs I ascribe to master wizards. I know since Lord Pilka retains two of them."

"I don't think it would be a good idea to have Pilka's position in the cloister administered through them, then," Quint said.

"That might cause a fight, but Lord Pilka is a pragmatic man. He has needed to be with a domain that touches royal lands."

Kozak frowned. "Will he defend us against the Reds in Baxel?"

Gallia giggled. "Father hates the Reds."

"Gallia! Don't say such things," Olinz said.

"As long as he doesn't love the Greens, I hope we are aligned well enough," Dakuz said.

Quint used his hands to signal everyone to settle down. "I agree with Dakuz. We don't have to know Lord Pilka's alliances as long as he isn't our enemy."

"He isn't your enemy," Olinz said. "You can be sure of that."

They didn't say more on the topic but asked Olinz about Lord Pilka's domain the rest of the ride. It was dark when they arrived at the inn.

"I will bring the lord to you after breakfast. If he wishes to entertain you at his manor house, I will let you know," Olinz said.

Quint watched Olinz and Gallia disappear into the night. Everyone was tired enough to grab a few bites of snacks from the common room and take them to their rooms. Quint dressed for bed, laid back over the bed quilt, and stared at the ceiling. The day had been more alarming for him than the others knew.

His relationship with the world, and with some other world where gods lived, had changed him, and he didn't know how to handle it. Quint had kept the experience to himself, but he needed to tell someone, but who? Would anyone believe him? There was Grizak, Dakuz, or Sandy.

He wanted to tell Sandy, but his relationship with her was uncertain. Quint was uncomfortable about her expression of jealousy when Gallia showed up. Gallia had disqualified herself in his mind, and that was what he would share with Sandy. Grizak was too much the religionist to be tested on Quint's interpretation of his vision or whatever it was.

That left Dakuz, who was along for the ride. He was a monk, yet he wasn't. Quint considered him a teacher or a mentor who knew more about magic than him despite a relative lack of strings. Because of Dakuz's irascible behavior, Quint felt reticent to share with him, but he was the most objective of the three.

Quint dressed and stood in front of Dakuz's door. The glow of a magic light seeped from the bottom of the door. He knocked.

"Who wants to bother me?" Dakuz said from behind the door.

"Quint. I need to discuss something with you before we meet with Pilka."

After some grumbling, the door opened. Dakuz had thrown on his monk's robe. "Come in. It's got to be important if you're worked up enough to disturb me."

"It is," Quint said, walking in. "This is best talked about sitting down," he said to a standing Dakuz.

The older man shrugged and sat on his bed, his bare legs and feet sticking out from the bottom of the robe. "This had better be good."

"I don't know if it's good, but it is alarming," Quint told Dakuz about his experience with Tova.

Dakuz didn't laugh in Quint's face, which was a positive for Quint. "I noticed something," Dakuz said, "like a long blink, but my eyes were open. It happened twice in that room when you stood by the wall."

"You believe me? I thought you would scoff at my story."

Dakuz snorted and shook his head. "I saw the golden lady along with everyone else. Tova sent it?"

"Her creatures," Quint said. "They only last for moments, although moments to her might be something different than moments to us."

"What did Tova look like?"

"Ageless. She seemed larger than she might have been, radiating with the power she possesses. Beautiful, but in an angular way. Not a conventional beauty."

Dakuz smiled. "Like Pilka's daughter?"

Quint nodded. "Gallia is more conventional."

"Certainly, with plenty of curves," Dakuz said with a smile. "Your Sandiza's beauty is less conventional, but she can't let it blossom as a monk, can she? I don't think she was impressed by Gallia."

"That isn't the point of my visiting you."

"Yes," Dakuz said. "Your quest. When will you start?"

"Finding Tizurek? Not for now," Quint said. "Tova said I wasn't ready, and I can tell that I'm not. She mentioned an arch-enemy, too. I don't even know if Tizurek's bane is in our world or not."

"Perhaps something to find out in time. You are a religionist now?"

Quint stood. "I'm amazed you can sit there without jumping up and down and calling me a heretic!"

"I've never not been a religionist, Quint," Dakuz said. "But I'm not a fervent religionist like Grizak and his boys. What would you call yourself now?"

Quint sat back down and put his head in his hands. "I don't know. More like you, I suppose. I'm not a Tova or a Tizurek worshipper, especially now that I know they are both limited. That wasn't something I was expecting."

"I'd watch what you say about that. You think they are limited, and I think they are diminished, somehow, but she pulled you into a different world. Her power is vastly superior to anything in this world, limited or not. You'll have to remember that about Tova and Tizurek when you meet him. If I were you, I would make sure you know more about the conflict between Tizurek and his arch-enemy before you act."

Quint groaned. "How am I going to do that?"

"You are the researcher, Quint. You'll have to expand your capabilities and extend yourself as much as possible."

"Will you help?"

Dakuz laughed. "You know the answer to that. I'll help you prepare, but

I may be dead and gone before you can seek out Simo Tapmann."

"Or we may be ready and sailing to Volcann in less time than you think," Quint said.

"Let's not get ahead of ourselves. I suggest you keep your quest between you and me for now."

Quint nodded. "That is why I came here. As you put it, Grizak is too fervent, and Sandy is too…"

"You haven't settled on your relationship with her, so that I would be careful. Aren't you attracted to Gallia? If you are successful at the mill, Pilka may be seeking you out as a husband."

"I'm not going to lead the mill," Quint said.

Dakuz laughed. "I'm not god and not proficient at predictor strings, but I can promise you, the mill will be yours to command in short order. It's part of your destiny."

Dakuz's declaration brought out a sigh. "Can't we call it something other than a mill? It is a portal to Tova's world."

"For you, sir," Dakuz said. "Ask Pilka for a cloister name, and he will start out supporting you for leader."

"I don't need to lead, but I'd like to put us in the best position with the lord. I'll do just that."

§§§

CHAPTER TWENTY-FOUR

After breakfast the following day, Pilka took the seat at the head of the table in the private room and reviewed the agreement notes. Pilka demanded nothing but gratitude. He still would be building a mill downstream from the cloister with new machinery, making clear his relationship with the new cloister was of its prime benefactor.

"We'd like a name for our new cloister," Dakuz said, winking at Quint. "Since you are taking such a grand role in its creation, we thought you should be the one to decide what to call it."

"I talked to Olinz and my daughter about the golden apparition and the wonderful feeling the spirit emanated. In the tradition of Narukun cloisters, we will name it by modifying real words. Seensist stands for seeing a Sister making magic. Parsun was from looking into the setting sun from the cloister grounds. My impression is that the cloister could be a derivative of the feeling given by her spirit. Feel Tova. Toff means a place of refuge or a strong emotion in Narallian, so if we combine Tova and Toff, we combine common and Narallian; the name should be Feeltoff."

"Feltoff," Dakuz said. "Can't make it too obvious."

"Feltoff," Pilka said, smiling. "I like it, and it's easier to say. I will insist that you call the mill-making operation Pilka Works. Internally, but not to customers. I'd like my sponsorship to be noted somewhere."

Quint thought the names were both bargains for what Pilka was doing. "I agree. We will present that to the current monks," Quint said.

The monks accepted the name and the agreement. Pilka officially chartered Feltoff Cloister in a short ceremony in Zimton.

Grizak and Donnie returned with Pilka's son a few days later and entered the mill's courtyard.

"Parsun is no more," Grizak said. "Once the wall fell, the monks began stripping the stone for their personal building projects. Once that happened, local villages started doing the same thing. The old monks moved out, and Parsun is now a ruin."

"Are they going to come here?" Kozak asked.

"I doubt it," Pilka's son said. "I think all have retired and are joining in stripping the old cloister so they can build their cottages nearby."

"We knew it was going to happen," one of the original monks said. "It was a matter of time." He shook his head. "It's sad it has finally come to that."

Quint and Dakuz told the story of the creation of Feltoff Cloister. Grizak and Donnie would be founding members, along with the original monks and Quint's group. Dakuz described the appearance of the golden spirit.

Grizak sighed. "If I was only here to behold the beneficence of Tova," he said.

"It could happen again," Dakuz said. "A reason to stick around. We will reconvert the hall into a church dedicated to Tova and Tizurek."

"As well we should," Grizak said with a snort.

Pilka's son continued to his father's manor house to report.

"What do we do now?" Grizak asked.

"Get to work," Dakuz said. "Kozak is drawing up plans for a larger cloister now that the church will take away some of the usable space."

Grizak looked around. "We need a defensive wall," he said.

"I've included it. It's a pity Parsun is so far away. We could use some of their stone," Quint said.

"Mostly brick in Parsun," Donnie said. "And a lot of the brick has deteriorated being exposed to the sea. The monks did little maintenance for the past few centuries. I'd never use those materials. There should be plenty of stone in the mountain quarries."

"There are three quarries within a day's cart journey," one of the original monks said. "We might have to repair some roads, but we didn't need to expand when we first arrived."

"Then it's time to plan and then time to work," Quint said. "When Kozak is finished with the basic plan, we will have to hire a builder. Kozak's next task is to get the mill running, and we will have to train ourselves to operate it."

"Then I have some good news," the monk said. "The village is still home to some of the millworkers. They are older now but have already offered to train us again if we start the mill."

"Perhaps we can also get some workers from the village," Quint said, "at least until we have monks arriving to help us set up the cloister."

"Do you want to do that?" Grizak asked.

Quint sighed. "It is necessary. We can't depend on Lord Pilka's largesse for the rest of our lives."

§

The courtyard was filled with tables celebrating the start-up of the Pilka Works. Walls of various heights and stages circled the mill with lots of growing room included. Kozak received most of the accolades and deservedly so.

Quint had learned a lot about machinery and making things. His father was a wheelwright but a solitary one, and Pilka Works had enough capacity for milling and shaping wood to make many wheels at once if the monks decided to do so.

Before expanding the business, Feltoff Cloister would begin by selling milled wood to builders and furniture makers. Grizak, Quint, and Dakuz were on the council, and they found that the original monks weren't interested in running the cloister as much as running away from Parsun. They were happy with the new situation and encouraged by what they told Quint to be forward decision-making.

Grizak took on the duties of the caretaker of Tova's Chapel, as the church was now being called. He and a few bodyguards were blessed to see another golden apparition. The positive feeling remained and Grizak took it as an acceptance by Tova of what they were doing at Feltoff.

Villagers began to arrive for services, which another of the bodyguards volunteered to conduct. The chapel was still too large for the congregation, but Grizak decided to partition off part of the chapel and begin collecting religious works and histories. Dakuz helped him select the proper works.

Quint and another Seensist monk began teaching self-defense to the monks. He didn't consider himself a warrior, but he had been trained to handle weapons, and the threat from Pinzleport and possible threat for Baxel, the capital, remained.

For a few more months, there were increasing buyers of the mill's output,

Tova's congregation grew, and a few younger monks from Parsun began to arrive. All the old ones stayed behind. Quint spent some of his limited spare time with Sandy, continuing Narallian lessons and teaching strings to the monks. Andreiza Hannoko still pursued Grizak without much success. Donnie had been seen escorting Gallia Pilka around Tova's Falls occasionally.

The progress was steady, and everyone seemed to feel at ease as they built Feltoff Cloister until a familiar face rode into the crowded courtyard with six attendants.

Shinzle Bokwiz was taken to Quint's workroom, a small unused side chamber that was part of the ancient chapel.

"We have heard of your great work," Bokwiz said as he bounced into the chamber. Quint was repelled by Bokwiz's familiarity.

Quint looked up, surprised at Bokwiz's nerve to pretend nothing had happened. Quint was working with one of the original monks on his strings.

"We will meet again tomorrow," Quint said, dismissing his student. "See if Dakuz has any time." Quint looked up at Bokwiz, not feeling that the man deserved enough respect to stand. "Why are you here? Did you get kicked out of Seensist?"

Bokwiz smiled. It seemed more sinister than before, but Quint put that down to his imagination. "No. I'm still an advisor to Brother Croczi. We thought I'd be a better person to see how you are doing. We've known of your cloister for a few weeks."

"It's not my cloister," Quint said, "although I'm on the council. We haven't developed any factions yet." He couldn't keep the anger out of his voice.

"You seem to be a bit touchy. I suppose it is understandable since we didn't part on particularly good terms." The sentiment didn't seem the least bit regretful. All Quint could see was Bokwiz's continued arrogance.

"I wouldn't call it good at all," Quint said.

"I was interested in the golden goddess. Some say Tova has returned, and I had to come from Seensist to verify the rumor. You can understand my interest."

"Are you a religionist? I'm not sure you are," Quint said.

"Oh, I am. Did the goddess truly appear?"

"Not in this cloister," Quint said. "We have seen apparitions, but the spirits only last a few moments before disintegrating. There are witnesses, but it appears the truth has been stretched as it made its way to you in Seensist."

The room seemed to chill, and a man made of hazy mist appeared. The apparition frowned as it looked at Bokwiz. The frown sent shivers through both men. The spirit burst apart, the mist bouncing like tiny shards of ice on the stone floor before everything disappeared.

Bokwiz took a step back. "It frowned at me, but not you. I was so cold." His voice was hoarse with fear.

Quint was glad for the spirit and the fact that Tova had helped him out. He was still in part of the original church, and the spirits never appeared far from the old chapel. That seemed to be the limit to Tova's power, or she followed her own rules.

"Perhaps you need to return to Seensist and reassess where your loyalties should lie," Quint said.

"You saw it, too?"

"I did and felt the coldness of its message. This was my first time experiencing a cold apparition. The golden spirits exude warmth and comfort. I would term this experience as a warning, Bokwiz. You are not welcome here, and I would prefer if you left the cloister now. I believe Tova disapproves of your presence," Quint said.

Bokwiz's eyes grew with alarm. "Is Tizurek here, too?"

"How would I know?" Quint said. "All the spirits do is appear and emanate an emotion or a feeling. Your message was very plain."

"I will return to Tova's Falls," Bokwiz said, "but I will have to prepare for my return in Seensist first. I have some penance to do." Surprisingly, he bowed to Quint and left the building and the cloister without a word to his former congregation, taking his escort with him.

Dakuz was on his way through the chapel and looked back at Bokwiz, who merely nodded to Dakuz on his exit out of the cloister.

"Someone said Bokwiz was here, but he looked like he had seen a ghost," Dakuz said.

"An apparition appeared in the workroom. It was a man, and he frowned at Bokwiz. We both felt shivers."

"Tova didn't approve?"

Quint shook his head. "Not at all. I told Bokwiz that Tova wasn't happy he was here and Bokwiz's face turned even whiter. He really is a religionist, and he has been chastised by the goddess he follows."

Dakuz clucked his tongue. "I hope he feels like he is headed for the underworld on his way back to Pinzleport."

"I hope he does, too. I'm concerned his experience will only increase the curious and the pious. We could be overloaded with sightseers," Quint said.

"Perhaps we should build an external entrance into a section of the chapel for visitors," Dakuz said. "Maybe we should charge people to take a look."

Quint frowned. "That wouldn't be appropriate, would it?"

"It would cut down on the curious. The pious might be offended, but I imagine there isn't a good way to tell them apart," Dakuz said. "Serve them right."

"Who?" Quint asked.

"The people like Bokwiz. They don't have a right to be here."

Quint pursed his lips. "I'm sure he is a true religionist. I wasn't convinced before he saw the apparition, but I am now. What if the experience changes him?"

"I don't think the charlatan would change," Dakuz said.

"We probably have a difference of opinion," Quint said.

Dakuz darkened. "It wouldn't be the first time," he said, stalking out of the workroom.

Quint felt worse about his talk with Dakuz than he did about sending Bokwiz out. He knew Dakuz could be irascible, but he didn't think his friend would be so sensitive. He could easily live without seeing Bokwiz again, but Dakuz was another story. Quint needed someone unafraid to challenge him.

He walked around the little room and slapped one of the stone walls. He wasn't seeking inspiration from Tova, but Quint was seeking internal guidance. He hoped he had found it and walked into the courtyard where Dakuz was in animated conversation with Kozak.

Quint listened to the conversation without commenting.

"An external entrance and exit that doesn't allow the visitor to enter the cloister. Religionists may want special privileges, and I don't want to give them any," Dakuz said. He glanced defiantly at Quint.

"Let's not charge them for looking," Quint said.

Dakuz grunted.

Quint continued. "But that doesn't mean we can't provide them with a meal or snacks for their visit. I don't think Tova would mind caring for her followers."

Dakuz brightened. "We can open a shop with souvenirs or sell written accounts of encounters with apparitions."

"For the pious and the curious," Quint said. "I think the council should discuss it. Perhaps the popularity might subside after a while."

"Not a chance," Grizak said. "There are cloisters in North Fenola that claim to have relics from Tova and Tizurek. They charge believers to see them, but I agree with Quint. I'd rather not have strangers milling about the courtyard when we are a working cloister, milling wood and making things. One ancient wall is as good as another. The apparitions don't come through walls; they just appear."

"Then let's meet," Dakuz said. "Perhaps Sandy and Andy can run the thing." He turned to the carpenter. "What do you think?"

"I know just the route to take," Kozak said. "If the tour doesn't work, we can turn the passages into furniture storage."

§§§

CHAPTER TWENTY-FIVE

THE COUNCIL AS A GROUP WAS MORE ENTHUSIASTIC than Quint, but councils were a ruling group, and Quint accepted their enthusiasm. The two women were ecstatic about having a project of their own. The two boys agreed to help conduct tours, but both wanted to learn to be working monks and convinced Sandy that they would work halftime.

Kozak designed everything simply, and the pathway was protected, secure, and large enough to be converted into something useful later. Andy thought accounts of spirits could be posted along the route to give their patrons a better feel for their walk around the pathway than simply touching an old stone wall.

Two months later, when the weather began to turn cold, the pathway was finished. Kozak crafted a wooden visitors' building outside the cloister with a kitchen staffed by locals from Tova's Falls. Quint took Lord Pilka and his family for the first tour.

Pilka laughed after he read the first posted account. "You'll make more money doing this than your millwork!"

"Perhaps," Quint said. "But having two streams of support is better than one."

"Three streams. Don't forget I am a contributor, too."

"How could I forget?" Quint said with a smile, but there was one matter he had to clear up. "You are fine with us not charging admission? We went ahead on this without your permission."

"The council runs the cloister. I promised not to interfere. Your little food shop and the souvenirs are more than enough to support whatever you spent on this charming route."

Quint wouldn't use the term "charming," but Kozak had put some thought into the design, and the builders still working on the cloister walls were excited to make something more decorative than the rest of Feltoff Cloister.

As they approached the stretch of the external wall of the chapel, Quint felt his hair rise. Another visit to Tova? His fears were calmed when a golden spirit different from the previous ones appeared and spread the warmth he had felt before. She smiled at Pilka before she vanished in a cloud of golden motes.

Pilka took a step back and put his hands to his heart. "The rest of you saw that?" he said, breathing heavily.

Andy stepped forward. "Now you can add your own experience to our wall of visitations," she said.

"The feeling," Gallia said. "I'm not as religious as my father, but that feeling of warmth was heavenly. Literally. It was just as touching as the first one I saw."

"We have done the right thing," Lord Pilka said.

Dakuz patted Quint on the shoulder. Quint looked into the smiling eyes of Dakuz. "Told you," Dakuz said.

"That is the first spirit sighting since before we started this pathway," Quint said. "It is different for us than it was for the original monks, although their experience wasn't negative."

"No, it wasn't, but you know that Tova approves," the former lead monk said.

Pilka put his hand on the wall. "On the other side is the chapel. I wish we could open that up, but," he shook his head, "I think you are right. It would disturb the cloister and impinge upon the chapel's atmosphere as a holy place."

They walked back, speaking in hushed tones, but the voices picked up when they emerged close to the visitors' building.

"Shall we test the local fare?" Lord Pilka said to his wife, daughter, and son.

Quint had already done sufficient tasting and let other council members host Pilka. Dakuz ran to catch up to Quint as they had to walk around the newly built walls to the main gate.

"A success?" Dakuz asked with a grin.

"Not on my account," Quint said. "Tova had everything to do with it. I hadn't expected her to lend us a hand."

"Or whatever that apparition was made of," Dakuz said.

Before they reached the gate, Donnie stopped them. "A messenger has arrived. It's from the king of Narukun."

§

The messenger held the reins of his horse, watching workers move wood and build walls. Quint walked up to him.

"You have a message for me?" Quint asked.

"Quinto Tirolo, formerly of Racellia on South Fenola?"

Quint nodded. "That's me."

"You are a lot younger than I thought. I am Lieutenant Garswicz of the Royal Guard," the messenger said. He handed Quint an envelope made from heavy blue paper embossed with a golden device. "Our majesty, King Finir Boviz, extends this invitation."

"Invitation?" Quint asked. He looked quizzically at Dakuz and Donnie after he took the message and opened the sealed envelope. "I am invited to a private lunch meeting with King Boviz at his palace in Baxel in four days." Quint looked at the messenger. "How long does it take to get to the capital?"

"Three days. You'll need to leave before noon tomorrow."

"When are you leaving?"

"I was planning to immediately leave after I had something to eat. You are to leave no earlier than tomorrow so you will arrive at the proper time. I'm sure the locals know the way," the messenger said.

"Then I will go with you today," Quint said.

The messenger's eyebrows rose. "But you'll get there too early. It will be against protocol."

"Too early for what kind of protocol?" Quint asked.

The messenger didn't respond.

Quint tapped the envelope on his palm. "I don't know if you are truly one of the king's messengers. I don't even know if the device on the envelope is the royal one. So, since I've never been to Baxel, I'm leaving with you so I won't lose my way or run into bandits. Surely, you would like a little more protection."

"I-I don't need protection."

"You are going to get it anyway, Lieutenant Garswicz," Dakuz said.

In a little more than an hour, Dakuz, Donnie, Olinz, and Quint rode out with Garswicz. The lieutenant wasn't particularly happy, and a couple of hours later, neither was Dakuz, but they were well out of the mountains, taking the north road out of Tova's Falls, leaving the council, the monks, and Pilka's domain.

Olinz was well-armed. Donnie wasn't very adept with a sword but knew archery and carried a bow. Quint wore armor and traveled with a sword strapped to his saddle. The Lieutenant had the best horse and worst offense, carrying a serviceable long knife and a sword. He admitted the sword was for decoration and would only last a few blows. His best defense was the swift horse.

Quint kept his attention to their route. Olinz and Donnie had been to Baxel before and knew enough to keep the messenger honest.

The messenger stopped at a town and went directly to an inn. It wasn't the best inn, but Olinz identified it as suitable. They had an early dinner, and the messenger said his horse had traveled enough for the day and went to his room.

"We take turns watching him," Quint said. "Should we watch him here or keep an eye on his horse?"

"The stable would be better," Olinz said. "Garswicz treasures his horse. I'll take the first watch until midnight."

"I'll take the second," Quint said.

Quint had taken his boots off when Olinz walked into his room. "The lieutenant didn't waste any time. He's gone."

"Do you have any suggestions?" Quint asked.

"Return to Tova's Falls?"

"Maybe we should go to Baxel after all. I doubt if the invitation is genuine, but it wouldn't hurt to see the capital. Dakuz and I have never been. We only need to stay for a few days and then return. I'm worried that if we follow Garswicz, he could lead us to assassins."

"Knowing your history, you may be right. Shall we get more miles ahead of any pursuit?"

Quint consulted with Dakuz and Donnie, and the four of them decided to ride to the next town. Donnie brought up the fact that Garswicz knew where they were staying.

Dakuz grumbled and took a blanket from his bed, cut it up for more padding on the seat of the saddle, and had a stableman help him secure it before they left.

Olinz knew the way. The road was well traveled all the way from the town to the capital, and there were plenty of travelers in both directions. As the evening wore on, fewer were on the road, and they finally came to the town that Olinz had expected.

Dakuz looked exhausted, and it had been some time since Quint had ridden for such an extended time. Olinz signed in with a different name and paid for their rooms. Quint helped Dakuz up the stairs to their shared room, and they both fell asleep as soon as they got into their beds.

Breakfast was a quick affair. After checking the shape of their horses, they left the town, and now armed with a recently surveyed map, they headed northwest toward Baxel. Olinz suggested taking an unconventional route that would still get them to the capital the day before the lunch, just in case the invitation was genuine.

No route was unconventional to Quint since he had never been so far from Seensist Cloister. The traveling was a little faster on the third day since Dakuz's saddle pad helped him endure the journey.

Baxel was a bit of a disappointment to Quint. Nornotta, the capital of Gussellia and Bocarre, was bigger, but the king's palace put the other cities to shame. The towers were made of white polished stone and cranes and scaffolding enveloped the southeast end.

Donnie, who had been to the center of the city more than Olinz, found an inn close to the main square but off the main thoroughfares. Quint thought it would be best to get the rejection over, so Dakuz and Quint walked to the main gate and presented the invitation to the guard station.

"I am Quinto Tirolo," Quint said. He handed the invitation to the guard. "I received this some days ago in Tova's Falls under odd circumstances and decided I would visit Baxel before the date on the invitation if it were genuine. I expect it not to be."

The guard examined the royal crest. Quint glanced at the device on the guard's chest, and they looked the same. "Stay here. I'll slip into the palace and see."

The guard walked briskly across the large courtyard and disappeared in a ground-level door next to the main entrance that was up about twenty steps.

A uniformed man in a white wig accompanied the guard back to the station.

The wigged official looked at Dakuz. "You are Tirolo?"

Dakuz gave the official half a smile. "No, the young man is. I'm merely a traveling companion."

"The invitation is genuine, but the courier sent two weeks ago was found deceased along a lonely stretch of road with the invitation missing. His death is a tragedy," the official said, sighing. "We are surprised you ended up with this." The courtier handed the invitation back to Quint. "His Majesty hasn't replaced your luncheon on his calendar, and now that you are here, we invite you to come. You should find better clothes to wear."

"I will," Quint said. "Shall I be early?"

"Ten minutes will suffice." The official nodded to the guard and returned to the palace, but he climbed the steps this time, entering through the elevated main floor doors.

"I shall be on duty at the proper time tomorrow," the guard said. "I will recognize you. The invitation didn't mention companions, so anyone accompanying you must wait here until your luncheon is over."

"I understand," Quint said. He was used to being underestimated.

On the way back to the inn, they passed a clothing shop with fancy clothes in the window.

"We might as well get this over now," Dakuz said.

They walked inside, and after a half-hour of rejecting overly fancy clothing, Quint settled on a black and gray outfit that was simple and more fit for a visiting monk, in his opinion. He declined to purchase a wig.

Donnie and Olinz were in the inn's common room, swapping stories. Quint wondered what kind of stories Donnie had to tell, but the pair didn't look bored by the wait.

"Shopping? Was the invitation real?" Olinz asked.

"It was. The original messenger was found dead at the side of the road," Dakuz said. "The messenger was an imposter and would have most likely led us into an ambush just as we suspected."

"We aren't safe anywhere," Quint said.

"Speak for yourself," Olinz said. "What we don't know is who is behind the messenger. Is it from the south or from the capital?"

"Maybe I'll find out tomorrow. It shouldn't be the king if the courtier were honest with me."

"Not a guarantee," Dakuz said. "But you'll find out. We will be on the square with the horses, ready to leave as soon as you walk out of the palace."

"I'd appreciate that," Quint said.

§§§

CHAPTER TWENTY-SIX

THE BAXEL PALACE WAS GRANDER INSIDE than even Nornotta's imperial palace. Quint was ushered along by a different wigged courtier, a shorter, squatter individual with his brown hair leaking out from the sides of the wig.

The king's private dining room was on the next floor, but the main floor was two floors high, so it was, in Quint's mind, the third floor. When Quint was shown in for the "private" luncheon, he was confronted with six other diners with place settings for four more. The king's place at the head of the table was empty.

"This is the guest of honor," the courtier said. "May I have the pleasure to introduce you to Brother Quinto Tirolo of the newly established Feltoff Cloister in Tova's Falls. It is in the mountainous part of Lord Pilka's domain.

One of the attendees snorted and said, "Pilka." Quint didn't like the derisive demeanor, but he tried not to show it.

The courtier introduced the other men. They were all ministers. Quint hoped he would remember their names.

"The king!" A guard proclaimed as he stepped through a side door. The empty seats were quickly filled before the king entered the room.

The others rose, but Quint was still standing, so he was ahead of everyone else until they gave the king a salute and bowed. Quint was caught off guard by the salute, a fist to the chest, and the arm extended along with the fingers. He hoped his bow was good enough.

"Your first time at court?" one of the attendees asked Quint.

Quint was sure the attendee was being rude, but he played along. "It certainly is," Quint said. "I've never been in such a palace before."

"Are all the monks at Feltoff country bumpkins like you?" another lord said.

"Lords," the king said with a tone of reproof. "Be seated."

Quint took his seat midway down one side when he saw his name scrawled on a card at his place. Luckily, there wasn't a ceremony attached to the seating, so Quint sighed quietly.

"You have met Brother Tirolo?" King Finir Boviz asked.

"We have been introduced, Your Majesty," a lord said. "Met? Not really."

"I assembled this lunch because of the issues that might arise from a Cloister in Lord Pilka's domain," the king said. "Brother Tirolo has claimed that the old structure on the property dates back thousands of years and has been graced by sightings of the goddess Tova." The king looked at Quint. "Give us a quick introduction and history before you describe one of the visitations. You have witnessed them, my people tell me. We will eat while you talk."

Quint gave the briefest of personal histories. At his mention of being a master wizard, a few lords took deep breaths. Masters seemed to be intimidating to some of them. They gave him a few minutes to finish his lunch.

Quint continued a description of the present conditions at Feltoff Cloister. "I have been present for a few sightings. The spirits or apparitions are not Tova. They emanate an emotion. Perhaps Tova or some other spiritual influence initiates them, but they disintegrate after a few moments, leaving nothing behind."

"Could they be created with a psychic string? You are a master, after all. Could you have created the illusions to make a name for yourself?" one of the unkind lords asked.

"No," Quint said plainly. "The apparitions appeared before the monks ever moved in and before I arrived in Tova's Falls. The apparitions have different appearances, some male, but usually female. Their reactions are minimal. None can talk, and they don't last long. I don't consider them human, but spiritual artifacts."

"You believe Tova is behind them?" King Boviz asked.

"Again, I don't know. I have researched psychic strings and have never encountered any strings that do anything similar."

"Certainly, you've found mind control strings."

Quint sighed and nodded. "I have. There is a string that can be used to plant a spurious memory. I can't make one, but I suppose a master wizard could implant a suggestion to a single individual. Still, these apparitions can appear to groups of people who all describe the same experience. I would know if I was being manipulated," Quint said.

"Unless you were doing the manipulating," the same lord said.

"Not before I ever arrived," Quint said.

"I understand you have started conducting tours?"

"Partial tours," Quint said. "We have a visitor's shop that sells snacks and drinks. We don't charge for the tours. The cloister was being inundated with visitors. We don't let them into the cloister grounds but take them to an external wall. An apparition has been seen at that spot. We can channel the curious and the pious away from the day-to-day activities of the cloister. That is the principal purpose of the tours."

"I see," the king said. "Some of us were surprised you were able to attend the luncheon today," King Boviz said.

"I was told the original messenger was found dead on the route to Tova's Falls. Another took his place. I wasn't sure about him, so we left in the afternoon when he had arrived. The man claimed his name was Lieutenant Garswicz."

"That was the dead man's name," the king said. "Go on."

"When he fled at our first inn in the middle of the night, we decided to travel to Baxel as quickly as possible to arrive before my enemies could get organized. It was a successful strategy."

"Obviously," one of the other attendees said.

The king looked solemnly at the attendees. "I did not kill one of my own messengers to lure Brother Tirolo into an ambush. As the king of Narukun, I don't need to do that. But the Red organization has joined the Greens in Pinzleport on a project to end Tirolo's life." Boviz looked at Quint. "You know this?"

"I do. I will take a random route back to Tova's Falls," Quint said. "We are improving Feltoff Cloister and will have strong defenses."

"Like Seensist?" King Boviz asked.

The king knew everything.

"Seensist is strong enough to defend itself from an external force, but nothing is strong enough when the leadership of the cloister was Red and Green sympathizers and let faction fighters inside the cloister. My little band of followers decided to leave Seensist once the religionist sponsor gained the title of head prior of the council and revealed himself to be a secret member of the Red Faction. That was when it was time for me to leave for the good of the Cloister."

The antagonist diner snorted yet again. "For the good of the Cloister," he muttered.

The king raised his finger at the comment, and the courtier sat up straighter, visibly chastened by the Narukun monarch.

"You have a problem with the Red faction?" Boviz asked.

"Not really," Quint said. "I am against the Green's authoritarian bias. I believe people are happiest when they are left alone as much as possible to make what they will of their lives."

"Do you have a problem with the monarchy?" King Boviz asked.

Quint felt that was why he was summoned to the king's presence. "Not in principle. Someone must administer the armed forces, the social services, and most important, the laws that preserve the right to a relatively free life."

The King pursed his lips. "And that is where the nib of the problem lies. Who defines what 'relatively free' means."

"I agree, Your Majesty. The Greens advocate a very restricted vision of the public's freedom. As I understand them, the Reds have a more expansive view."

"It is deeper than that, Brother Tirolo. I want you and your friends to spend some time in the palace, protected, and discuss your philosophies with my staff. You can be as honest as you want, and I won't get my feelings hurt. The only boundary would be your advocacy of a revolution." The king stared at Quint. "Everyone has their eyes on you. Your role in the world seems robust, but predictor strings are inconclusive as to the how."

Quint looked at the eyes on him, waiting for him to respond. "I will be happy to do so if my friends, who are staying just off the square, are allowed to join me."

The king nodded at an officer by the fanciness of his uniform. The man left. Quint guessed he was sent to summon his friends. At that, King Boviz rose and left the room.

Quint answered a few questions from the ministers, but his presentation covered everything they would ask him, and he had to repeat himself.

The courtier who had escorted Quint to the luncheon arrived with his three companions in tow.

"I will take you to a suite in the palace. It might be where all of the interviews will take place."

"Interviews?" Quint asked.

"The king didn't tell you. He doesn't know what to do with you, and you will discuss various subjects with Narukun's leading lights. Hopefully, he will know what to do after you are finished."

The suite had five bedrooms. One was being converted into a meeting room when they walked in. Everything was what one would expect to find in a king's palace.

"Now, what happened?" Olinz asked.

Quint told them everything in detail, including the antagonistic comments. "King Boviz seemed to be a neutral party to it all. He said I would better know the difference between the Reds and the Greens, but he expanded that to all philosophies."

"That is another way of saying he is as much afraid of you as the others," Dakuz said. "But he wants to understand you and your thoughts before deciding what to do with you."

"You are with me in the palace for protection," Quint said. "However, we know no place is safe if we don't control it. We need to be prepared for assassination attempts in these rooms, and anywhere else we go."

"Inside and outside the palace and all the way back to Feltoff," Donnie said.

§

Three visitors arrived before dinner. Quint peeked into the bedroom that was converted to a meeting room with a table for ten.

"I have nothing to add that you can't tell me later," Olinz said. "I'll guard the door from the sitting room."

"You are invited along with the rest," Quint said.

"I know," Olinz said with a smile.

The visitors spread some papers on the table. Quint and Dakuz brought paper and pencils, but Donnie was good at observing.

Introductions were made, and of the three individuals, one was a leader of the Red faction, another was a religionist teaching at the Baxel Royal

University, and the third was an aide to King Boviz, who introduced himself as Phandiz Crider.

"What is your basic philosophy?" the aide asked Quint.

"He's a religionist. That's a wasted question," the professor said.

"I wouldn't consider myself a religionist," Quint said. "I'm not sure what I consider myself. As I told King Boviz earlier today, I'm more interested in allowing people of all factions the opportunity to live a free life. Government should lightly govern."

"King Boviz wouldn't like that," Phandiz Crider said.

"Why not? The more freedom, the fewer complaints by the common citizen. It makes for less unrest among the people, but I'm not so sure. Those in power like the approach," Quint said, turning to the Red leader.

"I can see your point, but how would you govern under those circumstances?"

Quint frowned. "I can't answer that. I have no idea how a government works. I just know how I'd like to be governed. You overestimate my abilities."

"But your potential…" Crider said.

"Is potential and nothing more," Quint said. "Whatever I am in the future, I'm not the same person today, and I'm not sure those casting predictor strings have any true idea of what I'll be like. I might be a power-hungry would-be tyrant in the future."

"That's not what the strings show," the professor said. "They only tell us you will be prominent throughout the world."

"The world," Quint said with a laugh. "I'm an obscure wizard. If it weren't for the predictor strings, I would still be at Seensist learning Narallian."

"A teenage master is unique in the world," Crider said.

"You are a wizard," Quint said to the aide. "A master?" The way the aide made the statement revealed the man's wizardry background.

The aide raised his hands. "You have exposed me," Crider said with a smile.

"You cast the predictor strings?" Quint asked.

The man nodded. "It is as you have probably heard before. You will be influential in the world, but exactly how is shrouded. The haziness of the string is highly unusual, and that creates a great deal of anxiety among political people."

"It does indeed. We don't know what to do. Should we follow you? Are you a threat to our faction?" the Red leader said.

"So, it is better to kill me than to find out?" Quint said. "Do you see me bringing disaster to the world?"

The wizard cleared his throat. "Not to the world, exactly."

"To those in power, then?" Quint said.

"That would be more to the point," Crider said.

Quint had to think quickly. "If power is involved, then negotiations can be made. Am I correct?"

"But the time frame," the wizard said.

"And that makes everything uncertain," Quint said. "How far does your predictor string go?"

"Twenty, thirty years."

Quint shook his head. "Anything could happen between now and then. Could we shorten the timeframe? What will happen in the next year? In the next five years? With respect, that should be a more appropriate focus."

"You are saying that you promise not to do anything for five years?" the professor asked.

"No. Do you object to my basic philosophy? Are people free to believe what they want? Does King Boviz have any plans on seizing personal freedoms soon?"

The wizard shrugged. "No."

"Then we are presently aligned. Feltoff Cloister will be making its way by milling wood and making wood products. We already have a master carpenter and a mountain range full of raw materials," Dakuz said, looking at Quint. "We aren't going to be training soldiers or seeking to expand our influence in Lord Pilka's domain. The religionists within our order have access to the old Tova chapel."

"It would appear you are, for now, benign," the professor said.

"And what are your objections?" Quint asked the Red leader.

"I'm not sure I have any. The Red faction in Pinzleport is more aggressive in taking over the country with the cooperation of the Greens. We are opposed to any alliance with the Greens who want to displace the king with a council populated by their own people dictating rules to the citizens."

"Then what do we do now?" Quint asked.

"Educate you," Crider said. "You don't know how to rule. We should spend a few days teaching you what rule is like. If you are not experienced, perhaps we can prove that we aren't your enemy."

Quint had no objection, but Dakuz had a comment. "Are you going to demand concessions from Quint for decades into the future?"

The wizard pursed his lips and looked at his companions. "There has to be a price for the education."

"Then we can leave without Quint being influenced by you?" Dakuz asked.

"No. The alternative would be something worse."

"Imprisonment?" Quint asked.

"I wouldn't go that far," Phandiz Crider said.

"I would," the Red leader said.

"Then educate me," Quint said. "I'll risk being influenced." Quint turned to Dakuz. "I want to have options."

"Good decision. We will begin tomorrow. I will be involved, but I will bring government specialists with me," the wizard said.

The meeting was over, and the guests left. They were to be served dinner and had to remain in their suite.

Olinz was all ears at the description of the meeting. "So, all you have to do is listen to what they have to say, and then you can return to Tova's Falls and do whatever you'd like?"

"I don't believe that will work," Quint said. "It isn't something I would do, anyway. Predictor strings are pretty accurate in the immediate future. If I did something the opposite way, as I promised I would, they would be able to see that. I'm not bound to do exactly as they expect, but I must behave in a similar way. They say they will give me the benefit of the doubt."

"And hope they do just that," Dakuz said. "It's a dangerous game."

"That has proven to be true so far," Donnie said. "I don't have a problem with King Boviz's rule. I think Quint is right. Find the mutual benefits to promise on."

"I think I'm more interested in what kind of education they give me. You two don't have to join me, but I'd like Dakuz to sit in as a check on their facts. They called me inexperienced, and they were correct. I'm learning but not fast enough," Quint said.

A knock was followed by servants opening the door and setting up dinner for four in the meeting room. After they ate, Quint and the rest began to feel tired from the busy day and went to bed.

Quint tried to figure out what he wanted from the tutoring sessions but still didn't know when he woke up the following morning.

The morning session of the first day was all about defining political factions. Quint had a general idea about the Reds and the Greens, but his instructors compared specific policies. They emphasized that among the factions there were factions. Feodor Danko's sub-faction was the most aggressive of the Greens. Danko's group advocated total dominance, and Danko and his daughter dedicated their lives to subverting governments around the world. Feodor had just started in Racellia before the civil war stopped his progress.

"Does he want to lead the world government?" Quint asked.

All four of his instructors, three men and one woman, shook their heads. "No," the woman said.

"He recognizes his weakness as a charismatic leader, which Danko feels is a necessary trait to the success of a world empire."

"Danko didn't mention that in his book on empires," Quint said.

"You read that? A pile of drivel. Although much of the history was good, Danko had already rejected most of his analysis. I managed to get through most of it at university," the woman said.

"Have you ever met Feodor?" Quint asked the four of them.

They all nodded. "Danko spent most of his early years in Baxel and then became a nomad professor, working at different universities in Narukun spreading his philosophy. Plenty of people believed him, even after his views began to change into a strident version of Green political theory," the wizard from the previous day said.

The subject was changed, and the afternoon was spent on agricultural and commercial policy as applied to Narukun. Quint learned how restricted Lord Pilka really was as the lord of his domain. King Boviz kept a tighter hold on the Narukun economy than Quint had thought. Cloisters were exempt from most of the rules, and Quint had lived in a state of economic bliss while in Seensist. Feltoff Cloister would qualify the monks for the same kind of exemptions.

Quint's energy was drained from the inflow of so much information, but he asked Dakuz if any of the lecturers had applied a persuasion string to the conversation.

"Not that I could tell," Dakuz said. "Did you learn anything upsetting?"

Quint shook his head. "The Narukun economy isn't as free as I thought. There seem to be licenses for everything, and those come from guilds. I don't think the king has crossed a line up to this point, but I don't know how long the situation has existed."

Dakuz shrugged. "As long as I have been alive. It hasn't gotten worse, and it hasn't gotten better. The rules for licensing and the tax scheme aren't strict enough to cause much grumbling, except in pubs where the conversation is less guarded due to the mental lubrication of alcohol."

"But if the Green philosophy took over the court?" Quint asked.

"Commoners' backs would be broken," Olinz said. "Lord Pilka worries about the Green pressure from Pinzleport spreading northward. He wants to keep the heavy hand of the government from getting heavier. It has succeeded so far because he is not the only one complaining, and the kings of Narukun have kept the communication with the common folks open."

"That is something to learn from," Dakuz said, yawning. "Time for bed. Who has the first watch?"

"I do," Donnie said. "Wake me if I fall asleep." He laughed and settled down, reading a book from the suite's library.

§§§

CHAPTER TWENTY-SEVEN

"Get up," Donnie whispered in Quint's ear. "We have visitors, and my magic isn't strong enough to do anything."

"No," Quint said. "Your imagination isn't creative enough. What magic have they used? I don't smell the suite burning." Quint put his clothes on, grabbed his sword, and sniffed at the doorframe.

"We are locked in," Donnie said.

"If they know we are in here, then why are we whispering? How did they get in?"

"Through Dakuz's window. I was concentrating on the front door."

Quint looked at his own dark, locked window. There wasn't any movement, and aside from the random lantern, there was no light. "Shall we use the same way to leave?"

"What about Dakuz and Olinz?" Donnie asked.

"They are after them, too?"

Donnie nodded. "I think they came in through Dakuz's window. One of them dragged Olinz into the sitting room while I backed up against your door, waving my sword."

"Which is where, by the way?"

"They heated it with a string and made me drop it."

"I'll have to remember that," Quint said. "And Dakuz?"

"I think they put him to sleep when they entered his room."

"Then I can wake him up, but that may take a while. How many burglars?"

"Two."

Quint sighed. He thought two wouldn't be enough for his group, but the others were sleeping, and Donnie wasn't showing much talent as a sentry.

Quint tried the door and found it sealed. He would have done the same if he wanted to isolate someone.

The window frame was unlocked, which was a mistake on the part of the intruders. He looked across to the other windows and spotted a ladder leaning against the ledge underneath one of the rooms on the other side of the sitting room.

"First of all, we will get rid of that," Quint said.

He cast a string that moved the ladder backward, out from the wall, and let the attacker's escape route fall to the ground. They were on the third floor, the equivalent of four stories high. Lighting the dimmest of magic lights, Quint could see the ledge that ran underneath the bottom of the windows was barely large enough to shuffle from place to place. He would chance it.

"You can stay here for now," Quint said to Donnie before casting a strong shield. "If there are only two, I should undo the wood joining string the intruders cast on my door in a few minutes."

A fire spear lifted three stories from below, lapping against his shielded ankles. Quint could see some men dressed in black milling below them. Their spears weren't quite powerful enough to reach him, but his fire string should be able to warm them up in the cool night.

Quint didn't bother with a warning, and when another spear was sent up towards him, he returned fire, striking the attacker. The conflagration that developed gave Quint enough light to burn two more black-clad figures. He heard the cries of guards running to the intruders and redirected his attention toward rescuing his friends.

Quint quickly shuffled across to the open window the burglars had used and slipped into Dakuz's room. The wizard was sprawled on his bed, asleep. He heard voices in the sitting room, for they had let Dakuz's door open. He paused to listen.

"Do you think they got the kid?" one of the intruders asked the other.

"I think there was at least one attack from up here," the other said. "What shall we do?"

"Let's see if he came through the window," the first intruder said.

Quint didn't attack the two as they approached him but shrank against the wall behind Dakuz's door. He created a sleeping string and cast it once the pair were inside the bedroom. The two men dropped senseless to the floor. The glow of a string faded from one of the attacker's hands.

Quint bent over to check on them. They were asleep. He toyed with the idea of tossing them through the window but ended up locking the window instead. He untied Olinz, who had been leaning against a wall in the sitting room.

"They put Dakuz to sleep but kept me awake to ask questions."

"Let me get Donnie."

Once Donnie was freed and Dakuz was carried into the sitting room, Quint asked Olinz what questions he had been asked while Donnie tied the two intruders and gagged them. Quint observed the bindings and made sure Donnie secured their hands.

Someone unlocked the door to the suite. Three guards and Phandiz Crider rushed into the room.

"Are you all right?" he asked. "Is your friend alive?"

"Asleep as are the burglars. Did you catch the ones on the ground?"

"One got way, three are dead, and one is in custody," a guard officer said.

"Let me wake up Dakuz," Quint said. "He won't be able to help if he was the first one put to sleep."

"What's this?" Dakuz said, sitting up and blinking his eyes. "Assassins?"

"They are angry wizards, that's for sure," Donnie said. "They also underestimated Quint, as is probably usual."

"Indeed, they did," Crider said. "From what I gather, they overestimated their power."

Quint nodded. "Their fire spears could only reach my ankles. I have a little more reach."

"Three dead by fire," the king's wizard said. "I think killing you on the window ledge was their strategy if they bound your door shut. They succeeded in luring you to the ledge."

Quint shrugged. "I have no way of understanding what they are thinking. Is there any way of finding their faction while they are asleep?"

"We could strip them," the officer said. "Some factions are partial to identification tattoos."

Quint sighed. "Then let's get to work." He cast another sleep string at each intruder and let the guards do the stripping.

Both men had the red outline of a circle surrounding a smaller solid black circle on the inside of their lower arm close to the elbow.

"Do you know this?" Quint asked.

"The red circle identifies them as members of the Reds of Pinzleport, and the black circle means they are the militia of that faction," the officer said.

"Do you get many of those in Baxel?" the king's wizard asked the officer. He seemed to be as clueless as Quint.

"Not many. The Baxel members of the Reds don't use tattoos, but that doesn't mean they aren't helping," the officer said.

"A Baxel faction that would willingly cooperate with the Pinzleport Reds?" Quint asked. "Someone had to let the assassins onto the palace grounds. They reached our room on a very long ladder."

"Assembled on the palace grounds, I was told," the officer said.

"Really?" the king's wizard said.

It was apparent Crider wasn't particularly well informed on what was going on. Quint didn't know if the wizard was acting, but if he was, his performance was convincing.

"They also had to know where we were staying and which room Quint was using," Dakuz said. "Someone was on the inside and communicated with the assassins."

"I'll have to chat with my Red friend you met yesterday. He might have a good idea who it was."

Quint could see the wizard's mind spinning as Crider said, "It could have also been a guard or one of the servants who prepared the suite for the meeting. We didn't keep the location a secret."

"And we will talk to them all, Brother Tirolo," the officer said. "We will take the intruders away and let you sleep for a few more hours. Breakfast will be served in your suite, and I'll make sure no one tampers with your food."

The visitors left, carrying the intruders. The four in Quint's group sat down before retiring.

"I can seal my own window," Dakuz said. "I'll help with the others." He looked at Quint. "I'm sure you can do your own."

Quint smiled. "I can. Has everyone recovered from the disturbance? Let me cast a string to eliminate anything the burglars did to you."

Quint cast his advanced string on Dakuz and Donnie. There were no reactions, but when he did the same to Olinz, the man fainted. Quint was able to wake him up with a string.

"It looks like someone was affected and didn't know it," Dakuz said.

Olinz rubbed his forehead. "They commanded me to put this in your food." He walked to a chair and lifted a cushion, revealing a tiny vial filled with a dark liquid.

"Poison," Dakuz said. He turned to Quint. "You'll have to teach Donnie and me that technique. I didn't know shield strings would remove compulsions."

"I didn't either," Quint said. "That is a spell I acquired in a trade in Seensist. It's the first time I've used it. I think the monk who gave it to me died in the battle. I didn't do any testing before I used it, but we should when we return to Feltoff."

"Is there a chance we won't be able to duplicate the spell?" Donnie asked.

Quint shrugged. "There is always that possibility. We'll give it a try with some testing. My shield string is a little different from the one Dakuz taught me."

"More power?" Dakuz asked.

Quint nodded. "Let's not talk about it now. Olinz gets another try."

This time, he was unaffected by the string.

"The shields should work until noon," Quint said. "I don't think they will wait around to strike again."

"But they will strike again. This group doesn't know how to give up," Dakuz grumbled.

§

Breakfast was a little tense, with new servers bringing in their meal. The king's wizard had promised it would be poison-free, but none of them trusted anyone in the palace after the attack the previous night.

The same group of experts trooped in with a new tutor, a very attractive woman. She looked younger than Donnie.

"Thera Vanitz is a warfare strategist at the University of Baxel," the wizard said during introductions.

"You know Feodor Danko?" Quint asked.

She shook her head. "He was before my time, but I was in university with his daughter, Calee Danko. She was a rabid Green back then. It was five years ago. No one liked her if that is what you are after."

"No, but I tend to agree with you. Calee only tried to kill me twice," Quint said.

Thera giggled. Donnie should have been in the meeting. Quint was sure she would captivate him.

"Where did you get your battle experience?"

Thera smiled. "Racellia isn't the only country with a wizard corps. Narukun does, as well. I have some talent. Nothing compared to you, Quint Tirolo, but enough to put me in the field at a tender age. I was a better observer of the processes of war than the implementation. They put me in the university and then in an office after they found my way of thinking useful. I left the corps but stayed at the University of Baxel as an advisor to Narukun's defense ministry."

"My experience was similar, but definitely not the same. Not many read my analyses," Quint said. "I was feeling good at my progress as an analyst when Bocarre became the center of a civil war and that brought me to North Fenola."

"Our gain, I'm sure."

"I wouldn't be so sure," one of the others said. "Tirolo is a magnet for attracting trouble."

"Trouble attacks you, or is it that you represent a danger to them?" Thera said.

Quint was glad the woman had the right attitude. "Maybe it's a little bit of both," Quint said. "There are other factors, especially in Racellia, where I was a target because I was a hubite."

"I forgot about that," the one who mentioned Quint being a magnet said. "You had to fight through all that?"

"'Fight' is the wrong word. More like resist. I had to work hard to prove my worth so they couldn't dismiss me for incompetence. If I had aggressively asserted my rights, I'm sure they would have proved that hubites don't have any. Luckily, I was able to work for some uniquely tolerant superiors."

"But not all were tolerant, of course," the king's wizard said.

Quint nodded. "Assassination attempts are nothing new to me."

Crider rubbed his hands. "Enough of your history. We are here to expose you to ours."

Quint smiled. "I've spent time with Brother Dakuz learning Narukun and North Fenolan history."

"What do you know?"

Quint knew they didn't have the time to discuss all he knew, but he gave them a summary of what he had been taught.

The wizard turned to Dakuz. "And he knows the details behind all that?"

"He does," Dakuz said. "I'd stick to current events and the interactions of the factions if I were you. I'm sure Quint would like to understand the dynamics of factions in the military and in the royal administration."

"Well, that puts a different light on things."

Quint grinned. "Then I hope I can see better when we're done."

Not all the tutors were amused, but the discussion continued. Quint learned that Pinzleport was a chronic center of Narukun dissatisfaction, and there was significantly less cooperation between Reds and Greens in all other locales.

Looking at the king's wizard, Quint asked, "Did you get to talk to your Red leader or the intruders?"

"One of them couldn't resist a truth string. They were instructed to kill you either when you were out on the ledge or by poisoning."

"Olinz was prompted to poison my breakfast." Quint handed the poison vial to the king's wizard. "This is what they gave Olinz to use on me. I cast shields on my companions and the string put Olinz under. When he woke, he remembered what they had done."

"Two more failed attempts, then," Thera said. "You are resourceful."

"And lucky. None of their group could project a fire spear much past the ledge."

"And you had no problem reaching them," she said, sounding impressed.

Quint nodded. "As I said, I'm lucky. Now, let's continue."

They worked through lunch and mid-afternoon. Phandiz Crider proclaimed Quint far enough along to decide regarding his fealty to King Boviz.

"Fealty? I suppose I can swear some kind of allegiance, but I'm not his subject," Quint said.

"And we are satisfied that you don't represent a threat to the king," another tutor said.

"I can swear to that," Quint said.

"In his presence," the wizard said. "We will leave you. The king has time tomorrow morning for an audience at ten o'clock."

Thera stayed after the others left. Donnie was interested in meeting her. Olinz didn't appear reluctant to chat with Thera and the others, either.

"I'm interested in learning more about exactly what you did in Racellia. I don't need to know secret information."

"There is nothing secret at this point. Racellia was in the middle of a civil war and about to be absorbed by the Gussellian Empire when I left."

"And Racellia became part of the Gussellian Empire after you left. The king was sent a letter regarding you."

"And he didn't arrest me?"

Thera laughed. "No. It was from an aide to the emperor, a Colonel Pozella. Did you know him?"

Quint couldn't resist a grin. "He is a friend that I thought was killed. That's good news. What did he have to say?"

"To keep care of you. He and the emperor believe that you are someone special, not because of any predictor string, but who you are now. The king was impressed, which colored his response to you and your request. You passed his tests, and I hope he won't be dissuaded from giving you and your cloister permission to operate."

"So that is why he summoned me?"

"He didn't want you to know and don't tell him you learned it from your tutors. Now, tell me, what kind of strategic work you did?"

Quint described the work he did at the strategic operations of the wizard corps and all he had learned from analyzing publications for Colonel Julia Gerocie. "I paid attention to what I was doing, figured out how to think at the wizard corps, and then applied it to what I did in Colonel Gerocie's unit."

"Including learning willotan, the willot version of Narallian?"

"I wouldn't even call it much of a version; they are so different. The alphabet is almost the same, but everything else is different," Quint said.

"I didn't know that. I was told the two languages were similar," Thera said.

"You can't believe everything you are told and what you read," Quint said. "I learned that analyzing publications, but I learned to sift much of the truth from the distorted writings."

"'Sift the wheat from the chaff,' I think the term is. The polennese have almost the same simile, but they talk about separating rice," Thera said. "My experience was enlightening for me, and like you, I learned how to analyze and became more adept at determining how truthful reports are. I'm sure there were lies and distortions that escaped you. There were and are plenty that I miss."

"Then we have something in common," Quint said.

Thera rose from her chair in the conference room. "We do, Quinto Tirolo. We do," she said on her way out.

Donnie walked her to the door of the suite. It was still guarded, and they let Thera pass.

"An outstanding woman," Donnie said.

"And smarter than you," Dakuz said. He stared at the door she had gone out. "I wonder what wheels are spinning in that girl's mind."

Quint nodded. "As long as her wheels spin in the same direction as our wheels."

§§§

CHAPTER TWENTY-EIGHT

THE GUARDS HAD THEM PREPARE THEIR BAGS FOR TRAVEL. Quint thought that was a good sign, and by mid-morning, they were led to the king's court. The audience was no intimate affair. They wore the nicer clothes provided to meet the king for the first time. However, everyone else in the room was dressed in court finery, and all four of them still looked like country bumpkins. Quint had no problem with that, but Donnie grumbled a bit about not bringing better clothes.

They waited as King Boviz addressed other issues, but finally, their names were called, and they were lined up facing the king, sitting on a throne.

"We have decided to send you back to Feltoff Cloister. Our people didn't perceive an immediate threat to Narukun, and the royal wizard feels the kingdom is safe in the short term." The king leaned forward. "I can't say the same about you, Brother Tirolo. The attempt on your life disturbs me. I wish I could send royal guards to protect your cloister, but my advisors rightly claim that too much attention could make your situation worse. I will send an observer along with you to Feltoff Cloister for a month or two to verify you weren't deceiving the crown."

The king waved his hand. "Thank you for seeking me out. I wish your cloister luck and hope to meet you again," King Boviz said. "You may go."

A guard showed them out of the court and into a side hallway. Thera Vanitz was there with their bags. She smiled at them all. "I get to learn more about Feltoff Cloister."

"Aren't you needed at the university?" Dakuz asked.

"There are no wars currently underway in the kingdom, so my services are less critical at present. It's only for a few months. I hope you have room."

"We have other women in the cloister," Donnie said. "My sister is there."

"She is a monk?"

Donnie laughed and shook his head. "No. She is after a monk, my best friend, Pol Grizak, who is a monk."

Olinz distributed the bags, and they followed the guard to the royal stable.

"Can you defend yourself, miss?" Olinz asked.

"I am a competent wizard lieutenant and trained with commoner weapons. I will have my arms with the horses, or so I'm told," Thera said. She frowned. "The assignment to accompany you was unexpected. I was told when you first entered the king's court this morning. My orders are to observe and report."

"You are unbiased?" Dakuz said, intimating that she might be just the opposite.

"Don't worry about me, Hintz Dakuz. I'm likely much less biased than you."

Dakuz laughed. "I hope to Tizurek's sake that you are."

They reached the stables. Their horses had been replaced with new ones. They were much more valuable than the ones they used on their trip. There were bags of more supplies and light weapons except for a pile of weapons close to Thera's mount.

"You do know how to use those, miss?" Olinz asked.

"Oh, yes. We can do some sparring on our way to Feltoff Cloister," Thera said.

§

"Now it's your turn," Thera said to Quint.

Donnie was out of breath and sat on a log in their campground. They were a day out of Tova's Falls and Thera proved to be in better shape than them all. She quickly dispatched Donnie, who admitted he was never great with a sword. Olinz, on the other hand, did not let the woman defeat him.

"You aren't that bad," Thera said to Donnie. "Most wizards don't practice manual arms. You are like most wizards."

Donnie looked dejected and sat down. Quint had more training. Although he wasn't as practiced as Thera, his bigger size made their sparring more equal than with the other monk. Dakuz begged off physical swordplay on the first evening, plus he was closer to twenty years older than Olinz.

Quint stretched a bit and prepared himself for another defeat, although he could tell his swordsmanship was improving, sparring with someone with a higher skill level.

"You haven't practiced much since you've grown in size, have you?" Thera said with a grin.

"Didn't have the time. I spent most of my time buried in publications, and then it was off to Seensist from Bocarre," Quint said.

They sparred more, and Quint finally got through Thera's defense for a touch.

"I won!" Quint said.

"She let you, lad," Olinz said.

Thera smiled. "I did, but you deserved a win. Marital arts is my hobby, and it's a passion of mine."

"Then I will have to practice more."

Olinz tossed a damp towel to Quint. "There is an excellent swordsman in Lord Pilka's guard. I'll send him over to Feltoff Cloister as a guard who will give you lessons."

"I can learn as well?" Thera asked.

Olinz shrugged. That's up to Quint and the guard."

Thera looked at Quint with a pleading look. It made Quint laugh.

"You can join us. I can learn from more than one person," Quint said.

"Can you take one more?" Donnie asked.

Olinz smiled. "Better four practicing than three. You can break into pairs." He winked at Donnie behind Thera's back.

"What will you do once you get to the cloister?" Thera asked.

"Make sure everything is going as planned. We were called away just as we were getting started. The visitors' situation was resolved, but the mill and manufacturing furniture will allow the cloister to grow," Quint said. "My father was a wheelwright, but there were too many restrictions in Racellia to make him truly successful. He was restricted in where he could sell his wheels, but we were careful and never starved. I'd like Feltoff to be more successful to attract monks and become a center for non-military wizards."

"So, I wouldn't be welcome?" Thera asked. There was a little coyness in her question.

"Any wizard is welcome in a cloister. I don't think you'd find it stimulating enough."

She frowned. "Perhaps not. Perhaps I'll get to see some success before I leave."

"You will," Donnie said.

§

Quint was relieved to see Feltoff Cloister intact. When they rode through the gate, they were surrounded by the monks.

"I didn't know if I was going to see you again," Grizak said to Quint. "I see you brought someone with you."

"Thera Vanitz. She is attached to the University of Baxel. She is here to observe."

Grizak's eyes were glued to Thera as she dismounted. Quint introduced her to the monks he knew, and Grizak seemed very happy to meet her.

"Anything happen while I was gone?" Quint asked.

Grizak shook his head. "No. How did it go in Baxel? You met with the king?"

"Twice. Let's assemble in the church, and I might as well tell everyone at once. Our trip was more exciting than it should have been. Find a place for Thera to stay. She will probably be with us for a few months."

"Months," Grizak said, smiling and nodding his head.

Quint washed up and walked out into the courtyard. He had expected change, but there wasn't much. Piles of lumber had grown, so perhaps Kozak had been busy.

Someone tapped Quint on the shoulder. He turned around and saw that Sandy had moved to his other side.

"You brought a woman with you?" Sandy said.

Quint nodded. "A former classmate of Calee Danko's."

"Older," Sandy said.

Quint smiled. "I'm sure she's older than some of us, but not Grizak." Quint saw Donnie on one side and Grizak on the other side of the woman walking toward Tova's chapel.

The monks assembled in the church. Olinz stuck around to hear Quint's presentation before heading to Zimton and reporting to Lord Pilka.

Everyone had assembled. Andy sat beside Sandy, but Grizak and Donnie still guarded Thera on each side. Andy kept looking in their direction as

Quint talked about their adventure starting with the messenger's arrival.

"Questions?" Quint asked as he stood before the cloister's membership, realizing how small their group was.

Most of the concerns had to do with the king's intentions. Pilka had visited every other day and wandered around in the chapel, perhaps hoping for a visitation by one of Tova's creatures. He was unsuccessful.

The meeting was over, and everyone vacated the church. The refectory hadn't entirely been completed, but it didn't stop the monks from eating underneath the finished roof.

Kozak gave Quint a tour of the mill. The master carpenter had been busy. When Quint exited the building, Sandy met him.

"The visitors center is finished, and the new visitation plaques are up," she said. "You should see it before you become inundated with issues tomorrow."

"Inundated?" Quint asked.

Sandy nodded her head. "We've kept everything from you, but there is a backlog of decisions that you need to make."

"What about the council?"

"They decided they couldn't make a significant decision until you returned."

Quint sighed. "Grizak didn't get anything done?"

"The mill. He spent most of his time with Kozak, and the original monks weren't up to being very independent."

Quint pursed his lips as they left the courtyard walls and walked around the outside of the wall to the visitors' center.

"You painted it!" Quint said.

"Andy and I thought it would look better."

"It does, but you'll have to keep it painted to look good," Quint said.

"We will. Attendance has been good each day. There is talk about building an inn on the other side of the river in Tova's Falls."

"Lord Pilka's idea?"

Sandy smiled. "You are so smart."

The center was closed, but they walked along the pathway to the church wall. A few visitors were looking at the stories on the wall, but they passed them almost unnoticed. Quint leaned against the wall when Sandy stopped. But he realized she had frozen. Quint touched the wall and was transported into the now-familiar room where Tova waited.

"You have returned intact. I wasn't sure you would. Danger follows you," Tova said.

"I've been told I'm a magnet for trouble. It better make up its mind," Quint said. "You have a message?"

"Be wary. Some old friends are about to visit, and they do not have your best interests at heart. I'd prefer you preserve yourself for your quest to find Tizurek."

"I haven't forgotten, but you said it would take years."

"Maybe not years," Tova said. "You can trust the new woman, but there will be contention. Be wary of that, too. I am glad you returned. I must be gone for some time, so there won't be any of my messengers visiting. Try to keep the expectations low."

"Whatever you say," Quint said, bowing.

He felt a shift and his head was touching the wall as his bow had persisted through the shift.

"What?" Sandy blinked.

"I dropped something," Quint said, picking up a pebble and quickly putting it in his pocket. "There." He touched the wall again. "Any visitations?"

Sandy sighed. "We would have told you."

"Perhaps with all the people, we will scare the spirits away," Quint said.

"Maybe, but we still have all the plaques and the live witnesses," Sandy said.

"Have there been any issues with the monks?"

Sandy looked up and down the passage once the visitors had passed. "Andy and Pol Grizak."

"Don't tell me," Quint said. "Grizak isn't showing sufficient interest in Andy."

"How did you know?" Sandy said with a faint smirk on her face.

Quint muttered. "You saw Grizak and Donnie smothering Thera Vanitz."

"That's what you call it," Sandy said. "I wasn't quite sure what it was. I'm increasingly listening to an unfortunate girl lamenting her love life. It's not going to get any easier."

"From my standpoint, once he entered Seensist, Grizak has never been taken with Andreiza."

"I've pointed that out before," Sandy said, "but it doesn't seem to sink in."

Quint rubbed at a rock in the wall. "Should we send her back to her mother?"

Sandy sighed. "I don't think that will be possible. Andy received a letter from her mother. She's been asked to sell her house and leave Pinzleport. The Pinzleport police have been forced to return to their old ways, turning a blind eye to the Reds and the Greens."

"She's coming here?"

"Andy said her mother doesn't know if she'll become a monk, live in Tova's Falls, or settle in Zimton."

"Does Donnie know?"

"He might by now," Sandy said. "This isn't a council matter, but you are involved."

"Grizak is on the council," Quint said.

"But only you two. Dakuz doesn't count," Sandy said.

"What can I do?"

"You are friends with Grizak and Andy. I can't intervene with him."

Quint groaned. "And Grizak, who lost his ardor for Andy when he became a monk?"

"It seems he's gained it again," Sandy said. "You know Thera Vanitz, too. I've only been introduced."

Quint didn't mention that Andy's brother, Donnie, was involved, but Sandy must have noticed that.

"I'm the youngest of everyone, and I have to come up with a solution?" Quint asked.

Sandy sighed. "I'm not sure you have it in you to solve this particular problem."

"Then why bring it up?" Quint asked.

"You need to keep it from exploding into something ugly. Andy can become emotional about such things."

Quint turned around and leaned against the wall. "Keep things placid on the top while matters boil beneath the surface?"

Sandy laughed. "I like that. You have grasped the situation. What are you going to do?"

"Talk to Thera. If I can limit the ardor, perhaps that might reduce the overall temperature," Quint said.

§§§

CHAPTER TWENTY-NINE

Quint thought that sleeping in his cell at Feltoff would be wonderful while he traveled home from Baxel, but the state of slumber escaped him. He rose in a surly mood and hoped washing up would rinse the confusion away, but that wasn't to be. The breakfast bell rang, something that wasn't in place when he left a week ago, and Quint headed to the refectory.

He looked across the hall to see Donnie, Grizak, Thera, and one of the original monks at a table. The three monks looked at Thera with bright eyes, hanging on her every word. He sighed and retrieved his breakfast, sitting at an empty table with a view of Thera and her admirers.

Dakuz and Kozak joined him. They followed his gaze.

"You are both a lot older than I am. What am I to do with that?" Quint didn't need to say what. The two senior monks shook their heads.

"I've never had to deal with women. That's why I'm a monk," Kozak said. "I'd send the woman back home, however nicely she brightens the place."

"Kozak has a point," Dakuz said.

"Can't do it," Quint said. "Thera is King Boviz's eyes and ears. She's here for a few months."

Dakuz glanced their way again. "Why don't you have a tournament? Whoever can beat Thera in swords wins."

Quint laughed. "Problem solved. Olinz is sending an expert swordsman. He can defeat Thera and then our issue is solved."

"No, it isn't," Dakuz said. "Look."

Andreiza Hannoko walked up to her brother and said something to

Donnie. She looked disdainfully at Thera and said something. From the look on Thera's face, it was something objectionable. Thera took Andy by the arm and led her out of the refectory.

"I'll be back," Quint said. "Don't follow me."

Quint walked directly to the table and told Grizak, Donnie, and the other monk to stay seated. He stalked outside and saw Thera bring up Andy short a few yards away. Quint stood, uncertain about what to do next, but he was in earshot and folded his arms, not taking a step closer.

"You are crowding in on my property," Andy said.

"Pol Grizak?" Thera asked. "I have no interest in him or your brother. They are pursuing me, not the other way around."

"Got your eye on the other monk?"

"Not one at my table, another one," Thera said. "So, by the end of today, you don't have to worry about me spoiling your setup in the cloister. I will be disappointing your brother, so tend to his wounds of the heart.'"

Quint could feel his cheeks get hot. He shouldn't have walked so close. This was something far from his business.

"Are we through?" Thera asked.

"Yes," Andy said, probably redder in the face than Quint. Andy returned inside the refectory, pausing first to give Quint a side glance.

"I didn't mean to eavesdrop," Quint said, "but Andy can get determined as far as Grizak is concerned."

"Likely a futile dream," Thera said, breathing a little heavily. "But I'm glad you heard what I had to say." She walked closer to him. "You, Quint Tirolo, are the other monk." She put her hand on his shoulder.

"I'm already taken," Quint said. He regretted speaking since even he picked up on the nervousness in his voice.

"Sandiza?" Thera asked. "I think she would be an admirable foe. I really do, but I won't be as obnoxious about my pursuit as her friend, Andy."

"I'd rather you forget me as someone to be interested in."

Thera gave Quint a crooked smile. "Not a chance."

"But you are so much older than me," Quint said. "You went to university with Calee Danko. She's at least thirty."

"I'm a bit of a prodigy like you are, Quint. She was late leaving the university, and I was in my first year. I'm younger than you think."

"Twenty-five? That's too old for me."

"You make a girl feel bad. I'm twenty-three. Younger than Andreiza Hannoko and closer to your Sandy's age. Whatever she's said, she hasn't been a teenager for a few years. Don't worry. I'll earn my way with you." She smiled confidently and walked back into the refectory, leaving Quint alone in the courtyard.

§

After being reassured that activities of the cloister were moving along during the week of his absence, and with Thera's talk with Andy doing its work to defuse Grizak's interest, Quint sequestered himself in his workroom. He sat at the table with paper and ink and began to think about his next steps. He felt he had painted himself into a corner by going to Baxel.

The responsibility to get Feltoff Cloister started was beginning to get lighter. Still, the king looked to him as the cloister's leader, and if he were to leave too soon, he had doubts about retaining the support of the royal government. Of Lord Pilka's support, Quint had no questions, but he now had the complication of Thera Vanitz's declaration of pursuing him. Was she any different than Andy pursuing Grizak?

The problem was not only was she monitoring the cloister, but she was specifically monitoring him, and he decided that Thera's observations were vital to satisfying the king. Quint sighed as he stared at the blank sheet of paper.

He stood at a knock on the door and opened it. Vintez Dugo, the neutral party during the hasty exit from Seensist Cloister, stood with a half-smile.

"Can I come in?" Dugo asked. "Am I disturbing anything?"

Quint shook his head. "No. I'm thinking, and the only thing I have to show for it is a blank sheet of paper. Is something new happening?"

Dugo continued his smile and walked into the room, letting Quint shut the door behind him.

"What is it with the new girl?" Dugo asked.

Quint snorted. "That's what I've been struggling with. She said she wanted a closer relationship with me. Closer than Sandy."

Dugo chuckled. "Not hard," Dugo said. "While you were gone, Sandy began making eyes at Grizak."

"Why didn't Pol tell me about it? Wouldn't she be upsetting Andy?" Quint asked.

"Sandy is a smart one. She chooses her opportunities, and her approach is almost benign."

"Benign as in being a friend? Perhaps that is all she's trying to do."

Dugo shook his head. "If I've done anything in my life, it has been observing. I just wanted to let you know."

"You had a question about Thera?"

"I do," Dugo said. "She is the one who prompted me to talk to you about Sandy. I mean, I know Sandy has been partial to you, but Thera Vanitz picked up on Sandy within a day and chose me to tattle on her."

"You fulfilled her request. What does Thera expect me to do?"

Dugo shrugged. "I don't know. She is stirring the pot, but she was right about Sandy. I couldn't keep it in."

Quint sighed. "Perhaps you should have. Now, I can't deal with the problem without bias."

"Yeah, being in the dark and then acting doesn't suit you, Quint."

That brought out another sigh. "I'm not experienced in dealing with women or girls or anything. I've never had much luck in such a thing, not that I tried. All the girls I've known, except for Sandy, have tried to kill me."

"And Sandy? That happened before you returned."

"I'll do my own watching," Quint said, "but thanks for the observation. Let me know what you see from time to time about anything happening in the cloister. Another viewpoint won't hurt, no matter what I just said about not wanting bias. It's unavoidable, I've learned. Keep an eye on Thera. Do you remember the shield that I taught you?"

"I do," Dugo said. "Why do you ask?"

"Thera is a powerful wizard, as young as she is, and she might be casting a persuasion string. I'd be careful. I think I'll have a shield in place, myself."

Dugo left, and Quint did as he promised. He didn't like having to be suspicious in Feltoff, and the romantic entanglements made people do uncharacteristic things, at least they did in novels.

Quint wrote the names of the monks and Pilka's people on the paper. There were less than thirty, and he wondered if he would need to make a chart of affiliations. He didn't know if the analysis he completed for the first head prior had helped or hindered Seensist's stability, but Quint thought he might miss something if he didn't get things documented.

Thera was a complication but a temporary one. In a few months, she would be gone, and any damage she caused would hopefully fade away quickly. Dugo's observation of Sandy didn't seem right to Quint. She had taken on Andy as a friend, and Quint had never noticed her lingering around Grizak in Seensist or at Feltoff.

He stared at the wall. It was the one that was the original church, and Quint realized that he felt a tinge of fear in the staring. Quint decided to carve out another spot in the cloister for a workroom. He didn't want any female problems from a certain deity he had met in proximity to that wall.

Quint had spent enough time in his workroom. He decided to walk into the nearby woods and practice one-handed strings. Wizardry was one thing he had let go of when they arrived at Tova's Falls. Every effort was focused on creating a cloister, and then he was summoned to the capital. Perhaps some time outside the cloister would do him some good.

He found a thick stand of trees and moved through them toward a secluded clearing. Quint found no evidence of a camp or habitation on his walk and decided this would work for him. It reminded him of the clearing he used to sun himself once when out with the army. He removed his robe and tunic and stripped to the waist before going through strings to get warmed up. The trees never complained when he cast string after string to get warmed up, and then the real work began.

Quint put his left hand in the back waistband of his trousers and began to go through the same sequence using his right hand. Some strings worked, and others seemed to need two hands to craft the threads that were woven into strings properly. The hands never did the work, but the space between the two palms was required for the weaving platform.

As before, Quint realized that one-handed strings were more powerful. When he finished, he sat on the fallen log and struggled to jot down what worked and what didn't. After analyzing his results for a time, Quint now had a beginning point where he could more easily characterize why certain strings worked and others didn't.

The stage, as he now called the space above his palms where everything happened, needed space for strings that brought in different threads. The restriction had to do with the creation of threads more than it did strings. Quint's magical power activated the strings into magical effects.

Was that why men with bigger palms dominated wizardry? Quint had never considered string creation a physical phenomenon before, but a quick mental review indicated it might be. He had something interesting to talk to Dakuz, now.

It was now a matter of practice. Quint could tell some strings would never be candidates for one-handed casting, but of the strings he demonstrated, two-thirds could be completed, although with varying strengths.

He made a few more notes and let his skin soak in the last minutes of sunlight before shadows covered the clearing.

In the hour or so of day left, Quint picked up a dead branch and used it to do the sword forms he knew. Quint's muscles responded to the exercise, and he finally exited the clearing, fully dressed and feeling better about everything. He hadn't solved any problems, but perhaps the exercising and string practice had shoved everything into a better perspective.

§§§

CHAPTER THIRTY

"AND YOU ARE?" GRIZAK ASKED THE NEWCOMER dressed in armor and on a horse that matched his military demeanor. Olinz had brought him to the cloister.

"Omar Ronzle. I am Lord Pilka's champion."

Olinz chuckled behind the warrior's back. "He won the latest dueling contest at Lord Pilka's estate for the first time a month ago, but Ronzle is the best we have available. I can't beat him."

Ronzle growled at Olinz. "You ruined my entrance," Ronzle said.

"Good. Let me introduce you to the monks at lunch." Olinz looked at Quint, who was approaching. "You will invite us for lunch?"

Quint grinned. "Of course," he said. "Your timing is perfect."

The lunch bell rang as the horses were tied up.

Quint stood when most of the cloister was seated in the refectory. "You know Olinz from Lord Pilka's manor." Quint patted Ronzle on the shoulder, "This one is our trainer and protector for the next while. He isn't a monk, so treat him with respect. Get to know him. You will know him better if you choose to train in common weapons. I recommend that you all get some training. You all know what happened at Seensist, and we don't want a repeat of that at Feltoff Cloister."

Grizak stood and echoed Quint's invitation.

Ronzle and Olinz ate at the same table as Grizak, Dakuz, and Quint.

"I've trained soldiers before," Ronzle said. He gave them a quick description of his background.

"Then you can help Thera evaluate our defenses."

"Thera? A woman?" Ronzle asked.

"Yes," Olinz said. "And she'll give you a good sparring match."

"We get started this afternoon?" Ronzle said.

"No, tomorrow," Grizak said. "We will get you a cell to stay and find a corner to practice."

Ronzle smiled and nodded. Quint thought he was full of himself, but Ronzle had a much better sense of humor than his first impression, and he knew some battle strategy that Quint pulled out of him during lunch.

They walked outside, and Thera walked up to them.

"Remember me?" Thera asked Ronzle.

"Lieutenant Vanitz. Your first name is Thera, I hope?"

Thera shot Ronzle a smile. "It is, and we will be doing some work together at Feltoff. I'm here from Baxel to observe, but maybe it will be a little more hands-on than I originally thought."

She clapped Quint on the shoulder and winked at him. Quint knew what she meant. Her hand on him was the message. They walked through the cloister and realized that the best place to train was outside on the other side of the visitor's center. They passed the visitors center and the daily line of pilgrims.

"We can get a fence and a little roofing up in a few days. I have the materials," Kozak said. "Dimensions?"

While Thera and Omar Ronzle huddled, Kozak, Grizak, and Quint slipped away.

"Thera gets around," Grizak said, looking back before they went around the cloister wall.

Quint glanced at the group, too. Thera noticed him looking at her and waved. Quint nodded and continued.

"She is a lot to handle," Grizak said. "I thought she was different when I first met her."

"Different from whom?" Quint asked.

"Andy, of course. I don't like Andy's pushiness, but maybe Thera is just as bad."

Quint laughed. "I think she goes after what she wants."

"I'm glad she doesn't like me, then," Grizak said.

Quint stopped. "What did she tell you?"

"Thera told us all there was another person in her heart, and she just wanted to be friends with us."

"Last night at the table?" Quint asked.

Grizak nodded. "When we were about to leave. Andy was across the refectory, arms folded, glaring at us. I don't know if she was angrier with me or Thera."

"Why should you care?" Quint asked. "You haven't shown any partiality towards Andy."

Grizak smiled. "I've been successfully hiding my feelings," he said. "Thera initially had me on the edge, but…" He shook his head.

"I think you'd better do a little less hiding. Wannie is coming to town any day now, and it would be better to get a few things settled before she arrives."

"Andy said something about that, but she was coy, and I haven't spoken to Donnie…"

"Because of Thera?"

Grizak snorted. "Yes! That woman blows in like a storm and upsets everything."

"It's only been two days," Quint said. "Some of the storm has passed."

Grizak nodded. "I'll talk to Andy tonight. I must set some ground rules, though."

"She would prefer ground rules to no access, Pol," Quint said.

"What about Sandy and you? Are you two going to get together somehow? It seems she's the one beating about the bush with you. She's been reaching out to me as a friend, mind you, but it has been more like she's trying to pry. About what, I don't know." Grizak scratched his head. "No complaints, nothing other than a display of friendship that I can see," Grizak said, seemingly happy to change the object of the conversation.

"I've been too busy, but now that I'm back in Feltoff, I can see I don't have to run the council."

"Although everyone wants you to," Grizak said.

"If Sandy and I can develop a good friendship, that is sufficient for now. That's the way it's been since we met at Seensist."

"Good enough for me," Grizak said.

Quint hoped being on a friendship basis would be enough for both Sandy and Thera, but he doubted he was that lucky.

They walked through the gate into the cloister grounds to see a carriage and an overloaded wagon. Donnie was helping one of the passengers in the carriage down. Wanisa Hannoko had arrived before Grizak could settle things with Andy.

"I have to find Andreiza," Grizak said, rushing ahead, avoiding the new arrival.

Quint didn't have to worry about the Hannokos and headed for Wannie.

"Welcome to our little cloister," Quint said.

Wannie looked around. "Where is Andy and Pol?" she asked.

"Around here somewhere," Quint said. "I was just with Grizak, so he might have gone to find your daughter."

"Really? How nice," she said. "Can someone help me find a place in that lovely little village to spend the night? I don't want to impose, and we only knew to ask where the cloister is."

"If Olinz is still around, he can help," Quint said just before he spotted Olinz mounting his horse.

Quint didn't have to force Olinz to stop. He dismounted and gave Wannie a big smile. "Donnie and Andy's mother?" he asked Quint.

Donnie made introductions and asked if Olinz could direct Wanisa to an inn.

"I may be staying there for a while before I decide what to do. I may settle in Zimton. It's of a size that might be more comfortable for me," Wannie said.

"I'd be happy to get you a place to stay. However, I'd like to take you to Zimton to meet Lord Pilka after we do. I'm sure he'd like to meet you, and Silla, Lord Pilka's wife, will probably enjoy making your acquaintance."

"I can leave my wagon here?" Wannie looked at her son and then at Quint.

"We will find the space," Quint said. He watched Olinz lead Wannie's carriage out of the cloister.

When the carriage was out of sight, Grizak and Andy showed up.

"Where is Mother?" Andy asked her brother.

Donnie smiled and shook his head. "As much as she loves us, I think she is interested in how her adventure will continue in Lord Pilka's domain. Olinz has taken her to the man himself."

Andy snorted. "It's good that Pilka is married, or Mother might have designs on him. Should we follow?"

Donnie laughed. "Not at all. She will undoubtedly be back tomorrow. All her possessions are in that wagon."

"Not all, surely. I can imagine a wagon train stretching from here to Pinzleport," Andy said.

She gave Grizak a quick glance and smiled. "Can't you?"

"Oh, yes," Grizak said. "Your mother is a force."

To Quint's inner ear, Grizak thought the same thing about Andy, but he looked comfortable standing beside her. Something must have been said. He was glad Captain Olinko wasn't there to hear Andy's comment. He knew his former captain had designs on Wannie.

Quint wandered around as Grizak, Andy, and Donnie supervised moving Wannie's wagon. As he toured the cloister, Quint had an eye out for Sandy, but she wasn't to be found. He wandered past the visitor's center; she had left before lunch. One of the local women seemed to remember her saying she had an errand in Simton.

It was odd that Sandy would travel to the town without telling anyone. Quint chided himself for being worried about something that was probably none of his business.

An hour later, when Quint was looking over the cloister plans for another site for his workshop, Dugo, the informer, found him.

"More visitors. What a day! Sandy accompanied an older man and her daughter. They say they know you. She's talking to them in the refectory."

Quint left his surveying and saw a different carriage in the courtyard. He wondered if Dugo was referring to Lord Pilka and Gallia. He stepped inside the refectory and stopped. Quint wanted to rub his eyes but didn't dare. Feodor and Calee Danko drank wine while chatting to Sandiza Bartok as if Quint's enemies were her best friends.

§

"What are you doing here?" Quint said, trying to tamp his anger. He looked at Sandy. "How are you involved with these people? You know they tried to kill me."

"At this point, I'm glad I failed," Calee said, coughing.

Quint didn't believe her. He didn't feel bad that the father and the daughter had terrible colds and raspy voices.

"I was told Thera Vanitz is a monk here?"

Quint shook his head, upset at Calee's attempt to change the subject.

"She's not a monk. Sandy probably told you that."

Calee smiled at Quint. He could sense the coldness beneath the facade. "She might have." She had a fit of coughing and had to take a swallow of the wine.

Quint couldn't help but sigh. Tova's warning about a female's betrayal didn't take long to materialize.

"My question was, why are you here? I thought you were spreading murder and mayhem in some other hapless country of the world," Quint said.

"You are being unfair," Sandy said.

"You know who these people are? They are militant Greens. As bad as the Greens who we fought at Seensist."

"She knows who we are," Feodor said. "How else did we know you were here?"

"You are a spy for the Greens?"

Sandy's smile was no warmer than Calee's. "I've done my part. I'll be leaving with the Dankos," she said.

"Am I to expect an army to destroy Feltoff?" Quint asked.

"The simple answer? Yes, if we can't come to terms," Feodor said. His voice was as hoarse as his daughter's. Quint would have rewarded the person who infected them if he could.

"And that includes my death?"

Danko shrugged. "It might. Calee failed twice. Perhaps it's time for Sandiza to give it a try."

"Then get out," Quint said.

"Isn't there a council here? Perhaps you should see what they have to say," Feodor said.

Quint ran a hand through his hair. "What a day! What are your terms?"

"You come with us back to Pinzleport. You work for the Green cause and promise not to switch sides to the Red."

"And if I switch, that is where you kill me?"

"I told you he was smart," Sandy said.

She had told them everything. Sandy had done her job well, and Quint realized he was now surprised Sandy hadn't tried to kill him. She had plenty of opportunities.

"We already knew that," Calee said. "Sandy was an observer, not an assassin. We didn't return to Narukun until a month ago. Our first attempt was to kidnap you on your way to Baxel, and that was admittedly a pitiful attempt. Now that the opportunity arises, we can use Sandy in a more active fashion. She will be more reliable than the late messenger."

Quint looked into the teenaged face of Calee. "How old are you really? I heard you were thirty-five under your mask. Shall we find out?"

"No!" Calee said. "We must be going. We will return tomorrow morning at ten o'clock. Assemble your council, or something bad will happen."

Quint followed them to the carriage. Bound and gagged, lying on one of the seats was Wanisa Hannoko.

"You know what the something bad is?" Feodor said with an evil grin.

Sandy joined the Dankos, and they left the courtyard. Quint looked at the carriage, feeling furious and helpless at the same time.

§§§

CHAPTER THIRTY-ONE

OLINZ ARRIVED AFTER DINNER WITH LORD PILKA and a retinue of guards. He was bandaged and walked with difficulty. They met in Quint's current workroom.

"Sandy stopped us on the road to Simton. She said she had been kidnapped," Olinz said. He snorted and said, "Kidnapped," with more emphasis. "The kidnappers had ten men and killed the driver and Lady Wanisa's maid before trussing her up and leaving me beaten and bloody by the side of the road. I got a ride to the manor, and here we are."

"The Danko's have come and gone. They showed me Wanisa before they left. They will return tomorrow for a council meeting at ten. The Dankos are too confident not to have alternate plans," Quint said.

"We should find out who is in the cloister. They might have taken more hostages," Thera said.

"I'll send out some of my guards to see what kind of fighting force is out there. With the people I brought from Simton, we can adequately defend against ten fighters."

"I'll be of no help," Olinz said.

"You've already done your part," Lord Pilka said.

Donnie ran out to count noses, and they found that the two young monks in Sandy's care were the only ones gone.

"Can she be so cold-hearted?" Andy asked. "I knew she was always a little odd, but not that odd!"

Quint was embarrassed to have been so fooled. He had just suffered another female turning on him. What rotten luck, he thought. Quint noticed Thera looking at him and absorbed the punishment of a wink. Was she going to be the fourth?

"Let us know what we need to do," Grizak said to Thera and Ronzle.

"Ronzle," Lord Pilka said. "You'll earn your pay in the next few days. I'll drive those damned Greens all the way to Pinzleport."

"Perhaps a messenger needs to go to Baxel," Thera said.

"Are you volunteering?" Grizak asked.

"Not at all. I was thinking of paying a villager to go."

"That is something I can do," Olinz said. He turned to Pilka. "If you allow me to use your carriage, I know just the person."

"You'll stay in the village until this ends," Pilka ordered.

Pilka sat at the table and wrote a message to one of the ministers he counted as an ally, and then Olinz left in the carriage.

"Now," Pilka said, rubbing his hands. "Any ideas?"

Quint rolled out a plan of the cloister. Kozak marked the areas of weakness, and then Ronzle and Thera began sketching a plan.

"The first thing is to close Tova's path now. Get the women out of the visitor's center and board it up," Thera said. "We need to bring in anything of value inside the walls and remove anything the enemy can use for cover."

"Most of that is done," Kozak said. "Maybe a magician can seal the center?"

"I can do that right now. I've always considered myself to be a military strategist, but I concede we have two better," Quint said.

He left them and was let out of the cloister gate guarded by four of Pilka's men.

The women had already gone home, so Quint didn't have to worry about exposing villagers. He sealed windows and doors, but Danko's group, including Sandy and Calee, only needed to send a fire spear to burn the place down.

The pathway to Tova's wall was sealed. Quint used some of his power to shield the front door and wooden frame. He walked around the cloister walls and spotted a weakness. Someone, probably Sandy, had removed enough stones from the new wall to create a hole large enough for men to squeeze through. Quint didn't have time to get help, so he plugged the wall himself and sealed it with one of his one-handed strings. No one would be coming in from there. He looked up and realized that Danko's fighters would be milling about, and stones could be tossed over the wall if Kozak could make an inside platform.

When Quint was almost at the gate, someone called to him from the bushes on the other side of the road.

"You don't have to come to me. Olinz sent me. The messenger has been sent. There are twenty or thirty fighters camping on the other side of the village on the road south. We are assembling villagers to help, but we will need time to get organized. Olinz said you didn't expect anything tomorrow until mid-morning. That should give us enough time."

"Whatever you can do to help, but make sure you tend to your own safety. Tell Brother Tirolo that we are all behind him."

"I'll do that," Quint said with a smile. He jogged to the gate and slipped inside.

The planners were about done when Quint conferred with Grizak before returning to his workshop.

"I've done what I could," Quint said. "There was a hole in the wall with enough mortar removed to be pushed inside. I plugged it and used strings to seal the stones together. The hole will be a magnet for the Greens, so I thought we could make a platform and…"

Ronzle held up his hand. "We know what to do. Why don't you organize some monks to gather anything heavy to drop? We don't have parapets built on most of the walls yet, so that's a good call."

Quint wished he could do more, but he would be fighting. He wished the sun was still shining so he could get his power back more quickly, but he had the morning. Kozak went to work building the platform, and Quint had monks collecting building debris to toss over the wall.

He was exhausted after helping finish the platform after moving the debris. He welcomed his bed and didn't wake in the night. The sun had begun to shine into the courtyard and Quint took his shirt off along with the other male monks to absorb more energy for the fight that could come in mere hours.

Thera walked past, and suddenly Quint felt naked.

"You aren't built so bad for a wizard," Thera said.

Quint grunted. "I suppose you've seen plenty of wizard chests."

"I have," Thera sighed. "Unfortunately, Sandy proved true to type," she said.

"Type? You knew she was a spy?"

"Not knew," Thera said, "but the strings indicated a betrayal of someone close to you. We didn't know how close. There is so much fuzziness when predictor strings are applied to you. I thought she didn't act like she was really interested in you."

"You knew this from one day with her?"

"I did because I was looking for it. I talked to Donnie while we traveled, and that's how he described her. He never liked her fickleness. He said she would disappear and then return."

"She did. That was a warning sign that I never picked up."

"Olinz didn't either," Thera said. "He was around her enough to suspect. We are all surprised by different things."

"When do we get our assignments?"

"After breakfast." Thera squinted into the sun. "In an hour or so. Get as much sun as you can. I have other things to do, but I wasn't like you, expending magic last night. You did a great job in such a short time, doing wizardly and physical tasks. I'd cast a predictor string, but," she shook her head. "Unlike most strings that are clearer the closer they are to the time they are cast, your future string, as cloudy as it is, is more stable, and everything closer is a mess. I don't think it's worth the energy. The Greens won't be any better off."

"I hope," Quint said.

"So, do I. I'll see you later." Thera smiled and waved. Quint closed his eyes and moved his arms to get more skin exposed.

After breakfast, Quint was assigned to the most solid parapet above the gate, which was the weakest point in the cloister. Thera assigned most of Quint's bodyguards to burn any ladders that showed above the wall. With so few people, the best fighters had to roam along the walls, including Ronzle, who had grabbed Donnie as his fighting partner.

Now, it was time to wait. Thera and Ronzle ran the defense. Pilka and Dakuz sat in the refectory, ready to receive reports. Kozak sat at the gate to the mill with thirty buckets filled with water to help dampen any fires cast at them.

Quint thought of the two strings he had learned when he moved in and out of Tova's realm. They were so different from what he knew. Quint identified both as strings that could be cast one-handed, but he didn't know how they would operate away from the Tova's wall. Quint spotted a cobble left at the side of the road outside the cloister and decided to see if the string worked in his world.

He wanted to learn it one-handed since it wasn't even an experiment. The threads that he called from his magic felt different. They were more active, squiggling around like worms. The string was clearly imprinted in his mind, so that was the easiest part. He held a swirl of strings in his hand and cast it via a force of will at the rock.

Quint cringed and closed his eyes, ready for an explosion, but nothing happened. He peeked over the edge of the crenellation and couldn't see the cobble. Quint wondered if it was sitting in Tova's office.

He wasn't about to find out, but he saw a squirrel on a tree outside the cleared area, quickly created the string, and willed the spell at the squirrel. With his eyes on the animal, it disappeared. There wasn't a flash or a sound. It was there one moment and gone the next.

Quint tried the same string on a block of cobbles on the road, but nothing happened. He concentrated on another single cobble, and it was gone. The string had controls on it. One item at a time. He tried the other string he had learned, but it didn't work. Quint didn't have time to find out why. It was half past ten, and a carriage surrounded by twenty guards rolled along the road.

The carriage stopped fifty yards from the gate. The Feodors, Sandy, and a gagged Wannie Hannoko emerged. Wannie's hands were bound. The guards spread out across the road.

It was time for Quint to shield the gate. He didn't know how long that would last, but it would provide some protection from fire spears. The only person who would know what would happen would be Thera if she had chanced to cast a predictor string, but she had said it wouldn't do them any good.

On the other hand, Quint might have more luck, but he dreaded casting a predictor string that included him. They had planned for most situations other than another hundred fighters. He watched Feodor and Calee walk toward the gate. Something didn't seem right about the Dankos, but Quint put that down to his edginess. Sandy stayed behind, holding onto a rope that ended with a noose around Wannie's neck. Quint could strike Sandy down from that distance, but he didn't think and escaping Wannie could outrun pursuit by the Green soldiers.

He met Calee's triumphant eyes and gazed upon the smirk on Feodor's face. Their arrogance repulsed him, but they were protected by Sandiza Bartok, his one-time friend's grasp on the noose around Wannie's neck.

§§§

CHAPTER THIRTY-TWO

ALL EYES IN THE COURTYARD WERE ON THE PAIR when they walked through the narrow opening in the gate. Grizak escorted them to the refectory, while Quint descended from the wall to join the council.

Quint wanted to wipe the smiles off the Danko's faces, but he couldn't. He looked at the others on the council. He didn't see any friendly indications from any of the council members. It would be a hard decision to make. Lord Pilka sat behind the councilors. He was glad that Donnie was with Ronzle and Andy was on the wall to give her mother some moral support from afar.

"Shall we get started?" Danko asked. He pulled a document from his coat and slapped it on the table. "Quint should read this aloud so all can hear him explain how he made this happen."

"I'll do it," the original head of the cloister said.

"No. Quint should read this," Feodor said with his raspy voice. No wine was offered this time.

"You don't tell us what to do," the monk said.

He picked up the paper, and immediately, the monk's hands burst into flame. The monk screamed. Quint was the first to cast a water string on the monks' damaged hands.

"Whatever vote you cast, I submit a 'no' for whatever they want. I don't care what it costs," the burned monk said with teeth clenched in anger and pain. Another original monk took the injured man out of the refectory.

Quint felt terrible for the man who had initially supported the cloister. Quint was shielded, and nothing would have happened to him. He considered

Danko's act, one of pure evil.

"There stands a man and a woman formed of pure darkness," Dakuz said, reflecting Quint's thoughts. "Wanisa Hannoko doesn't deserve the end she will get, for I also vote 'no' to whatever you propose."

Grizak grunted.

Quint sighed. "I vote "no."

The council was unanimous except for Grizak's abstention.

"And guess what that makes you?" Dakuz said.

Calee shot a fire spear at Quint, but it splattered on his chest.

Quint cast a string to strip the mask from her face.

Calee shrieked. She was incredibly homely, and her natural face had not aged well.

Dakuz killed her with a fire spear. Her shield didn't hold up to Dakuz's attack. Feodor held his hands in front of him. "No! No! We have more troops in the woods. Your only hope is to let me go."

Feodor's eyes opened as he fell forward with a knife in his back. Vintez Dugo, who had walked into the refectory after standing in the doorway until that moment, put an end to Danko's life.

"He doesn't deserve life of any kind after what he did in Pinzleport and wherever else Feodor Danko tainted the ground he stood on." Dugo gave Quint a grim smile. "I'm not always an observer." Dugo washed Feodor's body with fire.

"To the walls!" a voice cried out from the courtyard.

"The bodies are spoiling Tova's ground," one of the bodyguard monks said.

Feodor and Calee's charred bodies were lugged up the stairs and tossed over the parapet. Quint fired a fire spear at Sandy's feet, who dropped the leash and ran behind the carriage. Wannie, now unrestrained, tore the noose from her neck and ran to the gate amidst the shocking conclusion to the Danko's influence. Quint was glad he was mistaken about how swiftly Wannie could move.

Grizak ushered Donnie's mother inside and locked the gate again.

The Green fighters coalesced around the carriage. Quint fired three more fire spears and set the carriage aflame. He wouldn't leave an easy exit for Sandy. However, Sandy ran along the road and out of view amidst the smoke, flames, and retreating guards.

"More soldiers are coming!"

Quint looked across the river before vegetation blocked the view and counted another twenty soldiers marching toward them wearing their green tunics. An officer rode a magnificent horse behind them.

A squad of villagers attacked the flank of the new arrivals, and the fight quickly became a melee. Quint was surprised to see wizards fighting on both sides.

"Attack!" a mounted officer raised a sword. The guards who escorted the Danko's reversed course and ran toward the gate.

"There are men at the rear of the cloister!"

Quint wanted to run to the back wall, but he knew he was needed at the front. His first fire spear pushed the officer off the horse before the Green discipline broke down. Another sheet of fire was shot from the roof. Quint turned to see Grizak's angry face. Fire came from a Green wizard, hitting Grizak in the chest.

The fool hadn't been shielded and fell backward off the wall into a cart pushed against the door. Grizak groaned as Lady Wanisa ran to his aid.

A man in a black cloak trimmed in green casually strutted down the road, impervious to everything the monks threw at him. He spotted Quint and frowned. Quint could see the master's eyes narrow before he dramatically created a string and cast a fire spear that grazed Quint's shoulder, piercing the shield Quint thought was as impervious as the master's shield below. Quint threw everything he could at the man, but nothing stopped the master's pace toward the gate.

Quint had one wizardly arrow in his quiver. He created the string and cast it at the wizard, who vanished. Seeing their wizard gone, the soldiers stopped fighting and stood motionless before turning and fleeing down the road into the arms of more villagers who had joined in the fight.

The rocks and debris had done unexpected damage to the Green attackers in the rear, and within minutes, the enemy was mostly dead or swimming back across the river for their lives.

Quint ran down the wall, past an amazed Thera, to the refectory now serving as an infirmary. Grizak was still breathing. Quint did what he could, which wasn't much, but anything would be helpful.

"He will live," Ronzle said, inspecting the survivors. "It won't be an easy recovery. Others were not so fortunate."

Quint thought of the monks. The head prior of the initial group had survived his burns, but there were at least four others who lost their lives and two of Pilka's guards. The Feltoff Cloister was mostly intact. Outside, the grounds were littered with battered and burned bodies. Forty-four Greens, including Feodor and Calee Danko, were dead.

Quint stepped outside and walked around to the back. There were a few bodies not yet recovered, which made it forty-seven Greens plus a few monks. Sandy wasn't a casualty, but she was lost to the cloister. He didn't know what happened to the two young monks. They hadn't added much to the cloister's activities, being mostly in Sandy's charge, and Quint speculated that they might be Green sympathizers if not spies themselves.

He leaned against the exit door to Tova's path after he unbound the wood.

"Quite a victory," Thera said. "We might all be dead if you hadn't killed that master."

Quint moved his shoulder, feeling the burn that barely injured him, but it was enough of a shock to have forced Quint to use Tova's spell.

"What was that string?" Thera asked.

"Tova inspired it," Quint said. "It is a vanishing string that removes one object at a time. I have no idea where he went. I moved a squirrel and a couple of cobbles this morning before the fight when I tested the string."

"Can you teach it to me?" Thera asked.

Quint shook his head. "I don't know it well enough. I wouldn't want you experimenting with it and disappearing."

"Aww. You thought of me," she said with a little mockery.

Quint grunted. "Not really. I don't feel much like talking right now."

"Still feeling the sting of Sandy's betrayal?"

Quint nodded. "It may take years to remove that sting, Thera," Quint said. "I have to reverse these defenses. There will likely be more pilgrims tomorrow, praying for their dead sons, husbands, and fathers of those villagers who helped us win."

"I may seem a bit callous, but I'm not," Thera said. "What we had to do today is why I left the Narukun Wizard Corps and retreated to Baxel University. I can fight, and I do it well, but…"

Quint merely nodded. He didn't know if he believed Thera or not, but the sentiment was right.

§

Olinz returned from the village early the following day with a body bag draped over his saddle.

"Sandy's body. There is a perfect hole burned right through her chest."

"The wizard master is probably the only one who could do that," Quint said, looking at the wound. "He probably felt offended we had the audacity to kill the Dankos, which lured him into the fray. I wondered what happened to the two little monks?"

Olinz shrugged. "That will be a mystery. The boys weren't found, and I hope they are running as fast as they can all the way home."

Quint sat in his workroom with his head against Tova's wall, but after an hour of thinking about what to do next, and with no visitation, he walked into the courtyard. He looked around the courtyard, watching Andy and Wannie help Grizak walk to the refectory.

None of the monks deserved to be dead or injured, and none of the villagers did either. Quint felt the cloister had changed after the battle, and he didn't feel part of it. Perhaps that was Tova's message. He decided he would have to leave Feltoff to keep everyone safe from a repeat occurrence.

Quint would prepare for his departure and talk to Lord Pilka about it.

He got the chance at lunch when Pilka motioned him over to his table. Ronzle, Olinz, and Pilka's most senior guard were already seated.

"You don't look like the conquering hero," Pilka said with a wide grin.

"I don't feel like it. I'm afraid Feltoff has lost its savor. Death does that to a person."

Pilka frowned. "You are moving on? I thought you might join my family for dinner. Gallia would like to hear a kinder version of what happened from you."

"Leaving is exactly what I'll do. I expect things might be different in Kippun."

"Different is right," Olinz said. "Kippun doesn't even have a central government. The country has been cut up by constantly warring warlords. Just like ancient Pogokon and Slinnon used to be. A bunch of hubites playing as if they are polennese."

"I've taken history courses," Quint said.

"Reading about it and living in it are two very different things," Ronzle said. "I grew up on the border and sneaked into Kippun plenty of times in my youth."

"I'll chance it. I don't think it will be any more hostile than Narukun with the Greens and some of the Reds after me. That's not going to change."

"Running away suits you?" the guard asked.

"No. Keeping people I know safe does," Quint said. "I don't consider that cowardice. Would I be brave to stay here and attract something worse than what we experienced yesterday?"

Pilka lowered his head and raised his hand. "I can understand you. I suppose the Hannokos would support you staying, but you are doing them a favor by leaving."

"My life goes on," Quint said.

The rest of the lunch consisted of stories about Kippun. Their points of view were quite different from Wannie's. Although Quint wouldn't mind visiting, he couldn't seriously consider living the rest of his life there. If it wasn't for the Greens hating him, he could see himself staying in Narukun, especially after eliminating the Dankos as a threat. But others were behind the father and the daughter, including the black-robed master wizard. He had made Quint feel totally inadequate after tasting the wizard's power.

Besides, how could he stay here, the place where Sandy turned against him and where she died? Quint wasn't sure if he could erase the sour taste of betrayal with the sweetness of good memories of Sandy as he passed the visitors center and Tova's pathway.

He returned to his workshop and began to plan for his departure. Quint didn't feel he could leave until the cloister was repaired and the memories of the battle began to fade. He paced the room and leaned against Tova's wall in despair.

"I should be angry at you," Tova said when Quint realized he was back in Tova's domain.

"Why? I protected your church," Quint said, quickly collecting his wits.

"That wizard master you sent me! What a horrid creature. He tried to kill me. Me!" she said. "I had to immediately banish him to the underworld. I wish I didn't gift you that spell, although the little squirrel is cute." She shrugged. "I just want you to know that's the last thing you'll get out of me until you return with Tizurek."

"I'm supposed to bring him back to you? What if he doesn't want to return? Tizurek is doing a fine job of hiding."

Tova had a pout on her lips. "I may send him to the underworld, too."

"Where is the underworld?" Quint asked.

The question brought a smile to Tova's face. "Wouldn't you like to know?

I'm not going to tell a living mortal."

"Then where did I send the wizard master? He was the most powerful wizard I've ever confronted."

"Maybe in your world, but certainly not mine," Tova said. "Anything you send my way with that little string ends up in a holding place, I suppose you'd call it. If you send a subject there, I am obliged to move them on. Being a goddess, I can see into their life and give them a proper reward."

"And he didn't deserve a reward?"

Tova laughed. "A curse, of course. You are different, Quinto Tirolo. Only a few humans can withstand my domain and live. Those that do become stronger."

"I don't feel very strong at the moment," Quint said.

"Aww. Poor baby," Tova said. She waved her hand. "You'll get over it. You've certainly been betrayed before, but the deaths, I suppose, make it worse."

"It does. The responsibility for all the lives in the cloister and the village is a heavy burden," Quint admitted.

"Something that you will learn to live with, but it takes practice. Your journey isn't over, so continue on your way. I won't tell you which path will be the best for you, but in my observations, moving ahead is better than wading around in a stagnant pond."

"Feltoff is stagnant?" Quint asked.

Tova shook her finger at Quint. "You won't get any more answers from me."

"So, this is it? I'm on my own? What if I decide this has been a hallucination? Quint asked.

Tova frowned. "Give me your hand."

Quint walked closer to the goddess and could feel her power raise the hairs on his arm. She touched the inside of his wrist.

"You can also show that to Tizurek when you meet him. He'll know it's from me," Tova said.

"But I need some guidance!" Quint said as he backed up a few steps from the goddess.

"Only if you are lucky. Goodbye."

She waved her hand, and Quint blinked when he realized he had been dismissed. If he was hallucinating, which was possible, he supposed, it was a very consistent hallucination, and the string that Tova implanted in him had saved them all.

Quint had wondered if Tova would visit him before he left Feltoff. He didn't know, and at this point, he realized he would certainly stagnate, as Tova put it, if he remained in Feltoff waiting for encounters with the goddess. That was a life Quint didn't want.

The inside of his wrist began to hurt. He looked down to see two small black outlines of triangles, one pointed side up and the other pointed side down connected by a red line. Tova had marked him seemingly for Tizurek and Tova. How could he deny he ever met her?

He stayed away from the wall while he thought and wrote what supplies he would take. Quint wouldn't leave immediately, but he wouldn't dawdle. He'd move ahead. After all, that was what he had done ever since he was pressed into the Wizard Corps.

§§§

CHAPTER THIRTY-THREE

THOSE THAT DIED WERE BURIED ON THE OTHER SIDE OF THE RIVER in an unused plot of land that Pilka owned. Quint walked among the graves. Those who died on Feltoff's side had stone grave markers, and the Greens were buried beneath wooden ones.

He had asked Olinz, who had supervised the little cemetery, to use a stone grave marker for Sandy but bury her with the Greens. Quint wondered where Tova had sent her soul. He hoped he never found out.

Calee and Feodor Danko's bodies were marked as plainly as the lowest soldier killed on the other side. In a moment of uncharitable thinking, Quint wondered if their bodies should be dug up and tossed into the river.

As Quint left the graves, he noticed bushes shaking at the edge of the plot, and the face of one of Sandy's boy monks peaked out.

"You can come out," Quint said. "I promise I won't hurt you."

One of the boys beckoned to the other, and both looked like they had been sleeping in the open for weeks. It had only been eight days since the fight for Feltoff Cloister. Quint wondered how the pair survived.

"Quint, can we return to the cloister?" the older one asked.

"It isn't up to me, but that depends on what happened. Why did you leave with Sandy?"

The younger boy looked up at the older and nodded. "Tell him."

"She wanted us safe from the battle," the older said.

Quint nodded. He could see how two relatively defenseless boys would find that reasonable coming from someone they trusted.

"Did you know you were to be hostages?"

"Not until Master Jelnitz arrived. He told us we'd be killed if the cloister fought back."

"You believed him."

Both boys shook their heads in the affirmative. "Sandy confirmed it when she apologized after she ran away when the battle started. She came to the camp where we were kept and told us we'd have to run. When the soldiers were getting prepared to kill us and getting battle instructions from the master, Sandy cut a hole in the back of the tent and told us to run."

"And you ran?"

"We did. When we had reached the bushes that surrounded the camp, we looked back and saw Master Jelnitz kill her," the younger boy said.

"We kept running," the older said, putting his arm around his friend's shoulders. "Neither of us knew if we'd be killed the next second."

"What have you done for eating and sleeping?" Quint said.

"There are lots of little farms. We stole enough to live, but we don't want to become bandits," the older one said.

"Come with me. I don't know if your story is true, but I'd like to believe it is. Let the council decide what to do with you. But don't worry, you won't be punished. At worse, you'll have to go to another cloister or something. It's not up to me to decide."

"We'd rather stay in Feltoff," one said.

"We both know how to guide visitors along Tova's pathway," the other said.

"You will note that I had Sandy straddle the line between the Greens and the Cloister. Ultimately, she thought more of you than she did of her life. Remember the sacrifice," Quint said.

"We've talked about that," the older one said. "She told us she loved us as much as if we were her own children." He wiped away a tear.

Quint took them to Grizak, who was more mobile because of common and magical healing treatments. The boys told their story, and Grizak assured them they had a place in the cloister if they didn't show any allegiance to the Greens.

"Not after what they did to Sandy!" the older one blurted out.

That was enough for Quint to believe their story.

With the mystery of Sandy's death and the disappearance of the boys solved Quint knew he needed to leave the cloister. He decided to depart in two days, and it was time to tell Dakuz, Grizak, and Kozak.

They assembled in Quint's workroom. Thera showed up along with Wannie, who had temporarily taken over the responsibility visitor's center. Wannie had yet to decide where she was going to live.

"You have something to tell us?" Dakuz asked.

"I'm leaving Feltoff Cloister in a couple of days. I've thought about it since the battle, and I must remove myself to keep all my friends safe."

"Where will you go? Parsun Cloister is a ruin," Kozak said.

"I thought I'd see what Kippun is like."

Wannie clicked her tongue. "We've told you that you won't like it there."

"I don't think I'll stay, but I can see what polennese-style hubites are like."

"Worse than polens, but we've talked about that," Wannie said.

"You've talked to everyone about it. We just didn't know when you'd go. With everyone buried and the two little monks returning," Grizak sighed. "I'll hate to see you go."

"I need to move on before I stagnate, someone told me. That might be part of my motivation to leave now. Feltoff is close to being where it needs to be."

"But we need you," Kozak said.

"For what? I don't want to have to fight again and put you all at risk because of me. I haven't kept this a secret."

"No, you haven't," Dakuz said. "I think you've been too open about it."

Quint turned to Thera. "Will King Boviz be upset?"

"Delighted that you'll be out of his realm is a more accurate description. You are making the right decision," she said.

Quint smiled. "Can anyone give me a reason to stay?"

"Other than losing a friend to the unknown?" Kozak said.

"Good. Now I won't have to hoard food and collect traveling things in secret," Quint said.

"No, but you should take one of the horses. We acquired too many in the battle, and Tova's Falls doesn't have a large enough market to sell them all at once," Grizak said.

"That is an offer I'll accept. Perhaps two horses and use one of them to pack my things?" Quint asked.

"Twist our arms," Kozak said with a grin.

Pilka arrived the next day with Gallia, Silla, his wife, and Olinz to say goodbye.

"I don't want to let you go. You are the glue that bound this cloister together, unwittingly or not," Lord Pilka said. "I want you to be able to stay in an inn if you need some comfort on your journey."

He handed Quint a purse. A quick peek showed the color gold mixed in with the silver.

"Thank you," Quint said.

"Are you taking anyone with you?" Lord Pilka asked.

Quint shrugged. "I've always thought I'd be traveling alone. I don't want others exposed like we were, traveling from Seensist to your domain."

"You might want to rethink that."

"I will," Quint said to placate the lord.

After Pilka and his entourage had left that evening, Quint sat in the refectory, rolling a glass of wine between his palms.

"Seeing if you can turn wine into strings?" Vintez Dugo said. He sat down across from Quint.

"No," Quint said with a smile.

"I'd like to come with you," Dugo said. "I'm healed enough to be useful as a servant if nothing else."

"I've already had to turn down half the cloister tonight," Quint said.

"Think about it. I'll not force you. Kozak wants me to learn how to handle wood, which feels like a prison sentence."

"A good reason since I feel somewhat the same." He smiled.

Dugo looked at a life of stagnation; at least, that was how Quint interpreted his friend's statement.

"Then get your things together. I can't promise you a good time," Quint said.

"I'm not looking for one."

§

Dakuz woke Quint, sleeping fitfully in his cell after midnight.

"You want to come with me, too?" Quint asked.

"I came to Feltoff because of you, and I'll not let you leave me behind," Dakuz said. "I'll be riding with you when you leave or catching up after you've gone."

"Dugo feels the same way. He said he'll be restless in Feltoff."

"I don't blame him," Dakuz said. "I'm not going to ask you to take me with you. I'm telling you that I'm following you, like it or not."

Quint rubbed the sleep from his eyes. "Then I guess I'll learn to like it. Having lots of followers defeats my purpose in leaving."

"But your survival may require some backup. Be realistic," Dakuz said.

"I just said I'd let you come with me," Quint said.

"What?" Dakuz looked dumbfounded and then grinned. "I guess you did. It's too late at night for an old man to make demands."

"You aren't that old. I thought you'd want to hook up with Donnie's mother."

Dakuz laughed. "Not a chance."

Quint wasn't interrupted again, and by the time he woke for his last day at Feltoff, he was happy he had slept better than he had in a week.

He checked with Dugo, giving him the good news and Dakuz. They would be ready to leave in the following morning.

A few others hinted they would like to join him, but Quint said no. At dinner, Grizak said he was willing to leave Feltoff, but Quint rejected him more forcefully than the others. The cloister needed a strong leader, and Grizak was developing into one. He needed Quint gone to grow into a proper head prior, and he needed to stay to protect the Hannokos.

Quint waited for the cloister to go to sleep. With his bags in hand, he sneaked out of his cell and saddled his horse, once the mount of one of the Green officers. The cloister was silent as he unbarred the gate and led the mount outside. He turned to look at Feltoff one more time. Quint's would-be companions would be disappointed, but Quint still felt he shouldn't be responsible for any followers. Besides, he didn't want to go through all the goodbyes that would probably take up most of the morning.

He mounted his horse and led the pack horse across the bridge. Three riders emerged from the bushes. Quint created a fire spear string and was ready to throw it when one of the riders lit a magic light.

"Don't fight us, Quint," Dakuz said. "We will stick to you like glue."

Quint saw the faces of Dugo, Dakuz and Thera, of all people, looking at him. He let the string dissipate and let his shoulders droop.

"Then let's ride out of here and not look back," Quint said.

He urged his horse on, and the four riders rode through a sleepy Tova's Falls and headed north toward Baxel. And then, if Quint could shake off Thera in Baxel, they could leave Narukun. He knew Dakuz and Dugo wouldn't let him proceed alone.

§§§

CHAPTER THIRTY-FOUR

BAXEL DIDN'T LOOK ANY DIFFERENT from the few weeks he had been gone. Quint had cast a disguise string to change his appearance before they entered the city, and with Thera's identification, they didn't have to show any of their own. Thera took them to her flat not far from the Narukun Military Headquarters. It was a two-bedroom affair, but it was large enough to be comfortable while they were in the capital city.

Their horses were stabled behind the building, and they decided to lug all their possessions up one floor to Thera's flat.

"Do you want us to clean this up?" Dugo asked. "You don't know when you'll return."

Thera smiled. "Don't worry about that. However, I will add a bit to our packhorse's burden. My family owns this building, and I don't have to worry about not paying rent," she said. "I'll have to tell them I may be gone for some time."

"You don't have to be gone," Quint said. "You've fulfilled your orders."

Thera gave Quint a crooked smile. "I haven't given up on you yet. And your obvious try to leave me in Baxel won't work."

Dugo grinned at Quint behind Thera's back. She was right. It was a lame attempt. He'd have to think of something better, but could he come up with something that would work with Thera? She was a much different person than Amaria Baltacco, Calee Danko, or Sandy Bartok. There was a bigger problem in Quint's mind. He didn't think of her as a romantic interest. There was no attraction that he could discern within him, and he wondered if that was an advantage if she stayed with them or would it become a liability at some point farther down the road.

"I'm reporting to headquarters, and then I may have to do the same to the king or one of his ministers," she said to them. "You should be safe enough on the streets around here as long as Quint is disguised."

She left, and the three of them did, too. Dakuz had been to Baxel before, so he wore a shapeless hat jammed over his head. Dugo had never set foot in the capital before, and Quint was disguised. They ate at a tiny restaurant and got directions to a local market where they would buy a few more clothes worthy of Baxel.

When the three returned to Thera's flat, she hadn't returned, and they proceeded to find open spaces where they could take a nap.

In the twilight of the end of the day, Quint sat up on the couch as the door opened. Thera walked in with someone else. There wasn't a squad of guards behind them, so Quint remained sitting as she walked in. The other two companions struggled to wake up and rubbed their eyes as Thera lit a few magic lamps.

"We can leave after an audience with the king's cabinet. King Boviz is out of the city," Thera said. "I am relieved of my duties at the university and resigned from the military. I am all yours."

"And your friend?" Quint asked.

"This is my former boyfriend," Thera said. "He will be our escort at the palace."

"How former?" Dugo asked.

"We realized that we weren't a couple after six months of trying," the officer said. "We are still friends."

"What is expected from our meeting with the cabinet?" Quint asked the boyfriend.

"Good question," the officer said. "Phandiz Crider wants to make sure of your motivation to leave Narukun. The king's internal strategies change if you are no longer in the picture."

"You are still relying on the accuracy of predictor strings?" Quint asked.

"That is the best approach we can think of. Thera's input has supported your leaving us. Removing a high-level Green wizard at the battle of Feltoff Cloister changed much of the short-term outlook. That is due to your survival and your decision to vacate Narukun," the officer said.

"Then it won't take long to talk," Dakuz said. "I can't wait to be on our way."

"None of us can," Quint said. He was about to exempt Thera from being on the way with the others, but the woman would see the comment as too clumsy.

In the morning, they were taken to a different meeting room. Quint recognized a few ministers from lunch with King Boviz, including Crider. Their faces seemed pinched and looked like they were all wound tight. Something unpleasant seemed to thicken the air.

Thera's officer guarded the door once they all sat down.

"We are facing a crisis," the prime minister said. "King Boviz has been kidnapped and is being held for ransom. This isn't an ordinary ransom. The Greens have done the kidnapping, and the ransom consists of splitting Narukun into two states."

"Why are you telling us this?" Quint asked.

"Because we are asking you to help save him," another minister said.

"What can we do that the army can't?" Dakuz asked.

"We don't have Quinto Tirolo."

"Do you know where the king is?" Dugo asked. "We have to get going on our way."

Quint smiled at Dugo's comment.

"We know where he is, and we have been unable to get through their gauntlet of wizards."

Quint sighed. "How many? Are they as good as the one we defeated at the gate?"

Thera frowned. "Nearly as good. Five masters. We can't think of anything to stop them other than a full assault, and that will result in the deaths of hundreds of soldiers. King Boviz will likely be a casualty before we can get to him."

"We should start planning now," Quint said. "The master who confronted us at the cloister had a shield I couldn't breach. If these wizards can produce shields as strong, we won't be able to help you."

"But Thera told us you defeated the master."

Quint took a deep breath. "I used an unusual string. I don't know if I can produce five of them. If we fail at any step, we risk the king's life."

"Then use the string again. We will have to fight these wizards again if the Greens take over the southern half of Narukun," the prime minister said.

"Then we shouldn't waste any time," Quint said. If he wasn't involved, he could cast a predictor string, but his magic was as murky as others regarding him. "I'm going to want an agreement that we can leave Narukun without any difficulties if we rescue the king."

"And if we don't rescue the king?" Dugo asked.

"Then I probably won't be alive to worry about it," Quint said.

§

The abandoned keep looked very secure, sitting on the prow of a plateau looking over a vast fertile plain to the south. The location of the king's prison was one and a half days west of Baxel. The keep was secure on three sides, with cliffs rising a few hundred feet from the floor of the plain.

From Quint's strategic point of view, the keep would be suitable for observing what happened on part of the plain, but much of the surrounding area was lost to view since the keep was built fifty yards from the edge. In Quint's eyes, it gave whoever held the land above or below no advantage other than making it difficult to approach but a perfect place for sequestering the king.

Quint didn't know any good invisibility strings if there were any. He would be trying to send five Green wizards to Tova one way or another.

"Where are the wizards?" Quint asked.

"They have moved around," Thera's officer said. He claimed he oversaw the military operation. They couldn't bring an army, or the king would be killed.

"What if we scaled the cliffs?" Quint said.

"Not me!" Dakuz said.

"We don't have rope long enough," the officer said, "or we would have tried. The wall is sheer and unclimbable."

"Then it's a frontal assault from the top," Quint said. "We will have to move fast and do it at night."

"We came to the same conclusion," the officer said. "Can you eliminate the wizards?"

"I won't know until I try. Fighting one is different than confronting four or five."

If the five were close in capability to the master at Feltoff, Quint had no chance, but the royalists had no answer for the Greens, and Quint couldn't abandon half of Narukun to the Greens. That would only be their first step toward a total takeover of Narukun and maybe all of North Fenola. He would have to find a way.

The small army was behind a screen of trees that started a few hundred yards away from the keep. There was nothing to do until nightfall, so Quint and his friends retreated to a village near the keep and bought black clothes. They needed any kind of advantage during their operation.

Dugo and Dakuz were support troops and were tasked with lagging, out of range but within sight, although everyone hoped there was little to see.

Thera and Quint would go in. Quint needed a powerful wizard at his back, and although he didn't ever test Thera's power, he trusted her intellect.

Quint stood just inside the treeline, looking at the sunlight slide up the tallest tower of the keep. It wouldn't be long before they would go into action.

"Are you nervous?" Thera asked Quint.

"I am," Quint said honestly. "I'm going to give this a try, but five wizards?" He shook his head with dismay.

"You don't have to kill them all." Thera pulled out a contraption from within her bag. "This is something we have developed but never implemented," she said.

"I've seen hand-held crossbows before," Quint said.

"It isn't the crossbow, but the string that makes it work. The bolts are generally too slow to penetrate a magical shield, but if they are shot with a string that I'll teach you, the bolt moves fast enough for most shields. The big problem is cranking the bow back far enough. It takes too much time to be a battlefield weapon."

"Show me the string," Quint said.

He observed the process of thread creation and string weaving closely and understood how it worked.

"Now, shoot a bolt," Quint said.

Thera struggled to draw the bow with the little crank, but she could do it and slipped a bolt in the channel. The string was cast on the bolt and when Thera pulled the trigger, the bolt moved fast enough to be heard as it sunk halfway into a nearby tree trunk.

Quint tried it. The bow was harder than he thought, but it was still easier for him than Thera. He applied the string, and his bolt missed the tree that he aimed at, but it found another trunk to stop it. The metal fletchings were all that showed.

Thera whistled. "The power of a master," she said.

"Let me try something else," Quint said.

He took another bolt and laid it on the bow without drawing it back, aimed, and invoked the string. The bolt sang through the forest, hitting the tree where Quint aimed.

"I don't know if you can do that enough to penetrate a magical shield," Quint said, "but you won't have to spend a few minutes cranking more power into the bolt."

Thera tried it and the bolt stuck into the bark, but not deep. "It would work on an unshielded person," she said, almost to herself. "I just happen to have another pocket crossbow."

Quint took it. Among her things she also had another bag of bolts. "I can get more before we leave."

He walked over to the tree that had taken his string-only bolt. It had gone in almost as far as the bow-enhanced string. He tried using a string to remove the bolt and found the only one that worked was the same string that Thera had just taught him. He only had to make a minor adjustment on the string for it to move in the opposite direction.

The bolt shot out of the tree toward Quint, who threw himself aside. The fletched side of the bolt grazed his upper arm and stuck in the tree behind him, but not far enough that he couldn't remove the bolt. He scratched that string from his list of possible ones to use on his foray to retrieve the king.

He removed his tunic and examined his damage. The bolt had drawn a tiny line of blood, looking like a scratch. Quint took out his handkerchief and wrapped it around his arm.

"What happened?" Thera asked.

"Nothing. I scratched myself, removing one of the bolts. It's not worth using it without more practice."

"You didn't need to do that," she said, handing him a bag of bolts. "My officer friend would like to talk strategy."

The officer had explained the futile attempts so far. "You are right in assuming you can only attack the keep from this side."

"I don't want to attack the keep," Quint said. "Thera and I will sneak in and take care of a few of the wizards before rescuing the king. Since we have no idea what we are really facing, that is as far as we can go. A red magic light will mean we have succeeded, and a double light will mean the king is dead, and you can proceed without caution. A green light triple light will mean we have been defeated."

"Let's hope for one red light," the officer said. He looked into the darkening sky. "You are free to do your intruding at will. I'll get a few fires going here to think the attack will come from this direction."

"Good idea," Quint said.

"Actually, it was Hintz Dakuz who suggested it," the officer said, smiling.

Dakuz grunted an acknowledgment from behind Quint.

§§§

CHAPTER THIRTY-FIVE

Thera and Quint, followed by Dugo and Dakuz, crept behind the tree line. Quint hoped the trees and the black clothes would cover their position. Quint stopped at a likely starting point. There were more rocks between the keep and their position than other approaches. He cast a disguise string on Thera and himself and felt ready to go.

"Stay behind the rocks," Quint said, "but you can peek out to see what is happening.

"From the side, not from the top of the rocks," Dakuz said to Dugo. I'd rather us both survive this."

Quint nodded and set out, following Thera slowly through the rock field. Quint felt a presence off to his side and touched Thera before putting a finger to his lips. He pointed toward the shadow up ahead that was too smooth to be a rock.

The sentry's role in the foray made Quint uncertain.

"Let him be," Thera whispered. "Stay here, and I'll tell Dakuz and Dugo to come as far as we are now."

Quint nodded. He thought he could go by himself, but Thera might be better at silent movement and did what she said. He had to trust her from this point on.

His eyes were on the sentry, who moved when something cracked toward the others. The shape detached from close to the rocks.

Quint followed with an enchanted bolt sitting in his undrawn crossbow. He aimed at the sentry and invoked the string. The dark figure didn't even have time to hear the hissing of the bolt and crumpled to the ground.

Making his way to the victim, Quint looked down. The sentry wore a black cloak over the green tunic of a Green soldier. He stripped the cloak and tunic from the dead man, heard voices, and used the direction of the sound to reach his three comrades.

"The sentry heard your movements and went to check," Quint said. "You don't have to worry about him anymore. I brought a couple of souvenirs. I think this will fit Dugo better than Dakuz if you are confronted. Dakuz is to hide, and you, Dugo, play the part of a sentry."

"What is this sticky stuff?" Dugo said as he put on the tunic.

"Luckily, I hit him in the back," Quint said. "No one will see it in the dark."

Dugo shivered, but it was for effect more than anything else. "I hope it doesn't taint me for life."

"Just hope you have a life to taint after all this," Dakuz said.

"Way to cheer him up," Thera said.

Quint wanted to laugh, but he knew better. "You can follow closer," Quint said.

He took Thera's hand and led her toward the keep.

"My, you didn't even ask," Thera said behind him.

"No sounds from here on," Quint said, letting go.

About one hundred yards from the keep, they spotted a dark canopy. Underneath was a dim magic lamp. Quint could make out green piping. It was the same outfit that the Green master in Feltoff wore.

"Master ahead," Quint said.

"I saw the green," Thera whispered. "There may be traps between us and the keep."

"We are going to let the wizard sit while we go inside," Quint said.

They circled around to the right edge of the plateau and carefully walked through the grassy field. Thera was the first to find a trap.

"I can sense the magic," she said, looking down at a rock.

"Like the agreement that Feodor Danko insisted that I touch?"

"The poor monk," Thera said. "The insistence should have alerted him."

Quint created a simple string and cast a small blue light on the trap. "Others might not be as sensitive to magic as you," Quint said.

As they walked closer to the keep, they came across more traps and were soon up against the keep's walls.

"No magic on the stone," Thera said.

"Perhaps they think their traps will be sufficient. Let's walk around and see if there is another entrance other than the front."

The traps intensified once they faced the plain. The view must have been stunning in the daylight. As it was, Quint could see puddles of tiny lights in the distance with a few larger puddles for towns.

The rear door, protected by a drawn-up, iron-clad drawbridge, was fronted by a ditch full of weeds and ancient garbage. The door almost glowed with magic, and Quint suspected magically enhanced spikes might still be covered by the weeds.

"Should I try to defeat the enchantment?" Quint asked.

"As long as you don't blow us up. It's a risk."

"So is confronting the wizard master sitting in the front of the keep."

"I'm going to make the door disappear," Quint said. "Can you jump across the ditch?"

"I can," Thera said.

Quint nodded and decided to use a one-handed string to send the door to Tova's domain. It was headed to Tova's holding place, so he hoped no one would be injured when it arrived if that could happen.

He cast the string, and the drawbridge simply disappeared without a sound. The following string eliminated the door, exposing an open gap in the wall.

"Now, no whispering unless absolutely necessary," Quint said into Thera's ear.

He jumped first and barely made it. She followed, landed a half-foot short, and began to wheel her arms, ready to fall backward. Quint leaned forward and grabbed an arm as she moved it in front of her and pulled.

She slipped and the only thing that kept her from falling into the ditch was Quint's hold on her. Quint struggled. He kept his mouth shut, but it was difficult to grab Thera and drag her over the transom.

"I might have splinters," she whispered in his ear.

Her voice, so close to him and so intimate, almost shocked him, but he ignored the sensation and brought Thera to her feet.

"That will be enough of that," A voice said behind them. Quint turned to look into the eyes of two black-robed wizards approaching Quint and Thera. The green piping was identical to the one who visited Feltoff Cloister.

Thera clutched him still, to keep her balance, and there was nothing they could do. Quint felt they were lucky the Greens weren't using them as pincushions.

The crossbows were taken from Quint and Thera as they were in the bags hanging from their belts, but the bolts remained.

"Bind one of their hands," one of the wizards said. "That will be enough to keep them out of action, and we won't have to spend as much time minding them."

Quint had thought they would just kill them, but he wasn't about to argue the point.

They were led down a single flight of stone steps into a dungeon. A cell door was open, and they were tossed into the same cell.

"Who are you?" a voice came from another cell.

Quint recognized King Boviz's voice and realized their disguises were still intact.

"Friends," Thera said, pointing to her face and making an "X" in front of it.

"You are wizards with one hand bound?" The king chuckled, but it wasn't a good-hearted chuckle. He held up his hand tied up like theirs. "They think I'm a wizard too."

"I thought you were," Thera said, changing her voice.

"Not much of one. Enough to entertain the ladies with a few parlor tricks. I was able to do four strings. No more." There was a pause. "You came to rescue me?"

Quint nodded, but there wasn't much light in the dungeon. "There are lots of traps in the fields surrounding the keep."

"Is that where I am?"

Thera told the king where the keep was.

"Useless except for holding the king of the land, eh?" King Boviz said. "You are useless, too, with your hands bound. I suppose you think your power is much greater than mine. At this moment in time, we are equals."

"Perhaps," Thera said.

She wiggled her fingers beneath her wrapped hand and gave Quint a frantic look.

Quint used a one-handed string to break her bindings. He then removed his own.

"You can do one-handed strings?" Thera asked breathlessly. "I thought that only applied to your special string?"

"A gift from a wonderful lady," Quint said.

"Who?" Thera asked.

"I'm not telling, but she's related to one of Feltoff's monks," Quint said. He turned to the king's cell. "What can you tell us about the keep?"

"Not much. I was out on a tour with too few guards. I was captured and hooded. I rode for a day until they pushed me down these stairs and put me in here. They feed me enough, but the cuisine isn't appealing without my spice bag. It is cuisine, though," the king said drily.

Thera was able to use a thermal string to open the cell door.

"Careful, it's hot," she said to Quint in her disguised voice.

"I am visited by Feodor Danko every morning," King Boviz said.

"You can't be serious!" Quint said.

"Oh, I am. Quinto Tirolo thought he had killed him at Feltoff, but those were two imposters with facial disguises."

"So, Calee isn't as ugly as I thought," Quint said.

"Tirolo? Is that you? I knew I recognized the voice but couldn't place it until now. What is your plan?"

Quint chuckled. "Plan? We don't have any plan. How could we when no one remembered much about the interior of this keep? We came to rescue you."

"And were captured yourselves."

"We found you, Your Majesty," Quint said. "They took us right to you, didn't they?"

"No titles here, Tirolo. Boviz is fine. I won't even get upset if you call me Finir."

Thera opened the king's cell door, and Quint removed his bindings.

"We are out of the cells. Now we take it step by step," Quint said. "My companion and I are not without resources."

"I'll say you aren't. Lead on, and I will follow," Boviz said.

Quint lit a brighter light.

"You are disguised, too."

Quint managed a smile. "I got the idea from Calee Danko. One of my brothers knew the string."

"Can you disguise me?" Boviz asked.

"I don't see why not. Who do you want to look like?

"Surprise me."

"Without a mirror, that might be difficult," Thera said.

"Quite," the king said.

Quint gave Boviz the face of Oscar Viznik, the monk who initially let him into Seensist.

"The court ladies won't be as anxious to meet your acquaintance," Thera said.

The remark made the king smile. "Good. Let's hope that repels Green wizards, as well."

"I think Brother Oscar was a Green sympathizer," Quint said.

The king shrugged. "We go up the steps to freedom?"

"Let's hope," Quint said. He palmed a bolt. His shots wouldn't be as accurate, but they would be almost as lethal and even more silent.

They slipped up the stairs and almost intruded on a squad of four guards playing dice.

Quint didn't say a word but put them all to sleep. None had magical shields, but Quint didn't expect that advantage to last on their mission.

"Do you need a weapon?" he asked the king.

"If you don't mind." The king tested the swords and sighed. "This is the only one that is barely passable. Are those pocket crossbows hanging with the keys?"

Quint followed the king's eyes and saw their weapons. He gave one to Thera and took the other. The palmed crossbow bolt had been enchanted with the propulsion string and placed in the channel. He wouldn't draw his bolt, but he helped Thera draw hers with the crank.

"I can do it myself," she said.

"But I can do it faster," Quint said.

Thera shrugged and accepted Quint's help.

The king spotted a dark cloak hanging from a peg and threw it around his shoulders.

"My clothes are too fine for this place," the king said. "I don't mean to steal."

"Consider it compensation for the kidnapping," Thera said.

"I will," the king said, looking pleased with the idea. Quint thought the king was joking about the stealing.

Quint peeked out the door. No guards were in sight, so Thera quickly ran down the steps to the dungeon and extinguished the light since the king said they put him in darkness every night. He had been gone for a week.

They made their way to the back of the keep to the open door only to find the king's captors had nailed boards over the opening. Quint tried to move the boards, but only one disappeared. Quint couldn't move separate boards to Tova's holding place quickly enough to use that as an exit.

"That won't work. We will have to walk out the front," Thera said. "You will have to teach me how to do that!"

Quint didn't respond.

They hugged the edges of the courtyard. They heard voices, and a door opened, throwing light into the dark courtyard.

"Don't worry. I will interrogate them tomorrow morning," a voice said. "We won't feed them tonight or tomorrow. That should be enough discomfort for the king."

That was Feodor Danko's voice. Quint made a face in the dark. The man defined deceit, but he shouldn't have been fooled by the fake Danko colds.

An officer bowed to Danko and walked across the courtyard and through a door. Two sets of guards patrolled the courtyard, but they were quickly put to sleep.

"We can leave?" Thera asked.

Quint shook his head. "Danko needs to be executed again," he said.

"You can put the rescue in jeopardy."

"No. I want to see the man hanged," Boviz said. "I'm with Quint."

Quint grimly smiled. "Two against one."

Thera was assigned to knock on Feodor's door, but Quint would rush inside. The king would watch from the porch.

Calee came to the door. "My father is not taking visitors until tomorrow morning," she said.

Thera nodded. "That is your voice," she said as Quint rushed in and put her to sleep. He erased her disguise to see an older face, but it was Callee.

'Who is here?" Feodor asked. "I asked not to be disturbed."

The man had changed into a dressing robe and spoke from his bedroom door.

Quint erased his disguise. "Fancy meeting you here," Quint said.

"Calee, kill this man! You've tried twice, but you must succeed this time," Feodor said.

"Calee has gone to sleep already, Danko," Quint said. "I'm ending your career of death and disruption tonight."

"No, you aren't," Danko drew a knife, but the king slipped into their rooms and ran Danko through with the sword and cut his neck. "That ought to do it."

Quint attempted to erase Danko's disguise, but he wasn't wearing one. He had to step aside to avoid the blood rushing from his wounds.

"What will you do about Calee?" Thera asked.

"I have just the place for her. She will join her father by a different route," Quint said before he sent Calee to Tova.

"Where has she gone?" Boviz asked.

"A place of no return," Quint said. "That's the only answer you'll get out of me. Time to go."

Quint turned toward the courtyard when they heard shouting in the back of the keep where the dungeon was.

"We can't go that way!" Boviz said. "But we'll be trapped."

"I wouldn't come to that conclusion," Quint said. "Let's stall them."

Thera bound the wood to the outside door of the Danko's quarters. It was up against the wall, and Quint went to a backroom, once used for storage but recently cleaned. It was there he began to remove the stones just like he had done at the back of Feltoff until a hole had been made large enough for them to leave.

They picked their way through the traps and found Dakuz sleeping while Dugo watched.

"Take the king to the army," Quint said. "I have to go back and dispose of some evil wizards."

"You don't have to do that," Thera said.

"My last gift to Narukun. Help Dakuz." Quint ran back to the hole in the side of the keep and slipped inside. It was time to signal the army. He stood in the middle of the courtyard and shot a magic firework into the air. The courtyard was figuratively ablaze with the red light of a massive firework that exploded high in the air. Quint expected the light could be seen for miles into the plain.

A spear of fire hit his back, knocking him forward. He twisted around and returned fire. The shield of the wizard couldn't withstand Quint's attack. Quint was surprised that his target was a black-robed wizard. So, they all weren't invulnerable.

Arrows and crossbow bolts bounced against his shield. He returned the favor and realized his magic was starting to fade. He thought that perhaps he had been a victim of hubris again as another fire spear licked against his leg. This time he had to cast a water string to extinguish it. The wizard was too close to him, and Quint reached through the wizard's shield and put him to sleep. The wizard's shield ended when he slid to the ground, and the next wave of projectiles missed Quint but killed the wizard.

Quint's shield was losing strength quickly. Another fire spear splashed against his shield. Quint took cover behind a wagon and cranked the crossbow. He crept to the side of the wagon as the wizard began approaching. He steadied the crossbow on the driver's seat edge and shot. The crossbow's magically enhanced bolt went through the magician's chest, throwing him back. He lay sprawled on the ground.

He hoped that accounted for all but one wizard, the one who sat outside, waiting for the army to attack. Quint had to reach him before the army was attacked.

He threw the front door open, seeing torches and magic lights emerge hundreds of yards distant from the treeline. The wizard rose from his chair and shot a mighty fire spear, hitting a cluster of advancing soldiers.

"Stop it!" Quint said.

The wizard turned around. "A Boviz flunky? You think you are powerful?" The wizard master sneered. "You have no power compared with me," the man said. He drew back his robe to reveal a green tunic. "We are to rule the world," he said. "I suppose you killed Feodor Danko. Was that part of your mission? I certainly hope so. I couldn't stand his smug attitude. He thought he would lead the Greens, but I'm the one to do that. Prepare to die."

Quint channeled as much of his energy into his shield as he could. The spear from the wizard enveloped him in green flame, eating away at his shield. He screamed as his shield began to fail. His left hand burst into incredible pain; his right thigh was next. Quint poured more magic into his shield but felt his magic flame out like a candle snuffed by a mighty wind.

The flames felt like they had attacked him forever and finally stopped. "Have you had enough?" The wizard gawked at Quint's injured hand. "I see I have destroyed your ability to fight back," the wizard said. "You are impotent without two hands, whoever you are."

The wizard watched Quint crumple to the ground in pain. He drew back to administer the killing flame, but Quint held a bolt in his right hand. It was enveloped in Tova's power. It hadn't extinguished like his mortal magic. He created a string from the power on the bolt and shot it. The wizard's mouth opened, but no sound came out as the bolt struck his heart, throwing him twenty paces and cartwheeling the victim into the air to land, face down, on one of the traps. Without his magic shield, the wizard was obliterated as the trap exploded.

The army advanced, and in a moment, they ran past Quint and into the keep.

"Give no quarter," the officer said, standing over Quint.

As Quint sighed and gritted his teeth, the pain overwhelmed him.

§§§

CHAPTER THIRTY-SIX

QUINT WOKE IN A BRIGHT, WHITE ROOM. His first thought was to find out if he was in Tova's holding area or somewhere similar. Quint didn't know how long he had been asleep, but the burns were barely a memory. He looked at his left hand, expecting to see a gnarled knob of angry flesh, but he could wiggle his fingers, although they were incredibly stiff. The pain wasn't excruciating, but it told Quint he hadn't become Tova's yet. He counted that as a good thing. He wasn't so sure he trusted the goddess.

"How? I thought I had mostly burned to death," he said, but there was no one to listen to him.

A healer walked into the room. "I hope you are worth it," she said. "The king ordered every healer and wizard in the capital to administer to you over the last month."

"Month?" Quint sat up, but his head felt woozy, so he laid back down.

"Yes, month. Of course, we are happy you saved the king and killed the Green wizards who wanted to take over our country. I suppose that is enough," the woman sighed, but Quint could see a smile spread on her face.

"There was talk the king wanted to make you Crown Prince, but you aren't properly from Narukun," she said.

"That's fine with me. When can I get up?"

"Now. We've kept you asleep until you can."

§

His new skin was stiff, so stiff it would make many things he used to do impossible. He would have to work hard at getting his fingers flexible.

Thera showed up in a few days, along with Dakuz and Dugo.

"The healer said we could help your rehabilitation. You need to move to get better."

"Are you here to watch or to help?" Quint said.

"Help," Thera said. "Everyone lamented that you had lost your magic. I can't sense it in you like I could before. That hasn't made the predictor strings any clearer."

"The magic I was born with is gone forever, I think," Quint said. "I poured it all into my failing shield. A lot of good that did."

"Then how did you survive?" Thera asked.

Dakuz leaned over. "I'm interested in how you did it, too. I've waited a month to find out if I guessed correctly," he grumbled. "Does it have anything to do with the new tattoo we found on your wrist when we brought you back to Baxel?"

"I'm not sure, but I found a different resource," Quint said. He lifted his tattooed left arm, willed a set of threads to blossom, formed them into a magical string, and sent a flowery scent into the air. "My magic didn't leave, it changed."

§§§§§

The End

STRINGS OF EMPIRE: CHARACTERS & LOCATIONS

CHARACTERS

THE WIZARD CORPS

Quint Tirolo - Fifteen-year-old boy with magic awakening inside him.

Zeppo Tirolo - Quint's father

Master Geno Pozella - magic trainer

Amaria Baltacco – junior officer in the Wizard Corps

Colonel Sarrefo - commander of Strategic Operations

Field Marshal Chiglio – Army commander

Specialist Gaglio - old friend of Pozella

Pacci Colleto. Master Wizard in the Gussellian army.

General Emilio Baltacco - over the Wizard Corps military arm. Amaria's father.

Zoria Gauto - assistant to Colonel Sarrefo

Marena Categoro - housekeeper of Quint's shared flat

Colonel Julia Gerocie - head of the Military Diplomatic Corps.

General Obellia - Head of Military Foreign Affairs

Henricco Lucheccia - Racellian Foreign Secretary reporting to the council.

Calee Danko - daughter to the Narukun professor.

Fedor Danko - Narukun professor teaching at Racellian University.

Grand Marshal Tracco Guilica - War Minister and Head of Racellian Forces

Horenz Pizent – Purser of Narukun ship

Captain Goresk Olinko – captain of Narukun ship

THE CLOISTER WIZARD

Oscar Viznik - The monk who saved Quint

Sandiza "Sandy" Bartok – cloister guide

Eben – Seensist master gardener

Hintz Dakuz - librarian and teacher

Pol Grizak - Cloister monk

Tizurek - God of the world

Tova - Tizurek's handmaiden

Shinzle Bokwiz - religious leader

Croczi - religious supporter

Kozak - cloister carpenter

Wanisa Hannoko - citizen of Pinzleport

Andreiza "Andy" Hannoko - Wanisa's daughter

Dontiz "Donnie" Hannoko - Wanisa's son

Vintez Dugo - injured monk

Zim Pilka - local lord

Olinz – Lord Pilka's aide

Silla Pilka - local lady

Gallia Pilka - lord's beautiful daughter

Criz Pilka - lord's youngest son.

Finir Boviz - King of Narukun

Phandiz Crider - Aide to the king

Thera Vanitz - military strategist.

Omar Ronzle - Pilka's soldier

Master Jelnitz – Green master wizard

LOCATIONS
CONTINENTS – COUNTRIES - RACES

Amea – last expanded into by gran race - an offshoot of hubites

Honnen

Progen

Chullen

Lekken

North Fenola - Oldest settled - by hubites and polens (or polennese)

Pogokon – polens

Slinnon - polens

Kippun – hubites who have assumed polennese customs.

Narukun – hubite

    Pinzleport – Southern port

Seensist Cloister

Baziltof – large village to the north of Seensist

Zimton – the principal town in the Pilka domain

Tova's Falls – village at the edge of mountains

Parsun Cloister

The Cloister Wizard

Feltoff Cloister

Baxel – Royal capital of Narukun.

South Fenola – Willots pushed most hubites out of continent

Barellia - willots

Gussellia - willots

        Nornotta - capital of Gussellia

Vinellia - willots

Racellia - Till's home country home to willots, hubites

        Bocarre - Capital of Racellia

        Fort Draco - wizard training

Resoda - Most recently settled - first by grans, but the other races followed

Volcann - all four

Akinnonn - gran/hubite

Logedonn - gran - hubite

Wippadann - gran - polens

Loppodunn - willots - polens

Frosso – most recently settled by grans. Willots coalescing in New Balloo

Boxxo - grans

Loppo - grans

New Balloo - Willots

A Bit About Guy

With a lifelong passion for speculative fiction, Guy Antibes found that he enjoyed writing fantasy, as well as reading it. So, a career was born, and more than fifty books later, Guy continues to add his own flavor of writing to the world. Guy lives in the western part of the United States and is happily married with enough children and grandchildren to meet or exceed the human replacement rate.

You can contact Guy at his website: www.guyantibes.com.

†

BOOKS BY GUY ANTIBES

STRINGS OF EMPIRE
The Wizard Corps

JUSTIN SPEDE
An Unexpected Magician
An Unexpected Spell
An Unexpected Alliance
An Unexpected Betrayal
An Unexpected Villian

~

GAGS & PEPPER
Plight of the Phoenix
The Wizard's Chalice
A Tinker's Dame
A Spell Misplaced
Comrades in Magic

~

THE AUGUR'S EYE
The Rise of Whit
The King's Spy
The Queen's Pet
The Knave's Serpent

~

THE ADVENTURES OF DESOLATION BOXSTER
Prince on the Run
Theft of an Ancient Dog
The Blue Tower
The Swordmaster's Secret
A Clash of Magics

~

WIZARD'S HELPER
The Serpent's Orb
The Warded Box
Grishel's Feather
The Battlebone
The Polished Penny
The Hidden Mask
The Buckle's Curse
The Purloined Soul

~

MAGIC MISSING
Book One: A Boy Without Magic
Book Two: An Apprentice Without Magic
Book Three: A Voyager Without Magic
Book Four: A Scholar Without Magic
Book Five: A Snoop Without Magic

~

SONG OF SORCERY
Book One: A Sorcerer Rises
Book Two: A Sorcerer Imprisoned
Book Three: A Sorcerer's Diplomacy
Book Four: A Sorcerer's Rings
Book Five: A Sorcerer's Fist

~

THE DISINHERITED PRINCE
Book One: The Disinherited Prince
Book Two: The Monk's Habit
Book Three: A Sip of Magic
Book Four: The Sleeping God
Demeron: A Horse's Tale - A Disinherited Prince Novella
Book Five: The Emperor's Pet
Book Six: The Misplaced Prince
Book Seven: The Fractured Empire

~

POWER OF POSES
Book One: Magician in Training

Book Two: Magician in Exile
Book Three: Magician in Captivity
Book Four: Magician in Battle

~

THE WARSTONE QUARTET
Book One: Moonstone | Magic That Binds
Book Two: Sunstone | Dishonor's Bane
Book Three: Bloodstone | Power of Youth
Book Four: Darkstone | An Evil Reborn

~

THE WORLD OF THE SWORD OF SPELLS
Warrior Mage
Sword of Spells

~

THE SARA FEATHERWOOD ADVENTURES
Knife & Flame
Sword & Flame
Guns & Flame

~

OTHER NOVELS
Quest of the Wizardess
The Power Bearer
Panix: Magician Spy
Hand of Grethia

~

THE GUY ANTIBES ANTHOLOGIES
The Alien Hand
SCIENCE FICTION
The Purple Flames
STEAMPUNK & PARANORMAL FANTASY with a tinge of HORROR
Angel in Bronze
FANTASY

~

Printed in Great Britain
by Amazon